M000309796

The I.F. Zones

Rufus Williams

Based on a story by
Rufus Williams and Keith Williams

Copyright © 2020 by Rufus Williams

All rights reserved.

The I.F. Zones is a work of fiction. Names, characters, places, events and incidents are the product of the author's imagination or are used fictitiously.

ISBN: 978-1-7353699-0-7 (paperback)
ISBN: 978-1-7353699-1-4 (E-book)

Contents

FORWARD: A WARNING ON TINKERING AND MANIPULATION   i

1   EIGHT WEEKS AGO   1

2   THE INVISIBLE AMERICAN   12

3   THE FISH OWL   18

4   JFK DHS   23

5   LEAVING HOKKAIDO   27

6   AGENT JOHNSON   30

7   TOKYO   33

8   AGENT SHANKLIN   40

9   NARITA AIRPORT   44

10 MASSACHUSETTS GENERAL HOSPITAL   50

11 A CALL TO HOME   52

12 WALLENSTEIN DEBRIEFING   55

13 RETURNING HOME   59

14 USAMRIID   62

15 THE KAZAKHSTANI PARLIAMENT   66

16 CDC EMERGENCY OPERATIONS CENTER   70

17 HOME   75

18 RURAL CHINA   79

19	THE GRIM REAPER	87
20	ATLANTA AGAIN	90
21	MARINE ONE	94
22	THE KRETSKY FACILITY	99
23	HARDBALL	104
24	FBI INTERVIEW ROOM 209	106
25	THE GEORGETOWN SUITES	109
26	BACK TO JAPAN	112
27	FAMILY	117
28	A KISS GOODNIGHT	120
29	PROTOCOLS	121
30	DEPARTURE	126
31	LOGISTIC RESPONSE	128
32	MARSHALL	136
33	SFO	138
34	MINISTER GORSHKOV	143
35	TARAS	146
36	SAM MOREN	150
37	GUERILLA WARFARE	152
38	GREATER SAN FRANCISCO	155
39	HOT ZONES	160
40	THE AMERICAN EMBASSY	165
41	IN THE TRENCHES	167
42	A CONUNDRUM	171
43	ANOTHER BRIEF	178

44 BIOLOGICAL SAMPLES   183

45 PRESIDENT WEN WU   187

46 PHARMACO   189

47 PRESIDENT POLLACK   192

48 FIRE ROAD 8053   197

49 THE RED CORVETTE   201

50 RATIONALIZATIONS   206

51 INTERROGATION   211

52 LANGLEY   216

53 CAPTAIN GREEN   218

54 LEAVING USAMRIID   219

55 I-270   225

56 COLLISION COURSE   230

57 THE BLOODBANK   234

58 PLASTIC COFFINS   240

59 HUNTED   243

60 CAMP DAVID   248

61 ELLEN'S OLD WEATHERBOARD   250

62 DAVISON ARMY AIRFIELD   256

63 SETTING MARSHALL STRAIGHT   262

64 THE BIG OPEN BLUE SKY   264

65 CHINA   265

66 THE WHITE HOUSE   269

67 RAFFLES BEIJING HOTEL   271

68 WEI LIN'S FACILITY   273

69 30,000 FT ABOVE THE PACIFIC OCEAN   275

70 TIME TO SLEEP   276

71 INSIDE THE WALLS OF THE HEART   279

72 THE SHOWDOWN   282

73 DECISION TIME   287

74 HOKKAIDO AGAIN   290

FORWARD: A WARNING ON TINKERING AND MANIPULATION

Humans like to tinker. We always have, it's in our DNA. Our ability to do so, and harness the results, separates us from the rest of the animal kingdom. It has allowed us, as Sir Isaac Newton noted three hundred years ago, to see further by standing on the shoulders of Giants.

Ironically, like a child playing with matches, our toying with complexities we do not yet fully understand may well prove our blazing ruin.

+

It is fitting then that fire ranks as one of humanity's earliest toys. Initial advances, however, came slowly.

Though paleontologists believe we have manipulated fire for well over one million years, the advance to utilizing heat in food preparation is more recent. Earliest indicators suggest that it was 230,000 years ago that hominids first definitively used fire to cook—the specific indicators being scorching patterns around the teeth and skulls of animal remains consistent with the barbecuing of brains from hunted game. Extending fire to use with vessels—ceramics, initially—does not, however, present itself until around 25,000BC.

Concurrent with these advances, Australian Aboriginal fire management practices saw swaths of that country's bush routinely scorched for yet another reason. Early season fires were deliberately lit to mitigate the risks of devastating late season infernos. That custom that marked mankind's first significant efforts at disruptive biological intervention; fittingly, considerations of side-effects secondary.

The watershed event in humanity's deliberate and systematic altering of the biological makeup of the world around us stands with the advent of our move to agriculture. Dates vary among the various corners of the globe, but 10,000BC is a good global ballpark.

The proverbial stove under humanity's raw curiosity was lit.

Agriculture was the beginning of genetic engineering. Seed selection and selective breeding were our first methodical attempts at tinkering with biology, attempts that over the course of millennia have proved unimaginably successful.

Corn, for instance, originated as teosinte, a drought resistant grass up to ten meters high. Edible and easy to farm, it still took thousands of years of human artificial selection to turn the small un-clustered kernels protected by a tough shell into two to four rows of seeds firmly attached to a cob. And even then, at about 5000BC, the cob was but an inch long, with as few as 6 seeds.

By the start of the twentieth century ears of corn were substantially closer to today's size, though hybrid breeding continued to improve yields so that average harvested cobs now contain 400-600 seeds, and up to 1000.

The biggest improvements in the twentieth century, however, came not from the size of the cobs themselves, but by improving the density of planting. Those improvements were ushered in with hybridization, and later, by engineering resistance to pests with genetic modifications that added insecticidal genes to the leaves, but not the corn itself.

Mimicking corn, most early history of mankind reads as a sequence of intermittent, but colossal technological advances interspersed with massive periods of relative stasis. Present-day revolutions happen, by contrast, almost daily. To even the casual observer, it is clear that the frequency of advances are inextricably linked to expanded education of our global population and the ever-increasing arsenal of tools we have proliferated. Old tools are the parents of new ones, and knowledge begets knowledge.

In short, our rate of advancement is exponential.

Unfortunately, these accelerating developments dramatically increase the risk of spinning off the racetrack.

+

Beyond our ever-increasing velocity of progress, are the changes in the sheer scope of the progress. No longer is mankind's tinkering limited to crops and livestock.

Beyond a simple understanding of the blueprint for life, the second half of the twentieth century brought an increasingly refined ability to manipulate that DNA. That underpinning knowledge opened the door to tinkering with the foundational building blocks of all manner of life. Unlike our ancestors we no longer play with just plants and animals. In the new world paradigm, we play with humans on one end of the spectrum and viruses on the other, and the dangers of tinkering with the latter are now magnified by many apparently unrelated advances, perhaps most notably those in transportation.

Air travel and the truly global economy have already shown their power to scatter far and wide. The SARS outbreak that started in November 2002 in Hong Kong, led with alarming speed to 8422 infected, ultimately killing 916 people, and reaching 37 countries, all by early 2003. Doubly troubling was that, lethal though SARS was, the deadly pathogen lacked airborne transmissibility. It was an evil genie, but not one with wings of her own. An airborne transmissible disease will, by contrast, transform ventilation systems in aircraft and shopping malls into lethal dispersal units, thus spectacularly amplifying humanity's technologically induced ability to propagate infection.

+

Of some comfort is the knowledge that humans are not blind.

Indeed whilst hybridized versions of crops often bear infertile seeds as a lucky by-product of their development, more recent agricultural monocultures have been engineered this way as an insurance policy against the unexpected. And, though scientists' careful engineering of this so-called terminator property in seed stocks has been assailed by the public for the dependence it shackles farmers with (specifically to the likes of seed giants such as Monsanto), these genetic safeguards are the least we should hope for. The terminator property is the sort of eminently sensible precaution against the undesired proliferation of unexpected and deleterious traits we should demand.

Unfortunately not all areas of biological research have fail-safes built in. And so it is that far from ethical concerns, the chief reservations stem cell researchers have around implanting stem cells into patients is the potential for runaway cells to grow cancerous. And though cancer is not known for its contagious properties, it is illustrative to consider the Tasmanian Devil.

That four-legged Australian marsupial neared extinction when a rogue cancer mysteriously passed through the native population. As we later discovered, the bite from an infected animal was enough to transmit the disease to the next. The ensuing population decline was nothing short of catastrophic. Thus we learned: some cancers are contagious.

The salient point is that, irrespective of the designed intentions, once a biological twist escapes, nasty pathogenic effects can be impossible to contain. Thus, cold war anxiety about the relatively isolated effects of a nuclear bomb pale as preposterously alarmist when compared with the global pandemic the age of biotech threatens to unleash.

The bottom line remains, all tinkering, by definition, yields unpredictable outcomes.

Sometimes superb leaps forward are accomplished.

Sometimes the results are simply uninteresting but at least benign.

But sometimes really bad things happen.

The nature of our ever-growing knowledge means simply that outcomes of every shape and size are occurring with increasing frequency.

Tinkering took our global population past seven billion people, but it will not always remain that way. Regrettably, concerns about disastrous byproducts are no longer academic.

What follows is the story of a program initiated in early 2013, a program ill conceived by its architects.

The inevitability of events such as those described herein is difficult to overstate.

Chapter 1

EIGHT WEEKS AGO

"Take your temperature," Ludmila pressed.

Jean Michael just looked at her blankly. The fever had descended on him like a tropical downpour, and she didn't like the way the red veins in the whites of his eyes looked; a snow covered landscape with streaks of lava erupting from his pupils.

"Dr. Michael," she tried again for his attention.

"Ou e Francais?"

"You're in Kazakhstan."

"Le ciel est bleu."

"English, Jean Michael." The international language of science was their only common tongue.

"Ouuuaaah ..." Jean Michael groaned slowly. "Blue skies."

"What?"

"It is the color of your flag."

Ludmila looked at the Frenchman, none the wiser about his ramblings. The Kazakh flag had a yellow sun against a blue sky, but what that had to do with anything ...

"Is how the Americans describe our work," he continued.

Ludmila shrugged, "Welcome to the world of biotech." It had been a bumpy road transitioning him from the Ivory Tower.

"This is the world outside academia?" Sweat matted his grey un-styled academic hair, as he clutched his head.

"Without conservative state restrictions," she smiled at him.

"Soar like an eagle!" He was babbling. "Your flag, it has an eagle."

Well that was true, but other birds were the really dangerous killers— ducks and geese. They shunned artificial man-made restrictions, freely crossing borders at will. "You made a quarantine?" her statement was a question.

His eyes traced the perimeter of the doors and windows, and he held up a roll of black duct tape.

"You taped the gap around the door?"

"Oui." This was good, his mind was focusing with the details.

"Only filtered air in? Only filtered air out?"

"Oui," he nodded, swaying in time with his nod. Then words joined his rhythm, "In. Out. In. Out. In-out. Dual purpose ... I am ... delirious." His observation was but a brief moment of clarity.

+

Kretsky was Dr. Ludmila Serik's company, and though others had vested interests—more than just financial stakes—safety protocols stopped with her. She had been watching the Frenchman for fifteen minutes now.

His head lolled about, "Tweene fiff degrees."

His accent gave her trouble at the best of times, add a slur and the glass wall between them ... she followed his eyes to the thermostat on the wall and 'twenty five' suddenly made sense.

"No. *Your* temperature. Put thermometer under your tongue."

He looked at her quizzically, and then somewhere deep inside those blue eyes a lightbulb flickered. "The sun is up?"

"Sun?"

"Oui, like your flag. Sun is a killer." More incomprehensible babble.

"Take your temperature," she repeated.

Jean Michael met her eyes and wobbled to his feet, steadying himself on the lab bench. She could see dark patches below his armpits. He almost certainly smelt bad too. Thank god for his quarantine.

A glass beaker toppled, spilling a clear liquid. The Frenchman watched it dribble off the side of the counter and onto the floor.

"Biological laydown," he mused "...her waterfall of worlds."

"Jean Michael!"

He knelt down on the floor and sniffed the puddle. "Teeny adjustments. Such different outcomes."

"This is true," Ludmila agreed to herself, "In people and in petri dishes." A single particle trapped in the lungs could cause a fatal infection, and a lone scientist could change the course of the world.

Jean Michael was sniffing god only knew what! The man was lost in a clouded world of his own; what to do?

Her phone rang. It was a welcome distraction summoning her to the front of the building, and she left her sick patient to his own devices again.

+

It was 6:30 in the morning and Ludmila walked Magjan Iglinsky back through the building. A one-time college hockey player, his presence was still intimidating, even if his skin held less tightly where muscles now waned.

"Tell me what's happening." Magjan pressed, "When did you put him in quarantine?"

"No. Actually, he put himself in quarantine." Ludmila corrected herself. "He called me 4AM this morning. Was delirious. Staff will be showing up in next hour."

"Do you know what it is?"

"No. He does not know too. He is somewhat incoherent."

They reached the lab Jean Michael had appropriated. Magjan looked through the window at the sweating Frenchman. "He's duct-taped the doors and windows, can he breathe?"

"There is plenty air coming in from laminar flow hood, and vents all have HEPA filters on them. Breathing is not problem."

"Is that really necessary? The duct tape."

"Maybe he has flu," she conceded without actually agreeing.

"The French, huh, always melodrama." Magjan smiled sardonically.

"I wasn't sure I should call. He just—I've never had a scientist ... " she trailed off, unsure how to describe the situation.

"No. No, it is good." Iglinsky nodded. "Good. Good." Academics were all the same, excessively sincere, and they took care. He liked that they reverted to analysis, even when the fox was already walking through the henhouse. That certainly wasn't his instinct, but he appreciated it in others. They could be relied on to play by the rules. It probably had to do with their ingrained practice of peer review, even in those who no longer shared their work freely.

He liked both Ludmila and Jean Michael. They were different, but he liked them, both of them. The Frenchman's expertise was in GIs and ICEs (Genomic Islands and Integrative Conjugative Elements) both of which had long been critical to recent discoveries concerning conferring transmission and drug resistance of genes between different bacteria. They had moved well past bacteria now. 'Horizontal transfers of GIs and ICEs' was the buzz phrase, though Magjan hated high-falutin terms. Call it what it was: Cutting and splicing chunks of DNA. This technology had the potential to supercharge the stem-cell program and open the door to new frontiers in regenerative medicine.

Magjan gazed through the glass.

What had happened? In the lab, the erstwhile esteemed Professor of Paris' Ecole Normale Superieure had not even noticed their arrival. Magjan rapped solidly on the window. "Professor Michael. How are you feeling?"

Vacant, glazed eyes met Magjan's. Jean Michael struggled to his feet, "I want to go home," he pleaded.

Magjan's prized recruit was no longer playing god with human genes.

"Sit down and relax. We can't send you anywhere. Obviously. Have something to eat." Magjan suggested as he turned to Dr. Serik, "Does he have food in there?" and then back to Jean Michael, enunciating clearly through the glass. "Do you have food in there?"

The Frenchman coughed as he produced a packet of roasted chestnuts from his pocket—not completely incoherent Magjan noted happily.

"We are going to fix you." Magjan assured him. They had to.

The power in today's world was neither in gold, nor a rod of plutonium. Physical commodities were assets from another time. Today's priceless objects were knowledge and expertise, and the expensive Frenchman was a reservoir of both. Even if, now slumped on a lab stool, he looked homeless, Jean Michael was not an expendable investment.

Magjan turned back to Ludmila. "Talk to me about safety protocols. Should you be in quarantine too? What about the rest of the staff? Is it safe for me to be here?"

"You will be fine. Unless I'm already infected–"

Magjan took a step backwards.

"We don't know what he has or why is he quarantined himself. It is not a weaponized biological laydown." she paused.

"What is it?"

Ludmila was lost in thought. She didn't answer.

"What is–"

"What is *it*?" she repeated rhetorically, "We don't know."

"No, what are you thinking?"

Then realizing his question pertained to her pause, she answered "Jean Michael used the same term a few minutes ago—weaponized biological laydown."

"So?"

"It is foolish thought. If people working here forty years ago knew then what we know today, the power dynamic in the world might be very different." Ludmila relaxed, they were back on hypotheticals, "We will swab everyone. We will contain—it is probably not airborne contagious. It is very unlikely."

"Professor Michael has taped the air outlets."

"Better to be safe." She really believed what she was saying. "Sun alone kills most airborne material." Talking about the science calmed Ludmila Serik's anxieties. If the devil was in the details, he was a soothsayer.

"Alright. What should I tell the brass in Astana?" But Magjan's question was interrupted by Jean Michael who was now coughing violently.

Magjan and Ludmila turned to see his arms flinging wildly.

"He's having a seizure!" Magjan panicked.

"No" she corrected him. "He is choking."

Jean Michael dropped his crumpled paper bag of chestnuts.

"A chestnut," Ludmila concluded. "He is choking on chestnut."

So much for the soothsaying devil, the divine sociopath was toying with their emotions. And in an instant the devil's roller coaster—led by Jean Michael's awkward slapping at his own chest—was hurtling them down a new precipice.

Ludmila watched detachedly as clarity of purpose pierced through Jean Michael's haze. The man needed to breathe!

In her mind the basal instinct to help save her asphyxiating colleague competed with the higher order necessity to maintain the quarantine. She could feel his panic infecting her as he beckoned their help with wordless gesticulations.

Damned if she did, damned if she didn't.

Jean Michael approached the door.

"Help him." Magjan instructed.

Ludmila shook. Her face was ashen, immobilized.

"He's choking!"

Suddenly she was running, "Watch him! I will return."

"Quick! That man cost half a million Euros!"

                                    +

Ludmila returned with a barrel-chested scientist, masks, latex gloves and, ten paces behind them, a younger woman trailing in a billowing blotch-stained white lab-coat—a comical version of a hysterical bride, she was nonetheless pretty.

"Doctor Serik!" she cried, "What's happening?"

Ludmila ignored the woman, focusing instead on Jean Michael who was now tearing at the duct tape around the doorframe. "He was suffering a fever. He quarantined himself."

"He what?" the bigger man asked as they returned to–

"Magjan Iglinsky, Ivan" Ludmila introduced the men, even as she handed Ivan gloves.

The bride caught up to them and gasped at the sight of Jean Michael, "Oh my god!"

"Stand back." Ludmila instructed Mica.

"Has someone called an ambulance?"

"He's got a chestnut caught in his throat." Magjan told Ivan, ignoring Mica.

"He looks terrible! I'm calling an ambulance," Mica declared.

"No!" Iglinsky countermanded firmly.

"No?!"

It was a small mercy that Jean Michael, who had fallen to his knees, still didn't understand much of the Kazakh language. Even so, given his incapacitation, and the glass wall between them, it probably didn't matter much anyway. He looked up with plaintive panic in his eyes.

"No." Iglinsky reiterated, elaborating, "It'll take ten minutes, and unless we can dislodge the object—focus on the problem."

Ivan pulled the mask over his chubby cheeks and gloves over his stubby fingers. He was kicking at the door, which barely opened an inch; the duct tape around its edge was putting up steep resistance. The large man put his whole shoulder into his work.

Finally the recalcitrant tape relented and the door swung open.

Mica held her breath in disbelief, and Ludmila addressed Ivan calmly, "I will close the door when you are inside."

Once inside, the big scientist slapped Jean Michael's back, politely at first, but with rapidly increasing vigor. The nut unfortunately was solidly lodged.

"It's not working!" Magjan yelled unhelpfully.

Ivan turned the Frenchman over like a rag-doll and grabbed him from behind. Pulling hard in an attempted Heimlich maneuver, he flapped Jean Michael's arms up, but the patient continued turning blue.

Wide-open-but-fading eyes pleaded with Ludmila. She stood placidly, unnervingly composed.

Fogginess clouded Jean Micheal's vision and for a moment he gave up the fight, his eyes closing altogether.

"Somebody do something!" Mica insisted.

"Shut up!" Iglinsky snapped at her.

The pretty woman struck Iglinsky.

But before he could respond to her a thud came from inside the lab. Professor Jean Michael's body landed on the floor as he drifted from consciousness.

"Give him mouth to mouth!" Magjan directed.

"It won't help if we can't dislodge the blockage." Ludmila observed.

Mica reached into her pocket, "I'm calling the ambulance!"

"No!" Magjan was categorical.

"The man's dying!" Dialing the phone, she stepped away.

Behind the glass Ivan stopped his jerking motion to feel Jean Michael's wrist. "His pulse is weak."

Outside the room Magjan advanced on Mica, snatching at her phone. She dodged, but the athleticism of his youth was not completely gone. He grabbed again, knocking the phone to the floor, "It'll take twenty minutes to get here. If we don't clear the blockage, you can't keep him oxygenated." There was a clinical cut through to what he said, "He'll still be dead. And we'll be left with nothing but a lot of explaining."

"He's not dead yet!"

Inside the lab, Ivan stood suddenly. He scattered equipment from the bench. He was searching. Violently, he pulled at the draws, hands crashing through their contents.

"Ivan?!"

The barrel-chested man tore a scalpel from its sterilized packaging, and brandishing the blade, he turned back to the glass, "I need some help in here!"

"Stop!" the young woman shrieked. She lunged for the door, but before her hand reached the handle Iglinsky grabbed her arm.

"Somebody get in here!" Ivan roared.

"What are you doing?" Ludmila screamed through the glass.

"Opening the airway."

It was Magjan who connected the dots first. He turned to Ludmila, "Get in there. Help him."

"There will be blood." Ludmila protested.

"The man is dying!"

"Blood carries infections. It is ultimate carrier!"

"So put on gloves," Magjan Iglinsky's voice turned to ice, "and be extra careful."

+

With giant paws, the man ripped Jean Michael's shirt from his prostrate body, exposing his pale neck. He touched the tip of the knife to the valley just below the Frenchman's Adam's apple.

As Ludmila entered the room, Ivan glanced up at her. "Hold him," he instructed.

Pulling a second pair of latex gloves over her first, Ludmila bent down and placed her knee firmly on Jean Michael's unmoving chest. "I have him."

The blade stretched the skin ineffectually.

"Push harder," she encouraged.

And then, with a jerk, it pierced the surface.

"Fuck!"

Blood pooled out, not fast, but enough to gurgle as Ludmila's knee sank on Jean Michael's chest.

For five minutes they continued as a team, frantically working to keep the airway open. But the initial bubbles were the only evidence of oxygen reaching Jean Michael's lungs. Nothing worked. Eventually, the blood flow slowed, already coagulating around the edges. Jean Michael's skin was now had a visible blue hue.

The genuine attempt to save the Frenchman curiously eased the panic about a potential biological exposure, but that was all it achieved.

Iglinsky looked through the window at Ivan who was still working on Jean Michael. He rapped on the glass, "Give up. He's gone."

Ivan checked for a pulse one last time. Nothing. He nodded his head in agreement with Iglinsky, and everyone stared in disbelief.

"Oh shit!" was all Ludmila could say.

"Take a deep breath."

"This is . . ." panic was rising in her voice again, even as words failed her. She turned to Magjan, "This is–"

"This is unfortunate." Iglinsky tried to calm her. "Accidents happen. It is unfortunate."

Ivan nodded agreement. "You can cure cancer, but death finds a way."

With all the exotic threats in the world, people habitually forget that simple accidents still did plenty of killing. People worried about Ebola, but the leading cause of traumatic death in men over fifty was a fall from a roof! Falling and choking each accounted for two of the five leading causes of all traumatic deaths.

"Get out of the room," Magjan instructed them. The situation was still precarious for a multitude of reasons, and disposing of Jean Michael's body required careful consideration.

$+$

Twelve hours later, under cover of darkness, puddles of rain spat off the asphalt as Iglinsky pulled through town. Soon the run-down city periphery gave way to quiet wooded roads. Thirty miles from Kretsky he hadn't seen another vehicle for ten minutes when he pulled the car onto a small dirt road. "Discretion is important," he thought to himself.

The sentiment had merit. So-called 'dual-use' technology—technology with both positive and untoward applications—invariably attracted an abundance of scrutiny that those bending rules preferred not to see.

Political ties helped. But if an outside investigator never found the body . . . they might even believe that Jean Michael had been out of town on vacation.

Magjan Iglinsky had felt it in his bones that day, but he could hardly have anticipated just how insignificant this death would later seem. Ten months into this job and nothing had become more apparent than that the study of science was unpredictable.

Unpredictable even in its unpredictability.

Chapter 2

THE INVISIBLE AMERICAN

"Don't look over," Magjan coughed.

"Jeans and jacket? By the window?"

"That's him. Don't look at him. Has he been watching me?"

The falafel vendor shrugged, "Maybe. Not sure." He finished wrapping the lamb shawarma in lavash and the whole roll in foil before glancing up again, "Yeah, he was looking just then."

He handed Magjan the food.

Magjan gave him 1500 Tenge and coughed again, "Thanks."

It had been eight weeks since Jean Michael died. There had been heat in the beginning, but it seemed to have blown over. And then, for a while now, it had felt like he was being followed though he could never quite put his finger on why.

He took a bite of his meal and, mulling things over, gazed up at the ceiling of the lazy-W building—the affectionate nickname he'd given the Almaty airport terminal in reference to the roof, which from the front resembled . . . well, a lazy "W".

Turning quickly in a bid to catch his presumed tail by surprise, he found the man by the window watching a plane on the runway. Magjan felt childishly naïve, stupid even. So he'd seen the man in Dusseldorf two days ago; the guy was probably on his flight here. Big deal!

What exactly would a tail look like, anyway?

People no doubt underestimated how difficult it was to run an effective tail, himself included. Cliché concerns about being spotted more or less presupposed the man by the window was part of a very slick operation.

Magjan had purchased his own ticket to Almaty at the last minute, and it was the last in coach. At a bare minimum the window watcher would have needed a well-heeled team behind him. One that could both cover the first class fare here, and, at the drop of a hat, have a car ready in Almaty in the few short hours it took their unexpected flight to arrive. Of course that was probably the sort of logistic difficulty that made the job interesting.

The man was no longer at the window. Magjan checked around. He was gone altogether. So much for the paranoid spy stuff.

Magjan walked to his gate. It was a short trek. Though Almaty was a busy airport, much of that traffic was cargo transport.

Surveying the lounge, Magjan was about to sit when he noticed the man again. It was one thing for the guy from Dusseldorf to appear in Almaty, it was another for him to also be heading from here to JFK. Magjan decided it was time to confront his anthropomorphized paranoia.

"Keshiriniz" Magjan prodded as he reached the man.

The man looked up from his book.

"Keshiriniz–"

"Sorry, I don't speak Kazak." The accent was American.

Magjan switched effortlessly to English, "Sorry. You were in Dusseldorf two days ago?"

"Do I know you?"

"Magjan Iglinsky," Magjan extended his hand.

"Gerald Stein," the man reached up cautiously.

"I thought I saw you in Germany a couple of days ago."

"Yes, I flew in here yesterday."

"I didn't see you on the flight. I also flew in yesterday."

"I was in first class." Gerald gave a thin smile.

"They're the last seats to go." Magjan quipped. He was used to reading people and he watched Gerald's reaction carefully for tells. Nothing. Either Gerald was professionally trained to evade or there was nothing untoward in his ticket purchase.

"You do much work in Germany?" Gerald interrupted Magjan's thoughts.

"There and America too." Magjan responded while indicating their flight details above the desk by the gate. Again, no sign that Gerald felt caught out. Magjan's thoughts turned back to the flight, first class would have given Gerald the jump on collecting his car. Magjan saw another tack with double meaning, "At least all three countries drive on the right side of the road." The observation felt more forced as he spoke it, and Magjan quickly followed up with the ruse question he was leading to, "Did you drive here?"

"Yes. Cars are cars."

"You rented?" Magjan pressed. "What did they give you?"

"A silver Camry."

Nicely non-descript, even in Kazakhstan. The old boxy red Lada Riva that Amanet had picked Magjan up in—the shit-box on wheels from another era—would have been a cinch to tail. And the plane ride would have permitted a few hours easy sleep; it was too public a place for anything interesting to transpire, and nobody would be getting off.

Transitions must be key to the work of a spy. With first class and the ubiquitous Camry, Magjan would never have noticed him.

"You're Kazak, right?" Gerald broke Magjan's thinking again.

"Yes."

"But you work outside the country a lot? Your English is excellent. What do you do?"

"I'm in biotech."

"Really?" Gerald's eyes lit up, "My brother works in biology. It's not something I understand well, but it is fascinating."

"Yes it is," Magjan agreed.

"Tell me more. What do you do?"

"I oversee international collaboration. And how about you? What do you do?" Magjan felt a small burst of pride at turning the spotlight back on Gerald.

"Nothing so interesting," Gerald shrugged. "Ink jet printers."

Gerald took a sip of his coffee. Magjan had the floor for questioning, but he wasn't sure what to ask. Gerald filled the void, "It pays the bills."

"And you get to travel."

"Yes, though that doesn't often make me popular at home." Gerald glanced at Magjan's left hand, "Do you have someone special?"

Again, Magjan felt he was losing control of the conversation. "No."

Gerald held up his own left hand and wiggled a wedding band with his thumb, "Twelve years."

And so their chat continued. Gerald had taken control, deftly steering the discussion through a sequence of small talk, until the flight steward at the gate called for the 'one-world alliance customers' to board.

Suddenly, Gerald stood and extended his hand again. "It was a pleasure meeting you Mr. Igansky."

"Iglinsky," Magjan corrected. "And you, too."

They shook hands again and Gerald was gone.

On the plane Magjan buckled his seatbelt. A seasoned headhunter he might be, but an international spy he was not. Gerald had taken control of the conversation and Magjan had failed to discover anything about him. Hell, he might as well have admitted to the statistical average of 2.2 kids.

+

Before collecting his bags, Magjan trudged forward, leapfrogging his carry-on another small step moments after setting it in its previous new position. The line to the customs officer snaked forward, slowly, and inexorably. 125,000 passengers every day, or so he'd read in the inflight magazine, JFK was a popular gateway to American soil.

Looking around, Magjan spotted Gerald Stein. The man waved to him. Magjan reflected that spy or not, he'd probably never see Gerald again. If indeed Gerald Stein was even the guy's name.

Magjan neared the customs officer, the check-in-chick as an Australian scientist he'd once tried poaching had called them; 'check-out-chick' was apparently Australian vernacular for supermarket cashiers, but the woman in front of him rang tourists into the country.

"Name?"

"Magjan Iglinsky."

She took his passport and papers, "Business or pleasure?"

"Business."

She swiped his passport and adjusted a digital camera to capture his likeness. Click. She looked back at her screen, and in that moment Magjan noticed her break from the monotony of what must have been her day. Her computer pinged.

"Is everything alright?" Magjan asked.

"Sure," she glanced at the screen, "Mr. Iglinsky, you've been selected for a random search—the department of homeland security will–"

"Mr. Iglinsky." A voice from behind interrupted her. A DHS officer had materialized from nowhere. "Can you please come with us," the officer had a partner too, both armed.

From four lines across, Gerald Stein watched as Magjan was escorted away. Had he known this was coming?

+

The two DHS lackeys dumped Magjan inside a windowless interrogation room, leaving him to stew. There was no sense creating a scene, and he didn't. He did, however, need to think very carefully about how to proceed from this point.

The nature of his governmental facilitations in Kazakhstan bordered on nefarious. Sure, traditional headhunting was a worldwide trade that all states engaged in, and, mercantile considerations were widely viewed in the 70 billion-dollar-a-year biopharmaceutical industry, as the most powerful lures.

But they were not the only ones.

Not everyone was motivated by financial compensation alone. There were reasons Magjan Iglinsky was not a formal member of the Kazak political system.

Transforming former infrastructures in a timely fashion and enticing talent—that could as easily work wherever in the world they chose— required special incentives. Incentives that more advanced and better funded countries couldn't afford, the sort of incentives that had to do with the parameters under which the actual work would be done.

Magjan's job was to entice the cooperation and enthusiasm of the most powerful states while poaching their talent with the lure of researching more "experimental" substance with more "experimental" techniques. The circles he inhabited understood perfectly that "experimental" was easily relaxed to explicitly banned when the talent in question, or the projected outcome, was important enough. Stem cells were but the tip of the iceberg.

The United States represented one of the most delicate lines he'd had to tread in the past, but it was the home of many actors who wanted results without questions. The difficulty lay in advertising your offerings without raising red flags with the authorities. It was a delicate dance.

Right now Magjan just hoped to hell that he hadn't inadvertently stood on the wrong foot and awoken a monster.

Chapter 3

THE FISH OWL

Jungles are where you find exotic diseases—Bolivian hemorrhagic fever, Ebola, Marburg. Category A diseases that melt your insides until they come leaking out various bodily orifices. Diseases that demand level four bio-containment, the labs adults play in.

Like countless budding biologists, Colonel Lucy Topp had started her career hoping to play with the big kids. The problem was "virus hunters" weren't exactly the Indiana Jones characters that Lucy had expected them to be; and Lucy really did prefer ropes, carabineers, quick-draws and the great outdoors, to tedious research conducted in the four walls of a sterile lab.

Besides, deadly though exotic diseases were, they were soft too. They tended to burn themselves out, or mutate to benign strains within a couple of generations. Rather than demand level four pampering for study, they required it.

In truth the deadliest threat to humanity wasn't a fragile category A disease that broke loose. The real danger was a pathogen that had already mastered the art of spread. The real danger was a virus that already moved through the human population effectively; one that with the slightest of genetic modifications went from benign today to lethal tomorrow, a hunter that finally learned to use its teeth.

So went Lucy's rationale. And it was a rationale good enough to plop her, precariously balanced, 70 feet above the forest floor in Hokkaido. She was an outsider who cajoled the system from within its power structures, but outside its walls.

"Are you almost done?" shouted a disembodied voice from below; her protégé, the one she'd had foisted upon her.

Lucy glanced down from her treetop perch. Major Ulman was standing beside a fast flowing pristine river. Liquid ice that sliced through old growth and boiled over rocks. No African jungle, this was riparian forest in northern Japan, and (but for her trying underling) it offered its own freedom from the human imprint.

"What's taking you so long up there?!" Ulman searched for Lucy amidst the billion bright stars that daylight made as sun pierced through the towering canopy in sparkling shards. Finally, following the Colonel's bright orange rope that lapped at the side of the trunk, she found her just as–

"Rope!" Lucy gave the obligatory universal call to let those below know you were dropping a coil of cord. It was all the warning she would give Ulman—maybe that would teach her to cool her boots.

The thump on the soft carpet of the forest floor elicited a squawk from her apprentice, and Lucy rappelled down with four bamboo birdcages clipped to her harness. "Back," she said with a smile.

"I thought we'd lost you up there." Ulman looked petulant well beneath her 26 years, "Some of us have stuff we'd like to get back to back home, you know."

"Enjoy the forest air. This is the best lab you'll ever work in."

"I'm not just talking about work." Ulman retorted. "Some of us have lives too."

Ulman had dark hair to Lucy's blond, but both women had the rugged fitness needed for this work. Unlike Ulman however, Lucy put less stock in applying her physique as a lure. She had seen serious attachments derail promising careers, especially for women, and she could easily guess the man Ulman was referring to. Mid-forties and handsome, he was a brief indiscretion Lucy had permitted herself last summer. She tested her theory: "Colonel Marshall's anxious for your return?" she asked with a cheeky grin.

Ulman blushed. "He warned me you'd keep us here forever."

"I bet he did."

"And that you're beguiling and that I should be careful not to fall under your spell."

Lucy raised her arms, "Behold my enchanting kingdom!" Men talk about meaningless flings, and then they get attached.

"I know he'd have something to say about that too."

Lucy grinned self-assuredly, "It takes two to tango!"

+

Up in the canopy again, Lucy looped an extra sling around a branch and clipped a quick-draw to it. She slipped her rope through the gate and kept climbing. Trees were whispering to her as the wind rustled through their leaves. Nature's simplicity held many mysteries, but it was so much more understandable than the complexities of human interactions.

Lucy shrugged off a fleeting flush of vertigo, and turned her attention to the last bamboo birdcage at the end of the branch. In it fluttered a panicked nuthatch bird, a small native of this forest that lived high in the canopy, but never ventured far.

Carefully edging her way out along the swaying branch, she moved with the grace and skill of an experienced climber. Her affair with granite rocks was truly meaningful, but she'd never really gotten past her first love, the more unusual and idiosyncratic climbing environment of trees.

At the bamboo trap hanging from jute twine Lucy uncapped the syringe with her teeth. What viruses coursed through this small bird's veins? She reached inside the cage, caught the nuthatch, but as she plunged the syringe for the blood sample a piercing shriek rang out behind her!

Whirling about, Lucy saw the shriek escalate to a thick cacophony of screeching before she was blinded. Hundreds of birds filled the air from the wall of leaves. Nothing stood out until–

Talons!

Lucy lurched backwards, her balance thrown.

And then she was falling!

She'd pulled a lot of slack climbing to the extremity of this branch, too much slack. It takes two mistakes to kill you—so the age-old hang-gliding adage went; the theory being you needed compounding errors to die. And as she tipped back Lucy saw, clear as day, that the slack she had pulled was being compounded by a bird of prey's misguided attempt to snatch her own captive subject.

Seventy feet is a death fall if you hit the deck.

With a snatchful of leaves, but no branch, in her hand, she fell.

If her muscular frame wasn't skewered by an inopportune branch, the earth below would, as effectively as Ebola, squish her insides through the lycra tank-top that clung to her lithe body. Time slowed. A glimpse of the owl, now perched on a branch high-above, felt long enough that she could see in its eyes the irritation of having been deprived the caged bird. It watched her contemptuously as she plummeted down, raggedy outdoor pants billowing like a parachute caught around her legs.

Twang!

Her rope went taut. 45 degrees taut. Her last clip, the one close to the thick oak trunk, yanked! Lucy jerked into a violent pendulum, right back toward the robust wooden pillar. She would never hit the ground, but a whipper with forty feet of slack–

Smack!

Her head hit the tree. Hard.

Stars blossomed in her mind and everything went fuzzy. In the distance, she heard the birdcage shatter on the ground below. Then everything went silent and black.

+

Still fuzzy, Lucy opened her eyes. She was thirty feet from the ground. Her head stung as if she'd been attacked by an elephant-sized hornet. Nonetheless she managed the simplest of smiles as she looked out from her gently arcing swing.

From a nearby tree, the giant owl perched on a branch and surveyed the scene. Lucy waved up to it.

"Colonel Topp?!" Ulman actually sounded nervous.

Lucy's forearm stung too. No wonder, the syringe was implanted in her flesh.

"Colonel Topp?"

Lucy dislodged the needle.

"Hor! Lucy-san." Miyake's voice on the other hand was laced with a sense of reverence. "You alright?"

Lucy turned and waved to her team below.

"You need help?" their wiry Japanese guide was always ready for what might come.

"It's my own fault, I let out the slack that made the fall possible. I'll climb myself," and with that she started her hand-over-fist climb back up the rope to her last clip.

Ulman gazed up at the canopy, "What was that?"

"That fish owl!"

"That big bird!" Lucy echoed Miyake, with the slightest hint of gentle mocking. Her head was clearing and she enjoyed the idiosyncrasies of language, especially those illuminated by a filtering through a second tongue.

"Very rare. Powerful hunter." Perhaps Miyake's reverence had not been for the ease with which she took her fall, but the cause of the fall itself.

Lucy rubbed the pin-prick on her forearm and looked directly across at the bird. There it was, the unexpected outcome; a needle jab was hardly what she would have expected from the error in judgement that was the extra slack in her rope!

She pulled her belay tight and paused to appraise her fine feathered foe. Miyake was right in his reverential judgment, the Blakiston's fish owl was impressive; a solid two feet tall with a wingspan as wide as Lucy could reach. She imagined it with a giant glistening trout in its talons.

The forest was teaming with vitality, but it was our human incursions that caused it to burst at the seams.

Modern life was a giant melting pot of pressures. Pressures to perform, pressures to advance, pressures to find love, and the sheer pressure of population, it was all part of what made Lucy's job so interesting. Life needs an environment to live in and with seven billion people on earth there was a lot of environment for the viruses that called humans home. Population pressure, like other pressures, forced shortcuts, and like the forgone clip she had just skipped on her ascent, shortcuts didn't always yield what you expected.

Chapter 4

JFK DHS

Agent Johnson stood in front of Doctor Wong. Doctor Wong was here to represent the Chinese CDC at an academic virology conference in Washington DC. He watched as Johnson scanned the inch of paperwork he had for the biological samples he was bringing in. They were a peace offering to a friend at the US CDC in Atlanta.

Like the customs officer who had met Magjan, Agent Johnson felt a big part of his job was ticking boxes. Once in a while though, he'd spend a day dealing with dignitaries, or individuals on watch-lists. It was those days that had inspired him to work for the Department of Homeland Security in the first place. Happily, today was shaping up to be one of them.

Johnson signed Dr. Wong's papers and handed them back to him.

"All is good?" Wong asked.

"Unless you know you're asymptomatically carrying the plague." It was a little joke, but the language barrier, or the unexpected humor from a DHS officer robbed Agent Johnson of the laugh he was looking for. He asked himself if he could really be the only DHS officer with a sense of humor; but as he'd learned back in college, there was no sense trying to force a joke. Instead he smiled and pointed to the door. "You're finished with DHS. Just make your way to the domestic terminal and enjoy DC."

"Many gratitudes."

"Welcome to America." Johnson offered his hand.

Doctor Wong took Johnson's hand and the two men gave a firm formal shake, even as Wong himself reflected on the sanitary efficacy of an elbow bump over the handshake.

+

Minutes later, Agent Johnson opened Magjan's door. And like the proper gentleman his wife had trained him to be, he stepped aside to allow Agent Sue Shanklin in first.

Magjan looked up from the bare desk where he sat; was she the bad cop?

Johnson opened a blue manila folder as he entered the room, "Good morning Mr. Iglinsky."

"So it seems to you."

The air in the room froze. It was not the right foot to start on, and Magjan regretted his terse rejoinder the moment he'd uttered it. Still, the agents had the upper hand and it wouldn't hurt to shake things up.

"Mr. Iglinsky, I'm Agent Johnson," Johnson said, proffering his hand. Magjan reluctantly reached across the table to meet him. Johnson had a solid grip which he only relaxed to indicate his partner, "and this is Agent Shanklin." Johnson's tone was firm and even.

Formalities were dispensed with and the two DHS interrogators moved right into specifics, but it didn't play out as Magjan had expected. They spent a lot of time running down dead-end alleys and beating about the bush. Were they just softening him up, or were they fishing. Perhaps he would walk out of this room in one piece after all.

Half an hour later, the fatigue of travel crept into Magjan's bones edging out his patience. His temper shortened and the interrogation began to sour. Finally Magjan snapped, contending caustically, "America has trouble navigating the intricacies of cutting edge technology."

"Really?" Agent Shanklin goaded.

"Yes. Your red tape cordons off new frontiers."

"I believe it's called a safe-guard."

"Ha!" Magjan retorted, "The betterment of mankind requires risks. But why take risks when you already have the best standard of living in the world?" he jabbed rhetorically, "That is what developing countries are for, right?"

"And yet here you are, visiting our shores."

"I never said you don't have expertise and resources."

"And you'd like to steal that expertise and resources?"

"It's not stealing. Everyone I meet with comes willingly."

"So you entice them away?"

"That's my job."

"You know a lot of people in your industry."

"Acquaintances are not a crime." Magjan snapped back. As his counter hung in the air, an association flitted through his mind, raising an ironic barb he could not resist, "It is not 1950. You cannot make lists like that now."

He was getting worked up, and his rancor excited a tickle in his throat. The tickle quickly cascaded into a distressed coughing fit.

Agent Johnson pushed his chair back. "I have enjoyed our chat today." He rubbed Magjan's shoulder insincerely. "Tomorrow we can discuss the unpleasant details surrounding your Awake Program."

Magjan brushed off Johnson's hands and with it his flagrant attempt at intimidation.

$+$

Six hours later, Magjan Iglinsky was sitting alone in another sparse room. A holding cell. He'd been moved to the Wackenhut Detention Center, an unfriendly industrial building occupying a whole street block. It was a short walk from the airport—only nobody walked here.

Outside the sun had long since set. Magjan coughed again and the lights went out.

Broadly speaking, of the multiple violations of international law Magjan had committed, or been an accessory to, there were three that might have triggered the treatment he was being subjected to; and without mentioning Awake by name until the end, the DHS agents had made abundantly clear that they knew his job intimately.

Could the Americans have known about Kretsky? Stranger things had happened. After eight weeks he had finally started to sleep soundly again.

Professor Jean Michael's death and subsequent cover-up had taken its toll on his psyche, but the trail back to him was clean. Hell, Jean Michael wasn't even American. More importantly still, the biological samples collected from his corpse—before Magjan had disposed of the body—had turned up nothing. At least nothing of known consequence. His death, it seemed, had truly been an accident.

Magjan was irritated with himself. He'd been too lax. Amanet had taken him to Kretsky's sister facility yesterday, but they hadn't found time to visit the main building. He hadn't spoken to Ludmila. And now he was left wondering if there was something he should have been told. He'd meant to ask about the animal trials. Had Jean Michael discovered something before he died?

It was possible that experts—such as Agent Johnson and Agent Shanklin no doubt were—would skirt alternate avenues in their first meeting, if not simply to soften him up, then to see if anything else might surprise them.

So much speculation. Magjan was very tired and he let his mind drift.

What of the other two clandestine incidents? Both had big upsides, and not just for Kazakhstan. The world stood to gain from the "dirty work" now being done in the former Soviet backwater. Big changes were afoot, albeit for the good this time. What was the saying: the more things changed, the more they stayed the same. At least this time, unlike in the case of the former weapons programs, Kazakhstan itself, and not the distant Kremlin, was in was in the driver's seat.

Magjan closed his eyes, he could think about the other possibilities in the morning.

The thought of waiting until morning was a nice one.

$+$

Unfortunately as the sun rose the next day Magjan lay very still on his bed.

He did not move when the guard entered his cell carrying a tray with oats and coffee, nor on the pronouncement of, "Breakfast".

The guard set the tray down and left; the tough act in the morning was not an uncommon play at bravado.

What the guard had not noticed was the eerie tight smile on Magjan's face, not the sort of smile a living man wears.

Chapter 5

LEAVING HOKKAIDO

A pinprick plague filled the air, the precursor to descending darkness. It was the tail end of the season, but mosquitoes were mosquitoes and Lucy slapped her exposed forearm. Whether the nasty critters would disappear tomorrow hardly mattered today. In any event, Lucy herself would be gone.

Others were being less philosophical.

"Are we almost done?" Ulman tried to hide the whine in her voice, but a return to the creature comforts of civilization had been calling to her for days now.

"You've got to make philosophical peace with the little buggers." Lucy counseled.

"Right! The bloody splotches on the nylon walls of your tent—that's philosophical peace?"

"You witnessed my triumph last night?"

"Yes, but unfortunately, the brothers of your vanquished foes are back for blood."

"Sisters," Lucy corrected, "only the girls bite. At least these ones don't have malaria or Dengue."

"I'm still buying an ITN if you get me back out here again."

ITNs—insecticide treated nets—were twice as effective at breaking the disease cycle as ordinary nets because mosquitoes tend to rest on walls between feedings.

"They don't stop the first bite." Lucy reminded her. But the future made no difference to the now, and Lucy relented. "Alright, keep packing and let's get out of here."

+

Two hours later, Lucy carefully stowed her stun-gun (an unnecessary precaution she'd brought, in case they encountered a Ussuri brown bear) and the rest of her field cases into the back of their 4WD. Then, she and Miyake piled into the front—there were advantages to driving and rank—while Major Ulman squeezed into the back with the supplies.

Darkness stripped the fall leaves of their color, and shortly thereafter of their shape too. Lucy relaxed as Miyake navigated his way along the heavily rutted forest road. The wheels squelched the last vestiges of the summer rains from the muddy parallel troughs as their Mitsubishi worked its way out of the majestic trees and back towards the human imprint.

As the road straightened Miyake reconsidered the question of Lucy's competence, "You close call yesterday."

"Pardon?"

"You fall out of tree."

"Ha!" Lucy retorted Miyake's statement of fact. "A bird'll need help if it wants to snag me."

"You need Hiroshi Sugimura. Hiroshi-san expert climber." There it was, more reverence in Miyake's voice. She knew this was the Japanese way, but, in a weird irony, it was harder to comprehend when faced with its undeniable authenticity. Lucy doubted there was anyone or anything Miyake didn't hold in high esteem when she realized that, by inference, her climbing was precisely that thing.

"Hiroshi Sugimura?" Lucy's mind sparked a loose connection.

"Yes. He is friend of mine."

"He's not an architect is he?"

"Yes! You know Hiroshi-san?"

"He has a sister? . . . Akako?"

"Hai! You know him?"

"No. Not really. I know her. Akako and I did our residency together. At Johns Hopkins. She used to tell me about Hiroshi's idiosyncratic views on improvements for hospital floor plans." Lucy paused remembering, "Apparently architects are curiously observant of how humans interact with their environments."

It was strange to hear this name from the past, a name she'd never actually met the bearer of. In today's connected world, six degrees of separation had plenty of implication to the spread of disease, but it equally implied multiple unexpected loops in your networks of friends. Social media sites regularly revealed such connections, but they still bubbled up once in a while in good old fashioned conversation.

Miyake was smiling at her, "Hiroshi-san is expert climber." The Japanese had their own way of being forceful.

"Really?" Having now connected Hiroshi with his sister, Lucy put less stock in the assertion of his physical prowess, "And you think he's what I need?"

"Hai."

"You did fall," came the unwelcome reminder from the back seat. "I'm just saying . . ."

And, as if tying the conversation in a bow, Miyake closed the subject, "Hiroshi meet us in Tokyo."

Chapter 6

AGENT JOHNSON

"There's a dead guy at Wackenhut?" Agent Ploukowski shook his head in frustration. "God damn it people! Holding cells are supposed to be safe!" He rubbed his temples. What a start to the day. "How'd he do it?" This wasn't the first time, and it wouldn't be the last, but the forty-year-old government career man from the department of Homeland Security wasn't satisfied with simply noting that people died.

He listened to the excuses from the other end of the line. The facts surrounding the death went some way towards softening his tone.

"Alright, maybe his heart did just give out. Those are some spooky cells." With that he concluded his call.

Glancing at his note-pad he left his office, and walked out to the bullpen, "Who had the slimy Kazakh headhunter yesterday?" A few heads turned to look at Ploukowski, "Cause he's dead."

From two desks away came the most helpful response, "Johnson, but he's not in yet."

"What about Agent Shanklin?" Ploukowski asked, "She was there too?"

The junior agent glanced at logs on a computer screen. "Yes. But she's not in yet either, and I already called her."

"You try her home phone?"

"No answer."

Ploukowski threw his hands in the air in despair.

+

A few miles away, in a leafy suburban neighborhood of New Jersey an old model Honda pulled into the driveway of a well—though not professionally—maintained front yard. A young woman got out and hurried past an abandoned tricycle. At the front door she slipped a key into the lock and let herself inside.

"Jennifer. Jennifer. I'm here."

There was no answer. The whole house was unusually quiet for this hour of the day, and in a moment of panic the woman tried to recall if she was supposed to meet Jennifer at the park.

"Mrs. Johnson, I'm here. Sorry I'm a little late." It was true, she was late, but only ten minutes, and that wasn't exactly unusual. They wouldn't have left without her would they? No, they would have called.

She called out again, still no answer. The woman put her bag down and walked into the kitchen where a cold pizza box sat on the counter, but no sign of breakfast. She felt the coffee pot. Cold too. She looked inside; it was empty. Confused, the woman made her way up the stairs to the second floor.

"Jennifer ..." Could that bundle of energy still be asleep? Typically she was bowled over at the front door; presented with a posy of flowers gathered from the garden while the little girl's parents dressed for the day, or a with a drawing of said garden, replete with a smiling nanny, herself, pushing a child on a swing under a sun-drenched sky.

She opened the bedroom door. Jennifer really was still asleep! In a tone of mock scolding the young woman approached the bed, "Jennifer, why aren't you up? Where's your mommy?"

But the little girl didn't move.

"Jennifer ...?"

She touched Jennifer and retracted her hand in an instinctual reflex; the child was cold and rigid.

"Jennifer!"

The recoil instinct abated and the young woman lifted the little girl into her arms. The child had an eerie smile on her face; muscles contorted, not in pain, but devoid of life.

Turning with the lifeless body cradled in her arms, she raced out of the room, down the hallway, and beyond that into the main bedroom.

There, also motionless, also smiling, and also dead were Agent Johnson and his wife.

"Mrs. Johnson! Oh my god!" Horror turned to fear. Had they been killed? Was the killer still here? No, the bodies were cold. They were all healthy yesterday. This was a crime scene and she was trampling all over it!

She screamed again. Panic rose in her blood. 9-1-1. She needed to call the police! But where could she put Jennifer?

She turned back to the hallway, still carrying the little girl in her arms. Thundered down the carpeted stairs. In the living room she spied her bag. It rested on the seat of the floral fabricked armchair. She traded the child for her bag and riffled through for her phone. Hands shaking, she dialed 9-1-1.

Mr. Johnson! It must have been his job.

"9-1-1. What is your emergency?"

"Homeland security," was her reflex response. "Wait. Sorry, I have the number," and with that she hung-up. Her fingers were like clubs as she searched through her contacts for Mr. Johnson's work number.

Could they have been poisoned? What had she touched? The pizza.

Suddenly her phone rang. She jumped! No number. She answered it, "Hello?"

"Ma'am, this is 9-1-1 we got cut off."

"They're all dead!"

Chapter 7

TOKYO

"Here, look at this." Ulman nudged Lucy with her phone. "He might be good for more than climbing."

Lucy opened her eyes, reflexively checking the bulk baggage area where their ropes and black equipment cases took a generous portion of the limited space. She accepted the phone from Ulman and scanned the wonderous fruits of her underling's search on google images. Hiroshi Sugimura was indeed a handsome man, and the bare-chested image of him hanging from a rock revealed a plentiful abundance of muscles.

"He's all yours," Lucy smiled at the Major, marveling at the scattershot energy of her junior assistant.

"You're not interested?"

Ulman awaited Lucy's response, but eventually realized silence was Lucy speaking, "If he's too hot for you to handle, I'll take him for a spin. I've got an extra night in Japan anyway."

"Hiroshi-san flying to America tomorrow." Miyake stated, apparently listening, and Lucy forced a smile to cover for Ulman's brazenness. Miyake smiled back at Lucy with what looked like a mischievous twinkle, "Same flight as you."

"Then I'll have plenty of time to talk with him."

"Yes," Ulman interjected facetiously, "you and Hiroshi can talk." She then switched attention to Miyake who was dozing by the window. "Hey Miyake, does Hiroshi have a girlfriend?"

Miyake smiled politely, revealing nothing.

Major Ulman persisted, taking her phone back from Lucy and waving it at their guide. "That's your Hiroshi, right? Is he single?"

Miyake shook his head, still demurring to answer, "Not Japanese way to talk about these things."

"Major ..." Lucy's tone was a gentle reprimand, "Remember, you're an ambassador of the US military."

There was a moment's silence and their bullet train skewered a new crop of rice paddies in a blur of sleek white.

Miyake closed his eyes and quietly shook his head at Ulman, "You and him are very different. I tell him fish owl. He very excited."

Smiling at poor Ulman's thwarted recon, Lucy returned her attention to the window where the rice paddies were giving way to lush green mountains.

$+$

Two hours later, the sleek white blur slowed to a shiny crisp sculpture as the Shinkansen pulled into Tokyo station. The doors opened and passengers poured out of the train.

On the platform—buried among the crowd—was the man himself. In person, Hiroshi Sugimura was short, but unquestionably attractive in a muscular sort of way. He had an air about him, a sort of gravitas, as if he were of Japanese royalty. Royalty with an understated but definitive swagger. He was wearing cowboy boots, no less.

Hiroshi scanned the passengers, his eyes eventually alighting on Miyake. The men waved measured waves and crossed to one another. Lucy followed and Miyake presented the Japanese cannonball to her and her underling. "Colonel Topp, Major Ulman, this Hiroshi Sugimura, my friend."

"Arigato gozaimasu," was close to the extent of Lucy's Japanese.

"Welcome Lucy-san. It very great honor to finally meet."

"You too," she agreed.

"Akako still talks about you."

Lucy grinned a Cheshire cat grin at Ulman who was clearly disappointed at having been uncharacteristically overlooked. Score two points for a reputation earned a lifetime ago. Lucy gave a bow, at once offering a cheeky snub to Ulman and deferential greeting to Hiroshi.

"Akako say you are remarkable in untold ways. She wish she were here."

Lucy rose from her bow, her smile broadening with Hiroshi's sincerity. Without warning she wrapped her arms around his solid frame, giving him an impromptu hug. "Send this along to your sister! I miss that girl too."

Hiroshi recoiled dutifully, "This is not traditional Japanese way."

"Not traditional American either." Lucy relished a quiet thrill over the Adonisian body hidden under Hiroshi's stylish attire, almost as much as she was enjoying the shock on Ulman's face. Snapping Ulman to attention, she gave the younger woman a quick directive to collect the luggage. Then, turning back to Hiroshi, she augmented her smile with a wink, "Miyake said you wanted to take me to dinner." It was a wild interpretation of Miyake's words, but Lucy was comfortable with that.

Hiroshi blushed, both at her candor, and the improper discussion Miyake had evidently already had with this beautiful and striking woman. She was, of course, correct in her assertion.

+

Inside the Japanese Steak house, meat sizzled on the grill as a chef in a tall black hat assiduously worked the flames. Ishihara, was an expert chef, whose focused proficiency juggling five meals on a hot plate of solid metal was impervious to the alluring American that accompanied Hiroshi. He greeted them with a sincere but measured bow of his head.

Lucy smiled at him and turned to Hiroshi, "So, how is Akako?"

"She lives with husband in Tokyo."

"Your sister's married!? "

"Hai. Kazuki-san." and with a sly grin Hiroshi added, "The right man can ignite fireworks."

Lucy laughed, "I don't need a man to create chaos in my life."

A flame flared on the grill and she looked up at Ishihara. The steak was calling to her. She pointed at the morsel he had just trimmed and smiled a smile that could open a safe. Ishihara responded with a small plate and deftly presented Lucy with the offering, the taste of which deliciously exceeded her hope and expectation.

Opening her eyes, Lucy caught Hiroshi's barely perceptible head-shake of quietly possessive astonishment at Ishihara. So much for Akako's insistence that Hiroshi really was unique, and, by being so, unusually suited to her. She stifled her internal amusement; men truly were the same the world over—they were either busy falling over themselves to help women, or shaking heads as they witnessed other men doing so; the only difference being: where the woman's attention was directed. Perhaps women would one day rule the world, if they ever decided it was worth the effort.

Hiroshi turned to Lucy, and, realizing he'd been caught, smiled lightly.

Lucy picked up the wet towel that had magically appeared in front of her. It was good to wipe the day's travel away, and she ran the cloth under the entire lip of her neckline.

Hiroshi glanced back up at Ishihara who honorably averted his eyes.

"So, Miyake tells me you're a monkey," Lucy said, catching Hiroshi off-guard. "You're an expert climber," she clarified.

This time Hiroshi demurred his eyes, even as he cheekily confided, "To a walrus everyone appears to fly."

Lucy grinned at Hiroshi's un-Japanese candor.

"Miyake say a fish owl knock you out of the tree."

"Oh really?"

"Fish owl is very lucky bird. This can be good omen." Hiroshi was entirely sincere, "Sometimes a fall is worthwhile."

"That may be, but I think it's time we set the record straight." Lucy's eyes glowed, "How are you with the chair traverse?"

"That is a climb? I am not familiar with this."

"You can find it in any restaurant."

Hiroshi glanced about, unsure what Lucy meant.

Akako had always insisted Hiroshi was good for some fun, and Lucy decided to test if that still held. "Here. I'll show you." And, well aware of the potentially embarrassing nature of what she was embarking on, Lucy delicately dropped underneath her chair, explaining the rules as she did, "Touching the floor is considered a fall."

With a skillful grace that defied gravity, she worked her way between the legs on the left side of her chair, into a hanging position directly underneath her seat.

"You have to pass through the legs of the chair, and climb out the other side and then back onto the seat. All without touching the ground."

True to her word, Lucy never so much as brushed the grey slate tiles of the floor beneath her. She did, however, openly revel in Hiroshi's quiet mortification. It was perhaps a childish game of tit for tat. Still, if he wanted to question her climbing prowess, she'd happily give the patrons of his favorite restaurant a show to remember.

Hiroshi ventured a furtive glance at Ishihara who himself was discreetly marveling at the wondrous feats of Hiroshi's supple guest.

That Lucy continued her conversation while elegantly hanging upside down, appeared to be part of the act.

Striving to maintain some level of decorum, Hiroshi attempted a switch of topics, "You are in Japan for research?"

She smiled up at him, "The army wants to know what happens when a foreign agent enters a new environment."

"You?" Hiroshi managed, while admiring the muscles in her forearms.

"No, malaria and some flu, H5N1 and a benign strain of H9N2."

"You bring American virus to Japan?"

Lucy shimmied her way through the right legs and out from underneath her chair. She finished her ascent back onto the leather seat, angling her legs, first as a counterbalance, and then delicately lifting them like a gymnast, all the while avoiding the floor. The whole display was as much contortionist as climber. She grinned at Hiroshi as she sat back at the counter. "Kazakhstani actually."

Ishihara presented a dish of BBQ to Lucy, who, following Hiroshi's lead, bowed her head in gratitude. Hiroshi , for his part, kept steering the conversation to safer ground, "I have been to Kazakhstan." Subtly, he surveyed his surroundings for signs of his expected imminent ouster but was as relieved to find none as he was hopeful that their dinner date might return to proper etiquette. Perhaps talk of Kazakhstan and work would tame the tiger seated beside him. "Kazakhstan is engaged in much construction too. It is a small world."

Lucy shook her head scornfully. "Coincidence just makes it feel that way. Kazakhstan has thrown a ton of resources at biotech. I'm sure they've put plenty of dollars into construction too." Then referencing her party trick she patted the chair underneath her. "That's the chair traverse. I rate this one a V2 climb. Should we order beer?"

Hiroshi demurred his head ever so slightly. He was glad to witness neighboring eyes returning to their own meals, but that didn't override his principles, "Sake is very good."

"But beer would go nicely with the BBQ."

His head remained bowed with forceful politeness. "Sake is very good."

So, the gentleman from Japan had some spine. No real surprise, he was Akako's brother. The mischievous twinkle flared in Lucy's eyes as she decided to test his resolve again. "You complete the chair traverse, I'll drink sake. You touch the floor, we drink beer."

Behind the steel hot plate, Ishihara's interest flickered. Lucy's native dexterity with chopsticks had obviously impressed him, but beyond her own violation of Japanese etiquette she was now attempting to goad Hiroshi to commit the same.

For his part, Hiroshi could feel Ishihara's eyes burning on him. But more distressingly, he also sensed the renewed attention of his neighbors at the communal counter. And yet, the decision was not as easy as it should have been. Akako was right, Lucy Topp was unpredictable and alive. The combination took him back to his crazy college days. She was an intellect and a woman with panache, but was he really ready to break protocol for her?

Lucy continued to scrutinize him, preoccupied by thoughts of her own. Akako's brother had the boisterous flare Akako had always attributed to him, and yet on the subway here he had regaled her with particulars concerning the gross discrepancy between our own visual acuity and that of our fine-feathered friends.

Learning that birds saw slow objects with as much fidelity as fast ones was all very well, but that fact took on a whole new dimension when Hiroshi noted that this meant they could see movement in the sun and the stars, and that it was that motion that migrating birds used to orient themselves! Lucy hoped Hiroshi's personality held similar surprises.

Random trivia he had covered, but she was curious to see the quiet samurai Miyake had hinted at. Lucy leaned in closer and whispered conspiratorially, "Are you really an expert climber?" The question was, of course, immaterial if he didn't have the gumption to prove it now.

Hiroshi ventured a final glance at the chef. He felt certain the liberty permitted his American guest would be less graciously surrendered to him. In fact, he had little doubt that accepting her challenge would usher in his unceremonious removal from what had come to feel, over the last six months, like his own dining room.

Then, Ishihara gave him a subtle but encouraging nod. It was all Hiroshi needed to throw care to the wind.

Lucy smiled. Hiroshi-san really was a Japanese cowboy.

+

At the conclusion of a gymnastic display, every bit the equal of Lucy's own, chef Ishihara placed two square cedar cups in front of them. He bowed to them both and, with two hands on the ceramic carafe, filled their masu with finely aged sake.

Hiroshi bowed his head in gratitude thanking Ishihara and the gods in one gesture. He then turned to Lucy.

Lucy smiled at him. Akako had been right all those years ago, her brother really did rise to a challenge. She raised her eyebrows at him, "So, are you going to escort me all the way to the plane tomorrow?"

Hiroshi grinned a sly grin as he raised his cup.

"Kanpai!"

Chapter 8

AGENT SHANKLIN

"Give me a minute."

"I thought you guys were quicker than that."

"You and the rest of the world."

His smooth hands delicately worked the pick past the torque wrench, sensitively feeling for the last of the tumblers in the lock. It was a simple lock and his hands—creased with age and wear, and stained with small splotches of grease and ink—had years of experience in them. There was a click as the last tumbler fell into place and the man turned the handle.

"Agent Shanklin?! . . . Sue?!"

There was no answer.

+

Four hours later the brownstone building was cordoned off with FBI crime scene tape. Across the street a buzz of reporters had gathered, collecting tape of the location and craning their necks for hints of which way the story was headed. Their agitation bubbled to a spike as Special Agent Williams, an FBI spokeswoman, ducked under the yellow tape and approached them.

And then the flurry of questions began.

The predictability and ineffectiveness of the barrage was comical to Special Agent Williams, and she wondered if any of the reporters in front of her had ever had success with this lemming-like drive forward.

She stood in silence. The technique so often deployed by Ms. Herd, her second grade teacher, remained the most effective in a wild multitude of situations.

Eventually the mob complied and she picked out the journalist she had identified as the least egregious; perhaps they could learn.

The young man launched right into it, "There are rumors a terrorist was intercepted at JFK yesterday and that both Agent Shanklin's death and that of her partner, Agent Johnson and his family, are all connected." There it was, the hyperbolic frame, and now the innocuous question that implicitly endorsed the frame. "Can you comment on the details of that connection?"

"The investigation is on-going. Obviously we're in early stages and all possible leads are being explored." Williams gave them ten minutes of boilerplate and then wrapped it up, leaving the buzz to shoot tops and tails before uploading everything to their respective studios.

CDC Biovigilance Report:

Unidentified Deaths with Tight Smiles

Topline Data:

```
Case Count              5
Laboratory Confirmed    0
Cases
Deaths                  5
Hospitalizations        0
```

Epidemiologic Data:

Geographic:

```
Isolated Fatality Zones    NYC
Reported Incidence         3 clusters around NYC
Noteable Developments      Apparently linked deaths,
                           contact and post mortem
                           indications
Timelines                  Less than 24 hours since
                           initial report, all NYC
Traceback Data             JFK?
```

Biological Indications:

Incubation Period   unknown if even contagious,
                                 < 24hrs
Symptoms   Rigid smile post mortem
                                 indication only
Mode of Transmission   Unknown vector
Notes   Apparent Patient Zero had
                                 contact with two others, who
                                 had subsequent contact with
                                 the remainder

Chapter 9

NARITA AIRPORT

Fatigued travelers wearily watched multiple wall mounted television sets as they slouched on the hard-molded plastic chairs in desperate attempts at achieving the unachievable: comfort and recuperation.

Even the business class waiting lounges on the mezzanine above—at least the one time Lucy had experienced them—were only marginally better with their cushioned seats. The problem was the one intrinsic to travel: stagnation. What was really needed was a means of exercising.

Happily for Lucy, last night's festivities had fostered a brinksmanship between herself and Hiroshi. So much so that she was beginning to wonder if Hiroshi might be the *genuinely* unexpected consequence of her fall in the forest! Their brinksmanship now extended to a newly accepted challenge; one equally at odds with their new environment.

A short distance away from the docile herd, Lucy and Hiroshi clung like monkeys to the thin trim on the underside of the sleek metal staircase that linked the main waiting lounge to a viewing mezzanine. Hiroshi swung from one arm under the man-made wrought iron overhang. The Japanese cannonball was apparently a goofball too—perhaps Akako had been more right than Lucy had given her credit for all those years ago.

Lucy matched his move, grasping the parallel support running up the underside of the other side of the stairs. Their physical activity was helping with her hangover in a way that coffee never did; exercise was definitely her panacea of choice.

And it was fun to play at giddy youth with this odd duck.

Then something from the real world caught her eye. Behind Hiroshi's fluid movement Lucy caught a glimpse of a television set. She stopped mid-climb. Hanging from one straight arm, she gently shook the lactic acid from the other while focusing on the screen.

On the monitor she recognized the brownstone architecture of a New York street she knew well. What caught her attention however was the incongruous sight of a body-bag-laden gurney situated between the apartment and the Japanese reporter in the foreground.

Nodding back at the brownstone building, the reporter spoke earnestly to the camera, and though his Japanese intonings were indecipherable to Lucy, his intended conveyance of panicked fear was easy enough to understand.

The TV cut back to the studio and a newscaster took up the bluster where the reporter had left off, a bold blood-red "7" showing on the screen beside him.

Lucy turned to Hiroshi, who was still concentrating on the climb. Hiroshi looked back at her and she matched his next move. Hiroshi smiled and extolled admiration he had reserved the previous evening. "You climb like ninja."

She smiled back and pulled ahead of him, lifting her head past the last stair and then the landing at the top of the staircase. The railing made an easy final hold, and a moment later she was standing on the landing she had just passed under. Again the television monitor caught her eye. This time, to her surprise, she not only understood the language, she recognized the man onscreen.

He had a solid build for fifty, with a salt and pepper buzz cut, and a clean shave. Below his face a caption identified him as Commander Krogen, USAMRIID—the United States Army Medical Research Institute for Infectious Diseases, Lucy's real home. Commander Krogen, very occasionally Bill to Lucy, looked squarely into the camera as military men tended to do, defiant and firm.

Lucy shifted her entire focus to the screen while below her Hiroshi hung from one arm and shook lactic acid out of the other.

"Bio-terror is just one possibility we are considering. The investigation is–" but the rest of Commander Krogen's words were swallowed in a sea of gibberish as the Japanese translation eclipsed his voice. Catching an occasional phrase here and there, Lucy gleaned little more than that there had been a spate of unexplained deaths back home.

Fascinating. And for Krogen to be taking time with reporters, there was sure to be more that was being unsaid.

The waiting lounge vanished from Lucy's consciousness. Her focus was complete. She had to know more.

From her pocket, she pulled her phone. The New York Times would have something, and if not a google search–

Wait—what the hell?!

To her amazement there was a missed call; from Commander Krogen's mobile number! The Commander didn't make social calls, and even less so when his time was already being assailed by reporters.

Lucy recalled the last time Krogen had placed such a call to her. She had been in Thailand, stranded at another airport. It was winter in the Northern Hemisphere, and erratic weather was playing havoc with the flights. Thailand had made her close to Southern China, where, of more interest to Krogen, a bubble was percolating in the form of a new strain of flu.

"I know H7N9 doesn't traditionally spread easily, but it does have a high death rate where it does spread. And–"

"And you want me to re-route to Guangzhou." Lucy had interrupted him, cutting to the chase.

"This is no climate change scenario." Krogen had signed off.

Compared with the sluggish progress of the climate change tanker— measured in decades if not centuries—disease was a high-speed coast guard interceptor piloted by pirates!

And unlike the last ice age, pandemics had significantly more recent precedents. The Black Plague of the fourteenth century had wiped out an estimated sixty percent of Europe's population. Though being the fourteenth century, that had limited the death toll to near a quarter of a billion people.

Lucy looked up at the Japanese newscaster who was now waxing lyrical beside an image of the trefoil-like biological hazard symbol and a red 1918.

1918, had been the Spanish Influenza. Half a billion people had been infected. A startling number to be sure, but Spanish Flu still lacked the advantages of modern kinetic intermingling. With trains, planes and automobiles, all a regular part of public life, the *next* benchmark biological disaster would kill billions.

Those were sobering numbers in any language.

Lucy looked back at her phone. Beyond Krogen's missed call there was a voicemail. Well, Commander Krogen had called and she'd missed the call, but at least some answers were waiting for her.

"Lucy-san?" Hiroshi stood, confused by her violent swing in disposition. But Lucy ignored him. Her ability to completely shut out lower Maslov priorities was a trait her mother credited as a superpower.

The call was one hour ago—1AM in DC. She pressed voicemail and an automated voice prompted her for her password.

Her *password*? Seriously?!

Sometimes she hated international travel. And herself. She had been thwarted by this exact problem on a trip last summer, and worse the message then hadn't been important enough to induce her to learn from her mistake. Why did you need a password internationally, if you didn't need one at home! She cursed herself, the phone company, and the capricious gods punishing her for recalcitrant laziness.

She had no idea what her password was.

"Can I help?" Hiroshi asked confused.

"No," she curtly brushed him off.

She tried her birthday, 0705. She tried her mother's birthday. No dice. She tried 1234 . . . 1111, 3141 or π, nope. 2718, the base of the natural log, nature's anchor for exponential growth, nope. Nothing. There were too many options to try.

Crap and double crap!

Lucy glanced up at Hiroshi again. Cogs whirring.

"Something is wrong?" he asked.

"I missed a call." She responded absently. She indicated the television monitor, "And I can't understand what they're saying."

Hiroshi turned to the TV, no clearer about the problem, "Is the weather report. There are floods–"

"No. There was a segment before that."

"Ah," Hiroshi nodded uncomprehending understanding.

Lucy cycled back to her phone. She opened the New York Times.

Front page! Second article: *Mysterious Deaths in NY*. Lucy scanned the first two paragraphs. Apparently there had been seven inexplicable deaths in New York, including two special agents from the Department of Homeland Security. She skimmed through the article; the writer was insinuating a potential link, even as the agencies involved were clearly being careful not to commit either way.

Lucy checked a clock on the wall across the lounge: 3PM in Narita. 2AM in Washington DC. She dialed Commander Krogen's number. It was only 2AM after all.

"You have reached the voicemail of Commander Krogen." Krogen wasn't answering.

"Hey. Commander, it's Colonel Topp. I got your message. I mean I couldn't access it—shitty passwords. Anyway, I saw you on the news here. What's going on? Our flight leaves in a couple of hours. If I don't hear from you, I'll try calling you again before we're wheels up." It was a garbled message, but it would have to suffice, and Lucy hung up. She glanced at Hiroshi again. The problem with emotional connection was that it put you in a coma. Surprisingly counter to her typical reaction, she didn't hold it against Hiroshi, who was now bowing to an airport security guard.

The guard glanced cursorily at Lucy, and Lucy smiled the same angelic smile she'd given Chef Ishihara. The guard shook his head with clear disapproval but left the climbers to attend to the three young girls who were chasing a cloud of soap bubbles in the waiting lounge below.

Hiroshi leaned close to Lucy's ear and intoned with a wry grin, "We must behave. No more climb."

But Lucy was distracted by the girls' mother who was blowing into the soap-film, and launching bubbles forth.

"It is good." Hiroshi assured her.

"Look at those bubbles," Lucy pointed, guiding Hiroshi's attention past the receding security guard.

A bubble drifted up towards them on eddies of hot air, oily rainbows swirling in the sphere.

Hiroshi smiled, "They are beautiful."

"Yes." Lucy's voice trailed off. "And they are also perfect pockets of air from that woman's lungs."

Hiroshi frowned, struck by his companion's odd way of seeing the world.

"Spherical vectors." Lucy mused.

They both watched the dreamy swirl on the boundary of the bubble, that mirrored the woman's invisible breath inside. On the floor below, more bubbles floated out over the rows of seats until the fingers of the girls popped them in splashes of soapsuds.

"That's a perfect illustration of airborne dispersal." Lucy marveled. "In 24 hours, her breath will touch four corners of the world!"

"So much for airport security." Hiroshi concurred.

Lucy nodded, "Mother Nature does as she pleases."

Chapter 10

MASSACHUSETTS GENERAL HOSPITAL

Dexamedetomidine was a spectacular 2-adrenoreceptor agonist that produced a sedative state resembling natural sleep; with the exception that patients, so drugged, were easily awakened from their hypnotic state to answer questions, take neurological tests and broadly respond to hospital staff and visitors. The patient remained calm, comfortable and lucid until the removal of the stimulus. And with the removal of stimulus they simply drifted back to their sleep-like sedated condition. So the description went, but Director Havamyer, the head of the FBI, was skeptical of medicines' extravagant claims.

An outstanding thirty-year veteran of the bureau, Director Havamyer was here for a face to face with one of the few Americans more lauded than himself. Content was paramount, but Havamyer had long believed personal appearance to be an equally critical a feature in any briefing. Presentation affected communication, and he was glad that—in spite of President Pollack's current condition—he himself had erred, as was his rule, on the sharper side of immaculate. He wore a dark suit, out of place in the hospital ward, but entirely in line with his own aesthetic.

He concluded his briefing with an analogy he had heard earlier that day—an analogy that had struck him as particularly insightful. "Sir, you wouldn't expect a country to surrender without a fight first, the body is no different."

President Pollack nodded, "Thank you Havamyer. Bottom line is: no symptoms means this is unlikely to be contagious."

"Correct sir."

Even under the lingering effects of the Dexamedetomidine, and from beneath the crisp white sheets of the recovery ward bed, President Robert Pollack had the ability to tersely surmise most anything thrown at him. His presidency was founded on bold decisions, diplomacy and an ability to read those around him. Director Havamyer clearly felt this crisis was dramatic, but not in need of presidential intervention, so, the Commander in Chief turned his attention to the three doctors who passed the suited security at the door. "Now what exactly have you fine surgeons attached to my heart?"

Happy to be dismissed, Havamyer nodded deferentially, and left the room. The President needed his rest, but there was a lot of work to do if the more dire prognostications on the current circumstances could legitimately remain withheld from him. If it was contagious and was more virulent than SARS, then there was no question that he had to be involved.

Chapter 11

A CALL TO HOME

"Pick up, pick up." Lucy felt agitated and annoyed. It was 5:30AM in DC, Commander Krogen had to be awake by now.

The woman beside her glanced at the red light above the aisle. The fasten seat belt sign had been glowing for minutes. Her neighbor was obviously about to put voice to her series of untoward glances when the captain jumped back on the speaker system with a directive of his own, "Welcome aboard again. Electronic devices should now be off and stowed ..."

"Commander Krogen," came the brusque pick up. "Colonel Topp, is that you?"

"Commander Krogen. Is it still local?"

This was what Commander Krogen liked about Lucy; no protracted greetings, she was direct, and invariably two steps ahead of anything anyone threw at them. "There's unsubstantiated speculation, but for now it appears to be contained in New York."

"Cabin crew arm doors and cross-check." The Captain interrupted again.

Lucy smiled through gritted teeth at the woman beside her, a forced apology of sorts. It was frustrating to be a civilian.

"Is your computer up?" Krogen asked.

"No. We're pulling back from the gate."

"Ma'am." A steward interrupted her, indicating Lucy's phone.

Lucy nodded compliance to the steward, as she pressed Krogen for more. "Contagious? An act of terror?"

"Still too early."

"What have you isolated?"

"Beyond the plane, we haven't isolated anything yet."

"The plane?" Lucy was confused, "What killed them?"

"Ma'am." The steward pressed, in a sterner voice.

"Colonel Topp, who's there with you?"

"I'm on the plane. We're taxiing to the runway."

"Good."

"Ma'am!"

Lucy could hear Krogen chuckle, "Safe travels. Get home fast."

"Wait, Commander–" but he was gone. Lucy glared at the steward, "There are no scientific studies, you know, that substantiate, in any way, that electronic devices interfere with the flight-deck."

"I don't make the rules ma'am." The steward replied diplomatically.

Once again perception trumped reality. Lucy shrugged grumpily at the steward, but stowed her phone. Speaking to Commander Krogen would have to wait for now.

"No news?" Hiroshi asked.

Lucy shook her head, "The public imagines silent release when they think of bio-warfare—a container left on the tracks of the London Tube. Some nasty microbe released by the arriving wheels of a train just as the crowds thronged. Or a contaminated air-conditioning system at a major sporting event, the NBA finals." It was true these were plausible seeding mechanisms for the dispersal of an infectious pathogen, but realistically most such opening gambits presented a high risk of turning around and biting the hand that seeded them. They were the purview of fanatics alone. "The smart adversary focuses on livestock and crops. Eliminate food and your enemy falls to their knees without a fight."

Hiroshi nodded thoughtfully, this made good sense to a man who spent much of his time considering the disconnects between the realities of how people interacted with space and their perceptions of it.

The woman to Lucy's left watched assiduously out her window, even as her ears burnt brightly.

Lucy read her irritated disapproval and, ostensibly speaking to Hiroshi, launched into a polemic diatribe that was purely for the benefit of the gallery. She finished by insisting that, "The media is not interested in the truth. Fear and conspiracy sell much better." adding inflammatorily, "There's something to be said for state controlled news."

The woman at the window audibly tut-tutted.

Lucy paused, a sudden pang of guilt sweeping over her, this woman wasn't the enemy. She turned to the woman and addressed her more directly, "I'm sorry. Really. That was an important call." She just wanted the woman to understand her actions, "People completely misjudge facts and statistics. I'm sure you've heard the claims; vaccinations cause autism, for instance. It's infuriating that the un-informed fools making such proclamations, never check the science, and conveniently forget the ghastly diseases these vaccines routinely prevent. Routinely. Fear blinds people and robs them of their sense." And here was the apology, "I too am people."

The woman awkwardly accepted the apology of sorts and turned back to the window.

"You are very worried about news report?" Hiroshi was having difficulty tracking when Lucy's indefinite articles referred to herself in the third person and when they referred to the general public.

"No." Lucy shook her head, "No, I'm not expecting a global pandemic. It just sounds interesting. But you never know, one day this will be the real thing and I will be prepared."

Around them the cabin lights dimmed and passengers snuggled under airline blankets. Whatever the reality behind the news reports, Lucy would have to await her stateside return for a report unembellished by sensational journalism—or, if it really was bad, for a report that didn't obfuscate just how dramatic the threat actually was.

The 747 made a turn at the end of the runway and lined up for take-off. The engines roared and the captain took his hand off the brakes.

Chapter 12

WALLENSTEIN DEBRIEFING

Pressed against a wall of glass was Magjan Iglinsky, or more precisely, a printout of Magjan's digital image from 36 hours earlier. Back when he was still alive. The photo was being held up to the glass by a young FBI agent.

On the other side of the glass window was Gerald Stein, aka Operations Officer Wallenstein. Operations Officer Wallenstein glanced at the face in the photo. It was a face he knew well. Indeed, by no coincidence, he had been standing less than half a dozen snaking queues across from Mr. Iglinsky the very moment this photo had been taken by the immigration official's camera at JFK.

Wallenstein looked past the photo, to the young FBI agent on the other side of the glass and nodded. "That's him. He made me in the Almaty airport." He might as well start at the beginning. "The CIA, through the NCS, has been interested in Mr. Iglinsky since he met with a French government scientist eighteen months ago. That scientist disappeared eight weeks ago. We expect he's dead. And we have reason to suspect foul play. Especially given indications he'd just made a breakthrough. Scientifically speaking. Anyway, the evidence was thin and no body has been recovered, so we've been shadowing Mr. Iglinsky for six weeks in the hope of something percolating to the surface. There's even hope a bigger fish might surface."

Jonathan O'Spaniel, an older FBI agent seated by his younger partner, pressed the button connecting the intercom between the rooms, and prompted Wallenstein further, "And?"

"You've heard of the phrase 'lots and none at all'?" Wallenstein asked rhetorically.

"Start us out with Almaty a couple of days ago."

Wallenstein shrugged, "Magjan Iglinsky was in Almaty to see an old friend. Yes there's biotech there, but that's not necessarily part of the 'lots' if you get my drift."

Agent O'Spaniel pressed the intercom again, "You think Almaty's a dead end?"

Wallenstein elaborated indifferently, "It's one place to start looking. A good one if you're trying to nail those perpetrating serious violations of ethical standards in scientific research. But the architects are further north, Astana."

"And what should we be looking for?"

"Look, PharmaCo and some other big drug companies here have been warning of the Kazak cowboys' approach to the work. Harness Mother Nature and all that. PharmaCo in particular has been helpful, but the Kazaks' aren't exactly running an open book. And hell, who listens to the big drug companies anyway?" Wallenstein's second rhetorical question hung in the air.

"You heard of the 2013 Novartis fiasco?" Wallenstein was unsure exactly how biotech savvy his interrogators were, "The Craig Venter Institute and Novartis were working on a new flu vaccine, based on a genetic sequence published by the Chinese CDC. Unfortunately for the project, neither thought to involve the Chinese. Big mistake. Contravened a key principle surrounding the publication of that work. And to add insult to injury, in Venter's case they actually involved the US CDC."

"I don't get it." O'Spaniel admitted.

"The private sector just took what they wanted and expected to get away with it."

"Oh."

"And you wonder why the public are skeptical of big pharma." It was familiar territory, but, like most issues, Wallenstein understood there were two sides to the equation, "It's weird really, because cynicism is a curious instinct to harbor against a sector upon whom our public health depends. Without industry, new drugs, and even fundamental research, are tough to fund."

"The drug companies seem plenty good at making themselves heard when it suits them."

"Right." Wallenestein was fighting rising impatience. "The trick is to make the rules of the playing field so that their interests align with ours."

O'Spaniel nodded as he grappled with the broad brushstrokes of the crib sheet Wallenstein was feeding him, "...so PharmaCo called the 'Kazak cowboys' out because the lax laws governing research there—in Kazakhstan—tipped the balance in their favor?"

"Lower operating constraints are a clear advantage." Wallenstein agreed. If only the whole world played by the same rules.

Wallenstein coughed again and switched to the subject occupying his own mind, "Listen, us agency guys don't like being locked up in a room by you Feds. Especially this crazy bio-containment room shit. Am I at risk?"

Agent O'Spaniel was unemotionally matter-of-fact, "We've quarantined your entire flight."

That information jolted Wallenstein like a lightning bolt. Up to this point he had somehow harbored the notion that this whole situation was actually about his surveillance job; that this was some sort of turf war. But entire planes didn't get quarantined for a turf war.

There was a knock at the door in the FBI agents' room. It was as if the universe knew Wallenstein's thinking and decided to underscore it theatrically by bringing the outside world into the scene. The door opened to reveal none other than Director Havamyer, a legend in the intelligence field, a man Wallenstein knew by sight, though they'd never met.

+

Havamyer—still sporting the sharp suit from his earlier presidential briefing—glanced at Wallenstein behind the glass. He gave the later, the slightly regretful nod you might give a recently diagnosed terminal patient, and motioned the senior interviewing agent outside.

In the hallway the Director listened intently to Agent O'Spaniel.

"There's a dead convenience store clerk who worked a few blocks from Agent Shanklin's place. Might be unrelated, but we're investigating."

"And Kazakhstan?" Havamyer asked.

"The team's assembled and flying out at eleven hundred. They fly into Almaty but most of the team will continue north to Astana. The CDC is sending a team with us. Mr. Iglinsky's flight hasn't yielded any more corpses, so for now he's still our index case."

"That's the CDC's position?"

"Yes, though the CDC and the RIID, haven't ruled out poisoning. They feel it's acting too fast to be infectious."

"And too cleanly." Havamyer added, echoing the earlier briefing he had been a party to.

"We're coordinating with Fort Detrick. They're setting up models and reviewing the field data as it comes in. Obviously they've got their own data, but we're sending them anything we get. Intel we collect from presumed and understood routes the decedents travelled in the last 24 hours."

Piecing together the activities of victims' final 24 hours was something the FBI did very well. Mostly it involved interviewing people—colleagues, store clerks, anyone who might have had contact with the deceased, accidental or routine—but it also involved analyzing CCTV footage and cellular records, reviewing web searches. Anything that might pinpoint a time and place visited by the deceased; data history from their car and phone mapping applications had been a particular boon in recent years.

The sentiment of one particular government report, compiled after the Weapons of Mass Destruction fiasco almost two decades ago, always resonated for Havamyer: "While the successful collection of intelligence cannot ensure a flawless product, the failure to collect information turns analysis into guesswork." Director Havamyer hated guesswork.

His phone rang and he looked at the number. Commander Krogen, the head of USAMRIID. This should be interesting.

"Thanks O'Spaniel," Havamyer nodded back at the interrogation room, "you can head back in."

Chapter 13

RETURNING HOME

As the CDC's Gulfstream destined for Kazakhstan hurtled down the Dulles runway, a much larger plane taxied towards the terminal. The commercial 747, on which Lucy sat beside Hiroshi and Mrs. Ford, the woman by the window with whom Lucy had since made peace.

At the immigration checkpoint, the 400 passengers merged with other incoming flights, and the thousands of bleary-eyed travelers got their passports stamped, snapshots taken and fingerprints digitally scanned prior to pushing their luggage ladden carts out through the arrival gates, dispersing like a scaled up model of a sneeze.

Waiting among the eager crowd was Ellen Topp, Lucy's mother. She spotted Lucy and her buoyant effervescence erupted to frantic waving. Lucy saw her just as she swooped upon them. Her embrace was full of love and warmth, and it lasted as long as a mother's want.

Once freed, Lucy turned to Hiroshi who was waiting politely, "Mom, this is a Akako's brother, Hiroshi. Hiroshi, my mom, Ellen."

"You're a handsome young devil." Ellen beamed at Lucy's companion, "You can have one too." And with that, she opened her arms and gave the reverential Japanese man a big welcoming embrace of his own, clearly demonstrating that the apple didn't fall far from the tree where adherence to social conventions were concerned.

Pinned in place, Hiroshi glanced around the cavernous atrium and was struck that this eagerness to befriend was apparently a modern-day epidemic in the West. Indeed, beyond Lucy's earlier greeting, Hiroshi reflected that he had seen the internet equivalent of this unfettered reception of strangers a year ago when a US colleague had sent him a link to a website called Chat Roulette. Software enabled you to connect with a random internet voyager. It was an odd intimacy, bringing a stranger into your home or office via a camera on your computer. Of course if you didn't like the random pairing, you simply pressed the "scan" button and a new connection was made.

It was nice that direct human interaction still lacked a "scan" button, and Hiroshi quietly reveled in the social discomfiture induced by his heritage.

+

"I've known Hiroshi's sister, Akako, ten years, but her advance press didn't do him justice." Lucy mused from the front seat of Ellen's car.

With not a hint of apprehension, Ellen ostentatiously ogled Hiroshi in the rearview mirror. "I'll say."

Hiroshi smiled politely.

"You be careful young man, my daughter breaks hearts."

Hiroshi forced a smile of quaint, if merely apparent, confusion.

"Hiroshi's just here for an architecture conference, mom."

Ellen grinned and Lucy began to blush.

"Stop grinning."

"Smiles are like chickenpox, dear; contagious."

Lucy smiled too.

+

Ellen stopped her car by a mud-caked Jeep and turned to Lucy, "Alright, out you hop. The rest of this ride is for the tourists."

Lucy turned back to Hiroshi who again smiled back at her, unfazed. "My meeting does not start until tomorrow."

"Great!" Lucy clapped her hands. It wasn't exactly a surprise to anyone that she needed to check in at the RIID before stopping at home, and Hiroshi could surely take care of himself.

Had they really just spent thirty contiguous hours together?!

Lucy shrugged and turned back to Ellen. She gave her mother a kiss and wished them well, "Happy sightseeing."

As Lucy opened the front door and climbed out, Ellen patted the empty passenger seat, indicating Hiroshi should move forward. "Come on, I don't bite."

Hiroshi exited the back and was about to take Lucy's vacated passenger seat when Lucy grabbed his arm. Winking at him, she gave a dramatic stage whisper, "You know she's crazy."

Ellen ignored Lucy's remark the way a loving mother does. "I'll return him for dinner on my way out of town. You satisfy your curiosity about what's going on."

"It might not be just curiosity, mom." Lucy chided.

"If you say so," Ellen dismissed her.

"Goodbye," Lucy waved, shut Hiroshi's door, and got into her own 4WD.

She watched them pulling away, blissfully unaware that her concerns might actually be well founded.

Your average citizen didn't see how close half a dozen deaths were to a global pandemic. They didn't understand measurements in logarithmic scales. Earthquakes were the same, 3 or 4 on the Richter scale is barely a bump, 6 or 7 flattens a city. The problem with biology was that 3 or 4 could easily be as close to 6 or 7 as the numbers appeared.

Chapter 14

USAMRIID

"Following on the heels of yesterday's ten mysterious deaths, New York was rocked this morning by revelations of twenty further deaths! Each accompanied by an eerie smile." The tone of the NPR announcer was alarmist enough to play on a commercial channel, which to Lucy's ear undermined the content. She turned the volume down as she rolled up to the guard's booth at the entrance to the USAMRIID.

Private First Class Alvin Smith glanced at the familiar mud-caked 4WD and waved Lucy in with an informal salute. "Morning Colonel Topp. Good to see you back."

Lucy parked in her reserved spot and passed the casual security at the building's entrance. Inside, she walked down a corridor full of collegiate atmosphere. Open doors and energized chatter filled the air as she rounded a bend and pulled out the card-key to her office door.

"Colonel Topp," Commander Krogen exclaimed, "just the person I was looking for."

Lucy returned his quick salute. She was about to jump into her list of questions when she noticed Colonel Marshall approaching. As always, he looked very pleased to see her, but also a little on edge.

"Look, it's the golden boy." Lucy quipped to Krogen, her longstanding reference to Marshall's uncanny ability to solicit funds from industry specifically earmarked for research.

"Colonel Marshall," Krogen saluted.

"Commander Krogen. Colonel Topp, it's good to see you back." The innocuous greeting, however preppy, retained layers of extra meaning.

Lucy turned and opened her office door. Marshall was fond of telling her that the world would change while she was on one of her 'jungle jaunts'. No doubt he was here to gloat. He had noted more than once, that a couple of day's head start for the wrong pathogen could easily cost millions of lives when the big one hit. What amused Lucy about this was the implicit implication that her presence would somehow make the difference. In the end though, point-scoring was really what was most important to him and he certainly looked pleased that the game had started with Lucy, not simply on the sidelines, but missing from the arena.

She placed her bags on the desk beside a folder marked H9N2, "What are the symptoms?"

"There are no symptoms, just a dramatically truncated serial interval." Marshall jumped in.

"What's with the guy from the plane?"

"The NCS had been shadowing him for–"

"NCS?" Lucy interrupted Krogen.

"National Clandestine Services, they're a division of the CIA. Operations Officer Wallenstein was actively shadowing him, had been for a couple of months. They've been interested in him over a year." Krogen pursed his lips and raised his eyebrows. "Wallenstein is being debriefed, but he has his *'integrity of the investigation'* to protect. You know how it goes, standard BS that wastes time. Still, we would have dismissed Patient Zero as a suicide if it weren't for all the other bodies." It impressed Lucy that Krogen was so comfortable admitting when a mistake might have been made.

"But no one else from the plane is dead?"

"No," and, anticipating her next question, Krogen continued, "And yes, our two Homeland Security agents could be the agents of death. But given they're both dead, and there's no symptoms to track, complete contact tracing is going to be a pain."

Lucy smiled at Krogen's play on the word 'agents', but in response she only shrugged possible agreement with him and continued down her mental list, "You have people investigating the agents' interactions from earlier in the day?"

Krogen nodded, "They worked at JFK! Came in contact with travelers from everywhere; China, Kansas, Australia, you name it, but as far as we know right now, they're all still living."

"Nothing else?" Lucy asked.

"Not yet. I need you to coordinate the data. Map the propagation."

Lucy crossed back to her door. "The raw's being uploaded onto the system?" she asked, referring to the untreated data.

"As it comes in. The FBI is sharing CCTV data and any Intel they gather on physical contact between the decedents. They're mobilized. As is the CDC's branch in New York."

"But the bottom line is, everything's emanating from the one point?" Her question was rhetorical, but significant.

Since John Snow's work on Cholera in the nineteenth century it was standard protocol to work the epidemiology of an outbreak. Time and again this proved the most effective way—indeed the only consistently reliable way—of attacking the outbreak of a new epidemic.

With H5N1 bird flu, for example, the apparent susceptibility of six-year-old boys in Thailand was simply a manifestation of the sociological fact that those kids were the social group most likely assigned the task of plucking dead chickens. That insight was of key driver in isolating the transmission point, and ultimately curtailing the epidemic. As was so often the case, seemingly innocuous idiosyncrasies concealed critical causalities. And so it was that CDC efforts nowadays coordinated with other agencies such as the FBI, and with teams on the ground who are deployed for the needle in the haystack door-to-door search.

The key observation was that every death so far could be traced back to one interaction.

Commander Krogen put voice to the obvious theory, "For all we know it's Legionnaire's disease in the Homeland security interview room, only it's super fast."

"Possible, though the apparent secondary cases look to be happening too quickly for viral transmission." Lucy countered.

"If the victims remain geographically contained to New York, this sounds more like media hype than impending pandemic, because JFK is the perfect international springboard if it's contagious."

"I'll check what the FBI and CDC in New York send through." Lucy gave Commander Krogen another quick salute.

"Thanks Colonel," he saluted back, and left.

Lucy shifted to Marshall who had been standing, quietly waiting the debriefing out.

"Are you busy tonight?"

Lucy waved at her desk and down the hallway Commander Krogen had just disappeared along. "I'm playing catch up."

"I'd be happy to help."

"Thanks, but I'll get more done alone. Besides, Major Ulman should be back soon. I'm sure she'll want to see you." She completed the terse brush-off by closing the door on him.

Chapter 15

THE KAZAKHSTANI PARLIAMENT

"We've quarantined the facility until we can get the right team in; one we can trust." Minister Gorshkov stood over the bundle of files and photos he had placed in front of Kazakhstan's top man. There were subtleties to the information he needed to communicate, but the key point was simple, "The outside world is focused on a biolevel 4 issue; Kretsky is a biolevel 2 facility. I'm hoping to keep it that way."

Prime Minister Maqtaly flipped through the files. "Did anyone else visit that day?"

"We're tracking it."

"And who else was involved with Kretsky?"

"The only loose end is Magjan Iglinsky, the hired gun who sourced a good chunk of the talent and technology. The good news is he won't be talking. The bad news is, he's the guy who died in US custody last night."

Maqtaly looked up from the desk, understandably concerned. "Will he be traced back to Kretsky?"

"We don't know what he revealed, but he was responsible for too many transgressions of international law to compromise himself willingly." Gorshkov could feel Maqtaly's concern, but panic didn't help anyone in a situation like this. Reasoned calculation and response was what was needed, and he had already formed his own theories. "I believe Iglinsky was detained for the work pertaining to stem cells, and that won't link back to Kretsky. Besides, while Iglinsky was at Kretsky two months ago when the Frenchman died, he hasn't been there in over a week. And while he saw Amanet the day of the incident, he flew out of Almaty *before* anything happened. The timing doesn't work for *him* to have known anything was wrong."

"And this has nothing to do with the Frenchman's death?"

"He choked to death." Gorshkov replied simply.

"But he was delirious before that."

"Sure. And that contrasts with these deaths; there's no evidence of symptoms this time." Gorshkov was confident of this, "This is unrelated to the Frenchman's death, excepting that it may have stemmed from the same scientific root cause. The new techniques they developed."

"So you really believe Iglinsky was in the dark?" Maqtaly grumbled.

"Unless there were symptoms. And there aren't. Iglinsky knew nothing of this catastrophe at Kretsky." Maqtaly wasn't convinced, but Gorshkov persisted, "It's a tight seal at this point. The stem cells red herring is a perfect dusting of snow to cover our tracks."

Gorshkov was doing his best to placate, but Maqtaly had a niggling doubt. The sort of doubt he had first experienced as a child when a stray dog had eyed an old meat bun in his hand. In the end, he had ignored his gut, proffered the bun and gotten his hand bitten for the effort. He smiled a thin smile as he reflected on his current position: you try and help mankind, and it bites you in the butt. He didn't like being bitten in the butt any better than on the hand.

Had Magjan Iglinsky really kept his mouth shut?

Gorshkov was talking again. Thinking aloud really, "The real question is whether someone brought something else into Kretsky. Something they shouldn't have."

"We both know the answer to that."

"But the things we know about don't account for the deaths of an entire lab."

Maqtaly remembered Iglinsky all right. He'd been necessary to move the Awake program forward in its early stages. Shifty characters had their place. Sourcing suspect materials, personnel and expertise had required that, but the program was ready to shed its nefarious roots, and Maqtaly was not altogether unhappy that Mr. Iglinsky would no longer be a factor.

"We have an opportunity." Gorshkov interrupted Maqtaly's thoughts.

"Really?"

"The history of biological cock-ups could work in our favor." As science minister, with a background in biology before he'd moved into politics, Gorshkov had his own perspectives. Around the world, investigators were focused on a biolevel 4 pathogen—the cases being lethal and as yet unidentified—but Kretsky wasn't even a biolevel 3 facility. Whatever pathogen caused the devastation at Kretsky shouldn't have been there! And in a perverse twist of fate, that very fact might save them now; people weren't going to find something they didn't think to look for.

"History?"

"Recent history. Scientific debacles happen more often than you think. The problem is not could this happen–"

Maqtaly interrupted "Good, because it has."

"And that's not actually surprising," Gorshkov persisted. "These things happen."

"Really?" Maqtaly objected.

"2003, a case in point. A Singaporean virologist infected himself with the SARS coronavirus. He was working at their Environmental Health Institute. Sure it was an accident—but it was also a textbook case of the compounding affects of sloppy lab-work. A level 3 lab had been set up in a lower level facility and the staff forgot to upgrade the overall protective gear. That alone could have caused serious trouble, but it was dramatically exacerbated by another unlucky happenstance. His West Nile virus sample was cross-contaminated with SARS." Gorshkov paused, re-collecting his train of thought. "The point is, people only noticed by luck that he was infected. If they hadn't, and they hadn't quarantined him, that could easily have become the benchmark case we compared this disaster to."

Maqtaly looked at Gorshkov, nothing he'd said thus far was reassuring.

"We just need to make sure no one lucks upon noticing Kretsky."

But Maqtaly decided to shelve Gorshkov's contemporary history lesson. The Awake program had stemmed out of Kazak oil money and the wish to be constructive with it. That this now appeared to have backfired in the most profound way ought to presage, not just Awake's, but his own demise. And yet somehow, Gorshkov was suggesting that the specific nature of the transmissions—of whatever pathogen was so wreaking havoc here and in New York—might end up saving them, if only people continued to miss the Kretsky connection.

"We have an edge." Gorshkov reiterated, "Kretsky doesn't even have biohazard suits. No one in their right mind would bring a truly nasty pathogen in there. All we have to do is offer a plausible explanation for what happened there." As he spoke, Gorshkov was forming his plan.

"You yourself have told me biohazard suits are only good if they're used right." Maqtaly shook his head. It was a problem inextricably enmeshed with the personalities of driven scientists, inevitably some of them got overconfident and pushed the limits too far. Awake; an ironic name for a program that had just put an entire lab to sleep, permanently.

"Yes. But I have a definitive way to hide Kretsky, for good."

"How much time can you buy us?"

Gorshkov's plan was fully committed, and it was definitive, "We can cover up Kretsky for good. Permanently. No evidence will be left."

Chapter 16

CDC EMERGENCY OPERATIONS CENTER

Lucy sat at her computer. Back in 2007, by comparing aggregated search query data against data provided by the CDC, Google had noted a strong, if hardly surprising, correlation between the public's interest in flu symptoms and the number of people actually experiencing flu-like symptoms. That observation prompted the launch of Google Flu Trends, a website that documented in-the-moment influenza-related incidence estimates.

Google Flu Trends and related sites were a windfall to health officials who had previously relied on more traditional means of collecting such data; means that suffered from up to a fortnight's time lag—the time it took doctors' logs to aggregate in central repositories, and anomalies to be flagged. A fortnight was an eternity in such extremely time sensitive matters—exponential growth implied that if each person infected two more daily, a kindergarten classroom outbreak engulfed the world's population in less than a month. Mitigation mattered! And these new data-crunching methodologies opened the door to the idea of using a plethora of other tracking terms.

It was emerging patterns among these tracking terms that had engaged Lucy's mind over the last few hours. The intricacies of information flow, and how it pertained to the spread of disease, was something she hadn't appreciated when starting out. And though she hated to admit dependencies, it was the coupling of that with clinical data that so often underpinned insights. Slowly, she'd grown to love population epidemiology and its implications for preventative and reactive health policy.

It was absorbing work, and it was only when she finally glanced at the clock in the top right corner of her primary monitor that she returned to the present. 2AM. She had cancelled her dinner with Hiroshi some eight hours ago; time flew when you were having fun she thought ironically, and all the more so when you were engrossed in what you were doing.

She pushed back from her desk and the various computer screens filled with graphs and charts—delta spikes and attendant bell curve tails that correlated with press releases and sensationalist media reports.

The corridors of the RIID were quieter at this hour. A body devoid of its life-blood, and yet, in contrast to a truly living organism, this cessation in the delivery of the basic essence of the system would be cured by the rising sun.

+

Lucy knocked and opened the door to Commander Krogen's office. Their salutes were as perfunctory as the hour made permissible, and Krogen skipped right to the point, "So what have you got?"

"The spikes in search words are correlated with press coverage. Nightly news segments. And they focus on curiosity factors, not searches about symptoms."

Commander Krogen nodded, so Lucy continued, "The FBI helped the CDC trace CCTV footage and other physical intel on potential paths of infection. With that as a proxy for contact tracing, the CDC put anyone who's had contact with a victim into quarantine, and they're working on second order connections now. The quarantines include the rest of the passengers on Mr. Iglinsky's flight, though no one else is dead or even symptomatic."

"Have we learned anything from 'recent associates' of the decedents?"

"Frankly, it's a bit of a mess. The effort has gone into quarantining and safety precautions; otherwise interviews are sketchy. And it's not like they're getting to interview the diagnosed, because right now the only diagnosing factor is death. We've brought in two homicide squads to help consult on how best to investigate mysterious and unexpected deaths."

"And victim profiles?"

"Sorry, nothing particularly helpful there either, they're all over the map. Well, literally they're obviously all New York and the environs, but there's not much else; we've got men, women, and mixed ethnicity and age, you name it."

Krogen continued to nod, absorbing Lucy's tidal wave of information. "So what's next?" The open-endedness of his question derailed Lucy's train of thought, and Krogen looked at her like the affectionate father figure that he was, "Why are you standing in front of me?"

That was easy, "I'm flying to Atlanta to check in with Doctor Moren at the CDC's Emergency Operations Center."

There was no need to talk this through, he knew well he couldn't change her mind if he'd wanted to, and there was rarely a reason to question her judgment anyway. Krogen smiled and saluted.

+

It was 7AM when Lucy entered the brightly lit building from the dark car park. Inside, she was quickly escorted to the Emergency Operations Center (the EOC) and Doctor Samantha Moren. To call Dr. Moren—the head of the CDC—an energetic woman, was like suggesting that Arnold Schwartzenegger, in his heyday, had some muscles. But her energy never swamped her presentation of information, and her delivery was always crisp.

Dr. Moren walked Lucy through the main room of the command center, a room filled with computer screens, big boards and a hive of activity. "We've enacted the pandemic response protocol."

"Commander Krogen wanted me to let you know he appreciated your bringing us in early."

"How is the Commander?"

"Still doesn't sleep." Lucy smiled.

"The burden of command." In the CDC director's quick accord was a barely disguised self-referential note.

Doctor Moren was the embodiment of what the EOC stood for, the role of the center being to analyze, validate and disseminate information irrespective of the crisis at hand. The EOC had been deployed over 60 times since its inception shortly after the 9-11 attacks and though it coordinated deployment of CDC staff, their mandate was not actually to run the minutia. Instead, it was tasked with the important role of supplying clear and consistent information about what was happening, and the best tactics for response. Specific communiqués were written to best communicate with various target audiences from the scientific community and emergency responders, right down to the public.

+

Dr. Moren began summarizing where their combined expertise had gotten them, "So, there's been a couple of deaths this evening–"

"But no tight smiles," Lucy noted, enthusiasm for her own role bubbling over, "and nobody within two degrees of contact of a previous casualty."

Moren nodded agreement and Lucy continued what they were both thinking, "That's just statistics, you get that any night."

Moren nodded again, agreeing with Lucy, "So what do you think?"

Lucy thought for a moment, "Give it 24 hours. It's about as non-specific as any SUDS case, which is to say we may never know why." Sudden Unexplained Death Syndrome was a general catchall for mysterious deaths. "Either that, or we'll find it's a freak mutation of an otherwise benign pathogen; highly virulent to the small group of people who've succumbed to it, who are missing some critical piece of their immune system that the rest of us have. It's unusual, but these things happen once in a while. They're not precursors to something big."

Again, Moren nodded agreement. A year ago, at a conference on H5N1 the two women had bonded over their accord on the sentiment that the real threat to the world was not some obscure tropical nightmare that we could stop with hand-washing, but rather a variation on a well-seasoned existing virus that could already fly.

Buttressing this sentiment was the observation that the diseases that took the big tolls throughout the world were often curable in the first world. Cutting back on the tolls was as much about understanding how common pathogens moved and mutated as about how lethal they were.

"Say hi to Commander Krogen."

"I will." Happy to have resolved the storm in a teacup, Lucy collected her bags, "I'll call you from the RIID this afternoon."

+

Lucy climbed down the stairs of the puddle-jumper the army reserved for non-critical flights. The late afternoon light looked gorgeous as it filtered through the trees that lined the southern side of the runway. It was a bonus to Lucy, who preferred to use Hagerstown Regional when she had the choice; beyond the light, it was both a few miles closer than Dulles, and much quieter.

Five minutes on the 81 South and another dozen on the 70 East, and Lucy was back at the RIID standing in front of Commander Krogen. Her return trip from Hokkaido had been . . . well it had been fun, but it had been exhausting too. Supplementing that with a feverish forty hours analyzing data and two further flights only exacerbated the fatigue. She was alive with enthusiasm, but she was ready to drop.

Commander Krogen smiled at her, beckoning a quick encapsulation of the state of affairs. Lucy happily obliged, "So we might see another handful of deaths if the incubation period extends to days, but the two Homeland security agents and their families were infected and died within 24 hours, which plays against that. Moreover, all branches off the primary node have been quarantined. Sam—Dr. Moren—is going to hold the quarantine for a week, just to be on the safe side, but at worst it's mopping up incidental leaks."

"So it's been contained?"

Lucy smiled and saluted.

Commander Krogen saluted back, "Great work. Now get some sleep."

Lucy turned, and in doing so, her mind swept back to Hiroshi.

Chapter 17

HOME

His hands worked quickly and efficiently, with a fluidity that comes from years of practice. The fluffy olive colored foam of the aerated liquid formed frothy bubbles near the top of the cup as the bamboo whisk worked it into a lather. Hiroshi had been missing a proper cup of green tea when he first heard the phrase "don't leave home without it", and he'd promised himself there and then never to make that same mistake.

Across the room, Lucy's fingers ratter-clacked at the keyboard of her computer. Relaxed but focused, her rapid-fire assault concluded. She pressed send and slipped her hands back into oven mitts, "Alright, that's off."

She ought to have come home and fallen asleep, but she opted instead to make good on her promise of an American burger to Hiroshi. Their "quick bite to eat" had now turned into a nightcap of sorts.

Rising from her desk, she passed Hiroshi who was concentrating on his ceremonial green tea, "Intriguing," she observed.

"Green tea requires traditional whipping."

Lucy smiled, wrapped her gloved hands around both handles of her glass-topped pot and induced the popping corn kernels to explode with a vigorous jiggle. "Pop corn just needs shaking."

"No rattle? No roll?" Hiroshi was obviously pleased with his pop-culture reference, albeit half a century out of date; the Japanese never really had tired of the King.

Lucy gave her rear-end a shake and returned her focus to the popping corn as it reached the top of the pot. "So what does Akako's husband look like?"

"I have photo."

Hiroshi pulled out an I-phone as Lucy removed the lid from her pot and turned to cross the kitchen. Intercepting her movement, he showed her an image of a young couple seated in front of a giant Ying-Yang poster.

Lucy smiled at the photo of the happy lovebirds, her old friend and her new husband, "He is handsome. They're a beautiful couple." Lucy observed as she poured the popped kernels into a bowl on the oak table. "I've got to call her."

Suddenly the dull persistent popping burst into the foreground; with the buffering layer of white fluff poured off the top, the now-exposed un-exploded kernels violently rocketed out of the almost empty pot. Lucy shrieked with laughter and swung the firing corn about in every direction.

Hiroshi dodged the shots, and, in a deft Aikido move, guided her hand and the pot to the underside of the kitchen table.

Their fingers enmeshed along the handle.

It all happened in an instant, but the seconds that followed felt much longer, and Hiroshi's graceful move lingered in the air as their close proximity sunk in. Hiroshi's hands had taken Lucy by surprise, but the surprise took on another dimension as the smoothness of his skin against hers radiated warmly through her climbing-calloused hands.

Then, Hiroshi's phone rang.

The moment was broken.

Except—he smiled and let it ring out.

But before either could say a word, Lucy's phone buzzed a disruption of its own. And its inexorable pull drew a quick glance. It was Commander Krogen, and the moment with Hiroshi was truly broken.

"Commander Krogen?"

Hiroshi watched her, still enchanted.

On the other end of the phone, Krogen's voice was devoid of humor, "There's 23 IF-zones. It's gone global in a big way." Like Lucy, it was the Commander's way too; download information succinctly, "Twenty dead in Sydney, and another hundred through Asia. All dead with tight smiles."

+

On the cobbled sidewalk outside her apartment Lucy handed Hiroshi a brown paper bag of still-steaming popcorn as the cab pulled up. Hiroshi bowed gently.

"I'm sorry about this," Lucy apologized, "You don't mind the taxi, do you?"

"You must work. We all must work. I will see you soon."

Then, as if by magic, resting on the up-facing palms of both his hands was a delicately intricate envelope. Surprised, Lucy took the proffered gift. She fumbled a moment, caught off-guard and gave him a slightly child-like hug, innocent, but with a deeper layer.

Hiroshi smiled, aware of the effect, bowed again and climbed into the cab.

+

Lucy put the key in the ignition of her mud-caked Jeep. But before she turned the engine over, she paused to open the envelope. Inside she found a postcard with a large bird on the front, a Fish Owl, wings spread in flight; it was a picture of power and grace, precisely what she was coming to expect from Hiroshi. She flipped it over to find exquisite calligraphy. The short note read:

> *Dear Lucy,*
>
> *It was a great pleasure to dine with you. I gift you this momento from your Japanese visit. Lucky you. Lucky me.*
>
> *Deepest Respect*
> *Hiroshi Sugimura.*

Lucy smiled, slipped the card into her satchel and started the engine. Hiroshi would have to wait.

GLOBAL INCIDENCE MAP

Notes:

23 IF-Zones, possibly more (deaths within same city assumed for now to be linked)

234 Deaths

Incidence centered on major travel hubs; predominantly in Asia, but includes significant presence in Europe and America too.

Chapter 18

RURAL CHINA

It looked like a rundown shack in a rural pastoral setting—big to be sure, but from the exterior there was nothing to indicate the state-of-the-art nature of the facility. It was a softer exterior than Kretsky's worn brick facade, but the bleached wooden walls housed similar contradictions, and modernizing the ancient land of dragons and emperors was no more linear than the path Kazakhstan was taking.

Among the first animals to be domesticated, pigs had been raised in China for over 10,000 years. They were part of the very fabric of the country, and, with 50% of the world's supply being reared there, they were certainly a part of its future.

For thousands of years single families and backyard operations defined pig farming in China. However, starting in the 1980s, industrialization began its inexorable creep across the land. Private equity transformed the landscape into a swath of huge, vertically integrated behemoths modeled on US giants like Smithfield. In spite of the negative press this revolution invariably garnered there were definite upsides; no longer were problems of quality control so dependent on individual skills of animal husbandry.

Nutrition was now the purview of specialists. With wheelbarrow trips to the local dump a thing of the past, feedlots were carefully calibrated to account for the individual stock's day-to-day ability to accrue weight.

And though the industrial farms cut corners with the use of antibiotics to increase population densities, they were less likely to slip an ailing animal through the slaughterhouse. In fact, commercial operations had built-in hospitals for animals suspected of illness, and they dedicated quarantine space for newly arrived stock to ensure an outsider could not jeopardize the entire facility.

But pig farms today were not just about food production.

+

Worldwide, approximately 60% of patients awaiting organ transplants die while on a waiting list simply because no appropriate organ ever becomes available. It was a statistic Wei Lin had lived, having lost his own mother ten years earlier to kidney failure.

Difficulties surrounding the search for viable donor organs had, across the board, been exacerbated by the advent of seat belts, air bags and random breath tests, each of which contributed their own delta drop in the once-reliable supply of healthy organs. Widespread automotive improvements were a catastrophe for those on organ waiting lists (and the promise of driverless cars only threatened an even grander drop in road fatalities). It was in this context that xenotransplantation— the transplanting of animal organs into humans—offered a glimmer of hope to a vexing and traumatic conundrum.

Being the closest relative to humans, chimpanzees had been initially favored, however the fact of their being endangered moved the search elsewhere. Baboons were the next obvious candidate. And indeed six baboon kidneys had been transplanted into humans in 1964, a baboon heart into a baby in 1984, and two baboon livers into patients in 1992.

Reviewing the literature, Wei Lin had been buoyed to see that although every patient had died within weeks of their operation, they did not die of organ rejection. Instead, they died of infections common to patients on immunosuppressive drugs.

Baboons, however, harbor many viruses, and their genetic proximity to humans increased the likelihood of zoonosis, the transmission of disease from one species to the next, including diseases not normally native to humans. This, combined with a variety of additional factors— including smaller body size, the infrequency of the type O blood group (the universal donor), long gestation periods and few offspring—had led researchers elsewhere again.

For long-term use, pigs were almost certainly a better option. In spite of their four legs, their anatomies were strikingly similar to that of humans and they were generally healthier than most primates. Beyond that, pigs had the pragmatic advantage of being extremely easy to breed, and of producing whole litters of piglets at a time. And that they were further from humans genetically simply reduced the risk of zoonosis, notwithstanding the very public outbreak of swine flu in 2009.

Whole pig organs had been transplanted into humans several times, dating back to 1992 when two women received pig liver transplants as "bridges" to hold them over until human transplants were found. In one patient, the liver was kept outside the body in a plastic bag and hooked up to her main liver arteries. Wei Lin had been excited to note that she had survived long enough to receive a human liver. In the other patient, the pig liver was implanted alongside the old deceased liver, to spare the patient the rigors of removing it. Although that patient had died before a human transplant could be found, there was some evidence that the pig liver had functioned for her.

Problems, however, still persisted. Immune responses were among the first problems, and, as with human organ transplants, powerful drugs were used to suppress the immune system's reaction. Without these precautions, a hyper-acute immune reaction could kill a patient almost immediately. Beyond drugs, there was the possibility of gene therapy, the insertion of human genes into pig organs, enabling the organs to produce proteins the body would recognize as human.

One technique that had been very successful over the past two decades was to preempt immune response reactions by fixing pig hearts with glutaraldehyde. Called bioprosthetic heart valves (BHVs for short), these reconstructions were now a regular fixture in open-heart surgery with 275,000 to 370,000 being performed every year.

Still, beyond immune suppression, concerns abounded; pigs run hotter than humans, for instance, $39°C$ versus $37°C$. And they had shorter life expectancies. Would basic questions of engineering matter, such as the different hydrostatic pressure under which pig hearts operate? To people who faced near-term death, these questions tended to feel like subordinate academic concerns, and having lost his own mother, Wei Lin concurred.

Still, nobody wanted to be responsible for the next swine flu, and there were two types of animal viruses that were especially troublesome: herpes viruses and retroviruses. Both had already been proven to be rather harmless in monkeys, but fatal to humans. HIV, for example, was a retrovirus believed to have leapt from monkeys to humans when certain African tribes ate the delicacy of fresh monkey brains.

Pigs were no safer, and some PERVS (porcine endogenous retroviruses) were embedded in the pig genome, meaning that you couldn't simply screen them out; they were part of the fabric. Although harmless to pigs, they might manifest in a new environment, humans for example.

In America, the FDA recommended that people having xenotransplants be monitored for the *rest of their lives*, and that if they ever showed symptoms they should be quarantined.

The advent of stem cell based therapies, which had their own issues— not least of which being the ethical crusade against them—had also dinted enthusiasm for xenotransplantation, particularly as there was evidence of heart repair by simply injecting (human) stem cells.

Xenotransplant advocates had however gone a step further, and trials were underway in rats and mice to model the idea of growing human organs in a pig by injecting human stem cells. The ultimate goal was to create a factory of patient-specific pigs akin to the farm of organ donors in Kazuo Ishiguro's book, and subsequent film, Never Let Me Go.

So it was that Wei Lin found himself overseeing the reconfiguration of the Baoding piggery for organ growth. It was a nuanced task with many variables to get right. Not least among the problems was containing Coxsackie virus outbreaks. With some luck the benign Coxsackie he'd picked up in Kazakhstan days earlier would solve that problem.

Wei Lin's phone rang and he answered.

The caller mixed his greeting with a directive, "Wei Lin, this is Feng, you must return at once." It was abrupt to say the least.

"Feng, it's nice to hear from you, but–"

"We need you back here."

"Alright, I'm just finishing up."

"Sir, bodies are piling up across the globe. Leave what you're–"

"Alright. I'm coming." Wei Lin assured his colleague, "Let me get into my car and you can brief me while I drive."

Wei Lin hung up and looked out over the indoor yards. Pigs in a sty always reminded him of stockbrokers in their own pit. When it came down to it, we really weren't so different, except that it was a lot easier to risk the lives of pigs in the name of progress.

+

A rooster-tail of dust wound it's way along the dry country road towards the bitumen of the 21st century; the link between China's agricultural past and it's burgeoning industrial cityscapes. Dry dirt gave way to a four-lane highway and from there on it was smooth sailing for Wei Lin's Toyota 4WD.

"Wei Lin, I have Chun, Siu, Hida and Shimura on the line."

Wei Lin acknowledged the collection of heavyweights that Feng had gathered. Their combined presence spoke volumes of the dramatic turn the situation had evidently taken.

"Wei Lin, where are you at with vaccines?" Chun demanded, predictably aggressive.

"Do you know the pathogen we're dealing with?" Wei Lin parried back.

"What?"

Politicians, Wei Lin thought, "You can't protect against something you don't yet recognize. We don't yet know what's behind this outbreak."

"Well what about Tamiflu? That works on everything, right?"

"Not quite. And it's a pain to police compliance; patients need to take doses every 12 hours."

"But you're ready?" there was edge in Chun's question.

"Yes, we have a stockpile, though not enough for everyone. We have also been stockpiling another drug called LANI, which does the same thing but with a single dose."

"Good, so we isolate the infected and dose them up."

"Easier said than done." It was Shimura who interjected this time, "we don't know who's infected until they're dead."

"So isolate everyone who has come in contact with a corpse!" Hida loathed the way scientific types had a tendency of beating around the bush.

But before Wei Lin could respond that that approach had a name—containment—Chun was back on the attack. "Do we have a plan for the dead?"

"Can't we just bury the bodies?" Hida groaned.

"Don't trivialize the problem of disposing of bodies. Mass graves don't just happen!" Wei Lin warned. "A few hundred thousand corpses is a lot of pathogenic waste!"

"Now you are getting ahead of yourself!"

"I have plenty of precedent. Even the conservative English planned freight containers during the 2009 H1N1 outbreak. They had plans to deal with up to 750,000 deaths in England," Wei Lin paused for effect, "and they made those plans after just 44 fatalities."

+

The arguments and education had lurched well past diplomacy.

"I'm got a recommendation in front of me that suggests hand hygiene and respiratory etiquette, surveillance and case reporting." Siu's tone was full of derision, "Writhing worms! This smells of a weak Western response. I don't want that pandemic in this country!"

"Then we isolate ourselves. Let the rest of the world do what they do," there was something callously disaffected about the way Hida spoke, "if they don't have the political will to react appropriately they will perish. That's natural selection, correct?" The question was framed rhetorically, the way politicians the world over liked to do.

Wei Lin looked out the window of his car as it wended its way through the still teeming streets of Beijing. Bicycles, motorized and otherwise, snaked through the gridlock of traffic that heralded China's ascension to the Western capitalist ideal of one car for every adult.

Their conference call ended with decisive plans.

A short time later Wei Lin looked down from his office window at the congestion below. He wondered what his Western colleagues were seeing out their windows; no doubt they too would be alarmed by the numbers that were ticking in—the mounting pitter patter of rain that portended the coming storm.

How were the Americans viewing this outbreak? They had a propensity for alarmism, but in this instance he had to agree that alarmism was probably a sensible reaction.

Equally pressing was how this might impact Wong's trip. He had not spoken to Doctor Wong since shortly before his longtime colleague had left for the summit in D.C.. Wong was someone he relied on, and if a tizzy in America brought him back earlier, it was so much the better.

Switching to a landline, he glanced at the smart-board again; the stats refreshed in real time, at least as fast as the field data propagated through the system. The numbers came in in triplicate; the first was a solid tally, the second, unsubstantiated interim reports, which had a tendency to vary wildly, and the third was a 48-hour prognosis—essentially meaningless algorithmically generated garbage at this stage, but a number that a week into an epidemic occasionally trumped his own intuition.

The numbers on the smart-board toggled higher and higher. The dot marking Tokyo flashed red followed by the triplicate (180, 220, 1056). Over a thousand deaths in the next two days! Wei Lin tapped the board twice at that point and the map zoomed in so that Japan filled most of the board. He tapped it again on Tokyo and the next zoom showed an aerial map of Tokyo city with clusters of red dots spread in clumps across the city. It looked to him closer to a random distribution than most untrained hands could draw—for some reason *random* citizens, when asked to draw a *random* distribution almost always spread data inconceivably evenly.

Beyond the impersonal details of the smart-board, the human toll had begun in earnest. Each red dot represented lives already lost. Tragedies. But their silent glow didn't speak of the details.

Wei Lin focused on a red dot just north of Tokyo central station, a major conduit of world travel. The location was scary, but the red placeholder gave no inkling of the hip young apartment in Ochanomitzu, an arty student district serving Tokyo University.

Nor did the red dot relate details of the inside of the Ochanomitzu apartment. Not the well tended bonsai garden, nor the bamboo floor matting, nor the giant poster on the wall—a crisp modern rendition of the ancient Yin-Yang symbol—that watched over the chaos ensuing in front of it. Two corpses lay askew on a couch, a young couple with smiles of terror on their faces.

Gloved hands zipped the bodies into black bags before transferring them to gurneys and wheeling them out of the apartment.

In the corridor bugged eyes, glued to the peepholes of neighboring apartments. They watched like a sea of Cyclopes through the portholes of a giant ocean-liner as the forensics team suited in disposable teal-blue scrubs washed the plague away ... only against the tide another empty gurney was already being wheeled in.

+

Back in his office, the smart-board flashed red on Singapore and (30, 32, 106) flipped to (284, 302, 512) and then immediately to (306, 310, 560). Wei Lin zoomed in and once again marveled at the beautifully random distribution of deaths. It was, no doubt, a function of the early data, and there were certainly clusters around the city that looked less than random with smaller numbers under them, seeded presumably by some unsuspecting carrier returning home infected, but the speed of the propagation bothered him.

It took an entire year in 2010 for 214 countries to show lab-confirmed incidence of H1N1 swine flu and the 18449 deaths, though it had been suggested in 2008 that there was a mere six-week window to vaccinate before things went badly.

But as he noted to Chun earlier, until you identified the causative agent all bets were off. Containment was the standard first response, and even that was predicated on understanding the underlying means of transmission, something specific to each disease.

Now Singapore had 306 confirmed deaths! This was not your normal paradigm.

The smart-board clicked higher over London, reflecting the collation of the previous nights' fatalities, which the rising sun brought with it. The English were above 44 fatalities, and freight containers were no doubt making their way up the Thames.

In some odd quirk of his mind's connective synapses Wei Lin reflected to himself that the Americans were largely asleep while this happened.

+

Excusing himself from the conference call that had grown increasingly frustrating, Wei Lin put that line on hold and dialed Wong's hotel with his cell.

Months ago Wong had spoken to him about hemlock water-dropwort, a perennial that thrived near Sardinian ponds and rivers. The inspiration source for Homer's term Sardonic grin, it had been used in ritual killings in Sardinia since before the 8th century B.C., now however it was being considered for its potential as a Botox substitute.

From Wei Lin's memory it had nothing to do with sleep, but the death smile was a link worth exploring and if Wong was interested there might be another connection he'd missed; Wong had after all also studied Laitai, a mysterious killer of otherwise healthy young Thai men, one that did kill its victims in their sleep.

Wei Lin waited for the line to connect.

Far away, in a room lined with gaudy old-world wallpaper that hotels deemed "upscale", a half-eaten room-service sandwich sat life-less as the telephone beside it appealed for attention. A couple of feet from the phone, Wong was similarly unmoved by the shrill bell.

Eventually, the phone rang itself out. The tight smile on Wong's face explicated the situation that Wei Lin was hoping against hope not to be the case as he left his urgent message. Whatever light Wong's years of experience might have shed on the situation was lost to this world.

Chapter 19

THE GRIM REAPER

An oversized dental mirror swung along the underside of his car as the guard inspected for sinister devices. It was a curiously obtuse reaction to a biological threat, but protocols were protocols and once an alert was sounded security increased.

As the driver waited, he reflected on just how effectively a conventional bomb—delivered at the epicenter of the coordinated defenses—would create strategic havoc, had the biological agent been engineered by an enemy state in the first place.

"All clear, sir," Private First Class Alvin Smith saluted.

Commander Krogen nodded appreciatively, and as the sun glistened over the horizon he pulled forward past another soldier with an M-4 slung over his shoulder.

Inside the building he found Colonel Lucy Topp with her head slumped on the desk, a consequence of the long night combined with inevitable jet-lag finally coming home to roost.

"Colonel!" was his sharp greeting.

Lucy looked up and in an involuntary reflexive response she returned his salute in kind. "Sir."

"China is cutting all flights."

Lucy looked at him askance.

"You'd better pull your head off your pillow," Krogen quipped as he handed her today's copy of The New York Times, whose headline boldly proclaimed:

"HE COMES IN YOUR SLEEP"

Two hours earlier the Times' chief editor had defended the reference to the grim reapers to the paper's owners with the curt observation that four hundred FBI and police officers were already dead. "There are no symptoms. You go to bed fine and wake up dead. It's peaceful if you're ready to die!" His ironic tone had had the intended effect of cutting short any argument. It was the story of a lifetime and he didn't want his reporters' caffeine propelled bustle dampened. There was energy in the air and he recognized the opportunity to make his career when he saw it.

+

As Lucy took in the headline, Commander Krogen kept them moving, "On your feet," he instructed as he turned down the corridor, "we're leaving."

Lucy scrambled her critical notes and satchel and chased after him. Krogen was not a man easily rattled, and he wasn't wasting time this morning.

The sun had just crested the horizon, but it was an abstract keeper of routine right now; Krogen certainly hadn't slept since the golden orb's last visit. The corridor down which they walked was a hive of activity; it reminded Krogen of what he had just witnessed at the White House. But as in the newspaper bullpens, there was excitement here too. And even if here it was mixed with more respect and trepidation for the invisible foe, it wasn't about to be tempered.

Lucy couldn't believe she'd slept the couple of hours she had! "It's not poisoning—nobody can disperse that much poison—but it's too fast to be traditionally infectious." Lucy enjoyed thinking aloud, and she knew the Commander found it helpful to have an intelligent analysis pour over him. "Which means: it scares the heebee geebees out of me." She was starting to wake, "It's starting to look interesting." She quipped ironically.

Krogen caught her infectious grin. "Scary is another word." That was a mild version of the opinions he'd heard expressed in the pre-dawn pow-wow with the government's other top brass.

+

Lucy followed Krogen into the belly of what she had always regarded as an oversized black insect. That they were being ferried by a thunderous

Black Hawke helicopter spoke clearly of the escalation of events; with Commander Krogen in tow on her second trip to Atlanta the USAPAT— US Army Priority Air Transport—had supplied their standard vehicle for moving senior leaders short distances.

Krogen stowed his sidepiece on the shelf above his coat jacket and caught Lucy's eye. He was not a man prone to traveling with his gun.

"Commander . . . ?"

"The public's emptying gun-shops."

Lucy reflected a moment, but finding her confidence, chirped as easily as she could force herself, "Second amendment. People have a right to defend themselves."

Krogen shook his head unmoved, "The panic may be as dangerous as the pandemic." It was an adage he had preached before, but just to emphasize his position he added ironically, "And sure, an AK-47 is a lot of help against a virus!"

In his off-handed remark, Lucy caught a potential deeper meaning. She looked at him, searching, but the Commander was sometimes a hard man to read, "Virus?"

"Your guess is as good as mine, probably better. It's certainly infective and induces some sort of catastrophic systems failure, probably the heart or brain. All we've really got is a cough and a smile."

Taken at face value, he was just as in the dark as she was. Then again, Krogen had intuitions he didn't always share.

Chapter 20

ATLANTA AGAIN

Doctor Samantha Moren was not just a leader in her chosen field, she had field experience. As a young post-doc, she had proven herself in the nether-reaches of Africa, back when that was the place to prove you had no fear. She had then moved to some pioneering research in China, just as the country was opening up, before returning home to a more managerial role. Lucy particularly admired her, and often wondered if she herself had what it took to manage both the science in a project and the invariably frantic people surrounding it in the way Sam did. Her crisp voice had the whole room's attention, "China has already placed a big bet that this is communicable."

"That's hardly an isolated perspective." Commander Krogen liked and respected Dr. Moren too, but he wasn't about to let the obvious pass without comment.

"Grounding planes doesn't seem that big a bet," Havamyer objected.

"Quarantining a billion people is a big bet," Moren countered, her tone classifying this as an indisputable fact, "At this point the case fatality ratio is 100%. We only know of dead victims. And the serial interval must be hours. Even SARS took a week to be infective."

The EOC had upgraded their response activation to level 2, thus this meeting. They had only ever had four level one responses, and of those only three had been biological in nature; Swine Flu in 2009, Ebola in 2014 and Zika in 2016.

Director Havamyer raised his hand again to slow proceedings, "Alright, can you please break that down for those of us without a PhD."

"Successive cases in the chains of transmission are happening fast." Lucy piped in, "Too fast."

"Unprecedentedly fast." Krogen went further. "If it wasn't so clearly spreading it would suggest chemical poisoning rather than a biological problem."

"Although with death as the only symptom," Moren noted, "the infection has without a doubt spread further than we realize."

Havamyer nodded slowly, digesting this.

To aid those struggling to keep up, Lucy added the clear corollary to Moren's observations, "If it's made Munich and Sydney, it sure as shit's made Atlanta and DC. We need to isolate ourselves. Hell, it may already be too late."

People shifted uncomfortably.

General Jackson, the army's Chief of Staff nodded approvingly at Lucy's sharp insight. He was as tough as woodpecker lips, and he'd always liked Colonel Topp.

Marshall too nodded concurrence.

Krogen continued, "As Dr. Moren noted, the first symptom is a dead body. With that in mind, we're devoting a lot of attention to autopsies. Unfortunately, autopsies haven't yielded further clues yet."

"Except that every corpse has H9N2." Moren reminded him.

Lucy smiled, and Sam registered the appreciation. Flu was their shared hobby-horse, and though Moren and the CDC were more focused on H5N1—bird flu as it was better known—she recognized and respected Lucy's reading of the mutation patterns in H9N2.

Marshall caught Lucy's smile and cautioned her, "Now's not the time to push pet programs."

"The H9N2 emergence is a fact," Lucy shrugged, "Nobody is implying anything causal."

"Because a nasty strain of H9N2 would also exhibit a ton of clinical symptoms." Marshall noted tersely.

"Alright, I'm not sure I understand the pissing match going on," Jackson interrupted them, "but it doesn't seem relevant; correct?"

"Correct," Commander Krogen confirmed, "H9N2 is flu, and flu doesn't kill like this."

+

Politics was in the air, and though not everyone in the room completely understood the specifics, the actions of those who did would be noted among themselves.

The sad reality was: for disaster preparedness, budgets correlated to previous season's fatalities and buzzwords. Unfortunately for funding, the last couple of years had seen pretty good health around the world. Everyone understood that catastrophes such as the Sendai earthquake of 2010 and the ensuing disaster at the Daiichi nuclear power plant energized spending on earthquake preparedness and new precautions associated with nuclear facilities. And beyond that, the lion's share of remaining dollars went to stalwart buzzwords like AIDS and cancer.

So it was that—with a core of the nation's power brokers in one room, and their attention on high alert—Commander Krogen correctly judged Director Moren's mention of H9N2 as priming the pump to be reaped when this event passed. H9N2 was Colonel Topp's specialty, but flu was flu, and while H5N1 was nowhere to be seen here, money for flu was always on Dr. Moren's mind. She was an astute politician and Krogen admired her for that, but it was a distraction and he didn't want it going any further. He shot Lucy a look that said as much.

Lucy understood all the subtexts. As an expert on H9N2, she could anticipate a funding bump, but she also knew when to let a subject die. Krogen—rightly to her mind—clearly didn't want to see this distraction get any more airtime.

Silent tensions settled for a moment, and Dr. Moren continued, "Bodies are piling up as the sun rises. We need ideas, people!"

Havamyer, undaunted by what had just transpired, tried his own hand at lobbying, "The postal service moves stuff anywhere humans exist; anthrax was widely dispersed after 9-11."

To Krogen's disgust, General Jackson turned to Director Havamyer. "Are you suggesting we tell the President to shut down the postal service?"

But before Havamyer could answer Lucy interceded. "The pattern of deaths doesn't fit that vector profile. Moreover, if you kill deliveries you severely limit the ability to quarantine the public in their homes."

"Really?" Havamyer was openly skeptical.

Lucy ignored Havamyer's provocative challenge, and turned instead back to Jackson, "But General, your mention of the President raises an important point: *he* must be quarantined."

"That makes a lot of sense," Marshall chipped in.

Admiring Lucy's pluck, General Jackson turned back to Dr. Moren and Commander Krogen, both of whom clearly concurred, "She's serious?"

Their unison nod sent the General's mind reeling in it's own directions. Turf war squabbles he could deal with—Havamyer would, no doubt, lay claim to this suggestion, and thus his need to be involved in its implementation—but there was the larger question of logistics, and the President himself.

Quarantining wasn't just a matter of securing the President from an outside threat. Isolated in the Catoctin Mountain Park, and protected by the Navy and Marine Corps, the Naval Support Facility Thurmont, aka Camp David, had long amply satisfied that requirement.

The problem was: quarantining was different. Once someone went outside the camp to coordinate with their own networks, they could no longer be let back in. Food and supplies naturally faced similar issues.

That matter was compounded by the fact that President, and many high-level officials he relied on, used personal communication as their modus operandi. The President, a man famous for valuing face-to-face briefings, was going to be a chief obstacle in implementing this plan of action.

It was testament then to General Jackson's long-term affection for Lucy, and deep respect for hers, Commander Krogen's, and Doctor Moren's intellect, that he saw the necessity of these actions. President Pollack's staff was either to be in the tent with him, or outside the tent. There was no middle ground.

Convincing the President was going to require a personal touch, and looking across the table Jackson had the inkling of an idea.

Chapter 21

MARINE ONE

Thick fog hung over the water, making it hard for the sentinel to see the joggers on the other side of the Charles River, let alone potential threats; and that was with the advantage of height. Still, he scanned the neighboring buildings one last time and made the call into his lapel mic. "Bring out the eagle".

A door opened on the far side of the rooftop and a bevy of black-suited men huddled out. In their midst strode General Jackson, and beside him, President Pollack who was none-too-thrilled about being roused from his quarters so soon after his operation. That the cause of the rousing was to move him to an even more remote facility only added insult to the injury. But Pollack was a tough man, and rather than shielding his face from the rotors' turmoil, he simply turned to General Jackson and groused "One minute I'm getting this flash new pacemaker installed because I may, or may not, have a heart attack some day, and the next I'm being quarantined because of some pandemic that may, or may not, be critical!"

"Mr. President, there *is* a pandemic out there. This precaution is the consensus recommendation of your science and medical advisors."

"You sure they're not just working for the opposition?"

Jackson was unsure of the President's meaning. "Sorry, sir?"

Showing a moment of levity President Pollack winked at Jackson, "That cabal will take any opportunity to sideline me!" and with a campaign-worthy ironic smile, he climbed into the helicopter.

+

Waiting nervously inside the chopper, was Colonel Topp. Briefings were not her forte, and she had never met the President before, but General Jackson had asked her personally, and Commander Krogen was happy to send her as the USAMRIID's ambassador.

Lucy glanced one last time at the red numbers covering the maps while President Pollack pulled on his headset and General Jackson made the introduction. "Mr. President, Colonel Topp will brief us."

Lucy bowed her head, "It's an honor to meet you, Mr. President."

"Please. Make the honor mine. Go ahead."

"Yes, sir," Lucy indicated the red numbers on the maps. "We have 68 IF-zones. And–"

And already he was interjecting. "If zones?"

"Isolated Fatality Zones, sir. Incidences of deaths where there is no obvious trace back to already documented events. You normally expect a few IF-zones at the onset of an outbreak, but 68 is unheard of."

Lucy saw President Pollack was missing the significance, but General Jackson gave her a nod, so she elaborated.

"Connecting IF-zones means tracing transmissions. That's how you find where everything started. And that's how you unlock–"

"Who's responsible," President Pollack offered.

Lucy paused, caught off guard. "It might just be Africa's latest Ebola or chickens from China. We simply don't know. Nobody does."

"I like your honesty. What do you recommend we do?" The question hung in the air as he turned briefly to his window to take in the Charles River and Harvard, his alma mater, behind it. "The Chinese have cut air traffic."

"Yes . . ." she was trying to indicate to the President how far they were from any understanding of what was happening, and he was looking for solutions.

The city of Boston was disappearing behind them and the Commander in Chief quipped lightly, "Well I guess we're not in China!"

General Jackson smiled calmly back at the President. "No, but we're gauging that as an overreaction to the heat they took for SARS."

"Or they know something." President Pollack turned to Lucy for effect. "Somebody always does."

Lucy was unsettled by the President's directness. No, it was more than that. He seemed to hear sound-bytes, but not the underlying meaning. And he needed to anthropomorphize their foe.

Like everyone else, Lucy had known the President through television interviews and public addresses, but she had expected that those were performances. She'd expected a more intellectual man. She looked right back at him, "Mr. President, with all due respect, I think you're missing the point."

General Jackson, who had a much longer history with the Commander in Chief, winced and watched cautiously as Pollack responded, "Really, *Colonel*? Help me."

"Biological warfare with Mother Nature requires routing out the enemy, but that enemy is small and often much more elusive than any human combatant."

The President nodded impassively so Lucy simply continued, "Chasing a pandemic back to its origins invariably produces clues that unmask the assailant, but there is a fundamental distinction between identifying the symptoms that we trace and the underlying causative agent. The public sees the symptoms, but easily misses the difficulty isolating the causative agent. This isn't the flu, it's more like the new AIDS."

"Call it what you will, it–"

But Lucy interrupted back, "Mr. President, this isn't a simple matter of nomenclature. A new flu is easy to identify, HIV took two years."

"Two years to identify?"

"Yes."

Were it not for the *thump-thump-thump* of the helicopter's rotors you could have heard a pin drop.

Lucy felt a forceful slap in the face as she realized that the President's apparent glossing over the most critical element in her debriefing was not willful; he simply *didn't understand* the biology.

The silence protracted as she digested this realization and the President absorbed her last remark. . . . Or was it more that he was taken aback by the interruption?

Fearing that the briefing had gone off the rails, General Jackson tried to diffuse the situation with the welcome suggestion that she elaborate her meaning.

Lucy took a breath, "New strains of the flu are simple because they are variants on an old adversary, it's like identifying a splinter group of an established terrorist organization. You know where to start looking and even more-or-less what you are looking for. By contrast, something like AIDS is like trying to locate an altogether new organization based on the wreckages of a few apparently unconnected bombings."

The President nodded, indicating he was willing to hear her out, "Alright, you have my attention. Talk me through AIDS."

AIDS had been a quick, indicative example in her mind, but the more she reflected, the more Lucy realized how fortuitous an example it was. It encapsulated the fundamentals of their current predicament.

The CDC had first reported AIDS in June of 1981 when five gay men in LA presented with pneumocystis pneumonia, only at that point they nobody had a handle on what they were dealing with. In fact, in the initial phase the task force referred to the cases as a Kaposi's Sarcoma and Opportunistic Infections, "They were just allusions to the known diseases with which AIDS was associated."

President Pollack nodded and Lucy continued.

"When the press termed the disease 'GRID' for Gay-Related Immune Deficiency, the CDC countered with '4H disease'. The four H's were a marginally more encompassing epitaph, referring to the apparently affected groups; Haitians, Homosexuals, Hemophiliacs, and Heroine users. Neither stuck. In the end everyone settled on the term AIDS, an acronym I'm sure you know stands for Acquired Immune Deficiency Syndrome." Lucy caught her breath, "That was September of 1982. But it wasn't until May 1983 that Luc Montagnier identified the causative agent HIV at the Pasteur Institut in France. That's almost two full years after the CDC documented the initial case. And that merely brought everyone to the starting line," Lucy finished, "only then did they know what they were chasing."

President Pollack gazed out the window. Colonel Topp had rubbed him the wrong way, even if she had neatly illuminated the situation for him. "There's still no cure for AIDS," he mused. "Right?"

"Right," Lucy agreed, "Though we do have therapies, meaning we can now contain the effects. Of course there are plenty more enemies like Malaria and Cholera who underscore the same problem—enemies for whom we already have wanted posters, and who nonetheless claim thousands of lives around the globe every day."

"So naming our adversary doesn't really help? Whatever it is will still be capable of wreaking death and destruction?"

Lucy tempered her frustration. He might not be with her yet, but she was making progress. "No, identifying the causative agent doesn't stop the problem, but it's a pretty important step. Until then, all you've got is the epidemiology, which is kind of like shooting in the dark. You might hear something, but by the time you turn and fire, the enemy has moved on."

Chapter 22

THE KRETSKY FACILITY

Makeshift work lights lit up the building, otherwise enveloped in the dark night.

As a teenager Taras Serik had wondered what took place inside the razor-wire perimeter of the Kretsky facility. He and his friends traded stories of the grim undertakings that were known to be overseen from afar.

Rumors spoke of offensive as well as defensive programs; bioweapons that included open air testing and the production of literally tons of plague, anthrax and tularemia (a bacterial infection common in rodents, but which had potential as an aerosol agent with a 5% fatality rate). He had always imagined the stories to be extravagant exaggerations fanned by the childhood game telephone. Only later did he realizes they were tame retellings by kids who could scarcely imagine the darker delvings motivated by the cold war.

Far from battle fatigues, the soldiers who now guarded the entrance to his wife's facility wore camouflaged spacesuits. It presented a curious juxtaposition: Kalashnikovs hanging like skinny lop-sided backpacks on their billowy Michelin-men suits; it was a juxtaposition that begged the question of the relative dangers of a bullet and an invisible pathogen.

The scene had given Taras pause when he'd first arrived to investigate why his wife had not returned home two nights ago. And the concern that now swelled in Taras' throat was far from assuaged by the Hazmat fire engines that had rolled up four hours ago as day had given way to night.

In the darkness he watched quietly from back in the forest, wondering if his wife's greatest fears were coming to fruition, or worse yet: could she be involved?

+

Taras had met Ludmila shortly after her return from graduate study in the United States. Theirs had been a slow and deliberate courtship, tempered by what he saw in her as a Western induced paranoia of the former Soviet era.

Still, even in him, certain details of her work resonated as concerning— the nasty lung infections, fevers and chills from the spring of 1997, and the subsequent state extermination of the local horse population in the villages radiating out from one particular state facility ... had that been Glanders? As they grew closer, Taras too had grown wary that the new biotech industry might somehow be subverted into something more sinister.

Pre-1990's memories, while accompanied by the innocent veil of youth, were nothing to which Kazaks wished to return. There simply were no "good old days," and emancipation into Kazak adulthood was fraught not just with the customary anxiety that one's parents might one day reassert their position of authority, but it had the layered, if similarly unlikely, anxiety that Russia herself might one day return as a power to dominate your life.

+

What had Ludmila not told him?

As he stared across at the chipped mortar of the former bio-weapons facility he reflected on the last time he'd seen her. He'd come to visit her at work. It was meant as a surprise, and that it was, only it was he who had been most surprised. Surprised to find Wei Lin, Ludmila's old friend from the Chinese CDC.

Why exactly had the Chinese CDC man been visiting? Had it something to do with the problems she'd been having with the animal trials?

Taras racked his memory for a clue.

Ludmila's stress had compounded dramatically over the previous three months. The power of the innovative techniques she was developing at Kretsky demanded checks and balances. She had dealt with mounting pressure, and the loss of a room full of animal models hadn't helped. In a grandiose moment she'd suggested to Taras that it was the same pressure she'd imagined the captain of the Titanic had suffered; with a ship this powerful it was imperative you checked, double-checked and re-double-checked your course, because by the time you spotted an actual ice-berg it was almost certainly too late.

Taras tried to recall the details of his encounter with Ludmila and Wei Lin. They'd been inside one of Kretsky's modern white-walled labs, one that starkly contrasted with the worn brick facade outside.

Taras was a meat and potatoes guy, he saw window-dressings as just that, and preferred to call it out when it was presented as otherwise. So, notwithstanding Kazakhstan's own reputation, or perhaps because of it, he'd never liked Ludmila's association with Wei Lin and China. When Ludmila had volunteered that, "Wei Lin is here for some samples." Taras had tersely replied "The man from the land of 'I have lots of patients who will try your drugs'".

More than the short fling that had happened between Ludmila and Wei Lin almost two decades ago—well before Taras had known Ludmila— Taras was disturbed by Wei Lin's connections to the trade in human organs. It had perhaps been guilt by association, but it was well known that organs from executed prisoners had been sold to so-called medical tourists in China, and Taras had overheard a conversation that spoke of organ transplants. Taras believed firmly in the sanctity of life; what he'd heard was cause for circumspection.

Such possible transgressions were more serious to Taras than the other boundaries of established practices that Ludmila pushed the envelope on. Wei Lin had openly reflected as much when faced with Taras' ironic stance, "When the wind of change blows, some build walls while others build windmills."

+

There was a sudden movement outside the facility and Taras returned his focus to the moment.

Fifty yards in front of him, six spacesuit-clad soldiers worked in pairs. Lugging human-sized black plastic body-bags, they disappeared inside the building. Taras waited. Five minutes later, the soldiers reappeared with empty body-bags in hand. The process repeated itself, and Taras wondered: nine bodies—if that's what they were. Had they brought more earlier?

The soldiers hurried back from the facility.

Taras Serik watched the men as they hunkered down behind a rock thirty yards in front of him. It was difficult to make out what they were doing when suddenly the building they had fled exploded into flames.

Serik stood instinctively, staring in disbelief at the flames that fanned out the windows.

Haloed in the glow of the flames, one of the soldiers rose to feet of his own. He was facing away from the spastic flaming inferno. He was looking directly at Serik.

Serik's eyes met the soldier's. Neither the distance between them, nor the glass bubble of the soldier's biological face-mask, hid the obvious: nobody was supposed to witness what had just happened.

The soldier raised his arm.

Taras Serik wasted no time. He turned for the surrounding forest. The billowing inferno fell back to secondary consideration when the first shouts of his armed pursuers clasped at his shadowy retreating figure.

"Toqta! Toqta!" but Serik kept moving.

The first bullet to zing into a tree cemented any wavering conviction.

"Toqta!"

There was no chance Serik would stop now.

He ducked and darted like a hunted animal. Leaves exploded around him into green-vapored nothingness. He felt the stress of a fox. And then fear escalated: did the soldiers have dogs?

Ludmila had dragged him on countless walks through these forests, but dogs could smell. He strained to hear . . . no barking.

With his concentration devoted to his pursuers, his eyes missed—and his foot hit—a gnarled root, slamming him off kilter and into another trunk. His cheekbone and jaw-line took the force of the impact in equal parts, splitting skin both inside and outside his mouth. Worse, he was momentarily dazed.

Whatever disorienting effect the collision rendered, it was short-lived. The next near-miss bullet was more than sufficient to refocus his basic survival instincts, and Taras once again fled deeper into the forest.

His pursuers were probably fifteen years his junior, but—thank-god—they were hampered by their protective gear. Their protective gear! Of course there were no dogs. You can't put dogs in Hazmat suits!

Serik pulled farther ahead, even as he reflected on the Hazmat suits. Suddenly, ducking in and out of sight, he saw an opportunity. Dropping behind a small embankment he switched course to a river-worn rut.

With the metallic taste of blood filling his mouth from the gaping split in his lip, he hurtled fifty yards along the creek-bed, searching. Searching for cover. He'd traced this river before, but what had he seen? He strained to recall the looming terrain even as rocky boulders cropped up either side. A small gully opened on left and he splashed down, churning the water underfoot.

Behind him, the gunfire had stopped, but thundering feet still pounded through the undergrowth chasing the main flow of the disrupted muddy stream.

Hunkered down behind a rock and he desperately tried to quiet his breath. The ruckus approached, and Serik watched them race by as he himself sucked in oxygen.

His pursuers, tracking the muddy water, shot past, disappearing into the forest towards the road below.

He was safe, for now at least.

Tenderly he touched the welt over his cheekbone. Using his sleeve, he wiped away the coagulating blood. He sent a quiet prayer of thanks to Ludmila for her love of the outdoors, a love that had consequented knowledge of the local topography. A love that had saved him today. And then his thoughts turned back to her in earnest ...

Was Ludmila still inside the now-incinerated building? And if not, then where was she? With Wei Lin? With Wei Lin in China?

Chapter 23

HARDBALL

"Kretsky has been taken care of."

Prime Minister Maqtaly looked across the oak desk at Gorshkov, "The threat has been cauterized?"

"Both threats; spread and discovery."

"Good," Maqtaly announced. "Information is power." It was a weapon: metaphorically but almost literally, too. It had long been so, as long as he'd lived. Nuclear technology had been no different to biological warfare, at least not to the politician. Just as there was power in the knowledge of the 'who', there was power in the knowledge of the 'how' and 'what'.

But sacrificing any potential knowledge of the *what had happened*—a scientific understanding of the catastrophe—was a necessary step in order to protect the *whos* behind the program—himself and a few core politicians. Kretsky was finished one way or another, but if the outside world had reason to look into it, he might well find himself finished too.

"You can't stop the flow of information, but you can affect the content." So the old adage went. Transmission of information required a listener, and listeners brought their own agendas and biases.

A simple alternative rationale for Kretsky's silence was required to send potential investigators elsewhere. "So it is an industrial accident?" the details were important to Maqtaly.

"Involving a gas leak. The facility burnt to the ground." Gorshkov was succinct which helped stifle any emotional misgivings that Maqtaly was developing. The rest of the world was uninterested in hearing about a fire right now, and so, that was precisely what he'd given them. Were there clues that might have helped curb the pandemic? Incinerating Kretsky removed the temptation of self-sacrifice for an uncertain bid at the greater good. He was a man who, once committed to a course of action, didn't falter or second-guess himself. Removing Kretsky, and the evidence it housed, had been necessary if he wanted to protect his own neck and that of his prime minister, the man seated in front of him.

Maqtaly in contrast was unemotional. He offered a rationalization more for Gorshkov than himself, "The first world didn't get where they are without some hiccups."

"So it is."

Maqtaly nodded, still eager to know all the details, "And the bodies were incinerated too?"

"Including dead spouses. Fortunately there were no children."

"Good."

"Taras Serik, Ludmila's husband, is still missing, but he's the last loose end."

"You know him, yes?"

"Yes. I don't think he's a big threat, though his wife is dead."

"It will be good to find him." It made Maqtaly nervous to see this giant of a man—both physically and, normally, in presence too—subdued. He gazed past Gorshkov, out the window of the giant blue trimmed Kazak Parliament Congress building. Lives had already been lost, and though many more seemed likely to follow, there was no need to add his own scalp to the list, especially not under the heading of collateral damage. "The Americans play hardball. The Chinese play hardball. It is our turn."

Chapter 24

FBI INTERVIEW ROOM 209

"The Awake Program is Kazakhstan's attempt to convert oil winnings into a biotech industry. They're moving fast and–"

Lucy pressed the intercom on the desk in front of her and interrupted Wallenstein. "I know," the last thing she needed was a refresher course on the international biotech sector, "they've poached a lot of talent in the last couple of years. I'm not surprised they lured Jean Michael, he was the kind of guy who liked to call safe-guards 'red tape'. They simply *obstructed* his work."

"You knew Dr. Michael?"

"Yes. He was a big believer in enlisting mother-nature's help to solve biological problems."

"He certainly wasn't on PharmaCo's most loved list."

"You tend not to be after you defect. Besides, big Pharma always prefer silver bullets to the unpredictable messiness of the real world."

There had been a growing consensus within the biomedical research community that single pills were not the answer to most problems. This sentiment was predictably less embraced by the pharmaceutical companies; educating people to eat right and exercise was a lot less lucrative than selling magic elixirs, even if the science was clear that the combined effects of all the factors were significantly bigger than the sum of their parts.

Lucy glanced at her notes to reorient her head.

"You said Mr. Magjan Iglinsky was dropped off at the Almaty airport."

"By an old college buddy of his. They spent the day together, his name was Amanet, I don't recall his surname off-hand, but I believe NCS is already looking for him."

"You have reason to believe he might be significant in this?"

"Not at the time. I didn't think Amanet was particularly significant to anything. From what I gleaned of their conversation it was old friends catching up, but he is in the biotech sector."

"In Kazakhstan?"

"Yes, he heads up a satellite facility of the Kretsky labs. It was located in Zhetygen, thirty or forty kilometers north east of Almaty. They are pretty autonomous of the main parent facility from what I gathered. In any event, he was apparently coming down to Almaty for a bio-safety in-house."

"Was Iglinsky interested in the bio-safety meeting?"

"No. He seemed more preoccupied with his own travels. It surprised me because he normally reads people very well, but in this instance he seemed unconcerned by his old friend's anxiety. Might just have been complacency among old friends."

"Alright." Lucy continued, "What about the rest of the flight? Did Iglinsky talk to anyone?"

"Mr. Iglinsky had a way with airline hostesses if you bought into his view of reality, and, if you didn't, then you would probably say he accosted the stewardesses throughout the flight. A dozen drinks, maybe half of which were consumed, but all of which required conversations . . . ."

Lucy stopped listening to Wallenstein. Her own mind was wandering again. Given the facts, Magjan Iglinsky looked more and more like a red herring, and yet something nagged in the back of her mind.

The last two weeks of his life had been turned over with a fine-tooth comb, and the result: nothing. What was bothering her? Was it the Frenchman, Doctor Jean Michael? Eight weeks was a long time ago, and linking Jean Michael to something that had transpired in the last seven days would take a lot of work. Maybe the FBI could connect them. She hoped it wasn't him . . . but if not the dead scientist from Magjan's past though, then who, or what?

The stem cell material on which DHS had held him was hardly a likely lead. Even the GM infractions were unlikely; symptoms simply wouldn't present the way the current crisis did. Sure, inherited side-effects might manifest in the environment as downstream effects of cross-breeding and tweaked genes traced along the food-chain, but these were not simple causalities and the side-effects that did occur wouldn't appear as this devastation had.

Magjan's true connection to the current crisis eluded her for now. He was their patient zero, but who or what had infected him? There was something she couldn't see, and she couldn't think what it was, nor even what she might *ask* this babbling agent on the other side of the protective glass barrier that might trip an insightful answer.

Perhaps it had something to do with the proliferation of I.F. zones? Magjan was an unusual patient zero. Maybe that was connected?

Lucy had every confidence she would figure it out. Work mind, work!

+

Suddenly her cell-phone chirped, interrupting Lucy's thoughts along with Wallenstein's prattling. Lucy glanced at the number and then back at the Operations Officer who nodded to her deferentially.

"I get it. You're busy. You squeezed me in before I fell asleep again. Just in case."

It sounded callous when Wallenstein put it that way, but only half an hour earlier Lucy had made the same argument to Director Havamyer when he protested that Wallenstein had just been subjected to a 36 hour debrief—perhaps she had been too hard in her assessment of his closing drivel.

The phone rang again.

Lucy nodded uncomfortably to the poor man on the other side of the glass and answered the phone, "Colonel Topp."

As Lucy's eyes brightened, Operations Officer Wallenstein's dulled; in his gut he understood that this might well have been the conclusion of the last real conversation of his life.

Chapter 25

THE GEORGETOWN SUITES

Hiroshi gazed down at the chaos. The serene and curiously sculptured tree in the center island of the circular valet drop-off stood alone in its tranquility. Those travelers attempting escape were being thwarted from the moment they checked out, assuming they bothered to take that potentially risky interaction.

He lifted his gaze to the historic red brick buildings that lined the edge of the Potomac River and watched as the sun inexorably dropped in the sky, kissing the rooftops and greenery that poked through them as it did. It was with a heavy heart that he had called Lucy's cell phone.

"Colonel Topp."

"Lucy-san?" Hiroshi's grave face brightened at the sound of her, albeit uncomfortable, voice.

"Hiroshi. I can't talk right now," though even as she made her objection, she registered something in his voice, something that augured badly for what he would soon tell her.

"There is much disaster."

Lucy paused, leaving space for him to continue. She couldn't talk right now, at least not until she had wrapped the interview. When Hiroshi left the open space, she filled it, "I know, and it's burying me. I'm in the middle of a debriefing. I'll call–"

"Akako-san dead." Hiroshi stopped Lucy in her tracks.

Lucy said nothing.

Officer Wallenstein watched her silence, her face suddenly drained of color.

At the Georgetown Suites, Hiroshi was on autopilot "Lucy-san?"—was she still there?—"There is last flight to Japan. In two hours."

"Akako is dead? How . . ." but of course she already knew.

"In her sleep. Kazuki-san is dead too."

"Wait, and you want to go to Japan?" Lucy was incredulous.

"I cannot stay here." To Hiroshi this was a simple statement of fact.

"But you can't get on a plane! That's insane!"

Hiroshi was surprised by the vehemence of her response, but he saw no other way, and responded very simply, "Lucy, I cannot stay. Food is running out. I see where this will lead. I have nowhere to go. I do not know anyone."

"You know me!"

"But–"

"You can stay with me. Getting on a plane is suicide!"

"My family–"

"I'll be your family."

"Lucy, you have much work. I will be one more problem for you."

"I can cope."

"I cannot be burden. I must fly home."

"Damn it, Hiroshi," Lucy reacted, "That's a terrible idea."

"Already society is to break down. Looters will be big problem soon. People will flee urban areas. I can do this in Japan."

"That makes no sense!"

"Hai. It does. Now is my chance to leave."

"You're talking about a chance to die!"

"Stay here is big risk too. You must see this."

"Stay with my mom."

"That will not work. It is too much to ask. Harboring foreigner will be endanger her. Besides, I must return to Japan. *My* mother needs me."

There was a silence. Logically, Hiroshi made valid points, but Lucy felt just as right herself. Her case was clear, "If just one person on your flight is infected . . . ?!"

"But if I make it, I can survive."

"Akako didn't!"

It had been a long time since someone Lucy knew had been killed by a communicable disease. Had it ever happened? Not on a disease she was actively working against, and certainly not at the hands of one she had yet to identify.

"Lucy, you cannot help me. Not here."

"Then why are you calling?" Lucy flared angrily.

"I am sorry."

"What do you want from me?"

"I need help. To get to airport."

"Damn you, Hiroshi! You want me to be your taxi-cab?!"

"I am sorry. When society breaks down, people protect themselves. It is most natural human reaction." His explanation was simple and clear. "If I did not need help, I would not need to go home. Foreigners are now shut out."

Chapter 26

BACK TO JAPAN

The sun dipped beneath the horizon and the sky blazed red. Hiroshi stared, wondering where the next twenty-four hours would take him. The previous ninety-six had been a whirlwind of connectivity, and while he was about to return home, he felt his life had changed irrevocably, and beyond the reasons for his return.

He packed his bags and closed the blinds as he always did when leaving a room. He left a gratuity envelope for the housekeeper. He was careful to avoid any interaction with the hotel staff and other guests, choosing instead to descend the fire stairs, exiting the building through a side door as Lucy had advised.

The dumpsters in the alley spilled onto the asphalt. It was impressive what just a day or two without garbage trucks did for the prevailing odor in the city. Was impenetrable the right word for this smell? Rank was certainly the colloquialism.

Back up the street, Hiroshi saw groups of stranded travelers frantically assailing the various neighboring embassies—Mongolian, Venezuelan and Saudi Arabian. Each man and woman was desperate to avoid the rest, helplessly listening to their respective cell phones. Negotiations were attempted with intractable guards. Even the most mercenary taxi drivers had decided the calculus of risk to reward was too great now, compounding the hapless travelers with more uncertainty.

Hiroshi was glad to have a friend, and especially glad that his recent interactions permitted him to call on that friendship. It was interesting that he still used the term friendship in his mind; he had moved at an unprecedented pace and–

Lucy's Jeep skidded to a stop and she flung the passenger door open revealing legs clad in well-worn-lycra. Hiroshi bowed graciously.

"Arigato Lucy-san."

"It's good to see you too, Hiroshi. Now get in."

Hiroshi complied with her directive and they pulled away from the curb as if the very fate of the world were at stake. Before he could strap in, they were tearing past the helpless tourists, leaving them in their metaphorical dust.

+

Lucy raced the Jeep through the empty streets. Past shuttered shops and deserted public parks. They passed two people on the sidewalk, faces respectively covered with a paper mask and a red handkerchief. Stripping D.C. of the politicians and their attendant staff would not have quieted the town this way.

"It's a graveyard out here." Lucy reflected.

Hiroshi paused, momentarily confused by the literal interpretation of her words. "People behave very differently. Very quickly. It is much worse than yesterday."

"Speed of spread depends on three variables; the rate of infection, how many are infected, and the co-mingling factor." Lucy recited the well established epidemiological mantra, "and the co-mingling factor is the only one we have control over once the genie is out of the bottle. It's a good thing people are changing their habits."

They pulled off the I-267 as a mid-sized aircraft roared overhead.

Hiroshi gazed after the plane. "Tomorrow there are no flights."

She touched his hand with hers, a simple act of reassurance.

"It is safe to touch?" he asked.

"What?"

"I could be infected." He looked at her, "this disease is traveling very fast."

"It's only been a day since I saw you."

"Many more people are dead."

"And it might be airborne infective too ..." Lucy squeezed his hand firmer, her reassurance underscoring the chance that she was already taking ferrying him to the airport. It was a brave face that masked the anxiety she felt about her earlier miscalculation; 36 hours ago, she had really believed the worst was past!

"We'll make it," she said, as much to reassure herself as him. They each glanced at the dashboard clock and Hiroshi nodded appreciatively.

+

Crossing under Aviation Drive, they hit gridlock. If the city was empty, the airport was a hub of activity. Though traffic was at a standstill.

"This is worse than Thanksgiving," Lucy worried, anxiety mounting as she looked about.

Hiroshi nodded, "Is worse than Tokyo."

Mayhem would surely have erupted by now, were it not for the armed soldiers with flimsy surgical masks patrolling up and down the road. Nobody got out of their cars.

But nothing stopped the ticking clock on Lucy's Jeep's dashboard.

Tick-tock. Tick-tock.

"I can walk." Hiroshi suggested.

Up ahead a car door opened. Three soldiers quickly descended on the vehicle and Lucy observed regarding Hiroshi's offer, "I don't think that will work." Getting Hiroshi to his plane was looking as doubtful as her need to return to the RIID was pressing.

With patience expired, she pulled the Jeep onto the curb. And were it not for the military decals on her doors' panels this might well have been the move to incite the fomenting riot.

Instead, Lucy flashed her credentials from the grassy shoulder of the road at the armed soldier rushing towards them. The young soldier pulled his weapon up to Lucy's vehicle, but he no more wanted trouble or contact with the Colonel than she with him. A cursory glance at her papers for the benefit of the other cars presaged a hand gesture that sent them through.

+

At the terminal curbside, Hiroshi had his hand on the door-handle when Lucy grabbed his arm.

"Hold on."

She reached into the back seat.

Hiroshi found himself unexpectedly electrified by her athletic display of flexibility.

She returned to the front with a bottle of antiseptic ointment and a mask, and smiled at him. "Hold still."

Hiroshi watched curiously as Lucy doused a swab. He permitted her to pull him closer, still unsure what she intended.

To the soldier manning the terminal entrance it could easily have looked as if he were submitting to a chloroform rag, though the application to his lips was too tender to render him unconscious.

Lucy let the swab drop, pulled Hiroshi closer still, and suddenly kissed him.

Adrenaline shot through both their bodies. The thrill of a first kiss was escalated by the stakes involved. A kiss of transmission could be a kiss of death.

They held the kiss.

+

And when they did release, Hiroshi gazed into Lucy's eyes. "You are dynamic woman."

You can tell a lot from a first kiss, and Lucy's mind was made up. This man needed to survive. She tore open a packet of filters, placed one in a face-mask she again retrieved from the back seat. She then pulled the whole thing over Hiroshi's head.

"Don't take this off for anyone."

Stunned by her unfolding actions Hiroshi nodded, acknowledging the apparent wisdom of her counsel. "Hai." She turned and reached deeper still into the back of the Jeep, providing Hiroshi, despite the context, an ideal opportunity to admire her taut buttocks. He smiled as she straightened, the masculine lines in his cheeks telling all that needed to be told.

Lucy held up latex gloves. "Put these on."

Hiroshi hesitated, unsure. "Today is before tomorrow. Tomorrow things may improve. You are a beautiful woman."

Lucy blushed. Without further comment she pressed the remaining half dozen fresh filters into his hands and pushed him out of the car.

"Go. Your family needs you."

+

Her actions were abrupt, and previous courtships had gone awry as a result, but today ... today Lucy sensed she'd found a man who, more than tolerated her sharp turns, seemed to take pleasure in them. It made her nervous.

She watched as Hiroshi presented his passport and the E-ticket on his phone to two armed guards with surgical masks of their own. He then disappeared inside the Dulles terminal.

There was no sense getting nostalgic now, and Lucy pulled away from the curb.

Time to get back to the RIID.

Chapter 27

FAMILY

"Thanks, George." It was time to end the call.

"Oh. Sure."

"You've been very helpful," she reassured him, even as the insistent beep of the other line intruded on her thoughts, "I don't want to keep you from your electron microscope. Call me if you find anything else." And with that Lucy switched lines. "Colonel Topp."

"Lucy!"

"Mom?" The traffic light turned green and Lucy accelerated through the empty intersection; with the empty roads, traffic lights seemed pretty redundant right now.

"I was about to hang up."

"I was talking to the CDC."

"You're still busy then." It was Ellen's way to call and hang up. That, or chat for an hour, "I just wanted to hear your voice."

"I've missed yours, too." It had been two days since she last spoke with her mother. The two were close and two days would have been a long span under ordinary circumstances.

"You're talking to the CDC?"

"The New York branch."

"Oh."

"They're the brains trust at the presumed epicenter of everything." Lucy elaborated.

"It is awful, darling. Did you hear Sheryl Lambert passed away?"

"Sheryl Lambert? Doesn't she live in Michigan now?"

"Yes."

"I didn't realize you were still close."

"I still have internet. Facebook. There's—Do they know anything in New York?"

Lucy smiled; Ellen had identified an opportunity for information, "They are as in the dark as we are about a possible causative agent. Have there been any deaths at home?"

"No. And I'm fine. People are keeping to themselves to be sure, but everyone here seems fine. Mostly, people are staying at home, but you still see people walking dogs and running. They cross the street when someone is coming the other way. Is there anything I should watch for? Are people really just dying in their sleep?"

Lucy drifted to the other side of the road to avoid a pedestrian on her side, and marveled that despite the light traffic, there were parking spots aplenty, "There is some evidence of a cough, but no consistent symptoms have been identified yet."

"People don't just die, sweetie. I've lived sixty-eight years and I've known but a dozen people in my life who went to bed fine and woke up dead. That's just not how it happens."

"Well, you witness a death, mom, and you call and tell me about it."

"You sound just like your father when you're frustrated."

"Yes, well you two always were a right pair."

"And how is *your* new man?"

"What?" Lucy marveled at her mother's switch of topics.

"Enough of the sturm und drang. Tell me about your new beaux. You have seen him again, haven't you? Mr. Hiroshi."

Lucy was surprised that even in the current circumstances she blushed at the mention of Hiroshi's name. But there was no point trying to evade Ellen's drive for details. "He's headed back to Japan."

"That's unfortunate."

"Yes," Lucy swallowed, "Akako, his sister . . . "

"Yes . . . "

"She passed away."

"Oh, I'm sorry, dear. Did you see him before he left?"

"I'm returning from the airport now. I just dropped him off."

There was a moment's silence, as Ellen was momentarily lost for words. It was an unusual occurrence.

"He'll be fine." Lucy filled the void, adding pragmatically "I made him take supplies. To protect him."

"He seemed like a sweet man. And I know you were close to his sister."

"Yes. Yes to both."

Lucy allowed herself to talk about Hiroshi for a handful more minutes before the guard's booth at the USAMRIID loomed in front of her once again, returning her focus to the task at hand.

"Mom, I've got to go." Was her signal that the topic was now closed.

"Did he–"

But Lucy interrupted "I'm back at the RIID. Call me when you wake in the morning." She'd learned years ago you had to be definitive to stop Ellen, "I love you, mom."

"I love you, too, dear."

Lucy hung up and stopped her car at the checkpoint. She sat for a moment, immobilized by the mission in front of her. Enigmas sat at every turn, and a deluge of information to process, and somewhere in its midst an answer.

It was 10PM. She'd just lost two hours' work, and to exacerbate matters she was feeling the fatigue of residual jet-lag compounded by four days of intense analysis. As she looked up at the lighted windows in the building, she suddenly realized it had also been over five hours since she'd last heard from Commander Krogen. Five hours was way too long for a man who demanded updates every sixty minutes.

Chapter 28

A KISS GOODNIGHT

The cream-colored silky sheets rustled gently as she lay watching him in the curtain-filtered moonlight. He twitched, an involuntary muscle spasm that heralded his descent to another world. Beside her lay the man she had met thirty-some years ago as a sophomore at Stanford. And yet, in spite of the those years together, the only memories his twitching muscles conjured in her mind were those of the tight smiles that now accompanied death everywhere.

Thoughts of mortality flooded her mind. It was true that any day could be your last, but—and perhaps this was just the scientific method so ingrained in her—she had always expected to see signs beforehand. In less than a week life expectancy had plunged like a base-jumper.

He twitched again.

She leaned over to him and kissed him gently.

It was 3 AM and he too was exhausted. Any other night he'd have been irritated by affection that brought him back from the brink of sleep, two hours before his requisite rise. But this, well beyond the unusual nature of her wee-hour advances, was no normal night.

Even in his drowsy state he recognized that well before he awoke, she herself would be back on the phone coordinating national security and public perception. Her caress signaled her anxiety.

He turned to her as she pulled him into an embrace, and for the first time in months, Doctor Sam Moren, the head of the CDC, and her equally important husband made love to assuage the unspoken "just in case".

Chapter 29

PROTOCOLS

"A mortician in Ann Arbor died two days ago."

"And you think that's significant?" Lucy asked.

"Bob was unbelievably careful." Krogen assured her.

"So it probably had nothing to do with his being a mortician. People are doing a plenty fine job of dying anyway. You knew him?"

Krogen nodded. "He'd autopsied forty bodies since everything started. I contacted a few morticians I know personally." Krogen clarified his grounds for having reached out to Bob in the first place, "I wanted to get a sense of sentiment from those on the ground."

"And?"

"At first, they were all excited to share what they saw—coroners aren't normally on the front line in a war, and everyone secretly wants to be where the action is—but ..." He paused, refocusing his scrambled thoughts, "Anyway, my point is, we need to get more incident-specific guidelines out there for handling cadavers and biological samples."

Lucy agreed. Corpses of sudden death victims in the past tended not to pose any risks during a post mortem, but though this rubric seemed to hold, who could say the current crop weren't contagious; there were certainly other agents of death that remained infective post mortem.

Coroners had been working overtime, but mostly in the dark. While the CDC and the public health institutions feverishly worked up victim profiles, and scientists ran tests on biological samples—all in an effort to isolate an angle on the disease—the morticians and other would-be Sherlock's had combed over dead bodies for any unusual signs. Death with a tight smile made identification of pandemic victims simple, and with the worldwide death toll cresting an unprecedented million just six days from patient zero, a surfeit of specimens lay on every other street corner.

"We need to get out guidelines for handling the decedents." Krogen reiterated, interrupting her thoughts. "I've spoken to Colonel Marshall and I want you to coordinate with him."

"He didn't want to take this on himself?" Lucy was surprised.

"Why?"

"He does love to be the face of the experts."

Commander Krogen looked at her crookedly.

"Sorry, sir." Lucy apologized, "His slickness sometimes gets under my skin."

"Colonel Topp, I want both of your inputs."

"Yes sir." Lucy suddenly had that awkward moment of being painfully aware she was being juvenile, and worse, in this instance she couldn't simply shift the blame to Marshall himself. Two heads were always better than one, but it made her wonder if Krogen knew of her affair last year.

Thankfully, Commander Krogen returned them both to the science in question, "So what do you think? About protocols."

Lucy frowned, "With the source of infection unclear, we're flying blind. The only truly safe precautions are maximum ones."

The Commander looked justifiably unimpressed with her completely hedged answer that was of little practical value given the scope of the matter; there being barely a dozen bio-safety level 4 facilities in the entire country, that would hardly suffice.

"The epidemiology isn't helping," Lucy tried excusing herself. "Isolating common themes from preexisting lifestyle traits—medical conditions, sex, age, occupation or travel history—has a tendency to be obvious or nearly impossible to spot, and unfortunately what we're faced with is leaning to the later."

Both the army and the CDC had scientists, on the ground, contacting and interviewing families and friends of victims and indeed anyone with whom the deceased had had recent contact. But as the pool of the decedents ballooned, a thorough approach was quickly rendered impossible. Given the magnitude of the pandemic, everyone but the world's most reclusive hermit now knew a dead person, and it all turned discerning patterns from noise into a very difficult game. That death was the diagnosis didn't help either; it was impossible to watch case studies play out. Realistically, the task had moved from containment to mitigation.

"Alright, forget the epidemiology." Krogen exhorted as a guide to their combined thinking, "How about other clues? From the clinical side? Toxicology?"

"The cadavers aren't helping like they should."

Krogen waved his arms in the air theatrically, "No: *'Let conversation cease, let the smile flee, for this is the place where death delights to help life'.*" The Commander was evidently quoting something ironically, but Lucy was in the dark and her look said as much. Krogen clarified his reference, "The motto on the front of the Medical Examiners building in New York. Particularly ironic, huh."

Lucy nodded, "So much for a fleeing smile, the corpses are still grinning at us."

At least the nature of this pandemic, with its lack of symptoms, meant that the hospitals had not been overwhelmed, a second tier effect of most pandemics that had the ability to dramatically—if surprising to novices—overshadow the direct consequences (suffering a heart attack when all ICU beds were already being used could easily be fatal).

Again Krogen returned to his initial question, "So what do we change? We need protocols that at least mitigate risks!"

"In a perfect world . . . " Lucy considered the example she had outlined to President Pollack.

AIDS had taken two years of consolidated investigation, reacting only to symptoms, before the underlying causative agent had been identified. However safe sex and needle sharing programs were instigated much earlier in response to observations around paths of infection; in spite of political opposition to the 'encouragement' of sex and drugs use. Again though, these programs were predicated on identifying chains of victims and idiosyncrasies in victim profiles, two key ingredients that eluded illumination in the current pandemic.

"We need guidelines for handling corpses," Krogen implored Lucy.

Lucy was caught up considering the lack of level 4 facilities (the only correct facilities in which to investigate a lethally infectious pathogen for which there was no known treatment).

But it was worse than that, the people handling the cadavers were people—doctors, morticians, police and all the way down to concerned civilians—with no expertise in dealing with pathogenic material. "Sorry, sir, but it's a massive blind fishing expedition," one that demanded countless skills in all manner of subjects—proteomics, glycomics, to name just two, genomics, metabolics—"And we've got trout guys on a deep sea vessel, guys who have no appreciation for the dangers they're facing. No appreciation for the dangers of working with an unknown pathogen. It's not a surprise that some of our fishermen, perhaps your mortician friend included, are making mistakes."

"Should we suggest procedures to inactivate samples?" Krogen asked, "We have to make specific recommendations."

Lucy shrugged her shoulders doubtfully, "Easier said than done. It's hard to inactivate a pathogen you have yet to identify, unless you don't mind destroying the material for analysis. On the bright side, there are extremely infectious agents like SARS for which simple precautions like masks and the avoidance of physical contact protect against. But then there are others ..."

Krogen understood this, he had a metaphor he often deployed when talking to political types. It involved the where-to-for of inactivating a captured terrorist suspect: Locking the suspect in a room sufficed to inactivate most of them, but there were people who could pick locks. Pathogens were even more diverse still; some had the proverbial power to blow the door from its hinges. Prions (such as scrapie type molecules that caused mad cow disease, or Kuru, for example) tended to survive anything short of incineration, even if they were unlikely candidates in this instance given their traditional gestation period of years.

"We still have some intrepid investigators," Krogen offered, "Through Colonel Marshall, PharmaCo has granted us access to anything we need, and there are other companies that, even now, see this as a potential goldmine."

"No doubt," Lucy smiled ruefully. Why did economics bother her so? Marshall was simply playing by the rules of the system, and her own research would itself be a downstream beneficiary of any success he had.

"Beyond that there are some functional labs left, and, notwithstanding flight restrictions, China wants to get their hands on some US samples. We need to recommend protocols. Investigators just want some sense of what precautions they should be taking." Krogen was asking for help, "What should we tell them?"

It was odd to hear the Commander so unsure, asking such open-ended questions. Lucy knew he respected her opinion, but he wasn't normally a man unsure of his own, and he certainly had a wealth of experience to draw from. It underscored the tough quandary they were facing; there were many ways to inactivate samples, be it chemical detergents, fixation by cross-linking molecules, gamma radiation or simply heat, the problem was that each of those risked rendering the sample useless for investigation.

At a minimum it would be nice to preserve the ability to do DNA, RNA and protein analysis, but to do so and work in anything less than a level 4 facility risked a fatal lab accident.

They were definitely stuck between a rock and a hard place.

Chapter 30

DEPARTURE

"CANCELLED" the departure board fluttered like an unstoppable plague that struck with capricious virulence.

On the grey floor a weird disjoint stochastic rhythm had set in as people with scarves across their faces huddled in corners and bee-lined only essential treks to sporadically manned check-in desks. Social distancing was impossible in an airport, but smaller airlines had closed shop which helped.

Hiroshi ricocheted a path from the towering, ominously angled, glass windows encasing the terminal. He gracefully sidestepped any time a stranger came within a couple of yards, and eventually he arrived at his check-in desk. The Tokyo flight was one of last still scheduled for departure.

Behind the desk, the attendant smiled bravely through a mask of her own, "Sir, are you sure you wish to get on this flight?"

"My sister is dead."

The woman nodded understanding and continued processing his ticket. Evidently his life was less critical to her than it was to Lucy. The thought of Lucy made him smile, and waiting for his ticket he reflected warmly that he was leaving with her blessing, albeit hard won.

+

Seventy minutes later, there was a distinct sense of unease among the passengers as the plane sailed down the runway.

Those unable to procure face-masks either hunkered down beneath blankets or dipped faces into their shirts, furtive eyes wearily scanning for signs of trouble while noses and mouths were carefully protected by the tenuous insulation their fabric garments supplied. Nobody talked, and no food would be served.

+

Somewhere over Kansas, as the few truly unshakeable passengers slept, a shirt fell from the nose of one such woman.

Only it revealed a tight smile.

From three rows back, Hiroshi watched as an airline steward, dutifully making his pass of the cabin, stopped by the woman. With nervous reluctance the steward gingerly prodded the woman's arm. The woman didn't move; dead people don't.

Chapter 31

LOGISTIC RESPONSE

The shrill scream of a kettle pierced through the linoleum corridor like that of a terminal patient in a hospital ward in the last moments of life. It continued until Lucy shut it off.

The sharp sound had been as helpful as she hoped the jolt of coffee would soon be in its own right. Coffee, that magic elixir. The earthy granules swirled in the bottom of her cup melting into the hot water; instant coffee was no longer the truly awful product of yesteryear.

Lucy watched the Brownian motion as she added milk. The chaotic eddies never ceased to amaze her, at once apparently random, and, yet, utterly beautiful; a choreographed swirl of nature that emanated from its central helix. The epidemiology of a pandemic outbreak had a similar allure.

A knock at her door brought her back to the present.

"Have you heard about London?" It was Colonel Marshall.

Lucy turned to him, barely registering his question "No?"

"Estimates of twenty thousand last night." The number spoke loudly enough, but there was an additional concern. "A dozen the first day, sixty the second, then two hundred, and now twenty thousand today! And there's no telling before you fall asleep if your number is up."

Lucy stood, stunned. It was as if the devil had placed an electric egg-beater into her coffee-cup metaphor.

"More people died yesterday than in the deadliest day of any war—ever."

"That's . . ." Lucy trailed off, unsure what to say.

"Look, there's a few of us are heading to my place outside Gatlinburg. Supermarkets are already being looted in D.C. and it's only going to get worse. There aren't as many people to infect you in the countryside. Finch and some of the CDC guys from Atlanta are meeting us."

"You can't leave." Her reaction was a knee-jerk one rooted in her sense of duty.

"I can manage quarantines by phone. You can't fight if you're dead, Colonel Topp."

Perhaps he was being pragmatic, and then–

"There's room for you."

Nope, he'd stopped here in a pathetic attempt to reconnect with her. "Really?!" she looked at him in disgust.

"What?"

"Try Major Ulman, she might be more interested."

"Lucy, people are dying everywhere." If his eyes were to be believed, this was a sincere gesture, "Make no mistake. This is the big one. We're all going to lose loved ones."

Lucy shook her head and turned back to her desk where the eyes of the fish owl on Hiroshi's card bore back at her.

Marshall's disappointment was obvious, but the cause was lost and he turned back into the corridor. Lucy watched him disappear around the corner at the end of the hallway. She'd hurt him just now. He was a good man, but he was kind of conventional. The hell with derailing her life, saddling up with a man.

Healthy or not, Lucy couldn't help the pull of the flame. Death wasn't something she actively courted, but it wasn't something she fled from either.

+

Lucy had barely lifted the phone to her ear when Hiroshi started at a mile-a-minute over the drone of his aircraft, "Lucy-san, many people die on plane. Many people. I must need your help."

"Hiroshi. Where are you?"

"I am in–" but his voice was drowned out by a burst from the plane's engines.

Lucy heard the captain's voice over the intercom, "Everybody, please remain calm!"

"How many people are dead?" Lucy grilled.

"Is maybe twenty." Suddenly the jet engines in the background cut out completely.

"Hiroshi, where are you?"

"San Francisco. Army is coming onto plane."

"What?"

"They have guns. Big guns. And they are in space suit."

"Biohazard suits," Lucy reflexively corrected, "How many?"

"Four. No, more are coming. They–" There was a disruption of cabin noise that distracted Hiroshi.

"What did they just say?" Lucy pressed him, "What are they doing?"

"They say not to move." Hiroshi relayed the soldiers' demands. "They are pointing guns at passengers."

"Ladies and . . . " Lucy could intermittently hear a forcefully authoritative voice addressing the plane, "we are . . . help . . . please . . . seated."

"They point guns at us."

"Hiroshi, slow down." Lucy counseled, "No one is being shot."

Hiroshi took a breath, he was more relaxed than Lucy had credited him, "You were right," he reflected, "flight was bad idea."

Lucy recognized what was happening on the plane, "They are simply showing overwhelming force. It will quell any panic-driven response before it starts. They don't want a riot, and neither do you." It was a genuine risk given the circumstances he had described.

"There are more people come aboard. Not just soldiers."

"Right. Emergency service personnel."

"They are move us to quarantine," Hiroshi continued to transmit the soldier's address.

Lucy well understood the procedure that was being enacted.

"Stay seated!" the soldier shouted loud enough for Lucy to hear.

"The service people, they have black plastic. Much black plastic."

"They're body-bags," Lucy explained. "They will bag and tag the dead." Then curiosity took over, "Hiroshi, are the dead all together?"

"No."

Interesting, Lucy thought, "Are they in clusters?"

"Yes."

"How many clusters of dead are there?"

"Two, no three—there is one row behind me."

"There are dead bodies in the row behind you?" Lucy was alarmed again.

"No, just *behind* me. They are maybe six rows behind."

Lucy breathed easier again. "And in front of you, how far?"

"Three rows."

That wasn't good.

"Across the aisle. They are give everyone masks." Hiroshi continued, appraising her of what was happening.

"You still have yours, yes?" Lucy judged he was still wearing it by the muffled sound of his voice.

"Yes, I not taken mine off."

"Good. Keep it that way." Biomedical masks afforded some protection against airborne pathogens, but just as importantly to the emergency service personnel, they should pacify unknowledgeable nerves too.

"They are move the front rows off the plane now."

As Lucy listened to Hiroshi, it suddenly dawned on her that in this case the dead bodies themselves were more or less irrelevant. The world was already littered with corpses, what was unique in this case was that twenty passengers had died in public. A fantastic opportunity had just presented itself!

"Hiroshi," she interrupted him, "you were awake the whole time?"

"Hai."

"And the nearest victims? The ones in front of you, could you see any of them?"

Hiroshi paused, considering, "Hai."

"Did you notice anything?"

"They are dead?" Hiroshi sounded confused.

"No. Before they died." Lucy pressed again, a sense of urgency rising in her voice, "Did anyone have a seizure? Did they make extra trips to the bathroom? Call out?"

"Ummm ..."

"Think Hiroshi. It's important. There are others with you, right now, yes? Ask them. Did the victims become incoherent?"

"I am avoiding contact right now."

"Forget that. You have your mask on, yes?"

"Hai."

"Great. Ask if anyone saw anything."

There were three hundred witnesses to twenty fatalities in a case where to this point all deaths had occurred in private. Perhaps a child had filmed something on their parent's phone. Lucky breaks did happen. But before he could respond, Lucy heard another soldier addressing Hiroshi, "Sir, you need to hang up that phone right now and focus on me." A soldier, no doubt.

"But" Hiroshi, tried to protest.

"Sir, this is not a game."

"Lucy, I must go."

"Call me as soon as you can." And the phone went dead.

Lucy worked her way down a phone tree at the CDC while shooting rapid-fire emails. Hiroshi would call back soon, but she wanted the schematic diagrams the investigative team produced the moment they had them. They would include important details Hiroshi hadn't noticed; air ducts, proximity to lavatories, and with a little luck, crude tallies of movement about the cabin. She made these files priority one among the myriad files of field data that were being fed to her system.

The air filters themselves would be bagged and shipped to a local lab, but she wanted to see everything; in the accumulation of so much data, pin-pointing the relevant nuggets was as much an art as a science.

+

Hiroshi finally called back. He, along with the other living passengers, had been escorted back to the terminal and subsequently separated by proximity to the dead bodies. And although Hiroshi had escaped the immediate neighbors' quarantine, he had still been lumped with passengers, some of whom must surely be infected.

"Hiroshi, ask the other passengers what they saw." Lucy started.

In the white-walled holding room, Hiroshi looked about. The strangers averted his gaze. "Excuse me," Hiroshi broke the silence. Some of his fellow quarantined travelers turned his way, while others backed away as far as they could. "Excuse me. Did anyone notice anything on plane?"

"You mean before we were escorted off by armed soldiers?" an old man asked rhetorically.

"What you looking for?" another woman asked, simultaneously pulling her kid closer to the blue plastic chair she was sitting on and taking the phone from his hand.

"Mom. I wasn't finished." The kid protested.

This was hardly a world-class quarantine room, but then how many airports around the world could afford extraneous rooms, never to be used except in emergency.

"Did anyone notice anything about the dead people?" Hiroshi clarified.

"Hiroshi, was that a child?" Lucy chirped in his ear.

"Hai," Hiroshi responded into the phone as the medic approached him.

"Sir, please sit calmly."

"I am just ask a question." Hiroshi responded calmly.

"Sir, we don't need anyone riling people up. Besides, you'd be better to be worried about yourself right now. Those people on the plane who died are dead already."

"Honey, how come you got gloves too?" It was the woman with the kid. "You got spares for us? Maybe I did see something, you know."

Hiroshi glanced at the latex gloves on his hands. The situation in the room had the volatile instability of a munitions cache on a dry summer night.

The medic glanced suspiciously at Hiroshi's hands too. "Sir, who are you? And where did you get those gloves?"

Hiroshi touched the mouthpiece of his earbuds with one hand, "From my friend from DC."

"And who is he?"

"Not a he. A she." Hiroshi corrected the medic's assumption.

"Then who is *she*?"

"She is works for the army. The US army. She is interested in our flight."

The medic glanced around the room, everyone was now listening to their conversation. "Sir, I'm asking you again. Please take a seat. There are proper channels if your friend is interested in your quarantine. Hang up your call."

The medic reached for Hiroshi's mouthpiece, but Hiroshi glided back.

In his ear Lucy sounded suddenly more urgent again, "Hiroshi, you need to get out of that room. Every minute you're in there cuts your chances of survival. You hear me?"

"But you want to know answers, yes?"

"Yes, but—Hiroshi, I want you to live more. That room is a tinder-box!"

"Hai." Hiroshi spoke into his earpiece. He then met the medic's gaze again, and in an effort to placate him, Hiroshi agreed, "I hang up." He then feigned clicking off.

"Thank you sir. Now just sit."

Hiroshi looked at the medic. He was just a man, numbed by the global catastrophe. "You have lost someone?" he asked.

The medic's eyes spoke what his voice did not, this pandemic had well and truly reached into his social circles. "I must fly to Japan," Hiroshi tried engaging the man, "My sister must have a funeral."

The medic shook his head, "Someone else is gonna have to organize that one, cause you just got off the last commercial flight in the US. You're not going anywhere." It was the same principle behind looting; in times of crises people looked after their own and left it at that. "It's like I said before, you should worry more about yourself right now."

If Lucy had been right that Hiroshi shouldn't have left DC, Hiroshi was right about how people would behave.

"Get—out—of—there. You—will—die—if—you—don't." Lucy's voice in Hiroshi's ear was clear and unequivocal. And then the line went dead.

+

In her office, Lucy put down her phone, "Hiroshi . . . Hiroshi . . . " she tried soothing herself with his name. She then crossed her fingers in a futile gesture, hoping that he would be safe, and also that interviews with the remaining passengers might turn something up.

Suddenly she looked up. There *was* something else she could try.

Chapter 32

MARSHALL

Lucy's feet screeched on the linoleum floor as she tore into the corridor. "Marshall!"

The door to the parking lot burst open and Lucy exploded out. She scanned the lot but Marshall was already climbing into his Mini Cooper on the far side of the asphalt expanse, his phone to his ear.

She tried his number again.

He glanced at his phone and ignored the incoming call as he plugged the device into its port in his car; Lucy could wait to apologize.

"Answer. Answer, damn it!" but there was nothing for it, the phone and her flailing arms were in vain. She had to physically catch the car!

The Mini turned to the automatic gates, erasing Lucy's charging form from the rear-view mirror just as Marshall glanced at it in reflex.

Keying off Marshall's indicator, Lucy switched course. She turned for the perimeter fence parallel to the road. There was a chance she could catch his eye as he headed east. Mid-way there she felt that chance slipping. Then she spotted freshly laid river pebbles on a small island of greenery in the car park. She diverted towards them and scooped up three rocks.

She hadn't thrown a softball in ten years, but she had never had the motivation she had now. The first stone hit the perimeter fence, already behind the car. She fumbled the third as she reached for the second, but with the Mini fast clearing her range there was no time to stop.

No outfielder ever put more into a throw than Lucy did with her last hurl. Like a crossbow her body stretched taut and recoiled dramatically.

The missile flew–

Sailing high in the air and then–

CRACK!

Marshall's head jolted right as he screeched the tires of his car. There was a chip on the passenger's window, and behind it, racing towards him, the fanatical woman who had just berated him.

+

"Are you insane!?"

No answer. Marshall was livid and it wouldn't help to interrupt him now. She'd given him the situation, and he needed time to digest it properly.

"Think with your head! The man just got off a flight with twenty corpses. He's right where he should be!"

Changing Marshall's mind was not going to be easy, "Marshall–"

"He's staying in quarantine!"

"Mr. Sugimura understands how people behave. He understand their environment. He is a valuable asset, and you yourself said you can't fight this pandemic if you're dead." Lucy had the floor now "He's got technical expertise! Don't make this personal!"

Whoops.

"Take a look in the mirror! You want to die, too?!"

Marshall gave her a withering look that said everything he had to say. He then turned, got back into his car and slammed the door.

If she hadn't felt Hiroshi's life was at stake, she might have laughed; slamming the door of a Mini was about as emphatic as pounding a table with a feather duster. As it stood though, her best bet to get Hiroshi out of the quarantine was accelerating away from her.

Lucy pulled out her phone again and dialed another number.

Chapter 33

SFO

Hiroshi looked at his phone, but it wasn't a service issue; Lucy had hung up on him. Her urgency was palpable, and he knew she was right. Waiting for her rescue dictated a lifespan akin to a death sentence; he needed to take the situation into his own hands.

"Do what it takes. Get out of there." Her words echoed in his mind like a command to be deciphered as he glanced around the clinical room.

To distract everyone, the medic had switched on a wall-mounted TV. The low volume did nothing to mask the enthusiasm of the show's host as he waxed lyrical about introduced species. "... Non-native biologies introduced to unsuspecting environments invariably yield outcomes as unpredictable as they are disturbing. The classic devastation caused to Australian biodiversity by the introduction of South American cane toads stands in as marked contrast to the successful introduction of the African Dung beetle as ..." On the screen, footage of African dung beetles engulfed the image.

Momentarily fascinated, Hiroshi felt himself sucked in. Faced with a hostile environment, these beetles had evolved internal mechanisms— as robust as their external armor—for dealing with waste products.

The television narrator continued his commentary on dung beetles, "the Australian native was out of its league when cows arrived ..." The picture compared the size of the robust dung beetle to a giant cow patty. The narrator concluded with mocking irony, "Kangaroo pellets don't quite prepare you." The dung beetles were now crawling through a huge pile of manure. Whether it was the beetle's blissful ignorance or disregard for their terrain of choice, or whether it was the David Attenborough-esque narration, Hiroshi watched his fellow quarantine cellmates being lulled into submission.

Fear slammed Hiroshi's mind again!

Would he smell the Nitrous Oxide if the authorities decided to subdue him and his fellow quarantine cellmates? Or was his concern simply heightened paranoia? Hiroshi scanned for the vents. He had read an article some time ago, describing how Spanish burglars had used such a similar technique to neutralize a house before cleaning it out. The concept had struck a chord in him. Either way, Hiroshi no longer had any intention of waiting it out.

The television narrator continued his prattle, "Of course the African dung beetle buries the piles elephants leave behind," and then he tied everything together, "Is our current plight just the latest example of a foreign invader?"

Hiroshi approached the medic standing by the door.

Tired and distressed, the medic clearly didn't want another interaction with Hiroshi. Hiroshi puts his hands together in prayer, softening the medic's attitude. And then–

A precisely directed, swift hand chop knocked the medic cold. Hiroshi gently lay the man's head on the ground, the way a longtime owner might lay to rest his cat, recently struck by a truck.

The rest of the room watched in silent awe.

In that moment of apparent victory, the door to the outside opened and a guard stepped in. Without breaking stride, Hiroshi repeated the "gently-gently" process, and lay the, now unconscious, guard beside the still-prostrate medic.

Again Hiroshi lifted his hands in prayer as he bowed his white-masked face to the unconscious medic and guard. "Most sincere apology."

Hiroshi quickly slipped the lanyard from around the medic's neck and rifled his pockets for his wallet and, more importantly, his flashcard ID. He then exited the room.

Outside the building, but still in his respirator and gloves, Hiroshi called Lucy as he moved quickly and efficiently along the empty pedestrian causeway, heading towards ... He had no idea where he was headed!

+

At Fort Detrick, Lucy peeked in the door to his office, but Commander Krogen was already occupied with his phone. He gave her a gesture that signaled "don't interrupt" but held up his hands to indicate he'd be done in five minutes.

She didn't have five minutes.

She tried again, but he made it clear this call could not be interrupted. Lucy scribbled a note that he should find her, and turned back into the corridor.

There was urgency in her step as she hustled past the deserted offices, desperately evaluating her next turn, when her own phone rang. It was Hiroshi!

"Lucy-san. I escape."

"You escaped?!"

"Hai"

"Where exactly are you?"

Hiroshi scanned his surroundings. "Baggage collection. Car park is across the road."

"Then get a car and get out of there." It was a flippant response, but it was also the right advice, the only question was how.

"I have no key."

Lucy paused in the doorway to her office. "Water, water everywhere, but not a drop to drink?"

On the other end of the line, Hiroshi's confusion at her initial directive was compounded by an apparently inscrutable metaphor.

Lucy continued, unequivocally definitive in her next command "Go to the parking garage." The call dropped. It was not surprising, calls had been dropping with increasing frequency over the last couple of days.

Hiroshi gazed for a moment through the window at the parking garage before heading in that direction. In the absence of a better idea, he simply assumed there to be logic to Lucy's proposal.

+

Two minutes later, their line reconnected, Hiroshi stared out at the throng of cars; in less than twenty-four hours the airports had turned from a hub of activity to a life-less wasteland.

"What's the oldest car you see?" Lucy pressed.

Hiroshi scanned the cars with purpose this time, and with reverence in his voice reported, "There is 60's Corvette."

"Excellent. Get inside."

"It is not my car."

"You wanna live? Get inside."

+

Hiroshi drove a brick through the passenger's side window. Ditched the weapon, and, in a graceful move that belied the awkwardness of the situation, glided like a nationally ranked gymnast, through the opening. He somehow avoided the seat with the glass shards and slid across and into the driver's seat.

"I am inside."

Lucy raised a hand to Commander Krogen who now appeared in her doorway. He had a grave expression on his face. She indicated he should enter and that this call would take but one more minute. "Pull the wires from below the steering column." Krogen gave her a quizzical look as she continued her tutorial "You see a brown wire?"

Krogen scribbled three words on the piece of paper Lucy had left in his office only minutes earlier: 'make and model?'

As happened intermittently in life, a sea of anxiety drifted away with the particulars of a childhood memory. It didn't surprise the Commander that Colonel Topp knew the specifics of hot-wiring a car, but it did once again endear her to him, and, for a moment, however brief, offered a distraction from the heartbreak he had come to share.

+

Inside the red Corvette, Hiroshi touched two wires together and the engine roared to life. He smiled with satisfaction.

"You can thank my father."

"Arigato Lucy-san."

"Now start driving!"

"Where?"

"Out of town! I'll call soon." And with that she was gone again. Hiroshi loved women with purpose, but never before had he met someone with Lucy's measure. It was very exciting.

What Hiroshi didn't know was just how badly Commander Krogen was about to knock the wind out of Lucy's sails.

Chapter 34

MINISTER GORSHKOV

Taras Serik looked across the room at his college roommate. Minister Yuri Gorshkov was not someone easily rattled, and yet here he stood visibly shaken. That Gorshkov was alarmed only exacerbated Taras' own growing neuroses. Gorshkov had just returned from a meeting with Prime Minister Maqtaly, and by his account it was the head of Kazakhstan who was faltering under the pressure.

"Maqtaly hasn't slept in three days, and neither have I."

"What is happening, Yuri?"

"People are dying all over the world!" Gorshkov had the wild look of a cornered animal. "And we're at the epicenter, my friend." He looked Taras in the eye, "How much do you know?"

"About Ludmilla?" Taras asked, "Not much. Just that the army torched Kretsky, and they shot at me!"

What could he tell Taras? That it had been an accident? That was the truth, but to a loving husband it would not have sufficed. How could such an accident have occurred? This program was supposed to have brought good to the world, and yet, with hindsight it was now clear just how ill-conceived their plans had been.

With a great effort Gorshkov met Taras' eyes again. It was important to be lucid and clear, he owed him that. "Your wife was already dead. They all died. Days ago."

"They who?"

"Everyone at Kretsky. The perimeter was sealed, but whatever it was had already escaped." Gorshkov crossed to the windows, and opened the doors to a small balcony. He beckoned Taras outside. "Look at this city, Taras. This country. I love these people. I have devoted my life to them ..."

This was not what Taras had expected. He hadn't known what to expect, and frankly not much had made sense in the last forty-eight hours, but this ... Gorshkov was breaking, his arms were gesticulating wildly as he approached the concrete railing and–

"Ludmila is dead?" Taras struggled to accept what was obviously the truth.

"And soon we will all follow."

"What ... What are you talking about?"

Gorshkov's eyes returned from the expanse in front of them, tracing the winding streets from the perimeter suburbs through the old city to the cold concrete courtyard below. His wild gesticulating had subsided and he rested his paws on the railing.

Taras watched his old friend, "Yuri ..." but the man's eyes did not waiver from the ground, twenty stories down.

There was an intensity to Yuri's gaze that pulled Taras out of his own grief. Suddenly, Yuri shifted his weight onto his hands. The railing was no higher than the back of a tall park bench and even for the bear of a man Gorshkov was, it was only a small effort to vault his leg up to the lip.

In reflex, Taras took a step back, "Hey! Whoa!"

Still, Gorshkov's stare did not waiver from the chasm below.

"Yuri!"

Torn between approaching his old comrade in a bid to console, and warily keeping a sensible distance from the madman, Taras was lost in an upended world. A week ago he had dreams of a future, and now— now his wife was dead! Millions of people had died, and in front of him, a man he admired was literally teetering on the brink.

Yuri Gorshkov looked back at Taras, "What have we done?!" His vision sparkled with fuzz on the periphery.

"No!" Taras' response was an emotive plea.

There was sadness in Gorshkov's eyes as he turned from the man who had grown with him. So many shared aspirations and experiences to lose. Tears—overwhelming emotion, or prosaic vertigo—the source of his blurred vision no longer mattered as he stepped off the balcony ledge.

In horror, Taras raced to the railing, but it was too late.

+

Behind Taras, the door to Gorshkov's office opened and Prime Minister Maqtaly entered. Maqtaly was a different beast to Gorshkov; folding his hand was never an option to cover his own tracks, and certainly not one to be taken over the sacrifice of others.

Taras turned back to the sound of Maqtaly's approaching footsteps.

Chapter 35

TARAS

"You can't just make the public guinea pigs in your big experiment." Taras objected.

"The public does not know what is best for them."

"Maybe not, but it's their lives."

"They live in society. They enjoy society. There is a price." Maqtaly's thinking was old-style Eastern-bloc. His force of personality corralled Taras, just as his physical presence blocked Taras from heading back inside.

"Infective vaccines can protect everyone. Holdouts no longer endanger the herd."

Taras knew Maqtaly's sentiment well, he and Ludmila, had argued many times about its merit.

"How do you think polio was eliminated?" Maqtaly challenged.

"I know about forcible vaccinations." Taras replied. Why had Maqtaly not crossed to the railing to verify Gorshkov's plunge to his death? It was strange.

"Infective vaccines save the conflict."

"Okay." To Taras, they were getting distracted, "That's all very well, but what does that have to do with this catastrophe? You're not helping. Tell me. What has happened?" Taras' sentiment change to accusation, "You're not protecting the herd right now!"

"Kretsky is gone."

"Because you burnt it to the ground! Someone will find out what you've done!"

Maqtaly stood motionless. "Look at this city," he implored Taras. Then, echoing Gorshkov's earlier gesture, he waved his hand out at the space beyond the balcony railing, "The world is full of fires right now. Nobody will look twice at Kretsky."

Taras glanced behind him. It was true, plumes of smoke billowed up from multiple points around the city. Fires, burning out of control. With the breakdown of emergency services . . . his mind wandered . . . but that wasn't good enough. Taras poked his own chest with his index finger, "I'll tell them."

Maqtaly shook his head slowly as he reached inside his coat, "No," and, producing a gun, he declared definitively, "You won't."

Taras bumped back into the railing. There was nowhere to go. "You wouldn't dare."

"You can save me the trouble." Maqtaly jutted his chin out towards the railing and the space beyond.

Taras laughed. The laugh surprised even himself, but the situation was so foreign and melodramatically surreal, it just happened, "You expect *me* to jump?"

Maqtaly made no answer.

There was a stalemate.

Taras appraised Maqtaly. First, gauging the older man's resolve, then the man himself. Maqtaly was of presidential age, maybe 58. His hair had lines of grey throughout and the flesh on his arms was not well maintained. To be sure, the arms would have strength, men of that age did—having lifted children, grandchildren and groceries for decades— but the same age made his reflexes slower, less physically crisp. If it weren't for the gun, there would be no contest. But there was a gun. Was Maqtaly really a cold-blooded killer?

The Prime Minister took a step towards Taras, raising the gun from Taras' chest to his head.

Both moves were obviously designed to intimidate, but the small tremor in Maqtaly's hand telegraphed another reality.

Again, Maqtaly took a step closer, desperate to display his control of the situation.

Like a cornered dog, Taras recoiled, but the railing blocked his path. Maqtaly was on top of him, the cold barrel of the gun in his face. Then, suddenly, Taras lunged forward at Maqtaly's hand.

Their limbs connected crudely.

The gun exploded, even as the weapon went hurtling over the edge and out into space.

The bullet screamed away ineffectually and the two men stood stunned.

Taras was the first to react, and his reaction was to flee.

+

Taras took the steps of the stairwell two at a time. He had no idea if Maqtaly was making chase, calling in support, or rooted to Gorshkov's balcony upstairs. Whatever the case, he wasn't waiting around to find out.

Get the gun, that was step one.

Taras exited the building at speed. But clattering across the concrete squares horror seized him as he approached the red mess that was Gorshkov's remains, his old friend. His feet slowed involuntarily as he gagged back vomit.

No time to mourn. He forced his eyes to scan.

Then, alighting on the gun, he forced his feet to move again.

Now what . . . ? Fifty yards across the square was a bike rack!

Taras carefully analyzed the safety on the gun as he crossed to the bikes. Figuring he had it on, he cautiously tried squeezing the trigger. Nothing happened. Good.

There were eight bikes at the rack. All were chained to the immovable metal structure.

Taras shook the flimsiest looking lock, but it was still a lock. "Damn!"

He was about to give up, when a wild idea hit him. Carefully, he pulled the gun back out of his jacket pocket and unflipped the safety.

He glanced around the courtyard, but there was no one there. To hell with it!

He aimed, shielded his eyes with his spare hand and–

BANG!

Clunk.

It was remarkably effective. The lock disintegrated and the chain links dropped to the ground.

The sound of the shot echoed for an eternity, but there was no sign of another soul. Taras wheeled the bike out from the rack and climbed aboard. Shooting a bike lock was crazy, but it was effective. And, though, just ten days ago, discharging a firearm in the public square outside the parliament building would have resulted in being swarmed, today, he was alone. He felt a surge of confidence; he was adjusting to the new world.

Chapter 36

SAM MOREN

Lucy looked up at Commander Krogen as she hung up the phone. In the circumstances, Hiroshi safely on the road was as solid a triumph as was available for the taking and she allowed herself a fleeting smile of satisfaction, "Problem's solved."

But the dead space in Krogen's eyes heralded a new concern.

"Sam Moren is gone."

"Where?"

"Gone gone."

"Sam–" and again, words failed Lucy. How quickly triumph turned to tragedy. The woman she had revered since the moment she first knew who to revere, was dead. Doctor Moren was invincible, or at least she had been in Lucy's mind.

"Most of the CDC is dead." Krogen continued, filling the space Lucy's bewilderment opened; he hoped she was still listening. "Their team in Kazakhstan is dead too. I'm sending one of our teams over, but it's a twelve-hour flight just to get there!"

Adrenaline coursed through Lucy's body. Her focus returned and she turned to a pile of notes on her desk, riffling through them frenetically. "Have them look for a guy—a guy named ...Amanet—no last name. He's connected with a facility called Kretsky. He apparently spent the day with Mr. Iglinsky before our patient zero boarded the flight from Almaty."

Krogen nodded appreciating the lead, but there was obviously more on his mind.

"Was there anything from Kazakhstan before they died?" Lucy asked.

"They're still a real bet for the index case, even if Operations Officer Wallenstein and the rest of the plane are still alive." Then, switching back to his original thrust, he continued, "Hospitals are collapsing too. Not because doctors are overwhelmed, or dying any faster than anyone else. They're simply fleeing."

"It's normally the surge that takes them down," Lucy noted abstractly.

"Sure; analysts blamed closed outpatient clinics for higher morbidity than SARS itself. Without any symptoms we might have hoped that wouldn't be the case here, but you still need doctors."

"Lack of symptoms doesn't stop fear." Lucy concurred "At least it might be saving some unnecessary transmissions."

"True, but I wouldn't want to have a life threatening illness right now." Krogen paused, "Anyway, given the problems at hospitals and the CDC we're taking charge."

"Who's 'we'?" Lucy stared at the Commander, bewildered again by his patently unrealistic assertion. "Colonel Marshall left a couple of hours ago. You and I must be the only people here!"

"I know. And you haven't slept in forty hours."

"And we've got no idea how to coordinate hospitals."

"Then we'll have to improvise."

"There must be ... "

"If you have a number for the cavalry, now's a good time to pick up the phone." Krogen looked at Lucy somberly, "Otherwise, now's the time for heroics."

"We're in charge?"

"We're in charge." Krogen reaffirmed, "There are still a few of us left. We will convene in a conference call at fourteen hundred hours. I'll send out a link." And with a salute he turned and left.

Lucy watched him go. They might be a bare-bones team right now, but if she had only one ally, Commander Krogen would have been her choice every time. He was a special man, and bouncing ideas off him had been a highlight of her tenure at the RIID.

Lucy leaned back in her chair and closed her eyes. It felt good to shut the world out, even if just for a moment.

Chapter 37

GUERILLA WARFARE

Shots rang out in the building.

She crouched by the exploded window starring at the dulled confetti. These were not the sparkling shards of the movies; the grime on the windows clung tightly to the fragments on the floor.

"Are you alright?" The blast had jolted her pensive gaze, but it was the Commander's voice that returned her to reality.

"Sure," nevertheless it was only then that it occurred to her to check, which she did, "Sure, sure."

She had been preoccupied tracking the mosquitoes that surrounded them for the last hour. With the state of the world their incessant zzzz—something that would usually have driven her mad—was weirdly comforting. How strange to be thankful for a small torture that helped stave off desperately needed sleep. She was actually *grateful* to the little bastards.

Krogen looked at her, "Come on, we need to move."

Lucy looked over at Caroline—Major Ulman. The M.I.T.-trained scientist was in her late twenties, and had thus seen almost no frontline, not that Lucy had seen a lot. Lucy really did like her, but she worried that in a situation like this, inexperience could be lethal. There was, however, no time to sit pontificating and she pushed Ulman after Krogen as another shower of bullets riddled the opposite wall.

They worked their way into the stairwell at the back of the building, putting distance between themselves and the sound of gunfire. They were sitting ducks if the enemy returned, and they were hopelessly under-armed. Not that it made a big difference, even the best supplies are inevitably ineffective against a surprise encounter.

War is daunting and all the messier when your enemy is invisible.

+

They sat hunkered down for two hours, ninety minutes of which was undisturbed but for crickets outside and the mosquitoes immediately around them.

"Should we make for the Humvee?" Caroline eventually whispered.

Krogen nodded silently. In total, they'd been pinned down for almost twenty-four hours now, and Intel was desperately needed. Lucy could guess his thoughts, but she also worried that the young soldier seated between them had little-to-no experience navigating a lethal adversary with the ability to turn the slightest of slip-ups into a deadly mistake. Simple actions mattered; never run smoothly from your adversaries' left to right—smooth tracking that way with an automatic weapon was too easy for a right-hander.

Krogen turned to Lucy "Take her to level 4".

"Up?!" Lucy looked back at the Commander.

"It's the only way we'll see what's happening."

Lucy's head swirled. Level 4: a window left ajar would expose them! And there was no doubt the adversary was vigilantly monitoring the perimeter. "She's never seen level 4." Lucy regretted expressing a visible lack of confidence in the Major as if she were not there, but it had to be said.

Krogen reassured his Colonel, "You're the best teacher I know. You've been there hundreds of times."

Lucy pulled out a roll of duct tape and started taping her gloves to her sleeves. The major looked at her quizzically, and fear rose in Lucy's throat, just as a hand touched her shoulder.

She coughed, blinked, and suddenly found herself looking down at the puddle of drool dribbling through the pile of papers on her desk. She looked across at the clock on her computer screen. She had just lost two hours. Standing behind her was Major Ulman.

"Colonel?"

Her world came flooding back. Danger still surrounded them. A war against a biological foe was every bit as dangerous as dodging bullets on the front line. And qualified or not, they desperately needed to get back into the lab; back into Level 4.

Chapter 38

GREATER SAN FRANCISCO

Hiroshi slowed the 300 horsepower V8 to a rumbling halt. He'd followed Lucy's advice, but leaving town had turned out to be no easy feat. In quarantine he had heard that the Golden Gate bridge was no longer open, so erring on the side of safety he'd started out south. He quickly discovered however the 101 was gridlocked—uncleared accidents from days ago left no room to pass—which forced him onto surface streets. That hadn't helped much. The surface streets were difficult too.

And so it was that five miles south of the airport he had been amazed to find the San Mateo Bridge open. He took his opportunity to get off the peninsula.

He'd been heading north for half an hour since, and was just clearing Berkeley when yet another checkpoint materialized in front of him. Having assiduously avoided six already, he had no interest in stopping at this one.

As the great Bard had noted centuries ago, albeit in an ironic context, discretion was indeed the better part of valor. With this in mind, Hiroshi pulled the nose of his red chariot to the left and commenced another three-point turn.

Unfortunately, a space-suited army officer was already approaching. The dusty mustard camouflage of his uniform was designed for the Afghan desert and looked as out of place on the neighborhood streets as the AK-47 slung over his shoulder; though no less ominous.

Hiroshi weighed the merits of a dramatic about face, one that required the dedication of rubber to the road, but instead elected to continue his subdued retreat, permitting the officer to reach his driver-side window. The plastic-like fabric of the spaceman's glove-covered hand squeaked as much as it rapped on the glass. His goggled eyes scanned from the shattered glass on the passenger's seat across the interior of Hiroshi's car.

Hiroshi deftly obscured the loose cables under the steering column with his knee. And somehow the officer's careful inspection missed the dangling wires.

Hiroshi tried not to fixate on the absent key in the ignition switch. And he tried clearing his mind, but his subconscious had other ideas.

Curiously one of the tenets of Sun Tzu's Art of War, a favorite of his youth percolated into his conscious. He decided to take the initiative, "This is a quarantine?"

The officer nodded. "You should return to your home." His voice was distorted by his gas mask.

Hiroshi continued his deception "I must find water; the plumbing is not working."

The officer scanned inside the car again. This time his eyes stopped on the broken glass on the passenger seat before thoroughly inspecting the rest of the vehicle. The rest, except the ignition-point that Hiroshi was now obscuring with his arm.

Hiroshi pressed on, "And I need gas." To Hiroshi this had already been a source of concern, making it an easy necessity to channel in his effect to play for sympathy.

The officer glanced at the needle on the fuel gauge. It was pointing to 'empty' and he—understanding the pervasive angst that immobility induced—took pity on Hiroshi. Turning, as if to see the location he was indicating, he gesticulated back up the road. "There's a gas station a couple of blocks back on the left. If there's anyone there, they might have water too, not that you should be driving about. Two birds with one stone if you're lucky." Then, deploying his eyes like a futuristic lie-detector test, he motioned deliberately at the shattered glass covering the passenger seat, the pink elephant that neither had acknowledged. "Everything alright?"

Hiroshi shook his head earnestly without breaking stride, "It is a grave time. Lawlessness is even at university."

Both men considered the veracity of Hiroshi's evasive explanation until Hiroshi's phone finally interrupted the silence. Hiroshi decided again that retreat was most advisable. He glanced at the number on his phone and blatantly continued his fabrications, "This my mother in Japan."

The officer stepped back from the car, there was something uneasy about this man, but if he seemed willing to about face—which amply satisfied the officer's own orders—then the officer in turn was happy to settle with waving the Yakuza back.

Hiroshi took the soldier's body language for what he wished it to mean, and answered his phone as he swung his purloined vehicle about. The, barely out of earshot of the officer, a man's voice could be heard on the other end of the phone.

+

The streets of Paris, the steps of the Opera House in Sydney, and Saint Peter's Square in Rome—where days earlier flocks had congregated to pray—were all devoid of people. At the Brandenburg Gate in Berlin, Victoria, the Roman goddess of victory had not looked down over such deserted a section of cobblestones since the days before Germany's reunification in 1989.

Hiroshi had been aware of the generalities, but talking to Miyake, and hearing of the specifics that pertained to Tokyo, his birth-city, brought everything home. How it was possible for Shinjuku Station—the busiest railway station in the world by headcount, with almost four million daily users—to be deserted was unfathomable. Almost as unfathomable as empty stores at the Tsukiji Fish Markets, which under normally moved in excess of 2000 tons of fish every day, again a world-wide benchmark. What were people eating? Where were they?

Without interrupting Miyake's descriptions, Hiroshi pulled his Corvette into the gas station that the quarantine solider had alluded to. The devastated attendant's booth in the center island disavowed him of any hope of finding food or water, its contents having been looted days ago.

Still, his thirsty steed needed fuel so Hiroshi pulled up to the gas pump. Glancing at the touch-screen, he was pleasantly surprised to discover life persisted; Todai, Tokyo's namesake university, was without power, and yet somehow this inconsequential gas station remained functional.

"Hiroshi, your engine has stopped?"

"I am at gas station, I need more fuel."

"You should have taken a rental car at the airport. They always have a full tank."

"The car rental was not open."

"So? They always leave the keys in the ignition. You stole the car you're driving anyway, right?"

"Hai," Hiroshi reflected, adding, "Things without all remedy should be without regard. What's done is done."

"What?"

"Is Shakespeare," Hiroshi clarified his quote, then grinning he added, "Anyway, I like my muscle car better."

The touch-screen on the pump begged for a card. A spark of thought doubled Hiroshi's gratitude to the medic he'd laid low in quarantine back at the airport; his own wallet had been confiscated on the plane by the space-suited personnel, but the purloined purse in his pocket would amply suffice.

Glancing about, and ignoring, the "no cell phones" sign, he pulled and swiped a credit card from the medic's wallet.

"You are an odd duck, Hiroshi."

"Hai."

"Speaking of ducks," and with that Miyake launched into an account of rumors of birds having infected the Tokyo water supply.

The gas pump prompted Hiroshi for the zip code on the card. Hiroshi flipped the wallet open again, silently praying the true owner had—like any Japanese citizen would have—retained a current address on his driver's license.

94122

Hiroshi waited while the screen processed his entry.

Miyake was now talking about 'avian fecal dust', something that, in spite of its alarmist appellation, was apparently often overlooked when it came to funding. The world had been complacent, but the fact was: dried avian excrement could easily pass on a myriad of diseases. And once ground to dust it became extremely airborne underscoring the issues it raised.

The screen blinked, directing Hiroshi to choose a grade of gas. Hiroshi breathed a sigh of relief as he flipped the 87 lever up and pulled the nozzle to the Corvette's tank. He pulled the trigger to engage the flow, but nothing happened.

At that moment the phone too cut out.

"Miyake?" but the line was dead. Actually, the phone was dead.

There was nothing to be done about the phone and Hiroshi turned back to the pump. Set back but undaunted, he switched to the 89 lever; Americans were cheap. ... It wasn't until the 89, and the 92 after it, both came up dry that panic began to creep back into his veins. Without gas he was stranded, stranded in a city in which he knew no one. In a city where nobody wanted to know him. And now, with no means of communicating with the outside world.

Perhaps it was the speed with which everything had happened, and perhaps it was simply the thrill of the chase, but Hiroshi suddenly found himself face-to-face with an abyss he'd barely noticed approaching. He needed a plan, and he needed it now.

Looking about, he scanned his surroundings.

At the back of the lot, the door to the workshop was open. Tools, tubes and spare parts were strewn everywhere. A lonely car sat stranded atop a pneumatic jack. There were other cars too, but hot-wiring was Lucy's expertise, and besides, Lucy's first instruction had been to find the oldest car he could; nothing he could see here pre-dated the 21st century.

He checked his phone again: definitely dead.

Hiroshi crossed to the car on the jack, and pushed a rolling ladder to its door. Climbing the ladder revealed an ignition switch as empty as his own. He stood there staring at the dashboard when he noticed the gas tank release lever. Leaning in the open window he pulled the lever, eliciting a satisfying "pop" outside the car. He descended the ladder, moved it, and re-climbed it to the open gas-tank hatch. He opened the cap and took a whiff. Never before had he been so thrilled by the smell of petroleum.

Minutes later he had siphoned the tank dry. His own tank was now three-quarters full.

Satisfied, he strapped in, touched the ignition wires together and roared out of the station. Where he was headed he still had no idea, but to stop risked contact.

Chapter 39

HOT ZONES

Whether you were wearing a level four *lab-styled* biohazard suit or a suit specifically designed for a hot zone out in the field, you were operating under pressure. Metaphorically, but literally too. The suits were all positively pressurized adding a layer of protection from foreign nasties in the surrounding air in the unfortunate event of a rupture.

Years back it had amused Lucy that this effectively made these suits one-way barriers; put an infected person inside a suit and rupture it, and they would spew out whatever contagion lent itself to airborne transmission. And that was *one* of the potential problems to encounter before you ever accidented your first rupture.

For another thing, they were hot.

And yet another, they made you antsy.

It didn't matter who you were, or how many times you had used one of the suits, it was difficult not to feel claustrophobic and paranoid. You might expect fatigue to numb these feelings, but accentuated anxiety was a much more common reaction. Bearing this in mind inspired Lucy to use her most soothing voice as she stripped off her clothes, hung her shirt, and folded her jeans and underwear neatly into her small locker.

Small talk had its value. Her casual manner prevented any excitement perceived connections might arouse. Idaho was Idaho, and if that was her newly enlisted protégé's birthplace, great; Lucy just wouldn't permit the conversation to veer towards downhill skiing. A background that included MIT was nice, but this woman was still in her twenties and Lucy remembered how the thrill of her own maiden voyage to level four had clouded her head.

"When did you first don a hot suit?"

Lucy balked. Had Major Ulman read her mind? "Umm ..."

"You don't remember?"

The incredulity made it impossible not to respond, "Sure. It was early 2002."

"Where? What happened?"

Perhaps Lucy was being unfair. Perhaps the Commander had correctly assessed Major Ulman; he was a great judge after all. The way Ulman had stripped down without emotion was reassuring. And so, in a 180 degree about face, Lucy decided to break the ice. Hell, maybe *she* was more on edge than her protégé.

"It was New York." Lucy handed the Ulman clean surgical scrubs and her first real smile. She could still remember when, as a young virus hunter, she'd secretly wished for the outbreak of a deadly pandemic. "There's nothing like a suspected outbreak to fast-track your career."

"Or a real one." Major Ulman smiled, "I thought that was why we all signed on anyway. Tell me about 2002."

Ah, hell with it, it was all context, "The CDC had been alerted to a fatality in the city. Near Bowery. A man had died suddenly and unexpectedly. And when the post mortem identified anthrax ..."

"In New York city?"

"Yeah, somehow they kept a lid on the investigation even if they did shut down three city buildings. I guess that's New York for you."

"And?"

"Human Intel from the FBI quickly identified apartment 12C as worthy of a *'predicated investigation'*—FBI jargon for a target on which to base further *'proactive inquiry'*." Lucy air-quoted the vernacular.

Ulman rolled her eyes, and once again Lucy could see her younger self in front of her.

"Thermal imaging determined the apartment was empty of potential suspects. However given the temporal proximity to the anthrax letter attacks, and interviews with the neighboring tenants, who described having seen lab equipment, 12C was quickly designated a hot zone." Lucy shrugged, an affect at nonchalance, "I was a junior member of the bio-investigative team brought in to provide further assessment."

"So you started in the field?" Ulman was surprised.

"It wasn't the first time I'd used protective gear, but yes, it was the first time I donned a bio-containment suit in earnest."

"Were you scared?"

Lucy nodded, "And we discovered a white powder too. As soon as we entered." Even now, over a dozen years later, her heart skipped a beat when she recalled that moment.

Ulman too drew a sharp breath, "And they kept a lid on this?!"

"The powder was cocaine. And the tenant in 12C was a small-time drug dealer who had fled at the first sign of the police." Lucy's pulse dropped again, "The drugs, it turned out, were entirely coincidental, as quickly became apparent when an FBI researcher connected the building's past use as a tannery with its present predicament. Leather and anthrax have an intertwined history, what with cows being a recurrent vector in anthrax's dispersal."

"Wait, so it was a false alarm?"

"Yes and no. Sure, the white powder was unrelated drugs, but there was anthrax." Realizing she had lost Ulman, Lucy elaborated, "The B. anthracis spores were released when a backed up toilet in 14A flooded and the liquid seeped through the floorboards of the old tannery from the 1920's. It's not always terrorists who create hot zones."

"Right. Sometimes it's Mother Nature. And sometimes it's wayward scientists." Ulman was smiling now, she was relaxed.

It was nice that Ulman was relaxed, but the spores used in the infamous mail attacks that killed five people in 2001 probably originated from a lab of responsible scientists, well one previously deemed so.

Lucy reflected on the age-old public quandary: Why would a scientist engineer a pathogen known to be lethal? To outsiders it often seemed implausible that a lab would deliberately mutate a virus to make it worse, but examples abounded, and would continue to do so.

As recently as 2011 there had been controversy surrounding the work of a Dutch group who had taken a strain of H5N1 bird flu with a 60% mortality rate but poor transmissibility, and tested what it would take to alter the later. Their study involved a ferret model (a good paradigm for replicating patterns in humans). After experimenting with a host of mutations they identified a strain within just 5 modifications—each of which existed on its own in the wild, just not together in one strain— that became airborne transmissible. That was to say, their new strain killed ferrets in neighboring cages with no other contact.

Particularly sobering was the thought that the Spanish flu, which killed 60 million humans in 1918, had only 2.5% mortality rate; one could only imagine the carnage an airborne transmissible flu with 60% mortality might cause in the modern jet-setting age!

Even more baffling to the public though, was the almost pathologically ironic defense scientists offered—of a study that examined potential outcomes of mutations—that being that the research involved a strain that was benign to humans, a trait meant to mitigate against the hardly unimaginable event of an airborne transmission to lab personnel.

It was but a small leap to see how scientific inquiry—the underpinning foundation of the enlightened approach to biological defense—could easily slip into the territory of research accident. From the Australian engineering of a lab vaccine resistant version of mousepox (a disease not unlike smallpox), to the CDC's reconstruction of the Spanish flu virus from a corpse buried in the permafrost of Alaska, there existed a rich history of scientists playing with fire.

And that didn't count examples of actors with nefarious intent. Actors whose sinister objectives prompted the elliptical words from a former Eastern block inspector that still echoed in Lucy's mind to this day: "You may use a knife to peel a piece of fruit, or to kill someone. So if I have a knife in my hand, what does it mean? It depends on the observer's point of view."

+

Major Ulman finished undressing her nubile figure while Lucy removed her grandmother's ring and tucked it into the clothes in her own locker. Lucy was far from sagging, but her muscle tone no longer matched that of her underling and whether it was just the fatigue or otherwise, she was surprised to feel it bother her.

"Here, give me your hands," Lucy directed as she tore duct tape from the roll.

Major Ulman slipped into the scrubs, pulled on latex gloves and held out her hands. As Lucy carefully secured Ulman's gloves to her suit, the younger woman ventured a question she'd been sitting on, "What exactly are we looking for?"

"A needle in the haystack," Lucy responded without irony. "Right now we're going to check a few leads,"—'few' was an understatement, but Lucy reasoned that Ulman could guess at most of the tests. The most likely exception to Ulman's undeveloped intuition was Laitai.

"Never heard of it," Ulman confirmed Lucy's guess.

"It's one of the closest known phenomena to what's happening right now. Only it's rare and not well known. I'm sure it's been looked at, but people miss things. The name, translates directly as 'sleep and die'. Kind of apt, huh."

Ulman nodded, absorbing the information.

"There are problems though. For one thing, although the afflicted are young Thai men who die suddenly in their sleep, they don't wear a tight smile the next day. Worse, the cause of Laitai isn't clear. One possible cause of death is Meliodosis. At best, I doubt it's more than a potential contributor. Have you heard of Meliodosis?"

Ulman shook her head again.

"It's an infectious disease that's caused by a gram negative bacterium Burkholderia pseudomallei. It's found in soil and water. So surprise, surprise Burkholderia pseudomallei is of public health importance in Thailand."

"Is it related to anything I *have* heard of?"

Lucy smiled at Ulman's instinct to file the new unknown appropriately. "It's closely related to Burkholderia mallei, which causes Glanders. You might have heard of Glanders from our efforts in the second world war, and, later, Eastern block bio-warfare research."

Ulman nodded this time.

"It's a long shot and the likely roads have already been reviewed many times over, but we're going to examine every possibility again."

Both women were now finished dressing. Lucy affixed their helmets and led them from the change room, into the decontamination room where they were greeted by jets of Lysol.

Despite seeing a lot of herself in this young woman, Lucy still wondered if Major Ulman, a woman apparently unafraid of jumping into her first hot zone, was a little too comfortable.

The doors to the decon room closed, and with the white noise of the Lysol torrent all around them, neither woman heard the buzz of the cell phone Lucy had just left behind, and they certainly didn't see the image of the caller glowing on the screen.

Chapter 40

THE AMERICAN EMBASSY

Locating the American Embassy was not as easy as Taras had hoped, and once he'd done so, he was glad for his newly acquired transport. If his own government wouldn't help, perhaps another would. He hopped on the bike and set off across the city.

The road was littered with a corpse here and another there, bodies ousted by the terrified survivors.

Stalin might have said: "one death is a tragedy, one million is a statistic," but it felt less simply statistical when you could name twenty or thirty of that million. And less again when a dozen were close friends. . . . Or was he conflating the millions with the death of one woman, his wife?

He rode past a burning building he'd seen from Gorshkov's balcony. It was surprising that the fire had not spread to neighboring structures, but it would be more surprising if, now that the afternoon winds were picking up, it didn't before nightfall. There seemed little hope a fire department might respond at this point.

Further ahead, a corner grocery store had a shattered window. Taras was hungry and he slowed his bike as he angled toward the storefront. To Taras' dismay, an unwelcoming man appeared in the window, rifle in hand. Taras waved acknowledgment, but elected to cross back to the other side of the street. His hunger could wait for now.

Ten minutes later he arrived at the American embassy.

+

Taras waited outside the spiked-metal fence while the guard reluctantly sought out Dr. Halpin, the only CDC personnel left. The skies drizzled a light rain, but Taras remained patient.

Eventually, a man emerged from inside the building. He popped up an umbrella, adjusted his face-mask and exited from under the awning towards Taras. "Can I help you?"

"Maybe," Taras responded, "But I might also be able to help you."

The man eyed Taras suspiciously, "Our CDC team got hit by what they were investigating. I'm the last man standing."

"They are all dead?" Taras was dismayed.

"I'm still here."

"What have you found?"

"Sir, with due respect, what is it you think you can help me with? Who are you?"

"My name is Taras Serik, my wife ran a biotech company outside of Almaty."

"Ran?"

"She is dead."

"I'm sorry to hear that."

"The facility was called Kretsky."

"That's the facility that burnt to the ground, right?"

"Did you investigate?"

"No, an industrial accident ranks pretty low right now."

"It was not accident. At least, not the fire. Everyone inside the building was already dead when it started."

The American cocked his head, trying to assess Taras, "And you know this because?"

"I watched the army set it on fire."

Dr. Halpin stood in silence, digesting the claim. He then turned to the security guard, "Let him in."

Chapter 41

IN THE TRENCHES

The sun set, but the fevered quest inside the BSL-4 lab at the USAMRIID facility continued to burn.

In her space suit, surrounded by white equipment, Lucy worked under fluorescent lights in a room with no windows to the outside world. Her eyes were bloodshot and weary from lack of sleep as she gazed at the Petri dish through the magnifying lenses of her Zeiss microscope. She did love her Axio Vert.A1.

What she saw was hard to comprehend. The tray was riddled with signs of H9N2 but otherwise there was nothing spectacular, and nothing else consistent. The problem was H9N2 just didn't account for the sudden death of the subjects she was examining. Different samples might yield a different result, and there were plenty more to check.

Lucy liked to believe she was master of her own destiny, but, when she was honest, she could admit it was rarely one genius that changed the world. There was no way to measure how often an incidental unrelated remark by a spouse had spurred a crucial insight. Or more mundanely, how a bevy of supporting cast permitted the tip of the spear to reach it's potential.

Right now Major Ulman was that enabling partner.

In a space suit of her own, she returned with new reagents for the umpteenth time. In contrast to their time in the Hokkaido forest, in the lab Ulman was every bit the asset Commander Krogen had suggested she would be.

Lucy smiled thanks, mimed a another request and was soon alone again. BSL-4 was an isolating environment and she had long ago made her peace with that fact. Her throat ached from an itchy cough, and she wiped her sweating forehead against the inside front of her helmet. At least the migraine, was subsiding with the Tylenol she'd taken. Or was it just her second-wind breaking through the fatigue. She blinked and did that tight-eyed squint you do to stay awake.

Exhaustion was well known as a contributory factor in attacks on the immune system, but even the most impaired systems showed signs of succumbing before death took a hold. Well not always. She mused with apprehension; the victims she was now examining had all died in their sleep, unexpectedly, excepting the global pandemic that made so little sense.

Sleep. How was that a factor? In one short week Lucy had become an expert on sleep and its potential as a contributing factor in death. There were three obvious lines to investigate: i) some derivation of a heart attack, ii) some sort of brain seizure, a stroke for instance, or iii) a sleep apnea.

In the first instance, victims tended to wake up during a heart attack, but there was no field evidence to suggest that had happened in the current crisis; none of those interviewed from Hiroshi's San Francisco flight, for example, had recalled anything remotely suggesting this. In the second instance, strokes were only occasionally fatal. And besides, strokes left ample evidence of their having happened. That left sleep apnea, which basically meant you stopped breathing.

The best-known sleep apnea was obstructive, which was a fancy way of saying a person's airways had closed, but there were others.

Central sleep apnea resulted from something going awry in the brain's breathing center; it was as if the telephone line was cut and the brain stopped sending the message to breath. This struck Lucy, as she was sure it had struck others, as a more likely candidate cause given the lack of post-mortem indications.

It was like a poacher was nabbing sheep before they could clear the fence once you were asleep.

Her mind was wandering again, but this time she chose to let it drift . . . see where it took her.

Medical wisdom contended that the body fell into sleep, not because it accumulated some sort of sleep inducing substance, nor through lack of stimulation, but instead through a specific change in brain function. Sleep was induced by a change in biochemistry. Moreover the changes differed according to the nature of the sleep you were experiencing; REM or not.

However, as Commander Krogen had noted earlier, sleep itself was not enough to trigger the fatal effects of the current pandemic. Somehow it was necessary to hit deep sleep.

"So an infected person can take a nap and live?" Lucy had asked him optimistically.

"As long as he or she doesn't hit deep sleep."

"Great! So the problem is solved." Lucy had dusted her hands and stood theatrically. "Thirty minute catnaps are to be nationally mandated."

"Right," Krogen smiled wryly, "don't let the public dream."

Their shared sense of humor always invigorated Lucy's thinking.

"Except, our damned bodies will adapt."

"I thought adaptations were supposed to be improvements?" Krogen quipped.

"If only! And in this case I'd rather mine didn't adapt."

The literature was clear on this, and they both knew it. Catnaps wouldn't mitigate the risks on a long-term basis. Studies consistently described how quickly the human body adapted to sleep deprivation; if all you ever allowed were short bursts of sleep the body became increasingly adept at dropping you into deep sleep without the prelude of light twitches.

"So sleep apnea ..." Krogen had trailed off, even as he attempted to return their focus.

"The electrical signals that keep you breathing properly during sleep are more critically balanced," Lucy began the brainstorming, "meaning that problems in sleep might well only manifest themselves there."

"You would look fine while awake, but head into all sorts of trouble during sleep?" Krogen asked, more or less rhetorically.

"Yes, and to compound that, dying takes just a couple of minutes of electric misfiring."

But sleep apnea didn't point at much for her to investigate in the BSL4 wet lab.

Krogen restated the one lead they had identified, "The autopsies have consistently shown an unusually high incidence of mild myocarditis," or inflammation of the heart.

Lucy had followed that hunch by checking for cytokines and chemokines that would naturally result from the lymphocytes and macrophages an invasion of white blood cells would deliver. The findings were truly overwhelming. All samples she tested showed raised levels.

What exactly this meant was much harder to interpret.

She had promised Krogen she'd have something for him by morning and she wasn't going to disappoint him. What he might make of the results was less clear.

+

As dawn inexorably broke outside the building, bringing with it another wave of corpses, Lucy pulled out her last 96-well plate from the DSX automated ELISA system. The matrix of yellow glowed back at her. It was the classic antibody-based diagnostic technology and the antibody she'd picked out was H9N2 specific. She contemplated the results. It simply didn't make sense. The H9N2 was ubiquitous.

Was this really just another example of the plethora of fireworks that presaged her birthday every year? A fluke coupling that was no more causative than a simple coincidence of date. Or was there—unlike the celebration of her birthday on July 5th, and the American celebration of Independence Day the day before—really some causative link? She'd been disappointed when as a six year old she had finally realized the fireworks were simple coincidence; it had scarred her, and coincidence had elicited a subtle sting from that day forth.

Suddenly there was a rapping from the viewing window. Lucy glanced up to find General Jackson.

His demeanor was unusually frantic for the unflappable rock that Lucy knew him to be. She paid close attention to his lips, the age-old mode of level 4 communication, but it was unnecessary; once Jackson had caught Lucy's attention he held a hand written note up to the glass. The contents of the note shook Lucy's world to its very foundations.

The note read, simply: "Commander Krogen is dead."

Chapter 42

A CONUNDRUM

Jets of Lysol engulfed Lucy from every side; you can't just walk out of level 4, it takes time to decontaminate. The protocols were safeguards, deliberately considered and composed in times when stress was not a factor, precisely to avoid accidents when it was. Seasoned visitors to level 4 learned to use the time to contemplate problems that required thought and little else.

Lucy turned her space suit slowly and methodically under the torrent of decontaminate. Inside her helmet, her eyes were closed, but her mind was racing.

Commander Krogen had alluded to a "Catastrophic systems failure." That was a fair assessment, as was the sentiment that all they had was "a cough and a smile", though the cough was far from ubiquitous. But when Doctor Moren had countered that every body had H9N2, Krogen had countered very quickly that H9N2 didn't kill like this.

Had his counter been too quick? Had she herself been blinded by his quick counter?

The jets stopped, leaving an eerie silence. Lucy unhooked her oxygen tube, which recoiled like a lazy yellow spring back to the roof. She opened the first door and air whooshed past her as she entered the airlock before the second decon room.

Five minutes later she removed her helmet in the locker room and, with speed that her relative safety now permitted, she quickly pulled her jeans back on. Outside in the corridor General Jackson stood anxiously looking at his watch.

When Lucy finally emerged from the locker room, Jackson gave her a supportive grimace and indicated the left side of the corridor, he took the right, "Join me?"

Lucy followed, giving a cursory explanation for her delay "Decon takes time."

"But this bug doesn't."

For a moment Lucy was silent.

"Are you alright?"

"It's just . . . the Commander, Bill . . . he was fine yesterday."

"You were close, right?"

"Yes. I mean we respected each other . . ."

"He was a good man."

"I know."

Lucy struggled to process the reality that Commander Krogen was dead. There was a lump in her throat and her chest felt unusually heavy. Her emotions were swirling. She was an analytic being. That was her strength, and it was so ingrained into her being that she occasionally forgot that she too had human needs.

+

They entered Lucy's office and General Jackson closed the door behind them. It was an unnecessary force of habit given the scant presence left in the building.

He shook his head, "Even suicide bombers play by some rules."

"It's playing by rules" Lucy assured him. "We're just not seeing enough of the puzzle yet."

"You really believe that," Jackson was assured by her belief in the order of the universe.

Lucy nodded; as pleased that he'd identified her religion, as she was that he understood her assertion.

"Maybe this will help." Jackson felt the sensitivity of what he was about to reveal and gave a reflexive glance at the door. "There's word the first death might have been Chinese. In China."

Lucy looked at him skeptically. "Really?" People underestimated the subversive power of rumors in the context of epidemics. Advertising and branding specialists understood how rumors could incite irrational behavior, and yet, "There are hundreds of unexplained deaths in China every week. And thousands more across the world. You have reason to believe the Chinese death is this because . . . it's convenient?!"

General Jackson made no effort to contradict her, so she continued, taking his silence as an implicit request for an expanded explanation.

"We've got no obvious vectors beyond spikes at major travel-ports." She turned to her computer and tapped at red dots on a map as she laid it out for him. "Don't lose sight of the DNA of this pandemic: There are too many IF-zones. Something is fundamentally wrong with the lens we're viewing this through. Epidemics have chains of deaths; and you trace the bodies back to case zero. Every IF-zone gives us a new case zero! How are the others connected to Magjan? We need to connect the dead bodies, but there are no symptoms."

"There's a cough." Jackson offered.

"In about half the cases, that's hardly definitive. Tons of people have a cough and they're not all dead. It's infuriating! If the body's a machine, this disease looks more like the power is simply being shut off."

Jackson looked at her wistfully, "The air-force lost a gem when you went biological."

Lucy blushed, but notwithstanding her forceful elucidation, it was worse than it sounded. "The evidence doesn't fit the paradigm of our world." Normally—and this was what the CDC's protocols were predicated on—you started by identifying the pathogen. Then, while working on a cure in the lab, you begun chasing the epidemiological trail back to the source. The source offered insights. It suggested solutions. Right now, both prongs of a traditional attack were helplessly hampered.

"Listen, there's something else weird going on that you need to hear about." Jackson broke her out of her thoughts.

'Something weird' was what she was after; new situations had their own idiosyncrasies and examining them was how you moved forward. "Go on."

Lucy listened carefully as Jackson described the situation up and down the West Coast. Tankers of milk delivered to San Francisco from Fresno had consistently caused spates of deaths. But the Intel was fractured, and the causality was difficult to understand, especially in light of a very low death toll in Fresno. Worse, apparently identical shipments from the same dairy were causing no corresponding spike in deaths in LA.

"So deliveries from Fresno are wreaking havoc in San Francisco, but the same deliveries are doing nothing to LA?"

"Right."

The obvious explanation was that it had less to do with Fresno, and more connection to the transit, "Where are the drivers stopping?"

"They're truckers, they don't stop on hauls that short. And right now, they're even less likely to stop. This crisis doesn't encourage random stops."

That the same milk caused no deaths in LA seemed to rule out the milk itself as a source, though obviously it could be the specific trucks that were at issue. Still, even that was unlikely; ten out of twelve deliveries to San Francisco had resulted in a spate of deaths that traced back to the deliveries, while no deaths could be traced back to *any* of the ten deliveries to LA. It didn't take a statistician to see that something other than a random distribution of infected trucks was causing an issue.

"And it's more pronounced than that."

"Meaning?"

"The two drivers whose deliveries to San Francisco that went through uneventfully had both literally taped themselves into their cabins and refused to partake in the unloading."

"So counting those, we're twelve for twelve to San Francisco, and zero for ten to LA."

General Jackson watched her as Lucy's mind traced the possibilities. He waited for her to offer a potential account for the discrepancies he was describing, but Lucy stayed unnervingly silent.

"It gets weirder." he opened his satchel and riffled through it.

Lucy looked at him eagerly; more information invariably helped with conundrums.

"The reverse problem has arisen from suppliers in Sacramento."

"The reverse?" Lucy was intrigued. "Trucks returning from San Fran are killing people in Fresno?"

"I don't know about that, but there's another reverse." The reports were scattered, but there was an underlying consistency: deliveries from the *Sacramento* area were resulting in clusters of deaths around LA, while having no effect on the population of San Francisco. No symptoms presented, but a clear correlation was emerging between deaths in Los Angeles and delivers from any Sacramento supplier, dairy or otherwise. "And here's what makes it doubly weird. Sacramento itself seems to be fine, as is San Francisco in the wake of deliveries from Sacramento."

Jackson removed a sheet of paper from his bag and laid it on the desk.

Lucy stared at Jackson's map. He was right, this was weird, but there was a clear conclusion to be drawn, "What is happening where those dotted lines are crossing?"

"Nothing." Jackson responded emphatically, "Well nothing anyone can identify, and we've devoted resources to it."

Lucy was skeptical that Jackson's subordinates knew what to look for, but there wasn't much point brow-beating him over it, and nothing else jumped out from the map right away.

Opening his laptop, Jackson pulled up time-lapse maps that showed classic blossoming chains of infection, textbook really: the initial seed was clear, and the resulting infection—or whatever it was—lit up as a succession of notches on the list of fatalities; motionless corpses with tight smiles. In some sense they were new I.F. zones, but at least they exhibited traditional chains from that point. And if you accepted the single source as the dairy farms, or something on the road in between Fresno and San Francisco, they all traced back to a single source.

"What do we know about Fresno and Sacramento?" Lucy asked.

"As I said, both cities look relatively untouched." General Jackson put his hands in the air defensively "I'm not trying to obfuscate. You now know everything I do."

Confused but feeling that a key was within grasp, Lucy turned to a smartboard map of the world and zoomed in on the US. "We've got tissue samples from all four cities?"

"I'm doing what I can. And yes, we're scouring the area near where those paths intersect." Jackson was obviously groping in the dark.

"There must be a blip somewhere in there." Lucy shook her head in frustration, "Double check Fresno and Sacramento haven't been mixed up. People might be dying in one of those cities."

"Both are fine."

Lucy didn't doubt they were; Jackson wouldn't have brought this to her without double-checking. She'd heard the upper echelons of the army complain about fighting wars in which it was hard to identify the enemy; guerrilla warfare, insurgencies. And for the first time in her career she really understood how they felt. Fighting an enemy you can't see felt futile!

"In the meantime, cut shipments from Sacramento to LA and Fresno to San Francisco. We can try re-routing if that works."

Jackson smiled at her, "You're a spitfire, but you make strong decisions. Fast."

"Let's focus on the section from Fresno to San Francisco, that's the shorter of the two routes. But I want shipping info you have for any shipments anywhere in California!"

General Jackson pursed his lips, formed a temple with his hands and touched the tip of his nose with the steeple his index fingers made.

Lucy could see there was something else on his mind. "What is it?"

"There's another reason I'm here right now," Jackson sucked in a deep breath, "President Pollack has ordered me to nominate a new head for the RIID."

Lucy's eyes popped wide open as the General put a warm hand on her shoulder. She had imagined one day but ...

"But ... what about Colonel Marshall?"

"Marshall's been a godsend to funding with his PharmaCo ties, but you're the best there is and we're in a crisis. Beyond that, I trust your temperament better. Congratulations, Commander."

Lucy's mind was reeling. For a moment the technicalities of Jackson's descriptions paled into the background as she wrestled with the elation brought home by a long-term goal realized. This was hardly how she'd envisioned it happening.

He turned to leave "By the way, the president will want to talk to you."

Lucy nodded, "Sure."

Then, as if on cue, her cell phone rang. General Jackson grinned, saluted goodbye and left the room.

Lucy took a deep breath to steady herself and answered the phone in her new incarnation, "Commander Topp."

Chapter 43

ANOTHER BRIEF

It was Saturday. Weekends were never meant to be like this, but then the days of the week were merely names at this stage. Call it what you will, a rose might still be a rose, but 'Saturday' was a name from another paradigm. The day still existed, but the meaning of the appellation was long gone.

He opened his weary eyes and looked about the store. That there were no cushions for sale had surprised him, but the pile of lacy panties he'd stuffed inside a silk camisole were as soft as they were brightly colored, and the thinness of the dressing gowns had been amply compensated by their abundance when utilized as a blanket.

It was curious that this store had not been looted, but then sexy lingerie did kind of lose its significance when the world was wracked by death. Mostly though, Hiroshi was grateful that the electricity was still working. He glanced at his phone; the charger from the nearby electronics store had restored four green bars.

He dialed her cell, a number he'd thankfully committed to memory. Two rings, three and–

"Commander Topp."

Hiroshi sat up straighter against the sales counter; Colonel had become Commander since they last spoke! "Lucy-san. You are Commander?"

On the other end, Lucy was flooded with relief. She wasn't yet ready to make a Presidential report, and she did wish to talk to Hiroshi. "Hiroshi. It's good to hear your voice." Actually, she wanted to see him, "Can you turn your picture on?"

Hiroshi fiddled a moment and brought his camera to life, filling Lucy's screen with color. "You are Commander?"

"I got promoted."

Hiroshi grinned. Behind the phone he spied a pair of oddly metallic silver panties. He reached for them and pulled them into frame for Lucy to see "Is, how you say, silver lining."

Lucy was as impressed by Hiroshi's English idiom, as she was confused by his whereabouts. "Where are you?!"

Hiroshi panned the camera past the racks of skimpy lingerie. The outlet stores outside Napa had been surprisingly devoid of people.

"It was first open store."

Lucy smiled, "Right! But in case you're shopping, I prefer purple thongs." She winked at him but her spirit waned. Everything was catching up with her.

"Are you alright?" Hiroshi asked.

"Just tired."

"Your mother is good?"

"Yes. Everything's just very isolating." She looked at Hiroshi sitting alone in the lingerie store, "Are you alright?"

"Nobody wishes to talk to foreigner right now."

"Have you heard from your family?"

"My parents are worried. It is chaos. Akako has not been buried."

Lucy got a lump in her throat. She had been going so hard that even with Krogen's death the human toll had felt like an abstraction. "I wish you were here Mr. Sugimura."

"I can drive across country." It could have been a flippant remark, but Hiroshi was serious. He had nothing to gain by staying where he was and there was no chance of returning to Japan. And Lucy looked very tired. He would like to cradle her head in his arms. The right pressure points would alleviate tension.

Lucy's silence spoke volumes; there was something else on her mind.

"Is there news?" he asked.

She stared at his makeshift bed, "Just sleep in short bursts." The thought returned her to the science, her standby emotional crutch, "it seems that you've got to hit deep sleep to die."

That explained the weary black smudges under her still-sparkling eyes.

"Beyond that," Lucy continued, "electrical storms within the body can stop the heart, but there's still no more than the tight smile post mortem as a symptom. It's some sort of muscle contraction."

Hiroshi knew a deeper explanation would swamp him. Lucy knew the same thing, but it was valuable to get an unsophisticated perspective on an intractable problem, the view from someone unwedded to the traditional position.

Her computer cycled through a red graphic of the death toll by location over time. There were patterns flowering and receding from LA up the coast, up to San Francisco. She ached to overlay the transportation vectors she'd requested.

Needle in a haystack was an enticing metaphor because it originated before the common abundance of strong magnets; with the right tools needles were not so difficult to find.

She gave voice to her minds' well-beaten path, "It doesn't make any sense, people are dying before they've shown any symptoms, and IF-zones continue to pop up inexplicably."

"Is Fucked."

"Exactly," Lucy agreed; Hiroshi had nailed it. "We don't even know what the problem is!"

"Is birds?" Hiroshi ventured, reiterating Miyake's concerns. It was a conjecture based on a 2007 paper that explained that H5N1 resided asymptomatically year-round in certain species of duck. According to Miyake viral loads accumulated over the winter when they jumped to domestic foul, making the ducks a proverbial Trojan horse. "They can disperse infection?"

"Maybe ..." Even laymen had biases, but birds didn't make sense, so Lucy explained why, "you'd see outbreaks clumping around migratory paths though. Or problems in the poultry industry. Neither is evident in the epidemiology we've got." Her mind returned to General Jackson's curious reports, "Something weird is going on between Fresno and San Francisco. Nobody's dying in Fresno or San Francisco, but deliveries between the two are triggering deaths, and the same is happening to those from Sacramento to LA." An idea occurred to her "Hiroshi, I need you to do something for me ..."

"Yes?"

"Drive to Sacramento." Jackson had put his people on the Fresno-San Francisco path, maybe Hiroshi could start in Sacramento; it was a short drive from his current position. It was risky, but he wasn't safe where he was anyway "You understand how cities work, how people move about them. Find what they're doing differently there. You see things a less trained eye will miss." This was more hope than belief, but why not have someone look at the source, and there was no one else to send on this wild goose chase.

Hiroshi read anguish in Lucy's eyes, and he wished he could return her earlier hug. Even as he found himself more alone than ever, Lucy was infiltrating his soul and it gave him a warm feeling. "Today is before tomorrow." He offered. "It will get better." The comfort of words would have to suffice for now.

Lucy smiled into the camera on her phone. Without question he was agreeing to what was patently a dangerous task. In his own quiet way, Hiroshi was as wild as she.

+

In the north Californian countryside Hiroshi enjoyed the thunder of the Corvette's engine as he powered along the empty highway. Up ahead a military helicopter was dropping a well-wrapped palette in a field. Emergency supplies presumably. A sensible way to avoid contact with potentially infected swaths of the country.

Further down the highway, a small group of people watched a house burn on the side of the road. They turned to Hiroshi as he drove by, a lone vehicle on a normally well-populated route.

Lucy's parting note of caution had been a warning that the problem could as easily be between the population centers as inside them. The sheer size of the populations wasn't necessarily critical in an epidemic that surfaced without defined contact trails. And though she had quickly ruled out birds as the vectors of transmission, she was focused beyond human-to-human contact. As she explained to him, the epidemiology almost demanded it.

Distracted by his musings on modes of transmission, he almost missed a quarantine checkpoint before he was on it. Almost, but not quite.

A quarter mile before the checkpoint, Hiroshi slowed his car and pulled onto the gravel shoulder beside the bitumen. He missed the tactile nature of a paper map, but was glad for his phone's ability to zoom in and out, and immediately pinpoint his location in this foreign land.

It would be impossible for the army to cordon off all thoroughfares, and he scanned further to the north—he'd already elected an indirect route to Sacramento, favoring a northerly, presumably less-travelled track.

Lake Berryessa sat at the base of a mountain range preventing easy access to route 16 on the other side. At first glance, avoiding the 128 looked like a long detour, multiple hours and gas he could ill afford to waste, but as he zoomed in closer a narrower route presented itself. Circumnavigating the lake there appeared to be a sequence of old fire roads that cut up east over the crest of the range.

Hiroshi put the Corvette back in gear and roared a powerful U-turn, retracing his path back to the lake turnoff. There, he disappeared down the canyon road toward the water.

+

At the quarantine checkpoint, Lieutenant Leon Watterson watched as his squad swarmed around their trucks lifting barricades to the ground. It was awkward work with the heavy breathing apparatus and thick plastic gloves. With their bodies covered in camouflaged spacesuits, Lieutenant Watterson watched his men nervously as they rolled razor wire along the ground.

"Careful with the blackberry vines! Those suits won't stop a butter knife!"

He was glad the old car back up the road had elected an about-face. Protect and serve he would, but if whoever that was had the sense to return home instead, so much the better.

Ten minutes later, he saw it, the glint of the dying sun reflecting off metal and glass, across the lake below, or was it an apparition. His Steiner binoculars would confirm either way, and he scanned the trees in search of—there it was again, undeniable this time.

Watterson returned to his Humvee to examine the maps. He had men sprinkled throughout the area and he well understood the importance of quarantine. No one would be getting through on his watch!

Chapter 44

BIOLOGICAL SAMPLES

The long thin knife slit up through the belly region, carefully avoiding the organs inside. He'd done this many times before and always found the familiar way that the blood glistened back at him from the white protective gloves to be curiously comforting. Gently, he laid the knife to rest in the metal tub that sat on the stainless steel table that also bore the two hundred pounds of still-warm pig.

On his other side were two ice chests, already packed with crushed ice, and beside them, sterile plastic bags lay filled with a critical perfusion liquid, ready for samples. It was delicate work, but it didn't help if you sliced the organs open and permitted an easy path for contaminants.

The meat packing industry was notorious for this, even if the standards they adhered to were dramatically lower. Of course the meat-workers themselves were more concerned with their own health than that of the cuts they were rendering. And understandably given that history had shown their wellbeing to be on the line. Q-fever (the Q stood for "query", and was a reflection of the politically motivated decision not to call it "abattoir fever" for fear of alarming the workers) took just a single bacterium of *Coxiella burnetii* to infect a slaughterhouse employee. That infection had spelt death in the past, even if industry workers were now vaccinated against this particular evil.

Notwithstanding historical concerns, the catastrophe at hand presented compounding problems, led by the undersupply of feedstock. Animals were stressed, and stress caused disease.

Industrial farming, like industrial living, was dependent on a consistent supply of food, and while the general populace resorted to alternative means of procuring sustenance, the pigs were, in alarming numbers, simply going underfed. Soybeans today were a critical component of the Chinese pig industry, but with almost three quarters traditionally imported from America and Brazil, the current embargoes had seen stockpiles decimated.

Small-hold farmers supplemented with corn, but the industrial farms were at breaking point. Acute infections would surface soon, not just among the animals themselves, but, in all likelihood, among those who tended them too.

He caught his drifting mind and returned his attention to the task at hand. Diligently working over the carcass, he extracted samples of liver, heart, brain and blood, carefully stowing them inside the ice chests. He secured the lids and exited the clean-lab to find Wei Lin and the farm's operator waiting. He placed the trademark blue Chinese CDC ice chest on a bench and removed his headgear.

+

Behind the technician, the farm's operator indicated to Wei Lin a row of 20,000 liter steel vats that lined the wall, "Everything is on track. We begin harvesting inoculants tomorrow."

Wei Lin nodded. It was rare that field tests went as smoothly as this one was going. It was less than a week ago, in a room full of liquid nitrogen freezers that he had watched as Ludmila Serik—his erstwhile student— dipped blue Cryo gloves into a steaming vat and extracted a vial. She had carefully deposited the vial into a cryogenic GT7 transport canister and sealed the top.

Wei Lin had watched her fingers deftly dealing with the instruments. She was millimeters from contact with a potentially lethal pathogen; biotech workers regularly were, "Negative pressure is your friend."

Ludmila looked back at him, "What was that?"

"Negative pressure, it is your friend. You are a short breath away from a nasty pathogen. Your containment hood protects you—with negative pressure."

Ludmila nodded and went back to her job.

Wei Lin reflected on the vertical draft containment hood. The simplicity that underpinned most safety protocols was beautiful.

More than physical barriers, negative pressure and its sister, positive pressure, had both been boons to the field of medical research; the simple act of sucking—or blowing away—air that harbored biological or chemical nasties was remarkably effective. Whole rooms were devised around the same sucking principle that underpinned the vertical draft containment hood. And on the flip-side, laminar flow hoods protected biological samples from any contamination the scientist might bring to the lab by blowing HEPA filtered air in a smooth laminar flow *towards* the user.

Of course pressurized air was all about airborne transmission. There were plenty of other ways to pass on infection right down to a simple handshake or pat on the back.

Ludmila removed her gloves and wiped the outside of the transport containers with a UV-C germicidal wand-lamp.

They had been in and out of Kretsky in less than an hour, including the uncomfortable contact with her husband. Half an hour after that, Ludmila had pulled her Mercedes onto the tarmac of the Almaty airport where she stopped the car by a private chartered plane.

And so the initial Kretsky samples had made their way to the Chinese CDC, a weigh station on their way here, to the Boading Piggery.

Wei Lin had not been entirely forthright with Ludmila as to the ultimate fate of the pigs her starter culture serum had been developed for, but then she too was evasive on other topics; specifically, the difficulties she was having with her own animal trials. It was curious how trust ebbed and flowed, even between long-standing friends who had once flirted and since been heavily involved in trade. Business was a delicate diplomacy.

On the runway, Wei Lin's Gulfstream IV had hurtled down the tarmac, lifted its nose, and receded into the distance.

Inside the jet, Wei Lin had sat near the pilot, both silhouetted in front of scattered fluffy clouds as the plane rose through them to open sky. Behind them, strapped to the cabin floor, had been the blue-topped GT7 transport canister, amply adorned with red biohazard symbols.

Wei Lin had glanced back at his precious cargo and his reflections on business had shifted to various auxiliary risks of international scientific collaboration.

With a liquid to gas expansion ratio of 1:694, liquid nitrogen made him nervous. He'd seen the BLEVE educational videos, and the acronym "Boiling Liquid Expanding Vapor Explosions" didn't really encapsulate the consequences nearly as well as the colloquial saying "Blast Leveling Everything Very Efficiently".

An accident at 35,000ft would have showered the countryside with him, his pilot and their cargo. It would have been a dramatic way to disperse a biological product. To distract himself, he'd turned to the window where he had gazed down at the countryside below.

Almaty to Bejing was a key part of the most famous trade route in the world; the great silk road. It's name derived from the lucrative Chinese silk trade, which began in the Han dynasty around 200 B.C.. Since then the proverbial road had become a conduit of cultural, commercial and technological exchange. It was one of the most significant factors in the development of many great civilizations including China, India and Rome. Indeed, it had been argued that it helped lay the foundations for the modern world.

Wei Lin smiled to think that he was the next chapter in that tradition. That his Kazakh visit had accomplished this with a speed inconceivable 3000 years ago only warmed his heart more.

Had Wei Lin had any real sense of the threat he had ferried out that day, he might not have felt so relaxed then. Nor would he have felt so relaxed now, as he picked up his new ice chest and thanked the farm's operator again. Despite the risks of what he had set in motion, he felt comfortable that the outcome would justify the gamble.

Chapter 45

PRESIDENT WEN WU

His Excellency, President Wen Wu was a complex man from family with traditional Buddhist leanings. Beginning life in the Beijing middle class just before the great urban migration, he was ahead of many of his peers before he started. His parents had great aspirations for him, and in consequence he grew up rubbing shoulders with the country's elite. It made for a formative experience that left him comfortable among the highest echelons, but oddly grounded with an appreciation of what it was to have less.

Later, after distinguished undergraduate studies at Tsinghua University, he rode a Fulbright scholarship to the American university equivalent. At Harvard he quickly connected with future world leaders and by the time he returned to China his integration to the Communist Party of China was a perfect fit with its place in the new world order.

The tragedy gripping the world had put him in a curious position. On the one hand, China was faring conspicuously better than elsewhere in the world—which made it automatically the source of suspicion—while, on the other hand, there were still downstream headaches that related to interconnectivity in the modern world. Attacks by foreign dignitaries, concerned for themselves and the welfare of their own citizens showed a lack of appreciation for his internal troubles, troubles that had already shortened his temper.

Finally, President Wu had had enough of the tacit insinuations he was being subjected to, "Your tourists fill our hotels. You co-mingle human pathogens that you bring us from around the globe. You worry about us making diseases, but you save us the trouble!" He took a cold breath, "If our industries or protocols were to blame we'd all be dead. Instead, it is the honorable Doctor Wong, our emissary to your DC summit on infectious diseases, who sat and faced your hot air and accusations. It is he who will not return home."

The silence on the other end was palpable.

So President Wu continued forcefully "We do not have your problem with H9N2."

In his office at Camp David, President Pollack looked at the green swath that was China on his electronic wall map. His own frustrations matched Wu's; around the world corpses were piling up, and yet China, except for closing its borders was apparently unaffected. In reflex, he adopted the icy timbre he used to send chills through his adversaries "You have too few deaths. The rest of the world has been powerless to stop the H9N2, perhaps you can share your insights."

"President Pollack . . . " Wen Wu took a deep breath.

But Pollack interrupted him, "Hold one moment." President Pollack's chief aide was standing in the door. The man knew well that Pollack was not to be disturbed during this call, and Pollack trusted him with his life. Even so, Pollack bore into the man's eyes with a stillness that amplified the significance of his words, "This had better be important."

"Sir. We have a breakthrough."

Chapter 46

PHARMACO

"Yes, your stake in this remains as we negotiated."

"Because without me—you understand there are other alternatives." Marshall had to be crystal clear.

"We understand." Hans Lichtman assured him.

"Excellent, then let's get on with this meeting."

Lichtman, the chairman of the board, opened the door and the two men entered the boardroom.

PharmaCo had been founded less than ten years ago, and the first four years of that had been devoted to strategy and planning, a calculated task, as consciously conceived around the intention of luring investors, as it was around laying any groundwork for the resolution of biological problems. And they had been successful in achieving their goals.

The founders were now millionaires many times over, and the facility—which housed some two hundred scientific researchers, and twice that number of infrastructure staff (business, legal and marketing to name just three core departments)—was state of the art. A sleek design firm had tastefully implemented a modern lab aesthetic throughout the building, seamlessly integrating sales and accounting with research and development. It was an interesting front that belied the truth of 21st century pharmaceutical companies, who actually acted as aggregators of technology, leaving smaller start-ups with the risks of development.

From those start-ups, the ones who scored, scored big, making their founders hundreds of multiples of their seed investment; unfortunately the vast majority simply lost everything. The big end of town on the other hand made fortunes, not so much as nose-bleeding multiples of their investment but in simple outright terms.

Colonel Marshall was a bridge between the government, specifically the military arm of the government, and the big end of the pharmaceutical business.

Industry heavyweights prized his ability to secure lucrative contracts for them, at fixed prices for drugs that needed stockpiling. These contracts kept manufacturing capacities at or near peak, but without the stress of over-capacity production. Meanwhile, at the USAMRIID Marshall was a hero for bringing in discretionary funds that enabled research in more esoteric areas of staff interests.

Since fleeing the RIID, ostensibly to the safer environs of Gaitlinburg, Marshall had actually crossed the country and spent the bulk of his time at PharmaCo, where the board was frantically pushing remaining staff to make the most of this remarkable opportunity. And not without success!

"Are there downsides to PharmaCo going public?" it was the question on everyone's mind and Hans Lichtman had finally decided to put it directly to Marshall.

"It'll invite external scrutiny to be sure. And that scrutiny will inevitably unearth the fact that Amanet spent the week prior to the outbreak here." Marshall had learned long ago that it was important to hedge responses to boardrooms, but he didn't want to dampen spirits too much, so he continued, "That, however, seems purely circumstantial, and any adverse publicity will in all likelihood blow over. Against the success you're already having with Tamiflu in Fresno, Los Angeles and San Francisco . . ." he paused for effect, "I'd say go for it. In LA and San Francisco, deaths dropped dramatically today."

"It's not every day we make a breakthrough on a topic de jour of the world!" PharmaCo's chief scientist, Dr. Waltham, was effusive.

"Quite so," Marshall cautiously endorsed Waltham's enthusiasm, "And when lives are being saved there's a tendency to look the other way."

"And you'll speak to Commander Topp?" Lichtman prompted Marshall.

Marshall nodded. There it was again, 'Commander Topp'. He was still smarting over the sequence of events that had seen the position he saw as his go elsewhere. Were it to have fallen the way it should have, the upcoming sequence of events would have flowed more simply. Still, he was a professional, "I will take care of Topp. She is curious and exacting, but she wants a breakthrough as much as we did. She'll see there are things in this for her too."

"And of course you know you have our backing," Lichtman enthused, "Feel free to dip into the discretionary funds pool as you need. The importance of this goes without saying."

"Thank-you sir, but with Topp there are more persuasive incentives than cash."

Chapter 47

PRESIDENT POLLACK

Lucy was in a realm she knew intimately; deeply immersed in a world of fatigue. Lab rats—the people who worked there, not the animals subjected to the experiments—invariably found themselves in the lab at 3 and 4am. It was the uncanny the way research tended to seep its way into those wee hours.

Understanding sleep deprivation struck Lucy as something that one could only ever achieve in the abstract. In the moment of the actual event your sensors failed to record properly to the brain's memory banks. This was easy to verify in practice as she'd noted to her own amusement when friends and colleagues started having children. The experiment was simple: ask any parent of a six-week-old child if they will ever have another child and they will, without exception, profess to being done with progeny. Then note how many of us have siblings.

This observation always amused her, but right now it made her wonder what other brain functions were being impaired by her serious deficit of sleep. Was there a connection?

She found herself googling sleep again. Studies were pretty definitive: sleep deprivation was never going to *make* you crazy, though that was a popular misconception. In actuality, it was a reversal of implication that held: insomnia was actually a common *symptom* of mental illness. Visual misperceptions, differed from hallucinations, or so the experts insisted, and you generally had to miss three nights' sleep before you began to misperceive.

On the plus side, sleep deprivation was so commonly associated with euphoria, particularly during the first night of deprivation, that it was used on a short-term basis to treat patients *suffering* from depression; one night of total deprivation improved symptoms in between 40 and 60% of patients.

The downside was an increased likelihood of making mistakes during routine tasks; and that made her nervous when she thought about lab work. Then there was of course the trouble with concentrating. Well this little foray onto the web was ample evidence of that.

Lucy sat there, zoning in and out of thought, when at last her phone snapped her firmly back to reality. "Colonel Topp," she flubbed, "I mean Commander."

"Hold for President Pollack, please."

Lucy blinked.

"Commander Topp? It's President Pollack. I believe you have moved up in the world since we last talked."

"Mr. President. Sir." Authority had a habit of calling when you least expected, or at least catching you off-guard. It was a curious ability. "Sorry sir, I was ... I've barely slept in–"

Pollack was unsympathetic. "The world has a new number one killer and you're sleeping?"

"Sir, there will always be a number one killer." It was a reflex retort she'd heard many times from Commander Krogen. Lucy sneezed.

"But this one isn't as benign as cancer." Pollack was a man well versed in wordplay.

Lucy sneezed again. "Sorry, I'm positive for H9N2."

"So am I," Pollack was still unsympathetic "but flu isn't the real problem, is it?"

Another symptom of fatigue was irritability.

Lucy could feel her ire building to bubbling over as Pollack needled her. Nobody liked being lectured to, and that the lecture was redundant and naively condescending only exacerbated the point.

"There are plenty of viruses in both of our systems that will out-compete H9N2 in its bid to kill us." She forced herself to agree.

"Coxsackie, for instance."

This time he'd surprised her, both by the specificity of his suggestion, but also because this specificity seemed like a crude stab in the dark. "Coxsackie doesn't fit the epidemiology, sir."

"Apparently it's difficult to detect unless you're looking for it."

There it was again, the baseless condescending insinuation.

Epidemiology was the rational study of the patterns and symptoms, not an attempt at random detection. Lucy's hackles were firmly raised, and, growling, she threw restraint to the wind. "Sir, Coxsackie might kill silently, but death is rare, and it doesn't kill like this!"

But Pollack, who was infinitely sure of himself, continued on his track "Commander Topp, Coxsackie wiped out an entire Kazak facility—two days *before* this pandemic broke in New York. Their Prime Minister–"

"What facility?"

"A facility called Kretsky. You probably don't know it."

"They engineer infective vaccines."

"Vaccines don't kill people!"

That wasn't strictly speaking true. But that's why you ran trials before scaling up. As had happened with an experimental SARS vaccine, they can be mostly effective, but trigger cytokine storms killing an unlucky few.

But Lucy had stopped listening to the President. For the first time, he had, albeit sort of inadvertently, exposed a new idea to her. It was information that required processing. It was wacky notions that shed light on mysteries, and coincidence always raised her antennae.

Wallenstein, the CIA man who had been tailing Magjan, had mentioned Kretsky too. So, who else was connected with that lab? Was it possible that the entire staff at Kretsky had been wiped out by Coxsackie? Had Krogen uncovered something before his death? She grappled with a thousand, suddenly pertinent, questions.

What unused bandwidth was left in her mind had no spare capacity to filter her thoughts as she simply responded to the President, "Of course vaccines don't kill people! They save lives, and infective vaccines, if we can make them, will distribute themselves. With a bit of luck, they'll revolutionize flu season."

Pollack reacted to Lucy's barb and his response was equally acerbic, "Not anymore."

"Coxsackie makes no sense!" Was he really missing the point so badly? She started a lecture she'd given as a guest speaker at Johns Hopkins "When you find six-year-old boys dying in Thailand, avian flu makes sense; they're the ones who clean domestic poultry." And then with synapses lighting up all through her brain she continued, thinking out loud, "Our pandemic isn't straight human to human either. There are too many I.F. Zones; something is jumping outbreaks from one location to another, and Coxsackie doesn't do that."

"It occurs in pigs."

True, but not close to a plausible explanation, "Pigs don't move about enough. Or have you got an explanation for that too? Pigs don't fly! Or are people are randomly carrying them about with them?! And even if they did, it's not easy to get from a pig into a person!"

"Perhaps you simply don't understand."

That was close to the bone! Of course she didn't damned understand! Nobody did, that was the point. Screw this sanctimonious pig. And his pigs! "Maybe I don't." she agreed tersely. Time to turn the tables of responsibility. She was just a lowly scientist after all, and he was the President of the free world. "Perhaps you, in all your wisdom, can shed light on the situation for me."

"No, that's still your job. But, I do have someone useful for you to talk to."

"Who?"

"Prime Minister Maqtaly, the Kazakh mastermind."

"Maqtaly. Who?"

"The Prime Minister of Kazakhstan. You'll be contacted by Commander Sandleman in the next hour. He will," and President Pollack paused to underscore the significance of his next words of choice, "He will *facilitate your discussion with our guest.* I expect to hear from you soon."

The line went dead.

Lucy was left hanging, grappling with the emphasis and implied double meaning Pollack had placed on the words 'facilitate', 'discussion' and 'guest'.

World Incidence Map

Epidemiological Notes: - high correlation with travel hubs
                        - surprisingly low correlation to sheer population density
                        - linear geographic veins of incidence within population centers
                           (as opposed to typical ripple propagation spread)
                        - unexpected bubbles of low incidence within population centers
                           (immunity?)

Chapter 48

FIRE ROAD 8053

Hiroshi was driving like a man possessed. Skirting north of the 128 to avoid the roadblock, he'd felt exposed as he circled around the shore of Lake Berryessa. The small, almost completely obscured dirt road on the east side had been a relief to find, and the padlock on the gate was no match for the combined impact of his muscle and the steel tire iron he found in his purloined vehicle's trunk. He closed the gate behind him and disappeared up into the forest.

He climbed the narrow mountain pass toward Fire Road 8053 (the one that would take him down the other side), uncomfortably aware of the glow of his headlights; they were beacons to anyone watching, and it was attention he did not want.

As it transpired, Hiroshi's fears were well founded.

+

Lieutenant Watterson, the man in charge of the quarantine station on the 128 to the south, had spotted the red Corvette, well before the sun had set. He then spent ninety minutes tracking Hiroshi's vehicle in the failing light, while simultaneously working his way through the two-way system, a system wracked by stress and under-staffing. The territory north of Lieutenant Watterson was deemed of secondary importance and it took tremendous persistence from Watterson to finally connect with his neighboring quarantine manager.

Finally though, he was patched through to the men on Fire Road 8053. Hiroshi's lucky evasive break was about to come to an abrupt end.

+

Cresting the ridge, Hiroshi pulled hard on the steering wheel to avoid the low clearance military Humvee blocking the road. With great skill, he squeaked through an impossible gap, showering the soldiers' bullet-proof windows with rocks and debris.

Inside the Humvee, Private Herd jolted awake. His ears filled with the tinkling as the rocks clattered back to the ground and his eyes latched onto the receding taillights of Hiroshi's Corvette. But before Private Wallace—his navigational companion—awoke, the two-way crackled to life.

"Private Wallace, this is Lieutenant Watterson. Do you read me? Over."

Herd picked up the two-way. "Private Herd here. We copy. Over."

"Private, there's an unauthorized vehicle headed your way. Over."

Wallace took the two-way from Herd as Herd revved the cold engine to life. "Sir. Private Wallace here. Your vehicle just passed our post. Over."

"Passed your post?"

"Sir, it had to be traveling at 45. This is a dirt road. Over."

"Private, you are running a quarantine check-point–"

"Sir, we are in pursuit. Over." And he wasn't kidding.

Dust clouds billowed in the Humvee's headlights, and through them, Hiroshi's red taillights winked past trees as the quarantine breaker fled the roar of the solider's engine.

+

Suddenly, from the blackness in front of Hiroshi raced an unexpected fork in the road.

Hiroshi applied the brakes, skidding wildly to a halt. He assumed the roadblock behind him was in full pursuit. That gave him, at best twenty seconds headstart, maybe thirty. But which way to fork?!?

He clutched for his phone and tapped the map on the screen. The phone was slow to respond.

Through the forest behind him, the Humvee's lights carved the trees aside as the vehicle hurtled forward.

No time for checking! Hiroshi put his trust in fate, picked right and floored the pedal.

Then, as if offering a judgment of its own, his phone chirped the sound of an incoming call.

Hiroshi glanced his rearview mirror. The gap to the Humvee had closed dramatically, enough to make the soldier's navigational conundrum a much simpler decision.

Glancing at his phone, he hit the green ACCEPT button, "Greetings."

"Hiroshi?"

Hiroshi fumbled with his phone as he wrestled his chariot around yet another tight corner. "Lucy-san! You must to call at different times." he shouted over the wind that buffeted his shattered passenger-side window.

"Hiroshi, where are you?"

"I am on a fire road, to avoid quarantine road-block. Is under control here. Are you alright?"

The storm clattering down the phone was in remarkable contrast to Hiroshi's calm voice and Lucy wasn't sure how to respond.

"Is there progress with you?" he asked.

In her office, Lucy glanced at the map on her computer screen. "San Francisco is bad, but many other cities have improved."

"You did something right."

Lucy closed her eyes, and wished it were so. Instead, she saw Akako, lying dead in a Japanese morgue. Whatever she may have done to help the situation on the West Coast, nothing was likely to have moved the needle on the bigger world picture.

"I haven't done anything. There're still I.F. Zones everywhere,"—this was the reality—"and although we've connected chains of deaths in a dozen cities to deliveries from Sacramento, no one is dying in Sacramento. Hiroshi, something is amiss in Sacramento and no one else can see it!"

"I will be there soon."

The surety of his voice was reassuring, but the loud clank that cracked into her ear was much less so. "Hiroshi?! ..." but there was no answer "Hiroshi, what's happening?"

In the Corvette, Hiroshi grappled for the phone, which an unforeseen pothole had knocked out of his hands. His head bobbed below the dashboard and up again, as the car fishtailed violently sending the right rear wheel spinning off the edge of a steep drop. The remaining three wheels clawed at the gravel, miraculously staying roadside while the free-floating rear rubber spun helplessly.

The Humvee exploded into Hiroshi's rear-view mirror just as the left tire pulled the right back into the brush. With renewed vigor Hiroshi shot forward.

Behind him, Wallace leaned out the window of the Humvee, his rifle trained on Hiroshi's car.

+

In her office, Lucy had the phone pressed to her ear as if somehow that would improve the chance of Hiroshi's voice returning. Instead, the loud and unmistakable sound of a rifle assailed her from the other end of the phone.

"Hiroshi! Hiroshi, are you there?"

A second shot cracked down the line, like another slap into her already ringing ear. They were sickening sounds. They were the sounds that accompanied the termination of a life.

Chapter 49

THE RED CORVETTE

The Corvette skidded out of control flinging Hiroshi's body like a rag doll, seatbelt notwithstanding. Underneath the vehicle, the rim on the ruptured back wheel shot sparks into the night air as the metal savagely dug into the ungraded road and violently clawed the car to a stop.

Behind Hiroshi's vintage muscle car, the Humvee, in just slightly more control, screeched to a standstill of its own. Herd and Wallace leapt out of the battle armored doors and warily approached Hiroshi's now-still vehicle.

The acrid stench of burnt rubber wafting up from the shattered and torn wreck that was once the rear tire stung Wallace's eyes as he passed through the cloud of dust and smoke and around the side of the fugitive vehicle. There was no movement from the driver's seat.

Hiroshi lay motionless, and in the grand scheme of things unconscious definitely bettered many of the alternate possibilities. He had blacked out when a violent jolt ripped his hands from the steering wheel and slammed his head into the frame by the car door, the upside of which was that the driver's side window was still intact. He came to to shouts from behind his car, which he gratefully noted had not disappeared over the precipice.

"Steeeer rot foth ee err!!"

Hiroshi blinked.

"Steep ouu tof erk arr!"

Hiroshi blinked again.

"Step out of the car!"

Hiroshi's focus returned on drawn rifles in his rear-view mirror.

"We will shoot." Private Herd was couching the serious nature of the situation in no uncertain terms.

Hiroshi turned slowly—the speed of his movement dictated as much by his condition as his desire to avoid misinterpretation—to see Herd's hand reaching for his door handle. But just as it was about to connect, Lucy's voice came shrill from the floor of Hiroshi's passenger seat.

"Do NOT open the door!"

Startled, all three men balked, but it was Hiroshi who first grasped the meaning of her advice, and, as if in slow motion, he turned and pressed the old door knob down.

Hiroshi looked up at Herd, a bedazed haze in his eyes, matched only by the confusion in Herd's own.

+

In her office, Lucy, her cell phone pressed to one ear, snatched the landline, dialed, and pressed it to the other side of her head. While the second phone rang she continued to bark counsel to Hiroshi. "Hiroshi, do not open your door to those men."

+

At the Corvette, all three men looked at Hiroshi's phone on the floor.

Wallace approached the busted passenger window.

But Hiroshi, feeling the soldier's threat, did the only thing left in his power: he revved the engine, sending a shower of dirt and loose rubber into the air. To the surprise of the soldiers, the vehicle lurched forward five feet and stopped again, fueling the already tense air.

"Sir, I'm going to ask you once more: Please step out of the vehicle." It was Private Wallace, this time adding a plead for reason, "We are here to help."

Lucy interrupted again, continuing to add tension to the situation as she reiterated her counter-counsel from the floor. "Toss the phone out the window and let me talk to them. I'll go up to the President if I have to!"

In awe, Hiroshi whistled respect that only confused the soldiers, "Hor. President-san. Big promotion!"

Outside the vehicle, Herd spoke into a LAV mic. Inside, Hiroshi slowly leaned down. As he rose he proffered the retrieved phone to Wallace who still stood two paces back. Wallace gave no acknowledgment of it, so Hiroshi gingerly tossed his phone through the shattered window. Instead of reaching for it, Wallace, stunned by the act, dodged the toss. The phone made a sharp crack on the ground and the screen went black. The three men were left in the proverbial dark that matched the moonless night surrounding them.

+

The cell-phone in Lucy's right hand cut out, just as the landline in her left connected.

Lucy desperately called for acknowledgement, "Hiroshi?! Hiroshi! ... Anyone?!"

"Colonel Topp? Is that you?" it was her landline.

"Commander." she corrected, "Colonel Marshall."

And then her cell phone rang again.

"Hold the line, sir." and without waiting for a response, she put him on hold, answering her cell with the other hand. "Hiroshi?"

"Lucy! You're still there!" it was Ellen, her mother.

But before Lucy could answer, a knock at the door joined the demand for her attention. It was General Jackson, and his knock was simply a perfunctory gesture as he entered the room, holding a map in his hand.

Lucy looked back from him to the cell phone still in her hand. "Hold on, mom." She nodded Jackson to take a seat. In her mind all she could see were the soldiers with automatic weapons trained on Hiroshi while they nervously fumbled their gas masks on. Her only viable response was the landline in her hand and she engaged it, "Colonel Marshal."

+

In the corridor outside the conference room he had reluctantly excused himself from, Colonel Marshall was irritated at having immediately been put on hold by the woman who had called him. That she had called seeking his approval for a violation of quarantine procedure that he had already denied did not help matters. And the realization that this would put his own head squarely on the chopping block only further aggravated the scenario. To add a final insult to injury, she had shown no embarrassment about taking the promotion that was so clearly due him.

With familiarity drained from his voice he rebutted her again, "Colonel Topp, you may be the Commander now, but quarantines are my call."

It was a terse reprimand, bordering on insubordination given the new balance of power, but Lucy was struck by the clarity of thought she had to Marshall's inflammatory statement: Marshall was tired, and sleep deprivation reduced emotional intelligence and constructive thinking. In this instance she needed to rise above him and any paranoia the situation was inducing in him. So she tried a new tack.

"Colonel Marshall, your quarantines have been in place in a multiple of jurisdictions, which ought to have caused a drop in fatalities–"

"And we've seen a drop!"

"Not the drop we should have. With this epidemiology, the infection should have burnt itself out, unless somehow there are asymptomatic carriers who aren't susceptible." It was a stretch, and this was by no means the only possibility, but it had Marshall thinking. Lucy kept going, "Virulent pandemics burn themselves out, and that just isn't happening here. Irrespective of the quarantines, something is already screwing with the infection cycle, and I believe Sacramento may offer an insight. So–"

"So send someone in who can appraise the–"

"That's what I'm trying to do!" Lucy shot back, interrupting him before he could finish. "Whoever it is represents a break in quarantine and frankly there aren't many takers right now."

"Commander, Mr. Sugimura was on an aircraft in which thirty people died!"

Lucy glanced at General Jackson. He was listening intently to one side of the argument. Lucy hit the speaker button, immediately bringing him in on the other side. "George, I've got a dozen cities pointing their fingers at Sacramento, and no one there sees anything wrong. Further, I've got a guy here who, unlike you, is prepared to physically face danger. So unless you want to change your mind and get on a plane yourself–"

Again he interrupted her! "For your information, I'm in Fresno."

"Visiting your friends at PharmaCo?" It was a wild guess, and probably right on the money.

"PharmaCo has made a breakthrough."

That stopped Lucy in her tracks, "Really?"

"They have been trialling preventative antibiotics with success. They already have–"

Bad reasoning! And the hackles on the back of Lucy's neck went up, "Antibiotics aren't a breakthrough! We need a cure, not a band-aid we can apply to a few thousand people!"

"You know full well we're hanging on by a thread. The soldiers at those quarantine stations aren't trained for this. Shit, they're probably already infected!"

Lucy looked at General Jackson, this was the first thing Marshall had said that she was in wild agreement with and she happily let Marshall continue.

"A single violation of quarantine is all it takes to unleash another wave of deaths. What you're asking is—is insanity."

"Hold on." Lucy saw her opportunity clear as day. She looked General Jackson in the eye, "General, I need Professor Sugimura in Sacramento."

Jackson smiled and took the handset from her and switched back from speakerphone, "Colonel Marshall, this is General Jackson."

Lucy could feel Marshall's face dropping on the other end of the phone, and she knew the problem was solved, she just hoped it wasn't too late.

Chapter 50

RATIONALIZATIONS

Lucy glanced at her desk. Strewn across it were wrappers from energy bars and two-minute noodle meals. A far cry from the rumors she had heard—rumors that spoke of people in cities cooking cats on spits—they still testified that her mother was right; nobody was eating well. But that hardly mattered.

She pushed back on Ellen, "Eat popcorn and preserved peaches if you have to. I know your cupboard can't be empty yet!"

In her old weatherboard house, Ellen smiled. She loved her daughter dearly, and not just for who she was, but who she reminded Ellen of, "You have so much of your father in you."

"Mom!"

"We were two halves that made a whole, your father and I. Your father made everything possible for me."

How did her mother's mind run so freely even in times of crisis?! Lucy was astounded.

And then Lucy's own concentration drifted. Having delegated Marshall to General Jackson, she'd assumed all was well, but was it? Lucy watched General Jackson across the room.

She noticed again the sheet of paper he'd tried to give her when he entered the room. It was still in his hand, and it piqued her curiosity now. It looked like a map of sorts.

More to the point, why was the general still on the phone? She wished she'd continued following the call with Marshall, but the situation would now play out as it would—there was little more she could have done.

If Marshall was putting up resistance, he was just doing his job, and frankly doing it well. Lucy knew she was a tough refusal for him but adding the General's weight would do the trick.

Her mind drifted further afield; she had always liked the Shakespeare's sentiment that: "things without all remedy should be without regard."

+

As it happened, General Jackson needed to do little more than remind Colonel Marshall that *Commander* Topp had the full authority of the President. Coming from the General, this amply sufficed to clarify what required doing, and done it was. Indeed, Lieutenant Watterson's earlier dusting off of the chains of command paid handsome dividends for Hiroshi who was surprised to find Privates Wallace and Herd standing down as the military maxim termed it.

+

"Lucy, is Hiroshi alright?"

"Mom, I have to go."

"Look after Hiroshi, dear. You need him."

"I don't need him." her reflexive indignation just underscored the way she felt about this accusation, "And I won't let a man derail my life the way dad did yours!"

"What–?"

"You had a career until you met him."

"I longed for a family 'til I met your father," Ellen corrected her daughter; this wasn't the first time they'd had this argument, "Just because that's not what you want, doesn't mean you shouldn't let love into your life at all."

Self consciously, Lucy turned to look across the room. General Jackson was waiting for her. His smile indicated Marshall had been dealt with. "Mom I have to go."

"Lucy . . ."

Too often their conversations were cut short by these words, but even if there were times in the past when they weren't entirely true, right now they were. "I love you, mom. I'll call later. Don't leave the house, okay. Promise me."

"I love you too, Lucy."

Lucy hung up the phone and looked across to General Jackson. He had been watching her for a good thirty seconds. She felt engulfed by her volatile emotions, and despite the context, she gave him an impromptu hug; they'd spent enough time in close proximity that neither was giving the other something they didn't already have.

Jackson reciprocated the embrace, "I'll have a chopper sent for her."

"And Hiroshi?" She looked up at him.

"He's already on his way to a city riddled with Coxsackie. That is what you wanted, right?"

A lump formed in her throat as her emotional roller coaster plummeted and she pushed back defensively, "Coxsackie doesn't kill overnight; it's a heart attack at the end of weeks of degradation."

General Jackson looked at her, awaiting the complete analysis he knew she was about to give him.

"We've got a tight smile which hints at a muscle contraction; some sort of electrics fault but . . . " she trailed off, her mind awash.

"Which might explain the observation that pacemakers are somehow prolonging life?"

"Maybe," Lucy hadn't connected that apparent data point, "That might just be a statistical aberration from a small sample size." She filed the thought for more careful evaluation later, "And either way, it doesn't explain the lack of pathology we're seeing in the heart and brain . . . " Whatever fleeting idea had interrupted her train of thought was gone again and Lucy frowned, "I know the autopsies haven't come up with anything beyond the H9N2, which can of course mess with the brain, but that, too—it takes time." And this was the salient point, everything was happening too fast! "There has to be another vector, it's not just human to human. And it's not following any birds' migratory paths. There's a clue, somewhere in Sacramento . . . there has to be."

Jackson handed Lucy the map he'd been holding. It was similar to the one he'd shown her earlier, only this one had many more shipping routes. He pointed to Sacramento, "Coxsackie or not, sending Hiroshi to Sacramento may still be a death sentence. Shipments from there are killing a lot of people."

His words lingered heavily in the air. Despite the benign shipments from Sacramento to San Francisco, *every* other route emanating from Sacramento was lethal. It was a truth hard to ignore, and Lucy, try-as-she-may to rationalize it, couldn't shake the thought that sending Hiroshi to Sacramento was a self-interested play.

But it was hardly self-interest that was driving Lucy's proposal; there was a world dying out there and she was simply doing everything in her power to stop that!

"He's also one of the few people who might see the discrepancy that is the other vector." she protested. Even this felt like a justification that put Hiroshi's life on the line.

Heroes should have the right to volunteer, not be volunteered.

+

Meanwhile, the man in question relaxed as best he could, sitting in his car while the two soldiers outside exchanged the torn shot-out-mess that clung to the rear axle with the spare tire from the trunk. His eyelids faded and his mind drifted back to Lucy.

She had a great faith in him, and, though she wasn't able to articulate specifically what it was he should look for, he was surprisingly at ease with the task assigned him.

Architects, were always being asked to define and articulate things that others simply felt. It was something he was very good at. She was right to entrust this responsibility to him.

Outside the vehicle, Private Herd ratcheted the last bolt back onto the wheel and Wallace released the jack. Far from the trigger happy zeal they had expressed during the earlier chase, the soldiers now looked at Hiroshi with a mixture or awe and apprehension. The man in front of them was about to drive into what was potentially the heart of the pandemic, to a war-zone filled with microorganisms you could never see, but who could nonetheless strike you down as effectively as any AK-47. The soldiers gave him a deferential salute and watched as the night forest engulfed Hiroshi's Corvette in the same way the curtains at a crematorium folded around a coffin as it entered the pyre. It was unlikely they would ever see this man again, perhaps nobody would.

Chapter 51

INTERROGATION

"Just to be clear, Jean Michael didn't die of illness?"

"No, he choked to death. On a nut."

Lucy consulted her notes.

"But he was sick before he died." Maqtaly continued, "Delirious."

"Well that's great," Lucy said struggling to suppress a tinge of sarcasm, "because that's not what Coxsackie looks like."

"I do not understand the sciences. Just big picture. But I have be told deaths at Kretsky are result of same techniques the Frenchman was using."

"And that's why you suspect Coxsackie?"

"They use those techniques to develop new strain of Coxsackie. And also, dead bodies, they are infected by Coxsackie."

Lucy cocked her head skeptically.

"We took samples. Before we incinerate corpses." Maqtaly didn't look as apologetic as he should have.

"And that was a part of your infective vaccines program?" Sandleman interjected derisively.

Lucy glanced at Commander Sandleman. He had arrived an hour ago with Maqtaly in tow. Since then, he and Lucy had repeatedly worked at cross-purposes. Interrogations or interviews, call them what you will, they were outside her expertise. What was just as clear to Lucy, was that Sandleman knew little about biotech.

"There are many applications of GM technology." Maqtaly countered. "Your country too, it has rich history in this space."

"And Kazakhstan helped China with genetically engineered rice. Is that correct?" Sandleman had evidently done some cribbing.

Maqtaly nodded. "Crops are tailored to regional conditions."

"And yet Greenpeace opposes all GM organisms?"

"Even when our GM-genes are only expressed in leaves." Maqtaly was conversant in the big talking points. "People do not eat leaves of rice. Conventional rice is sprayed three, sometime it is four, times in season! GM farmers do not need to spray anymore."

"Yes," Sandleman enthused, though Lucy detected the hint of an acerbic tone in his voice. "I heard about that too. Glowing rice. No, Golden rice."

"Right." Maqtaly seemed nervous, "Golden rice. It has yellow hue."

"How does it work?" Sandleman asked, "The technology?"

Maqtaly looked blankly back at Sandleman, "The details, I do not know them." And he turned to Lucy.

Lucy proved her expertise by giving color to the two men's superficial understanding, "You add a couple of new genes to normal rice. One from a daffodil. One from a soil bacterium, Erwinia Uredovora I think it's called. They both aid beta-carotene biosynthesis."

"Yes, that sounds familiar." Maqtaly agreed.

"And why bother?" Sandleman pressed. "Poor kids or something, right?"

Lucy could detect an undercurrent in Sandleman's voice. Or was she imagining things? The power of suggestion was amazing.

In her own eleventh hour study she had glanced several guide manuals on hostile interrogation. Build rapport was a recurring tactic—and they were doing an iffy job from her perspective. That, and bombarding the subject with irrelevant details, 'cognitive loading' it was called. Both reduced the subject's ability to employ counter-interrogation strategies. She assumed this was Sandleman's current tactic.

"Right," Maqtaly agreed.

Sandleman nodded silently. Lucy assumed he was creating room in the conversation for Maqtaly to boast, another strategy that commonly undid detainees, or so Sandleman had told her before they started the interrogation. "It's a basic spy technique."

Sure enough, Maqtaly filled the void. "Children suffer from Vitamin A Deficiency. VAD." His enunciation of the letters in the acronym placed an odd emphasis on an unimportant detail, "124 million suffer VAD. It is cause two million deaths in year, and half a million times of irreversible blindness. Opposition is simple willful."

"That was Greenpeace's biggest fear? Golden Rice as a Trojan horse that would open the door to the widespread use of GMOs?" Suddenly Commander Sandleman pounded the table, "What does this have to do with what's happening now?!"

"I do not know."

"You can do better than that." Sandleman stood abruptly and rounded the table, "I'm going to make you."

"Commander," Lucy interjected, caution in her voice, "Prime Minister Maqtaly is here to help."

Sandleman turned to Lucy, even as he lifted Maqtaly from his seat with latex-gloved hands, "This scum's responsible for millions of deaths. He lost his right to the benefit of the doubt when he torched the one place that might have had some clues."

Lucy put her hand on Sandleman's arm and indicated the door, "We need to speak."

Without warning, Sandleman slugged Maqtaly in the stomach.

The Kazakh leader doubled over involuntarily and Sandleman let him go, dropping him, crashing onto the table.

"Excuse us." Sandleman whispered coldly.

+

In the corridor, Lucy glared at Sandleman, "I don't know much about interrogating," she admitted acidly, "but I'm pretty sure torture doesn't help."

"Not with professionals." Sandleman concurred, "but this is a politician. I can induce him to be helpful."

Lucy stood in silence, processing.

"The President," Sandleman started, "Our President, he wants answers. And we're going to get them."

Lucy stiffened, physical combat was not her strength, and Sandleman could overpower her with one hand tied behind his back.

Sandleman turned back to the room, "Can we continue? Is that alright with you?"

"Sure" Lucy shook her head defiantly, "You continue. I'm going to splash some water on my face."

Her interrogating partner stared at her, trying to gauge meaning.

"I'll be right back," Lucy assured him. She was appalled. She understood that Sandleman, like everyone else, had lost people. But that didn't excuse his actions.

$+$

She crossed to the lab sink, figuring she'd better splash some water on her face. It certainly wouldn't do to raise Sandleman's suspicion as soon as she re-entered the room.

She stowed the dart in her coat pocket, wet her face, and left the lab. Walking down the corridor, she went over her plan in her mind.

Entering the interrogation room again, Lucy was immediately struck by Maqtaly's beaten face. She flinched, and hoped it didn't show.

Sandleman looked back at her, "So glad you could join us."

Maqtaly looked up at her, desperation in his eyes.

As casually as she could, Lucy indicated the Kazak Prime Minister while speaking to Sandleman, "Do you mind if I take a turn? Seems like you might have softened him up."

Sandleman smiled. Clearly pleased with his work, he turned toward Maqtaly, "Maybe there are things you will share with the lady."

But before he could turn back to Lucy–

She drove the syringe tip of her dart deep into Sandleman's neck. It caught him by surprise. He grabbed at her hand, but the ball-bearing plunger had plunged.

Lucy leapt back.

Sandleman changed tack and reached for the syringe. But the collared needle had a barb-like circumferential ring that improved retention and Sandleman struggled with it, fading motor skills frustrating his effort.

Lucy bade him, "Nighty, night." while hoping he was a big enough man, literally. With the dose of the stun-gun dart designed to stop a bear, it was plenty powerful to knock the Commander out cold. She just hoped it wouldn't do worse, because there was a risk of a cardio-pulmonary depression.

One thing was sure, Lucy was now committed to her course of action. As Sandleman slumped to the floor, she turned to Maqtaly, "Come on, we'd better go."

Chapter 52

LANGLEY

A dozen dead pigs were stacked in the muddy yard just outside the pathology lab at the Baoding piggery. They were nothing compared to the human bodies that littered the globe, but in a corner of the world largely untouched by the pandemic, they were still striking.

With no more than a face-mask, gloves and rubber boots, the owner of the farm returned with his small forklift and thrust the prongs deep under another carcass. He jerked the hydraulic tilt ram until the swine's belly rested against the load apron. He was experienced with moving dead pigs, but it still surprised him how high you had to lift the corpse in order to avoid dragging either end.

At the already half-filled dump truck, he further raised the forks to ease the carcass into the hold tray. A little more tilting and jerking was all it took and a hollow thud greeted the body to the truck. He put the forklift into reverse again just as Wei Lin's CDC 4WD screeched to a halt across the yard.

+

High in the sky a satellite recorded Wei Lin as he leapt from his vehicle and crossed to the farmer. The images were a lesson in body language; even from this high off-angle perspective, and without the benefit of sound (which would not have been helpful to Havamyer anyway given his distinct lack of Mandarin), it was clear Wei Lin was castigating the farmer.

In his White House office, Havamyer toggled back and forth through the footage, something was amiss, "That's a Chinese CDC vehicle, huh." Havamyer paused in thought, "And he's not happy about something."

At Langley, the agent in charge of foreign satellite surveillance nodded concurrence with Havamyer's opinion as he added details to the scene "The fork-lift removed forty carcasses."

Havamyer zoomed in on the satellite footage that showed another dead pig being dropped into the cargo hold of the dump truck. "And this is definitely unusual? That's an industrial piggery, right?"

"Yes, but slaughter takes place in a designated slaughterhouse, not on site. Those pigs aren't headed for dinner tables. We wouldn't have noticed, but as a precaution we've been following all traffic to and from the Chinese CDC."

"Do we know who the CDC guy is?"

"We believe his name is Wei Lin, and we're working to reconstruct his movements over the last two weeks."

Havamyer rested his chin on his thumbs letting his brow furrow in thought. "Pigs," he mused to himself. "We have no idea what their significance is?"

"We're investigating, sir."

General Jackson had relayed a sentiment from his scientific contingent that the pandemic was likely not simply human-to-human transmission . . . could this be the missing link?

+

Across the country from Havamyer, and across the Pacific Ocean from the Chinese piggery, Hiroshi scanned out his window as he cruised past an industrial piggery of his own. He was closing in on Sacramento, and the nearby slaughterhouse seemed like as good a place as any to start his investigation.

Chapter 53

CAPTAIN GREEN

He closed his eyes, reflecting on the day. It was a confusing mission, and although simple enough, it had left him wondering about the why. They had been scheduled to execute what was now an uncomfortably familiar routine: fly into a small township and investigate how and why the town had dropped off the grid. Occasionally this amounted to finding a community that relied exclusively on landline communication with the outside world, and that communication was now thwarted by downed lines or natural disruptions, but all too often the last week's missions had been characterized by the discovery of entire townships wiped out by whatever was sweeping the globe.

His dreams had been choked with nightmare scenarios that left babies as the exclusive survivors, and he, clad in his biohazard suit, responsible for their pick up and return to quarantine. They were images, no doubt influenced by *The Andromeda Strain*.

Today's mission had been equally specific, and though the surrounding residences were apparently unaffected by the scourge, his brief had been clear: return this one woman from the field.

Now, with the successful rescue behind him, he drifted to sleep. As he did so, events of his day played back on the inside of his eyelids like a fancifully distorted cauldron's contents. At 3:21AM his dreams ruptured into a slew of random fractured images that culminated in an explosion of white light. His face contorted, a tight smile pulling across his lips. And with no further fanfare, Captain Green, the pilot responsible for executing General Jackson's directive to return Ellen Topp to the safety of the USAMRIID, passed away.

Chapter 54

LEAVING USAMRIID

Lucy took a bright orange Racal biohazard suit from the closet. It was the protective gear of choice for fieldwork when there was a risk of encountering a level 4 organism. Positively pressured from a battery-powered air supply, it inflated to give a slightly anemic Michelin man cover around your body, though it's bright color ensured you would never be shot by accident.

She moved the Racal to her left hand and shouldered a sturdy, fully loaded backpack. Killing the lights, she turned out into the corridor. She threw a face mask to Maqtaly, "Put that on." If she were honest with him, this was for her benefit more than his.

She lifted her hand and beckoned Maqtaly to follow her, "we can't stay here." Having saved him, he was her responsibility now, and she felt stuck with him.

Footsteps from around the corner focused her attention back on the present. She changed her hand to a palm-up stop sign and cautiously, but quickly, crept to the corner and peeked around.

General Jackson was fast approaching.

Lucy reiterated her palm to Maqtaly and moved decisively into her only feasible course of action, deliberately careening around the corner, right into General Jackson's path.

"Commander!" Jackson seemed surprised by their collision.

"General Jackson?" Lucy too feigned surprise.

There was an awkward pause and then Jackson started again, "I was looking for you."

"Oh?"

"...but I didn't expect to find you." Jackson was speaking slowly and deliberately.

"Why?"

Lucy's eyes had purpose, but General Jackson was clearly harboring something of significance in his own. He opened with a remark that he knew would not be well received, "I just spoke with President Pollack."

Don't assume Jackson knows what you've done, Lucy reminded herself. Offense is defense, "And I suppose he believes the drop in deaths on the West Coast means everything's plain sailing now?"

"The President believes that Marshall is doing a good work with his quarantines." Jackson went to move forward, but Lucy blocked his path.

"His quarantines?! It's easy to believe you can empty the ocean with a pail when the tide is going out." The words were Dubois', but Lucy had always liked the quote, and she quietly delighted in her reflex use of the metaphor.

"From the President's perspective, you just willfully violated Marshall's quarantine."

"Hiroshi?"

"And ..." Jackson left space for Lucy to fill the void.

Lucy shook her head carefully. The world was dying, and Marshall was playing politics! "So bring Mr. Sugimura in, just don't put him in a room full of people exposed to the pandemic." Jackson shrugged, so Lucy continued, "God knows I'd feel better about myself. As long as it's my call, though, I say leave him out there to investigate, he might just find that anomalous something we're looking for. That something that might save the world!"

General Jackson looked at her soberly, "It's too late for that."

Suddenly the color drained from Lucy's face. Had her callous quest to save the world just cost Hiroshi his life? She barely dared ask: "What happened to him?"

"Nothing." Jackson reassured her, "As far as I know. It's what's might happen to you."

Lucy studied the General's face, what was he suggesting? Then, from around the corner, came the light sound of a disposable mask hitting the linoleum.

"Your second break of quarantine is a bigger problem." Jackson's eyes went to the corner to the neighboring corridor, "President Maqtaly, is that you?"

Lucy gasped. Jackson had known?

Jackson's eyes rested on Lucy, "You're being relieved of your duties."

"That's ridiculous!"

"Well, it's good to see you still have fight in your system." Jackson smiled, indicating he completely concurred with her sentiment. "But my hands are tied." Then he surprised her, "Commander Topp, this conversation never happened. I wasn't able to find you, or President Maqtaly. You must already have fled . . . but you can't come back without something big, you're on your own."

Lucy stood still. This was a solid vote of confidence, and one made at great risk to General Jackson's own reputation.

"Come on." Jackson urged. He about faced, and Lucy, bringing Maqtally with her, fell in line right behind him. Jackson made it clear that the efficiency of Lucy's continued forward motion was to countermand any traditional etiquette.

With the ungainly biohazard suit flouncing over her arm like a ridiculous prom dress, Lucy pressed Jackson, "The President called me. To tell me it's Coxsackie. Does he not realize that makes no sense? China is covered in Coxsackie, and they're so unaffected they're letting the general populace move about locally!"

"And cutting Fresno to San Francisco and Sacramento to LA somehow averted catastrophes in LA and San Fran last night." Jackson concurred that Lucy was making smarter analyses, "I would have expected that to buy you some political cover too; but it hasn't."

Lucy stopped again, "What can I . . . ?"

General Jackson put his hand on her arm and nodded at the battered and bruised Kazakh President, "Take him. I trust you over Sandleman to get results."

"He thinks it's Coxsackie too." Lucy conceded, nodding at Maqtaly.

"And maybe he knows something else he doesn't realize, something important." Jackson encouraged her.

Lucy glanced at the forlorn Maqtaly and then turned back to General Jackson; the General deserved acknowledgement for the risk he was taking here, "Sorry—I mean thank-you." She was dispirited, "Is there anything else I should know?"

"There's one more thing."

Lucy waited. There was something in General Jackson's disposition and tone that slowed time. "What is it?"

Still he paused, then forced himself forward, "Ellen—your mother—she's dead."

Lucy's face went totally blank. Her mother couldn't die. She couldn't be dead! She'd never died before! Lucy had spoken to her yesterday! Argued . . .

"Lucy . . ."

"My mom is dead?"

Jackson folded her in his arms, there were few times in his career that his professional armor had been pierced, Commander Lucy Topp was one of them.

"How?"

"The same as everyone else. The soldiers who picked her up died too. It's not clear if she infected them, but no one else died on the base last night. I'm sorry."

"I . . ."

General Jackson held her tight for a long minute, before gently moving her in front of him, "You had better go, they'll be coming for you." he checked to see she was fit to let go, "Be careful out there."

$$+$$

In the USAMRIID garage, Lucy packed three extra plastic Jerry canisters of gasoline into the back of her Jeep.

"Where are we going?" Maqtaly asked.

Lucy ignored his question, replacing it with one of her own, "You're sure everyone at Kretsky was infected with Coxsackie?"

"Yes."

"That doesn't make sense," Lucy was speaking more to herself . . . and yet, Coxsackie did kill silently, generally through a heart attack. She needed to know what really happened at Kretsky. Coxsackie took time to wear a healthy heart down, and there were precursor symptoms to death. But what if it was some form of activated Coxsackie?

No, there were large population centers—especially China—infected with Coxsackie, and no appreciable difference in death rate. Infuriating! "People are always ascribing meaning to coincidence; someone wins the lottery every week, but there's nothing more significant in the numbers than just that—that they change *someone's* life."

Maqtaly looked thoroughly beaten and confused, "I do not understand."

Lucy desperately wanted to dismiss Coxsackie as a biological lottery coincidence. "What is different now? What has changed in the system? What might leave both H9N2 and Coxsackie as symptoms?!"

"Coxsackie is change."

"Is it?" Lucy wondered. Perhaps the Coxsackie wasn't new. It wasn't something automatically tested for. It was worth checking. Suddenly, she knew where they were headed; somewhere she could review the recent history of Coxsackie.

Frederick Biologicals was the obvious first choice, but at just a few blocks away, that made a lot less sense given the recent turn of events—she needed to put some distance between herself and the RIID.

There were more facilities that she knew of, two on the outskirts of Washington D.C. They became her new immediate objective.

But beyond a blood bank, her broader destination was far less obvious. She needed time to clear her head. The routine of collecting samples promised an opportunity for that. Perhaps she would stay with—no, at—her mother's house. The thought that she had no one to turn to again brought Ellen's voice into mind, "I wish you had someone to share your life with."

Lucy closed her eyes. In spite of her record with men, she had always wanted the same thing, and Hiroshi . . . well she still held hope he might be her answer. The way her mother had watched the dashing Japanese man in the rear-view mirror of her car when she'd picked them up from the airport—Ellen's eyes had agreed with Lucy's own assessment; this one was a good match.

Their time together had been short so far, but duration was hardly the standard for love, and she'd never experienced popped corn the way she had that night; the way his hands had cupped hers . . . Lucy's eyes moistened. Her mother—her best friend—was gone, and to compound the emotional upheaval she'd just sent the first man she'd had genuine feelings for into, what some part of her still hoped to be, the eye of the storm on the West Coast.

"Commander Topp?" Maqtaly broke her thoughts.

"Yes? Right." She had plenty more pressing problems than personal brooding, "Let's go."

$+$

With her focus returned, Lucy pulled to a stop at the USAMRIID guards' booth. A makeshift sign on the gate read: "Do NOT open your window." And another in the window of the closed guard's booth stated simply: "Hold up ID." Neither direction had been necessary for Lucy who forced a brave smile for Tony, the Private she'd known two years. It was a nice gesture, but her bloodshot eyes spoke abundantly enough of her true reality.

From his booth, Tony gave Lucy a grim nod as he raised the gate. She saluted him and pulled away from her second home. She had never conceived AWOL might one day refer to her.

At that moment she had no inkling that just 15 miles away, two large black SUVs were hurtling north on the I-270 from Washington. On the dashboard of the lead vehicle a green dot bleeped its way from the USAMRIID perimeter on a digital map.

Chapter 55

I-270

Drowsy driving is a killer. A fact highlighted by the National Highway Traffic and Safety Administration who tally in excess of 1500 fatalities a year, and more than 70,000 injuries in their conservative estimate of 100,000 annual crashes caused by fatigue. Alarmingly, more than one in four American adults acknowledge to having fallen asleep while driving in the last year.

Lucy was unaware of the exact statistics, but she did know, both that she was exhausted and that driving this way was more dangerous than driving drunk.

Compounding the sheer volume of drowsy driving accidents was the problem that such accidents tended to be among the most serious, for the simple reason that drowsy divers were effectively asleep at the time of impact, and thus blissfully unaware of their predicament, which in most instances, led to a complete lack of evasive behavior. They plowed right into telephone poles, trees and on-coming vehicles.

The new and very personal emotional turmoil that Lucy was wrestling with exacerbated the effect of the exhaustion. And, as Lucy reflected in her haze, the other problem with comprehensive fatigue was that being consciously aware of it was no defense. She had tried conversing with Maqtaly, but the poor man had significant pain compounding his jet lag and exhaustion. Their conversation had petered out, and Maqtaly had fallen asleep. She really didn't need the tag-along.

Her ringing phone offered a new hope of waking her, especially given the specific caller.

She answered it, "Commander Topp."

"Topp, it's Commander Marshall." Marshall corrected her.

"What can I do for you, George?"

Marshall looked out the window of his PharmaCo office, this was going to be a difficult call for many reasons. "Lucy, I'm sorry."

"What for? For getting me fired or taking my job?!" She didn't entirely believe the sentiment she was putting voice to, but she could already feel the adrenaline of the fight she was baiting course through her body, and she was happy to encourage its waking effect.

But Marshall stopped her, "For your mother."

Lucy was taken aback by his sincerity, the adrenaline subsided as quickly as it had risen, though her mind at least was racing, "How did–"

"General Jackson told me."

"What exactly did Jackson tell you?" Lucy was confused, had Jackson played her somehow? Was he playing Marshall? Or was her tired mind over-reading the situation?

Up ahead, traveling north on the otherwise empty highway were two large black Lincoln Navigators. Ordinarily they would have suggested either a coincidence of two zealously protective parents in tandem, or some sort of government agency convoy. In this instance though, with the otherwise empty road, the later was the only sensible alternative. The drivers locked eyes on Lucy as they flew past; and it didn't look like their gaze was simple curiosity about a lone traveler on the deserted highway.

Lucy picked them up again in her rearview mirror.

"Topp?"

But Lucy was too busy to answer Marshall, her mind racing in a new direction as she watched the SUVs exit the freeway behind her. Time to get off the interstate herself.

She raced past the 117.

A quick shot across the I-370 would take her to the 355 that offered a reasonable alternative route to her destination, and if she spotted the black tanks behind her again, she knew the surface streets well in that area.

+

The green dot sped away from the center of the digital map on the dashboard of the lead SUV as it tore black rubber swaths across the surface of the local streets, navigating its way back onto the interstate.

+

"You spoke with the General?" in conspiratorial fashion, Lucy wondered if Marshall was somehow connected to the secret service she had just flown past.

"Yes. He told me you'd left."

Was he playing games with her? There was no risk of sleep anymore.

"Lucy, the world's falling apart."

"I'd noticed." She pulled off the I-270, onto the I-370. The 355 was just ahead and she'd pretty soon be harder to spot again, especially with the added safety of minor streets and tall buildings. "But what's changed? Why now?" The question was as much to herself as to Marshall.

"Coxsackie."

"And H9N2!" If the prevailing wisdom was going to be Coxsackie, she would continue to point to flu which was just as improbable. Then she added, "Can you think of anything that would leave both as symptoms?" It was a genuine question, and she felt there was merit to exploring it as she pulled off the interstate. "An ordinary pandemic should have burnt itself out by now—serial intervals are obviously shorter than our quarantines—and yet it keeps coming in waves, and we're still groping in the dark to make sense of what it is!"

She was aware her sentiment sounded as if she believed in Voodoo, and Marshall's silence only confirmed that he viewed her line of inquiry with skepticism at best.

"Right! We have a preponderance of asymptomatic carriers who aren't susceptible and a pile of corpses who are telling us nothing about how they died." Marshall was getting snide again.

Good. This would keep her awake. "What's different from a couple of weeks ago?" she prodded.

"Everyone is hungry."

Lucy's focus was so overwhelming, she barely heard the tenderness in Marshall's voice. What she didn't miss, though, was the glint of shiny black in her rearview mirror as she raced around a bend on Hungerford Drive. That wasn't coincidence, she was being tracked somehow; She hadn't noticed a helicopter in the sky, and a satellite was even less likely. Still she'd look for a covered parking garage now. If only there were some traffic to be anonymous in.

"The world is littered with IF-zones, but recent deaths are universally linked to some form of travel, even if there are no trails of corpses to follow." This was the conundrum, and she wasn't going to let it elude them regardless of what else was happening.

But Marshall was on his own kick, "People need to get food."

The phrase jolted Lucy in yet another direction; it was so close to the last words Ellen had spoken to her. She remembered her desk strewn with energy bar wrappers and two-minute noodle packets; hardly a hearty bacon and egg breakfast. Was this just an emotional reaction?

Two hundred thousand people died in New York City last week, but hunger took a lot longer than that!

Suddenly, as if some celestial being had decided to emphasize the point, Lucy saw a homeless man on the sidewalk a couple hundred yards ahead. He'd probably survived the last week on stolen Snickers bars. The man reached up pleadingly to a second figure—excepting the SUVs, the only other evidence of human life Lucy had seen in twenty minutes of driving—a woman, with a scarf covering her face. The homeless man was clearly faring badly, and though he may well have slept abundantly, he was obviously suffering fatigue.

In an odd juxtaposition Marshall's voice continued on the phone, "We're on the same side."

But Lucy was too apprehensively preoccupied to react.

Fatigue was different to drowsiness; it compromised your judgment to even obvious, albeit unusual, threats. Where drowsiness might inure you from checking the road ahead, with fatigue you see the oncoming headlights and continue careening towards them all the same.

"Come back in." Marshall's voice was a distant echo to Lucy, who gazed with horror as the scarfed woman suddenly brandished a gun at the homeless man. The situation ahead was escalating as Lucy closed in.

The woman was yelling at the homeless man. "Stay back!"

But he didn't heed her directive. Another step forward was his fatal last. Hunger, physical, and, no doubt, emotional stress were bearing down on his under-resourced brain. Fatigue was particularly dangerous in situations when a rare, but very salient signal must be adhered to; this was one of those situations.

"Help me figure this out." Marshall continued his plea, "it's not safe out there."

No truer word was ever spoken, as the blast of the distressed woman's handgun testified.

Marshall went silent.

Maqtaly gasped awake.

And the homeless man crumpled into a heap on the ground, a casualty of poor judgment.

Lucy's vehicle continued towards the gun-wielding woman, adrenalin guiding her foot to the accelerator pedal with the reflex response of hoping to pass the danger, but there was still half a block to cover as the lethal weapon turned and leveled on Lucy.

The woman—who, with her scarf and stance, curiously resembled a Western gunslinger to Lucy—screamed one last warning, "I'm serious as a motherfucker. I'm not going to die!"

"Lucy!?" Marshall tried.

But before Lucy could react to her erstwhile lover, or the gunslinger, the woman squeezed off two plugs from her hand-canon.

Chapter 56

COLLISION COURSE

It was important to everyone involved that the resolution was neat and without bloodshed, which was all very well, but there were normally a team of teams appointed to a mission like this. It wasn't like tracking a bunny with a bloodhound. And the target, if alerted would be a lot more cunning, and volatile, than any hunted fox. Still, notwithstanding an initial hiccup, they had been making good ground and there was reason to hope it might end well.

That was until the sound of gunfire cut through the air as they rounded the corner finally sighting the target properly for the first time since they passed her on the interstate.

Two straight blocks ahead of them, Commander Topp's Jeep careened forward, clipping the curve and rebounding wobbly back onto the road, revealing in the process, a dead man on the sidewalk and a crazed woman brandishing a gun.

"Was she hit?!" The question was shrill and penetrating, but the answer came in physical form as Lucy's head bobbed up in the front of the Jeep. She shot past the gun-slinging woman, who turned with Lucy's vehicle and unloaded two more rounds into the back as it passed.

The first bullet connected squarely with one of the metal Jerry cans strapped to the back.

The explosion of red flame and black smoke amply obscured the Jeep from line-of-sight as the gasoline vaporized under the compounding heat.

There was no time to think.

Explosions echoed in their ears and the demented weapon-wielding woman turned her attention on them. Fifth and sixth blasts ricocheted off the bulletproof windshield as Agent Davis pulled hard into the side street, one block before contact.

Davis' missing vehicle opened a line-of-sight between the second SUV and the gun-woman.

Two more bullets lodged in the engine and headlight before the driver of the second SUV could turn the wheel and follow Davis' turn.

+

The first bullet had shattered her side mirror, and by some stroke of luck the second had missed the Jeep entirely. Instinctively, Lucy had ducked beneath the dashboard as she careened forward, but, driving Braille, she was forced to react to the violent wallop of the curb against her tires.

"Lucy!?" was the last she heard of Marshall's voice as her earpiece ripped away; with the savage swerve the projectile phone smashed to the floor of the passenger seat.

Lucy tore the steering wheel hard out from the sidewalk and lurched the vehicle back onto the road. A furtive glance over the dashboard confirmed an alley up ahead just as her peripheral vision picked up the shiny black tail in the rearview mirror, the one she thought she'd already lost.

She passed the shooter and pulled hard to the right. A second peek over the dashboard revealed her estimate to the alley to be twenty feet on the optimistic side. Another tug on the steering wheel averted the brick wall that was rushing at her, but not the bullet behind her that ruptured the spare gas canister. A fourth—and final—bullet zinged by even as she completed the dogleg into the alley. From behind her a cloud of black smoke engulfed the front seat as flames licked the back of her neck with scarring heat.

"Get rid of it!" she shouted at Maqtaly.

"Is impossible!" he shouted back, shielding his face.

"Maqtaly!" she implored him.

"Cannot be done!"

There was no time to stop, but with Maqtaly cowering next to her there was no choice not to. She hit the handbrake hard.

Maqtaly slammed forward, cracking his head hard on the dashboard.

Lucy glared at his slumped and unconscious body. Damn it!

No time to deliberate. She lifted her left arm to her nose and eyes, and swung her feet up through the gap between the front seats. She put a solid boot into the oversized flaming Molotov cocktail at the back of the car! Gasoline spilled up, but the Jerry can stayed in place. A second solid boot, however, did the job and it toppled out the back. In spite of the bullet and consequent fire the Jerry can had held it's structure remarkably well.

Then, upended on the ground behind the Jeep, it exploded into a proper fireball.

With her balled up jacket, Lucy dampened the residue in the back of the Jeep. Having done so, she turned back to the front, where she shoved Maqtaly's body aside and retrieved her phone. Remarkably the line was still open, "Marshall?"

"Lucy, are you alright?!"

"My Jeep was hit—I'm fine."

"Lucy, I love you." It was an odd proclamation "Turn yourself in! Don't get killed! Maqtaly isn't worth it! Lucy!"

But Lucy felt the pressure of her pursuers, crazed and governmental; there was no time to chat, "George, I've got to go." And with that, she hung up, put the Jeep back into gear and left the inferno behind her.

$+$

Agent Davis glanced down from the road in front of him to the digital map on the dashboard. Once again he was speeding away from his quarry. He frowned and checked the tinted rear window. At least they had both evaded the panicked woman whose gunshots continued to reverberate in the receding distance; terrified bark with an aim too wild to hope for a hit, were there even something left to aim at.

The green bleep, which had stopped briefly, changed to yellow. Agent Davis picked up his ringing phone. "Davis."

"Agent Davis, it's Commander Marshall."

"Commander. What's your status?" Any Intel would help at this point, and Davis knew full well that Marshall had been in contact with the erstwhile Commander.

"She has the asset." Marshall confirmed.

Chapter 57

THE BLOODBANK

It was unclear exactly how they had tracked her, and there probably wasn't much she could do about it right now anyway.

Depending on who her pursuers were working for, it could have been as simple as eye-in-the-sky; there were so few cars on the road right now that even assuming they were understaffed she'd be easy to trace. But there could just as easily be a bug on the car itself. The thought unnerved her as she pulled into the eerily quiet parking ramp and did a three-point turn to face her Jeep back out to the street.

She pulled the handbrake and surveyed the scene in which nothing moved. There was no sign of life outside her car. On the bright side, that included her tail. Lucy forced herself to breath as she considered the situation. Abandoning the Jeep brought unwanted danger, but she was determined to get to the bottom of the Coxsackie conundrum, and the bloodbank, with it's dated samples, offered the best chance of a glimpse into the incidence of the disease in the recent past.

The problem now, was what to do with her unconscious companion?

+

The building ought to have been bustling with life, but the concrete edifice stood as still as a sheer cliff with millennia of unmoving stratified layers. She let go of the steering wheel, reached into the back seat and pulled forward the Racal biohazard suit. It had a black smokey residue on it but looked otherwise unscathed. With her phone and keys tucked into the pocket of her jeans she shimmied her legs into the one-piece orange shell. Getting out of the Jeep, she slipped the orange hood over her head and quickly taped the open cracks.

The double doors at the entrance to the building stood disconcertingly wide open but fixed in place by the glass shards wedged under their base. Even from within the din of her pressurized helmet, Lucy could feel the quietness as she crossed the open atrium.

A pigeon alighted from the guard's desk.

Excepting the risk of her earlier tail, this building should afford a relative safety, and perhaps even a lab to run some quick tests. There was little here a desperate public would want in the current world climate, but still, she decided not to use the elevators; they somehow seemed more likely to alert any lingering residents to her presence.

In spite of her caution, the crunch of glass beneath her feet, and the loud catch of the stairwell door as Lucy pushed it open, infiltrated the dreams of the two sleeping residents in the building's lobby; a man and a woman huddled behind a wall of potted plants.

The man was first to stir. Waking from his now-customary restless slumber, he took in the nightmare that was the present-day reality. Rubbing sleep from his eyes he found himself focused on an orange alien. Salvation or demon? It hardly mattered.

"Hey!" he shouted, inadvertently waking the woman beside him. "You! Stop!"

But, with the noise from her helmet, Lucy was oblivious, and continued through to the stairs, letting the door close behind her.

The man turned to the woman, grabbed their small bag of essentials, and her hand, and pulled her in pursuit of the interloper.

+

Four floors up, Lucy carefully opened the door from the stairwell and scanned the empty corridor in front of her. Once again she missed the desperate voice from below as the young couple entered the narrow stairwell.

Lucy breathed regularly to avoid overheating inside the spacesuit. There was a sereneness to the claustrophobia inside the Racal suit and she tried to relax and engage that inner calm.

A minute later she found the room she was looking for. It was filled wall-to-wall with squishy plastic bags of blood plasma, loosely propped against one another in stainless steel tray drawers, all encased behind the refrigerated glass doors. They resembled an odd smorgasbord, a sort of Starbucks convenience counter for vampires.

+

At the stairwell door, Aaron poked his head into the hallway. Scanning quickly, he found no one. He scurried to the T-intersection twenty yards ahead, but there was no one in either direction.

"Nothing." He turned back to his girlfriend "He's gone."

"I told you it was the next floor!" Vivian was already returning to the stairwell and Aaron followed.

+

Standing in front of the industrial fridge, Lucy pulled out another drawer filled with plastic baggies of red blood and yellow plasma. She carefully checked the dates, and transferred a few liters of plasma from different fridge units, and a dozen dates, into her backpack. Then, zipping her bag shut, she gently lifted it onto her shoulders. She turned and–

Her faceplate smashed red with blood!

Lucy wheeled about completely and took in the desperately angry man shouting at her.

"I'm talking to you!"

Apparently Lucy had missed the introduction.

"Who the hell are you! And where did you get that suit?!"

His anger was apparent, but between the whooshing air in her helmet and his obvious fright it was all but impossible to make out what he wanted specifically.

"We want space suits too!" Vivian chimed in.

Lucy had just one suit, and though it would no doubt withstand the hurled bag of plasma she was well aware how vulnerable it was. Armor against microscopic enemies it may have been, but it was hardly chain mail.

That she was here to help was clearly too abstract a concept to make a difference.

Aaron advanced on her.

Lucy backed away awkwardly.

The blood smeared on her visor impaired clear vision, but she grasped at a loose tray from the fridge and pulled it between herself and her would-be assailant. The blood-filled bags wobbled like jelly shots. It was hardly effective.

Aaron grabbed another bag and hurled it at her in desperately futile rage.

Vivian raised her voice, "Help us! Not just yourself."

Lucy held up her hands in a placating gesture, but Aaron continued to advance. With no real alternative available to her, Lucy turned and ran, tossing more trays and medical debris between her and her pursuers. She blasted through the doors at the far end of the room and spied another stairwell.

The upended furniture gave her a small lead, but behind her the chase was on. As she banged through the stairwell door she thought she saw someone below, but there was no time to check or second-guess, and she turned up to the floors above.

How the hell would she get out of the building? And how could she escape her pursuers? Did they know the layout? For all she knew they had worked in the building for the last ten years.

Her spacesuit made an unfortunate handicap against her clear physical prowess, but she was still able to bound up the stairs two at a time.

Two floors up she burst into another hallway. They were all the same! Modern buildings differentiated their corridors as subtly as the human body differentiated its own conduit veins.

She raced across the linoleum. The first door she tried was locked. As was the second. Thankfully, the third opened at her first touch and she found herself in a supplies room.

Behind her the stairwell door burst open again. Her panicked pursuers scanned the hall, but all was quiet. Lucy's door was firmly closed. Aaron went one way, pushing Vivian in the other direction and commanding her to, "Try the doors!"

Inside her room, Lucy slumped to the floor and pressed her back firmly against the door. Smudging the blood from her visor, she thanked her lucky stars she'd had the presence of mind to launch a bag of blood to the other end of the corridor before entering her makeshift panic room.

Shelves of equipment surrounded her. A *medical* supply room.

Suddenly there was a tugging at the door handle and Aaron's flushed face pressed up against the small reinforced window in the door. His eyes darted back and forth, but the lock Lucy had turned held. Aaron moved on.

$+$

Lucy forced herself to count slowly to sixty before moving across to the shelves. This was an opportunity, and she didn't miss opportunities. If she were to be out on her own for the foreseeable future it would be nice to have some medical supplies.

She stuffed a small bag with tape, gauze, and bottles of antiseptic. A roll of rubber tubing on the shelf above pushed her mind into overdrive.

Options for egress included an air duct in the ceiling—not the option of choice, but simply noticing it was significant; most people never looked up—the door she'd entered by, and another door at the far end of the room, blocked behind steel shelves. There was an emergency exits map affixed to the wall. Evidently, the second door connected to a corridor unconnected to the one she'd just entered by, but for an elevator bank that ran down the center of the building. Her path forward was clear.

The shelf, once emptied was still heavy, but not so heavy to withstand her very motivated assault.

Lucy exited the supply room.

She was cautiously approaching the elevator when the bell sounded, the doors clunked and, connecting to the inner mechanisms of the tired old mechanics, they started to open. The barrel of a gun revealed itself first, and Lucy felt yet another jolt of adrenaline.

$+$

Agent Davis hit the open button again in a plaintive attempt to speed up the doors' process. They had tried five floors already and the old elevator was getting on his nerves. The doors finally widened to an unobstructed point of view.

Davis surveyed the open seventh floor foyer. Nothing.

"Hold the door," he instructed his partner as he pointed across at the receptionist's desk, "I'm going to check the desk."

'The desk' was Lucy's cover. There had been no time to flee back up the corridor, and even as Davis stepped out of the elevator she was burying herself deeper under the rudimentary structure. Her mind was racing. Had the gun belonged to the panicked residents of the building?

Lucy could see the figure approaching, reflected in the trashcan and silhouetted by the elevator lights. Thankfully, her own location was the darkest corner of the lobby. She prayed his eyes wouldn't notice her reflection. To thwart an aural give-away, she'd already risked turning off the air blowers inside her suit that now sunk around her, like skin on a once horribly obese person. She stopped breathing; vision typically places a premium on movement and if her orange outfit wasn't enough to give her away, she didn't need a careless gesture to help out.

She could feel his black-gloved hand on the table above her.

"Commander Topp?"

Was this her highway pursuers closing in again? And if so, how were they tracking her! They were a lot closer than her car.

Had he seen her? No, there was a frustrated tenor in his question.

Davis scanned the floor briefly, his line-of-sight to Lucy obscured by mere millimeters as he glanced over the desk's top.

Suddenly Lucy felt the trapped feeling of a fugitive, moments before her capture. Then it struck her, she was that fugitive. The President himself wanted her taken into custody.

"Davis. Any sign?" It was the man in the elevator.

"Nothing." And with that Davis turned back to the elevator, "Just our luck she picked a ten story building! Cell phone GPS tracks beautifully, except for elevation!"

There it was, explicated for her, her phone! How could she have been so dense?! Definitely a drowsy driver!

Davis stepped back into the elevator and pressed eight.

Under the desk, Lucy strained to hear what was happening when, from within her protective suit, her phone began chirping. The suit protected against microbes and other pathogens, but the sound of the cell phone tore right through, and Davis heard it!

Chapter 58

PLASTIC COFFINS

Lieutenant Watterson's men escorted Hiroshi as far as the quarantine checkpoint on the perimeter of Sacramento, where they entrusted him to suspicious soldiers who wanted nothing to do with a man who had potentially come in contact with the unknown contagious pathogen. In consequence, he had been admitted to the Sacramento quarantine zone and from that point been left more or less to his own devices.

It was dairy deliveries that had formed the core of Lucy's specific data, so rather than doubling back to the piggery, Hiroshi typed dairy into the search bar on his mobile map. Happily, there was a signal and the phone returned information for a change.

+

An hour later he pulled into the driveway of the Willet and Smith dairy packaging facility where he was a little astonished to find half a dozen trucks—were these people unaware of the contagious pathogen on the loose? He was reassured though by the wariness of the onlookers as he pulled to a stop; a beat up muscle car one vintage older than its driver tended to inspire that reaction at the best of times, but right now, excepting a lack of wings, he might easily have been mistaken for a Kamikaze pilot who'd crashed, but not yet exploded.

Hiroshi sat collecting his thoughts. Did it make sense to approach the men? He had risked exposure while driving here, eschewing the mask for 50 miles figuring his skin needed some fresh air. There was that, and his supply of protective gear was running low.

As a man in milk-stained overalls split from the gang by the trucks and approached Hiroshi's vehicle, it was clear to Hiroshi that now was the time to re-fasten the mask and pull on new gloves.

The man delicately placed a long steel tire iron on Hiroshi's front fender, it was an ominous gesture of warning. "We don't want no trouble."

He was 220 pounds if he weighed an ounce, but—the implied weapon notwithstanding—Hiroshi didn't feel physically threatened. In fact the weighty tire iron was a reassuring sign; it was presumably the pinnacle of intimidation at hand, and Hiroshi had little doubt its presence only played to his advantage; Westerners loved action films, but they spent their youth playing baseball and basketball. "No trouble," he assured the milkman.

"Well how about you just turn yourself around then."

"But there is trouble here."

The man flinched. He was a trucker, not a fighter. He had big arms and could take care of himself, but if this foreigner was infected that wouldn't really matter. They had kept delivering milk throughout the crisis, but they'd kept rigidly to themselves because those who played loose—Dan Reid, Fred MacKay, Dustin Goodchild ... —guys who hadn't sealed their cabins like plastic coffins, they were dead.

"Your drivers have cause death in Los Angeles." Hiroshi always felt facts were important in any negotiation. This man looked as scared as he should have. He was working under the most stressful circumstances Hiroshi could imagine and that counted for his character.

"Nobody's died delivering to San Francisco. Seems like maybe its LA is the problem."

It was a reasonable retort, "but wave of deaths in Los Angeles start with drivers from here." Perhaps a more personal connection might diffuse some of the tension, they were after all both human, and both clearly wanted to help the greater good, "I am Hiroshi. What is your name?"

"John." The man poked the front of Hiroshi's car again with his tire iron, "How about you turn your muscle about Hiroke."

"I am here with army."

John glanced back at his posse, "Yours or mine?"

"I am here to investigate official business."

"Your vehicle don't look very official."

Hiroshi smiled reassurance and stayed put in his seat. For seventy minutes they continued to trade tense, but politely informative talk as Hiroshi gradually won John's confidence. The men behind John had largely gone back to their work and John himself was now sitting on an empty milk can whose scuffed and dinted old exterior well matched John's own psychological state. Hiroshi had not moved from his seat.

As the sky began to redden with dusk, another man approached John from behind, a plate of food in his hands. Hiroshi watched as the man whispered something in John's ear, neither man taking their eyes off the interloper. John nodded to Hiroshi, "You want some food?"

Hiroshi hadn't eaten anything more than a snack bar in twenty-four hours and the thought was very tempting, but perhaps not judicious. "I am sorry to burden, but do you have any cans?"

John smiled at the sensible question and a few minutes later the second man returned with a can of beans, a can opener and some sterile wipes. He placed the latter two items on the former, and the whole pile on the front of the car. John picked up his tire iron and pushed them within reach of the driver's window, "No need to get out," he suggested flatly.

The sentiment was one Hiroshi wished he could agree with, but Hiroshi felt that nosing about was now an imperative action. He'd read enough psychology experiments to know that subjects' self-reported activities were notoriously unreliable. And in spite of John's warming demeanor, there was no chance he was going to permit Hiroshi a guided tour of the facility.

His dialogue with John provided an invaluable framework from within which to work, but Hiroshi felt he must now view the environs of this transfer station with his own, albeit amateur, nonetheless independent eyes.

$+$

Half an hour later, and shrouded in darkness, Hiroshi bade his farewell and pulled back up the driveway. He could feel the wary eyes on the back of his vehicle as he turned towards the most densely populated collection of buildings he could see. Once obscured by the abandoned industrial structures he killed the lights of his Corvette and slowed to a gentle halt. He waited, this time fifteen minutes, but no one appeared behind him. He reasoned they had accepted his story, assuming him gone for good.

The trucks were due to leave in an hour, which unfortunately made his reconnaissance more risky than he would have liked, but he felt it important to view the plastic coffin cabins first-hand. He might not have felt so bold had he known there were, not merely tire irons, but two firearms on the premises.

Chapter 59

HUNTED

Lucy desperately clawed at her space suit to silence the phone, but it was a futile action with the damage already done.

The only saving grace: the men inside the elevator, like deer in the headlights, had reacted too slowly. They were beaten by the closing doors, and, in spite of their frantic hammering at the OPEN button, the elevator moved steadily up. Even as it opened on the eighth floor, Davis was pressing on the CLOSE button, as if it would somehow respond faster to his rapid jabbing.

+

On the seventh floor, Lucy had her helmet off. She dripped sweat everywhere as she whispered desperately into the phone,t "I'm being hunted!"

"Your imagination, it is wild." Hiroshi's voice had a gentle smile that seemed to be masking strain.

"I know what being hunted looks like."

"We find many things when we hardly look." Hiroshi crouched in his car, urgently pressing at a wound, "Lucy, I have been shot." It was a classic understatement that a cursory glance of the blood leaking through his fingers would put lie to, only Lucy couldn't see the blood.

"Are you alright?"

But before he could respond, a clunk from the elevators forced Lucy's hand. Instinctively, she killed the phone and regretfully skated it across the linoleum floor into a neighboring corridor. There was nothing else she could do from where she was, and her own capture wouldn't help Hiroshi.

The elevator doors opened, and Davis, his gun drawn in front of him, emerged swiftly, his partner following close behind. Davis' eyes landed on Lucy's phone, visible in the corridor entryway and he motioned his partner in that direction. Davis himself continued towards the nurses' station, this time carefully, and completely, rounding the structure.

But Lucy was gone!

He scanned further back into the office. There, hidden behind another desk, but reflected in a silver trashcan on the opposite wall, the orange spacesuit stood out like a beacon. With his pistol cocked and ready, he waved silent but definitive hand-signals to his partner. Together, they approached Lucy's hiding spot, and on a three-two-one of fingers, whirled on Lucy.

Only Lucy wasn't there either.

In jeans and her lycra tank top, she held her breath as if that would make her more invisible while she waited inside the elevator. The two men stood there, confused, as Lucy peeked out at them, silently willing time to speed up. Finally, the elevator doors began to close, rattling as they did.

Davis swung about from the discarded spacesuit, his gun aimed at the sound.

He was forty feet from the doors as his eyes found Lucy's. Instinctively, he recognized that his easy means of tracking her was gone. Plugging three shots into the elevator's call button was his last vain attempt at stopping her.

To Lucy's immense relief, the doors continued shutting.

She closed her eyes and slumped in exhaustion as the cubicle dropped toward the ground floor.

+

Back on the eighth floor, Davis' fist slammed the smoking call button twice in frustration. Then, he turned to the stairwell. The elevator was fast, and there was a risk it might stop on any one of the floors, but he and his partner were descending the stairs three steps at a time.

+

Lucy glanced up at the sound of Davis' pounding fist above, but the elevator continued to drop: five, four, three, . . .

+

In the main lobby, the two agents burst from the stairwell door, and guns drawn, stalked efficiently towards the arriving elevator. With a ping, the doors opened, only no one was inside. Three times she had escaped by the skin of her teeth. But where this time?! Which floor?

Davis looked at his partner and delivered his directive, "Take the stairs, and check the floors as you ascend. I'm taking this back to seven." He didn't wait for an audible concurrence. He simlpy re-entered the lift and closed the doors.

With a clank and a ping at level seven, he exited once again, only this time he pulled a chair into the door and wedged it open.

+

Clasping her bag of medical supplies, Lucy sat in silent darkness, the wet texture of black grease rubbing against her arm. Her movements were stealthy, but there was a shakiness in her hands that she wasn't used to. She had been unnerved by an apparition of Hiroshi in the dark void as she ascended again; even as she recognized it for the classic symptom of exhaustion that it clearly was.

Once Davis vacated the elevator, she carefully wrapped one end of the firm rubber medical tubing around her waist, looping the end back through a figure eight knot and leaving a healthy length for slippage. Intellect told her the makeshift rope would hold, but she couldn't shake the doubts that nagged in the back of her mind as she fastened the other end to the elevator cable.

Lucy glanced at the slim crack of light that spilled up from the opened doors underneath her. She was sitting on the roof of the metal box, silently contemplating her next step as she waited. Then, looking left, she saw him again. Lucy savored the hallucination this time. She leaned closer to kiss his lips, but in the last instant Hiroshi disappeared into thin air.

She turned back to the shaft, and peeked down at the dark void below. This was her fate. She eased her feet over the edge and again inspected the chasm below. Pushing off the edge, she somehow resisted the urge to squeal in delight and fright.

As the rubber reached its elastic limit her makeshift harness dug deep into waist and thighs. Then, with the first signs of contraction and silent bungeeing, a cheeky grin crept its way onto her face. Another triumph for reason over emotion; though, given that she was hallucinating, trust in her own reason ought *reasonably* to have been called into question.

Whatever the case might be, Lucy delicately reached out with her foot, maneuvering her way across to position herself above the neighboring elevator's roof. Still ten feet above the precarious landing zone, she weighed her options. She wished she could let slack out from her knot, but the tubing had irretrievably snarled with the catch of her fall.

Her mind drifted: that had not been Lynn Hill's problem ...

Once the world's preeminent climber, Lynn's career had been marred by a 75 foot fall. The story had stuck with Lucy since the first day she'd heard it. Lynn had been on the cusp of taking the women's world rock climbing title when just weeks before the competition she made the most rudimentary of mistakes, forgetting to tie the knot in the end of her rope. It was a mistake her belaying partner should have caught.

There's a reason *both* climber and belayer are supposed to check the knot; like hang-gliding it's compounding errors that kill you.

Wow! Lucy's mind was really wandering, but she couldn't stop it ...

Lynn had been lucky; and though the untied rope had slid through *her* harness, God's hand, in the form of a small tree, permitted her to dodge death. Ultimately, she'd recovered from her horrific injuries and went on to become the legend Lucy remembered now.

What was Lucy's mind trying to tell her?

She refocused on the task at hand. A few short meters was a far cry from 75 feet! And though undoing the knot was an intractable problem, what with her weight on the rubber tubing, the knife in her backpack would achieve the same goal.

She pulled the blade out, braced herself for the awkward drop, and sliced the rubber cord.

The liberated rubber recoiled upwards, and Lucy dropped.

A loud thwack echoed up the elevator shaft as the giant rubber band whipped the underside of its anchor point and Lucy plonked atop the second elevator. She ignored the reverberating noise, rubbed her ankle and turned to the the the access hatch.

She dropped to the empty floor inside, pressed the open button and—

confidence restored—she strode out and exited through the foyer of the building.

+

Approaching her car, she veered to the right to pick up Maqtaly from behind the dumpster, where she'd left him. Only he was gone. He'd been groggy when she left, but she was sure he'd understood the need to stay put. Where was he?!

There was no time for a search. She paused at the two black SUVs. She'd ditched her phone upstairs, but there was no reason not to take an added precaution, and she knelt down by the SUV's tires, pulled a scalpel from her bag, and drove it into the valve of two tires on each vehicle.

Still no sign of Maqtaly. Well, so be it. He was on his own now.

A minute later, she passed the body of the dead homeless man on the side of the road. In comparison to the crisis the world faced, her own difficulties were but an irritation.

As she drove, her mind returned to HIroshi. What had he meant when he said he'd been shot?

Chapter 60

CAMP DAVID

By themselves, politicians don't cause much harm, and for that matter neither do scientists, but together, or, as was pertinently the case in this instance, working against one another . . .

$+$

President Pollack unleashed a fresh succession of coughs. It infuriated him that, even as the world's most important man, he was still prey to the limitations of the human body. He had no need to experience illness to feel empathy for the citizens of the world.

He blew his nose and lifted the receiver of his phone back to his ear. "Go ahead."

"Yes, Mr. President." Director Havamyer paused a moment, assuring himself he had the President's full attention, "President Wu has been isolated longer than you, and no one on his team has died, nor are they showing any symptoms."

"There are symptoms?" it was a redundant question—not even his best scientists knew what they were fighting—but Pollack had learned long ago to cover his bases. Actually, the situation was absurd, though in the back of his mind there was a nagging analogy: terrorist acts too were on occasion difficult to assign blame for. Was this Mother Nature's version of modern warfare?

"Not in China." Havamyer responded to the question of symptoms.

China, there it was again. They may have had pockets of flu in the US, but China was devoid of *any* real symptoms. "They know something."

Havamyer affirmed the president's position. "They're still denying it, but we both know things change when you're in the room."

The President coughed again.

While President Pollack composed himself, Director Havamyer returned their discussion to its most critical point, "Who do we tell about your plan?"

Pollack's answer was predictably definitive, "No one."

Chapter 61

ELLEN'S OLD WEATHERBOARD

It was past midnight when Lucy pulled onto the pebbled driveway that led to her mother's white-trimmed wrap-around verandah. To a visitor, the big birch trees that surrounded the old weatherboard may have felt ominously oppressive, especially in the still darkness. To Lucy though, who knew them intimately, from the gnarled roots to the tips of the canopy, they were the welcoming arms of an old friend.

It was perhaps lunacy to come here given her mother's recent demise, but beggars couldn't be choosers as far as accommodation went, and Lucy was wanted by what was left of the powers that be. True there were, no doubt, other empty properties, but they were just as likely empty due to their own owner's deaths, and for all Lucy knew, she might well encounter an actual corpse. Besides, her mother had been fine up until the army picked her up, and those responsible were now dead too.

She smiled at her childhood home—still her only real home—as she climbed the front steps and opened the screen door. Wretched fatigue caught her like an unfamiliar barb in the hallway mirror; who was the woman reflected back at her? Black bags under bloodshot eyes. She'd never been overly concerned by physical appearance but her hair now looked like the extricated cause of a drain blockage.

A small picture on the hallway stand below the mirror caught her eye— her mother in more radiant times—and without warning an emotional wave flooded Lucy's body culminating in the blurred vision of tear-filled eyes.

"How are you dead?!" Lucy murmured, but the picture simply smiled back as tears rolled down her cheeks. Time stood still, or perhaps it fast-forwarded, because Lucy's next conscious apprehension was the wetness that enveloped the front of her shirt.

She removed the cotton top and wiped her face with it. In her mother's room, as a half-hearted nod to safety, she dug deep into the closet for a garment not recently worn. There, she found the old USAMRIID sweater she'd given her mother when she first took up a post with the army. It still smelled of Ellen, and Lucy pulled it on.

+

In the kitchen, Lucy found a jar of un-popped corn kernels in the pantry. It rattled like a rainmaker as she pulled it off the shelf, echoing the storm that had coalesced outside. She took it and turned to the stove where Hiroshi was proffering a glass-topped pot.

Numbed to the inexplicable, Lucy took the pot.

"I hope you're a hallucination and not a ghost."

Hiroshi's smile was charismatically comforting.

"There is no green tea here," she apologized, "but you can pretend." She was talking to a hallucination—telling it to pretend—and it really didn't bother her. In fact, more than anything she marveled at her mind's ability to simultaneously recognize and succumb to the illusion.

Once again they popped corn together.

+

Two hours later, Lucy was slumped asleep in a living-room armchair, a half-eaten bowl of popcorn on her lap. There was no tight smile, but she was too beaten to care had there been one.

Knocking from the front door did nothing to stir her.

"Lucy. Lucy! Where are you?" It was Hiroshi again.

Lucy's eyes remained firmly shut even as the corners of her lips tilted up in appreciation.

The audible click of the front door lock presaged its creaky opening, and to accompany that a slurred *woman's* voice "Commannnner Topp! Hiroshi aasss eeen shotttt."

The front door slammed shut and Lucy bolted upright, scattering corn to the floor. From the hallway, footsteps approached, increasing in speed, and with them the woman's voice came into brighter focus, "Commander Topp, is that you?"

Lucy scrambled to her feet, catapulting the remaining popped corn across the room, and crashing the stainless steel bowl behind the fluffy white confetti. Footsteps thundered down the hallway and into–

–the disoriented Lucy who turned and crashed into Major Ulman, as she entered the room.

"Commander Topp. Are you all right?"

Contrary to all appearances, Lucy placated Ulman with surprisingly easy assurance, "I'm fine."

Ulman didn't double check, preferring to plow forward, "Did you hear me? Hiroshi was shot. In Sacramento."

Lucy went white.

She wasn't religious, and she'd never believed in ghosts, and yet here it was, the experience the faithful always talked about. She looked about the room, but there was no sign of Hiroshi. Of course there was no sign of the man!

Lucy's eyes percolated with the bubbles surrounding the fish tank filter.

Major Ulman watched Lucy's disoriented grasping when she realized the cause might have been her own miscommunication, "Not dead shot, just wounded."

The fish lay dead on the gravel floor, unmoved by Ulman's change of implication.

Ulman continued, "General Jackson said he owed it to you to bring him back. He's arriving in an hour or so."

People were dying and resurrecting in the next minute, and Lucy was struggling to keep apace, "Where?"

"The Davison Army Airfield, near Fort Belvoir."

Lucy knew the airport well and her foggy mind was clearing with fresh calculations. It was a solid two-hour drive. "How did you find me?"

"General Jackson."

Lucy smiled. "Did he say anything?"

Ulman handed her a map showing Coxsackie incidence in California.

"He gave me this, and mentioned Kretsky again."

Lucy glanced at the map and pocketed it, the contents could wait. "What did he say?"

"Apparently Wei Lin, from the Chinese CDC–"

"I know Wei Lin."

"Well apparently he visited Kretsky less than two days before the first death in New York. Someone at Langley connected the dots after he was seen in satellite images outside a Chinese pig farm. A farm with a *lot* of dead pigs. It may just be another red herring ..."

But Lucy had stopped listening, her mind now racing through scenarios.

Interrupting Lucy's train of thought, her own agenda still incomplete, Ulman placed a cell phone in Lucy's hand. "It was Commander Krogen's. No one will suspect to trace it."

Lucy, looked at Ulman, "Thanks Major."

This simple gift solved a problem she had been wrestling with since she had abandoned her own phone. She was reconnected to the world. Better still, Commander Krogen's phone would have many of the phone numbers Lucy needed, but couldn't recall.

$+$

Hunched down against the torrential downpour, she crossed the now-muddy driveway, opened the door and jumped into the Jeep. It was not a moment too soon. Thumping helicopter blades crested the tree-lined hill as she fired up the engine. Shge engaged the gears and left a white-pebbled scattershot spray in front of the car as she reversed down the drive.

From the cockpit of the helicopter the co-pilot slashed the chopper's white searchlight across the wet canopy of leafless fall trees. Between the branches, swaths of liquid black reflected back from the asphalt surface of the road. One hundred feet below them, the still landscape whipped by ferociously—until the beam alighted on Lucy's Jeep.

"There she is!" pointing to the Jeep, the co-pilot locked the light in a fixed position, "Slow up."

The pilot eased up the throttle and settled in for the easy pursuit. The vehicle was speeding, but neither the darkness, nor the forest canopy obscured it from sight. And far from the tough task that finding her in the first place had presented, the linearity of the roads made tracking the car way too easy.

The pilot picked up the radio. "We have Commander Topp's Jeep. She's heading north. Maintaining contact. Please advise."

The radio crackled briefly as a voice came to life, "Do you have a clear shot?"

The co-pilot who already had the rifle in his hands nodded affirmation.

"She's got nowhere to go."

"Take the shot anyway, we want no more mistakes."

"Roger that."

The co-pilot nodded again, sighted the vehicle below and gently squeezed the trigger.

Chapter 62

DAVISON ARMY AIRFIELD

Four black SUVs tore down the tight country roads, converging rapidly on the spotlight that was no longer a distant speck, the LCD screens in their dashboards blipped in unison with a green dot lighting up at the top of each digital map.

The shot from the chopper had been a direct hit, and the small putty blob with a delicately whipping wire was transmitting perfectly. This time there would be no escape.

Nor was there. If the helicopter's spotlight hadn't already felt like a solid clasp, the speedily approaching posse of vehicles, both from behind, and now another bevy visible across the valley, made abundantly clear that this time the Jeep was trapped.

Swarming around Lucy's car when it finally stopped, the secret service vehicles spewed out agents in a grossly unnecessary show of force. At the wheel of the boxed-in Jeep, Major Ulman couldn't help but smirk at how well the simple ruse had worked.

+

Two dozen miles away Major Ulman's Tesla Model 3 carved through more rain. A sleek commitment to the environment, it struck Lucy as America's individualistic response to the Japanese bullet train. Indeed it had superseded Japan's own effort—the Prius—to solve America's heart of hearts struggle with the reality that public transport was the ultimate environmental solution.

Inside the vehicle, Lucy's eyes were tired and bloodshot. Two hours of sleep had been a much-needed respite, but it wasn't enough.

Waking was the toughest stage in the cycle of sleep deprivation. Mostly though, an hour after waking, the exhaustion dissipated. International travel, as Lucy knew well, often elicits the same feelings. Food was a good short-term antidote, and Lucy tore into the bagel Ulman had given her, like a lioness devouring a hyena. She glanced at the clock in the dashboard, not really sure what she hoped to find.

She had been awake seventy-five minutes now, and she was still every bit as exhausted as when she'd first woken from her brief nap. Perhaps this was why the Geneva Convention had such strict guidelines on the sleep deprivation of prisoners.

A memory made her smile. Her mother had quipped—when Lucy had told her that the Geneva Convention prohibited waking prisoners more frequently than every two hours—that "someone ought to give a copy of that convention to babies when they're born."

If this was what parenthood held in store, propagation of the human race suddenly made a lot less sense.

+

Twenty minutes later, having lucked across Wei Lin's phone number on Krogen's phone, Lucy was glad to have the phone to her ear, an extra source of stimulus to keep her awake. She was also excited by what she was learning.

"You have the Kretsky Coxsackie?" she asked.

"Yes." Wei Lin was affirmative, "And we have a sister company we work with, near you. They should have it, and they definitely have another, more virulent strain that they've amplified for us, for use in pigs."

Wei Lin told Lucy how the Chinese CDC had worked with Kretsky for some time, not just because the Kazaks were loose with the rules, but also because they had genuine capabilities with these state of the art technologies. He summarized the regrettable transpiration of events with a Chinese proverb, "Unfortunately, water not only floats a boat, it can sink it too."

"What about your sister company near me?" Lucy circled back to Wei Lin's earlier remark.

"They are a small biotech firm in North Carolina."

It was a small and very interconnected world they lived in. "Is there anyone there right now?" Lucy asked.

"Yes, but I assure you the Kretsky Coxsackie is benign; China is covered in it."

Lucy heard his objections, but she wanted to know what they were working on. Besides, this was her best prospect for a new hideout, and somewhere to test her recently collected blood samples.

As she neared the Davison Airfield she thanked Wei Lin and returned her attention to the surroundings she'd last seen eight years ago when she was still training in the air force.

The Davison Army Airfield was better known as a home of helicopters, indeed it had been the home of the Presidential helicopter until 1976.

It was a clever ploy by General Jackson to divert an airplane here, though Lucy guessed that the pilot had probably been initially instructed to fly to Dulles, or perhaps the Joint Base Andrews Naval Air Facility. It would have put a smile on her tired face to know that it was right now that Jackson was rerouting the flight.

Waiting on the edge of the tarmac with the green grass either side of her, and the big white chopper sheds nearby, she glanced at Krogen's phone sitting on the passenger seat. A thought alit in her mind and she picked it up. Turning the phone on, she flicked to the voice-mails and pressed play. There were thirty-eight messages and she listened to them systematically, skipping message after message until she came across something that piqued her interest.

"Commander Krogen, this is Agent Williams, you requested background whereabouts on one Amanet, surname unspecified, who returned to Kazakhstan August 28th. He was in the US just one week and spent the bulk of his time in Fresno, principally at a medical research facility called PharmaCo. Hope that helps. Let me know if you need more." There was a beep, and the next message was about to begin when Lucy shut the phone off, cogs whirring in her mind.

Short cuts often seemed benign, and in research they could amount to little more than skipping a check on results. But while others believed the Chinese use of Kretsky had potentially nefarious roots, Lucy felt that it was the ties between PharmaCo and Kretsky ought to be scrutinized.

On the one hand, pharmaceutical companies had been—particularly over the past decade—under extreme pressure to convert prospects into drugs, even when the path to the golden goose was expensive and fraught with risks. Kazakhstan, on the other hand, was the new wild west of biotech research; a willing enabler of industry.

Was PharmaCo outsourcing more problematic trials to Kazakhstan? Or were the Kazaks simply supplying materials? Were they perhaps the means of accelerating tests? And more to the point, what did Marshall know that he hadn't told Lucy about?

+

In front of her, the army airplane taxied to a stop. Lucy checked her surroundings again, but there was no one else to be seen, something she hoped to hell would stay that way. The roar of the engines wound down, the cabin door dropped open, and Hiroshi emerged, shading his eyes from the light.

Lucy smiled at him as he stepped off the plane, the first light of day fanning out behind him. He crossed to her, a heroic tenor to his limping stride. Her bloodshot eyes were glassy with emotion when he stopped in front of her.

"I am sorry about your mother."

Lucy clasped Hiroshi's face in her hands, "Hiroshi, I'm so sorry. I was wrong when I sent you to Sacramento. I . . ."

Hiroshi let his own hands rest on Lucy's forearms, "You are to try to saving the world." His fingers touched a rope-burn on her wrist, ". . . with one hand." Referencing the abrasion, he asked, "What is happened?"

"It's nothing. My arm got caught on some tubing. A rope of sorts."

She put her arms further around him, and tears from her weary eyes leaked out onto his shoulder.

"You are a complex woman."

"I'm scattershot but–"

Hiroshi cut her off, "But the whole is bigger than the sum of the parts."

Lucy pulled him deeper into a primal embrace, holding them together for a long time. When she did release him, it was only to pull back enough to kiss him firmly on the lips and sink her very being into his.

She had always scoffed at the Greek myth that held humans originally to be four armed, four legged and two headed. A myth that credited Zeus with splitting and condemning them to a lifetime search for their other half. It was fanciful stuff, and yet Hiroshi felt like no man she had embraced before.

For the first time she understood her mother's time-honored sentiment of her father, "we were two halves that made a whole. Your father made everything possible for me, and me for him."

And then it struck her! The rope burn! Lynn Hill! Hang gliding! Her subconscious mind had been trying to tell her!!

Lucy pulled violently back from Hiroshi. "Oh shit!"

Hiroshi looked at her confused.

"It's a combination!" Again her mind felt that injection of adrenaline. She was thinking double-time, her superpower, "How could we be so stupid?!! Hiroshi, every corpse has both. I have flu and you, you no doubt, have Coxsackie!"

"But–"

"I. F.—Is Fucked! Two distinct pathogens interacting! The Coxsackie and H9N2 must be acting in combination."

Hiroshi touched his lips, he did not understand the biology well, but one fact suddenly resonated . . . "And now we both have . . . both."

She stopped hearing Hiroshi as her mind spun in a dozen directions at once.

+

This was antithetical to every medical case she'd known; pandemics were single source functions. Sure, contributory factors existed, but the underlying pathogen was always a single source. Even AIDS, the classic counter-example—it not being the ultimate mode of death—spread as a single virus that opened the gates to a panoply of co-conspirators; it didn't team up with any one specific pathogen. To be sure, it mutated constantly in reaction to our attacks, and the environment in general, but you traced the infection as a single source.

Then the weighty realization struck her: this might very well be the last day of her life. There were unfulfilled dreams, unfinished projects . . . and there was Hiroshi.

He was here now. That offered some comfort, but what tragically ironic comfort.

Wait! What was she thinking! She wasn't throwing the towel in. Never! This was a major breakthrough, and there was nothing like a ticking clock to put the pressure on one to get results.

The airfield about her whirled back into focus. It was no wonder the IF-

Zones made no sense, this pandemic had no precedent. Well no direct one. But her fresh reasoning just opened an entire directory of new paths to explore.

Specific flu, you could vaccinate against, but that took time! Time she didn't have. If she was wrong, she was back where she started. But worse, if she was right, she had until she next slept to find a solution. Not a comforting thought given her sleep deprived hallucinations and overwhelming fatigue.

Lucy grabbed Hiroshi's arm and pulled him to Major Ulman's car, there was no time to waste!

Chapter 63

SETTING MARSHALL STRAIGHT

Hiroshi sat shotgun. He watched as the dark world outside streamed by the windows. The driving rain was back. It cloaked their passage and soaked the corpses ousted by frantic residents onto the streets; these houses were very different from his own home, but people were people and fear cut through most ethnographic boundaries. And then there were those who rose above their own doubts and apprehensions, the woman at the wheel beside him for instance.

Hiroshi looked across at Lucy. Again, she was waiting for her phone to connect. She'd already made half a dozen calls since she'd hurried him into the Tesla.

Lucy saw Hiroshi's gaze on her and gave him an affirming smile, the thrill of their new break had injected life into her. The phone connected and, with it, Marshall's confused voice, "Hello? Commander Krogen?" the man was supposed to be dead.

Lucy was emphatic, "It's Commander Topp."

Her clarity of conviction did nothing to alleviate Marshall's confusion. Lucy was AWOL, and not passively so, "Lucy?"

"Yeah, different phone. I ditched mine." She had neither the time, nor the inclination, to pussyfoot around Marshall's bewilderment, "Marshall, how is PharmaCo linked to Kretsky?"

Marshall felt himself entering the twilight zone. Lucy had returned armed with information. She was a terrier, or was she just venturing wild guesses. "What . . . ?"

"Don't give me that bullshit run-around!"

She had something between her teeth. "There is no connection."

"And you've never heard of a guy called Amanet?"

Marshall fell silent. He was surrounded by people he used to know, and Amanet was one of them, but Lucy was his more significant past, and her investigating made him a lot more nervous than any nebulous connection PharmaCo had to Kretsky.

"Lucy, PharmaCo has stopped the spread of whatever is killing people. Preventative antibiotics and–"

"They've halted the spread?" Lucy's skepticism rang out loud, "You know this because ..."

Was she digging or prodding? To Marshall, it didn't matter. He had the advantage of the machine's backing, "You've been dropped from the loop. Deaths have dropped." He took her silence as an affirmation, and continued haughtily, "So much so, that President Pollack has relaxed local quarantines."

Had Marshall seen the color draining from Lucy's face, Lucy's simple cold reply might not have taken him so by surprise. "He *what*?!"

Was she really questioning the President's authority?

"Marshall, there are two pathogens, and it's their interaction that is killing people. And my guess is that the H9N2 is PharmaCo's, care of Amanet." It was a big guess, but he needed some prodding to wake him from his slumber! "Reinstate those quarantines. Now!"

"You know this becau–"

A defensiveness re-entered Marshall's tone, but Lucy didn't have the time to tiptoe around his feelings, and she cut him off, "Where the hell is the President? And more to the point, what is that one man wrecking ball going to do next?!"

Chapter 64

THE BIG OPEN BLUE SKY

High above the earth's surface, the airways had been conspicuously absent of airplanes. Cloud formations lacked the tell tale crisscrossed vapor trails that spoke of man's ubiquitous presence there.

But there were still some planes in flight, and one of them was marked "United States of America". At that moment, Air Force One was midway across the Pacific Ocean. Inside the generously proportioned aircraft, President Pollack blew his nose and turned back to his personal doctor, "President Wu is fine and so am I. This is a mild flu, millions of people have it. It's not the problem."

Doctor Doupe knew Pollack well, and he wasn't about to correct the President over something that he had no good reason to second-guess.

President Pollack continued categorically, as if the force of his will could change the course of science, "I'm not dying. Just give me something to suppress the symptoms. We're closing in on China and I can't be coughing all over President Wu."

He was about to seize the bull by the horns, and it was important to project strength if, in person, he was going to elicit information from the Chinese leader that teleconferencing had so far failed to deliver.

Chapter 65

CHINA

Smoke exploded into the air when the massive wheels hit the tarmac. As the plane slowed to taxiing speed a flock of swallows lifted from the ground ahead of them. Notwithstanding the stasis of the other aircraft—at an airport that normally moved over one hundred million passengers a year—it was the presence of birds on the runway that sent the unnerving chill through the pilot's veins. Swallows were small, but so were starlings, and as every pilot knew, a flock of the latter had been responsible for a catastrophic crash in Boston harbor many years ago, one resulting in the deaths of 62 of the 72 passengers.

Beyond the avian welcoming committee, Beijing Capital International Airport was eerily silent, and without the assistance from the control tower it took pilot Colonel John Gateway some time to navigate Air Force One to the portable stairs.

Once inside the pristine car, President Pollack and his three innermost secret service, all wearing ignoble face-masks and gloves, were ferried along trickling highways into the heart of Beijing, stopping finally at the Raffles Hotel, President Pollack's own personal preference.

In dramatic style, a concertinaed isolation tube ran from the door of the hotel to the President's car. It was a tube of stylishly retro futuristic appearance; a blend of oversized vacuum cleaner hose and industrial garbage chute running horizontally, not vertically.

A more discerning eye might have questioned its true value, but Pollack simply coveted it as he walked its length and entered the building.

Half an hour later he and the Chinese leader met.

+

Together alone inside their bio-safe quarters, President Wu reached out and firmly clasped the US President's proffered hand. Both men were exhausted, and to complement Pollack's minor sniffles, President Wu had bloodshot eyes and a headache. They were, no doubt, counterpart consequences of their shared lack of sleep.

Their initial greetings aside, the Chinese leader opened proceedings with the empathetic pledge of solidarity you would expect from a leader of his distinction, "I am happy your casualties are falling, and I am sure together we can resolve this problem." He then added an attempt to break the ice, "Perhaps by now, either you are immune or you are dead."

President Pollack smiled, the apparent joke had lost something in the translation, but the sentiment was clear, "I guess we are both immune."

"Perhaps. But just in case, how do we deal with ..." Wu trailed off. It was disarming, but it reflected his own genuine mystification about the issue at hand.

Pollack tried filling the gap with wild speculations that were everywhere rampant, "The microbes from Mars. The monkeys from Africa. Or," and then he too trailed off, only not out of uncertainty. He placed satellite surveillance images of the dead pigs on the oak desk between them, President Pollack looked at Wu significantly. "What did your CDC learn from these pigs?"

Wu appeared honestly caught off-guard as he lifted the CIA photographs from the table, "I have no explanation for our relative health."

"These images mean nothing to you?"

"No. But I promise you, we will both know about these photographs tomorrow."

President Pollack's nod indicated that he was there until they got to the bottom of everything.

+

Lucy glanced at him, to check that Hiroshi was following, "The H9N2 must activate the Coxsackie—make it lethal. It fits perfectly with the epidemiology. Twin pathogens; and the homogeneous populations are fine. Without an interaction of agents there's no death." Lucy had sparkle in her eyes as she enthused to him. In spite of the obvious implications for their own health, she was giddily excited.

Hiroshi, wrestled furiously with the wave of scientific information. He desperately wished to honor his role as sounding board. And it seemed, the essential synthesis of Lucy's dynamic speculation amounted to, "No movement between populations equals no death?"

"It's very neat, isn't it."

Hiroshi understood the connectivity in the abstract, but it surprised him that the experts hadn't considered this possibility, at least not until now. It was apparently a rare example in which expertise blinded. What to the untrained mind was obvious, was obscured from the experts by a fundamental prejudice; twin pathogen pandemics simply didn't exist.

"So, I.F.-zone are where pathogens collide. But there are no trail leading to the massacre." He restated the basic tenant of Lucy's theory.

The implications were multitude. "We now have *two* opportunities to stop the pandemic!" Lucy enthused, "Neither H9N2, nor Coxsackie are particularly lethal. H9N2 has the potential to be, but deaths from a pernicious strain of the virus—typically pneumonia—would look very different to the epidemiology the world is witnessing right now. And China—which is overrun by Coxsackie—serves as ample evidence that the Coxsackie alone is not a threat."

Hiroshi nodded.

"But, if we can stop either vector, the H9N2 or Coxsackie, then we have a cure." Lucy smiled, "Unfortunately the best-case for making a vaccine is about four years, and even if we had one, we'd need it at scale."

"Hai."

"And in the meantime, all it takes to unleash a tidal wave of deaths in a population primed with Coxsackie, is the introduction of a single man infected with H9N2."

+

In the Beijing bio-safe room the world's two most powerful men shook hands again in a foolishly imprudent display of solidarity.

"I believe our meeting has been very productive."

The unfortunate double meaning of President Pollack's sentiment was lost on both leaders, and President Wu simply bowed with graciously before he left the room.

The door to President Pollack's wing opened and he too was whisked away.

In the ensuing hours both men consulted with their inner circles, safe in the knowledge that neither camp had, to this moment, experienced any deadly disruption. Scientists in protective gear swept the meeting room itself, and sent samples, under the tightest of security, to party labs where they were being prepped for analysis in the hope that a clue might emerge.

The curious simplicity of the oversight that followed was remarkable. It resided in the cleaning crew who disposed of the warm fruit cocktail and other unconsumed foods into the standard trash receptacles.

From there, a local vagrant devoured the contents of President Pollack's uneaten compote. His body then set about coaxing the virus back to full-blown infectivity before he carried it out to the city at large.

Before the night was over, a local night market thronging with life that existed now only in China, had the American President's flu.

For their part, Pollack's secret service attaché was collectively infected with Coxsackie.

Chapter 66

THE WHITE HOUSE

Havamyer looked at the number on the incoming call and picked up the phone, "Director Havamyer."

Lucy heard the uncertainty in his voice. She was starting to enjoy the disarming effect that calling from her erstwhile Commander's phone elicited. "Director, this is Commander Topp. I'm hoping we can avoid a catastrophe, but I need your full attention."

What became apparent very quickly, was, not only that Commander Topp knew of the President's whereabouts, but that she had explicit and justifiable reasons to question his safety.

"Suppose you have the flu." Lucy continued, "You get a sore throat, drink some O.J. and return to work. But imagine you bump into a friend when you're buying the juice. And imagine they have Coxsackie."

Her case was serious, and it was the first argument on the subject that Havamyer had heard that made any sense. It aggravated his nagging ulcers, but when the computer in front of him lit up with alerts of deaths in Beijing, and the insistent second phone line trying to break into his call *refused* to accept his snub, his stomach went from queasy to out-and-out nausea.

"Even your perfunctory hug is enough to trade the illnesses." Lucy was unrelenting, "That night, you both go to sleep and somehow the flu activates the Coxsackie."

Havamyer's screen showed hundreds of people had died in China. All in the last 24 hours.

"The next day you're both dead, and there's no chain of deaths leading to either of you; the person who infected you with the flu doesn't have

Coxsackie and the person who infected your friend with Coxsackie is still free of the flu!"

President Wu's security staff was dead.

"Certainly underscores the rationale behind quarantines. Right?"

Lucy's question hung there, unanswered. Director Havamyer was frozen with fear.

The insistent call on the other line was from the upper echelons of the Chinese leadership. "Excuse me Commander Topp." Havamyer didn't wait for her reply as he picked up the incoming line.

+

When Havamyer returned to Lucy's call he possessed of a profusion of unwelcome particulars. Near, but not at the top of his list, was the unfortunate passing of President Wu, China's much-loved leader.

Ordinarily this calamitous news would have trumped anything, but as he understood it, a majority of his own President's attaché was dead.

"Commander Topp, I have a call being placed to President Pollack's suite. The Chinese have agreed not to enter the room until I have at least attempted to make contact. The door is–" and at that moment the other line sprung back to life. Havamyer cut himself off "I'll call you."

The line to President Pollack's room connected, and Havamyer waited while the phone rang.

In the Presidential suite, Pollack lay motionless in his bed. The phone on the mahogany bedside table shook the stillness of the air. It rang once. Twice. Three times, before the leader of the free world stirred and lifted the handset.

Chapter 67

RAFFLES BEIJING HOTEL

"Rope!" The black-clad man gave his reflex call as he dropped the coil out of the open doors of his MH-60S Seahawk helicopter.

The building below was stately colonial, and would have looked more in place in London than the streets of China, but it was the Chinese way to host foreign dignitaries in quarters that made them feel comfortable. That said, comfort was not the high priority of the hour.

Fifty minutes after Director Havamyer's call, the two MH-60S Seahawk helicopters blasted the rooftop with downdraft. The lead pilot lowered his powerful bird, delicately dangling the umbilical cord that was the navy seals' rappel rope onto the concrete top. The black clad men clipped their D-rings into the line without hesitation and dropped away from the chopping blades.

Once on the roof, they unclipped and moved swiftly to a fire door that presented no obstacle to their entry.

Their path down the dark hallways and stairwells was lit by headlights. Ear-pieces delivered a stream of information from the command center that watched the teams' progress from the helmet-mounted cameras; night-vision goggles were a popular public misconception, shunned by assault teams who feared the disorienting brightness an ordinary room light could cause. Their drawn weapons were a superfluous accessory their training demanded. There was no sign of life to challenge their entry.

The building blueprints and general Intel had been excellent and ninety seconds after their initial jump, they stood outside the President's suite. The President's nervous security stood down under instructions from earpieces of their own.

+

Inside the room, President Pollack was dressed and ready to move. He had spent the last hour being debriefed and he hadn't liked what he had heard. Even less had he liked the sound of genuine surprise he'd detected in Director Havamyer's voice when he first answered the phone. Havamyer had obviously had every expectation of finding him dead, and his tone of voice was unequivocal when he addressed the President, "Mr. President, this is Havamyer. You need to listen to me very carefully."

Pollack opened the door when the Seals knocked. The rescue team then escorted him back through the building and onto the roof where he'd been less than ceremoniously attached to the winch and, to his mind, a trifle ingloriously raised to the hovering Seahawk.

The extended gloved hand of a seasoned—if temporarily awestruck—marine welcomed the President aboard. "It's an honor having you ride with us, Mr. President." It was a reassuring moment for Pollack; in spite of the turmoil, one thing remained constant, respect for him and his office.

The last Seal swung into the chopper's belly from the winch, and the helicopter thunk-thunk-thunked off into the distance.

+

China had cooperated admirably in light of the chaos, and the absence of their leader. The extraction was taking on textbook qualities, but nothing masked Lucy's underlying question: "with the eruption of death around him, how was the US President still alive?"

Chapter 68

WEI LIN'S FACILITY

Avoiding roadblocks and unwelcome attention had added unwanted time to their trip. What would normally have been a four-hour drive was now pushing six when Lucy finally pulled off the TW Alexander Drive and into the North Carolina Research Triangle Park. Traffic lights and a split carriage road at the entrance to the facility were the only clues that something significant lurked behind the forest just a few yards from the curb. Such were the trappings of modern business parks.

Square footage probably wasn't expensive out here, but even so, the building Wei Lin's directions led her to was big enough to give a solid sense of the commitment one particular Chinese company was making to this location.

Lucy was still on the phone when she pulled into a parking space and killed the engine. The news she'd just received was infuriating. "Just how much damage could the President do in China?!"

Hiroshi watched her closely for clues, as he exited the car and followed Lucy towards the thick glass doors of the biotech building.

On the other end of the phone, Havamyer was predictably defensive, "Our assessment indicated a strong probability that China possessed intelligence that could potentially resolve this crisis." He then ventured to include the president's rationale, "Diplomacy, as you know, can bring its own solutions and you yourself said the Chinese were stonewalling–"

Astonished that he might have the gall to try turning this back on her, Lucy interrupted him, "The Chinese–"

But Havamyer interrupted right back, "Might well be furious, but let me assure you they were happy to see him go."

"Perhaps we should have left him there." Lucy quipped acerbically.

"Be that as it may, how the hell is the President still alive?!"

Finally, a matter they both felt to be significant. It was the question that had been nagging at Lucy since she learned that Pollack had survived. She left a long pause before double-checking, "He slept all night?"

"Yes."

"Then he should be dead. Unless ... " she trailed off.

Lucy looked at Hiroshi, but her co-pilot on their one-way ride to the other side was in the thick of negotiations with a Chinese man of his own on the other side of the building's glass door.

Her phone crackled again, "You think he has some natural immunity?" Director Havamyer ventured, as much in hope as genuine suggestion.

"No," she answered him definitively. This was more than immunity. There was something else at work, and Lucy had a fair idea what it was. She smiled at Hiroshi, more sparkle in her eyes.

The Chinese man on the other side of the glass had folded his arms. Lucy turned to him and held her ID to the window. The man scrutinized is, and Lucy handed Hiroshi a paper medical mask.

Hiroshi looked at her, confused.

"It's for their benefit, not ours."

With a quick flourish, the man turned the lock and the door swung open.

Chapter 69

30,000 FT ABOVE THE PACIFIC OCEAN

The E-2 Hawkeye with its characteristic surveillance disk atop sailed majestically into the distance. Already four hundred miles from the aircraft carrier from which they'd picked up their consignment, they'd long ago reached a cruising speed well in excess of the slower Seahawk helicopter that had performed the initial extraction. This was a time-sensitive mission and all the stops had been pulled. They were flying at the jet's maximum capabilities.

Behind the cockpit, Doctor Neilson, a seasoned military medic, moved over to attend to the President who stiffened as he turned back from a window.

"I'm fine." If the obstacle of his own frail human form was not irritating enough, President Pollack was certainly not going to brook the extra doubting of this medic, "It's the people around me who keep dying."

"A bit of a god-complex?" Dr. Neilson had treated powerful men before, but this patient was in a league of his own.

"I'm the president of the United States," came Pollack's cool reply, "it's the closest thing we have on earth."

Chapter 70

TIME TO SLEEP

Lucy turned back to Hiroshi who was sniffing at a foul-smelling glass beaker filled with a murky liquid. General Jackson's concluding words from the call she'd just hung up still echoed in her mind, "Good luck and may God be with you." Though many in the armed forces were, Lucy was not a religious woman, and yet still she found solace in the allusion that had real meaning to so many.

Jackson was the consummate gentleman, and his assurance meant as much now as it had ever meant before. Without his assistance she wasn't actually sure her plan stood any credible chance of working. But there were still risks ahead, big risks, and a lot more needed to be done before the trigger was pulled. Her eyes moved up to meet Hiroshi's and she gave him a smile.

She took the beaker from Doctor Eastwood as he nodded his head to confirm that this was indeed the serum she had sought. Spacesuit-clad, Doctor Eastwood had—under Wei Lin's instructions from afar—already been of incalculable assistance.

A mass of electrical cables lay on the two beds that had been pushed together and Lucy crossed to what might become her final resting place if her conjecture proved mistaken.

Hiroshi followed her, still clasping his own beaker in hand, "This is a very bold experiment."

Lucy placed her beaker on a rubber-wheeled steel trolley laden with biomedical monitors and machines from which the mass of electrical cables streaming onto their beds emanated. Those wires would soon be affixed all over their respective bodies. To facilitate that end Lucy unbuttoned her blouse as she turned to Dr. Eastwood, "You'll revive us if we flatline."

Doctor Eastwood nodded his helmet, and Lucy climbed onto the bed. She began attaching the electrodes.

Her failsafe precaution was speculative at best—at this point it all was—but at least what data she had been able to cross-reference seemed to support her speculation.

Her theory chalked President Pollack's miraculous dodging of death to the pacemaker he'd had inserted on the day of the outbreak. If in fact Coxsackie was the root cause, and that causative connection was an electrical disconnect to the heart, then it made sense that jump-starting the heart might avert the catastrophe. Data from the field supported this theory, in as much as there were a handful of documented cases in which bearers of pacemakers had outlived relatives by an otherwise improbable couple of days.

It wasn't much to go on, but her hand had been categorically forced. She was exhausted beyond living memory and she had to make a play one way or another before she succumbed.

On the neighboring bed, Dr. Eastwood attached electrodes to Hiroshi's muscular frame. Lucy watched. She noticed a small scar just above Hiroshi's boxers that Dr. Eastwood avoided.

Hiroshi looked across at her and winked. "You like chestnuts?" Hiroshi asked, referencing the pattern on his boxers.

"No. Yes." Lucy blushed, "I was just noticing your scar."

"Hai," Hiroshi smiled, at the improbability of her pre-text.

Lucy's blush brightened and Dr. Eastwood delicately worked his way below the boxers, and around the blood-encrusted bullet wound on Hiroshi's powerful left thigh.

+

Hiroshi held up his murky beaker in a toast that was as much to their bravery as to the possibilities this liquid might hold.

"To good health and a long life." Lucy wished.

Without further ado, the two newly bonded lovers, whose lives now hung in the balance of a scientific hunch, clinked glasses and swallowed the inoculants.

Lucy puckered at the taste, and Hiroshi put voice to the myriad violent twitches he felt on the buds of his tongue, "It does not taste good."

She smiled and finally allowed her eyes to close, "Time to sleep and let Mother Nature make her choice."

Hiroshi watched a moment. There was something else on his mind. It was perhaps foolish, but what was life if not the opportunity to enjoy silliness? If this was to be the last day of his or her life then folly was reasonably doubly important.

Lucy looked back across at him.

Hiroshi held up a finger, beckoning Lucy to wait a moment. Then he reached through the web of wires lacing her body, nudged her and magically proffered a gift-wrapped box on his open palm.

"What the ...?" Lucy took the box. She pulled curiously on the tails of ribbons, releasing the bow. Inside, parting the delicate tissue paper, she was surprised to find a skimpy purple Victoria's Secret thong.

Hiroshi grinned, his smile rivaling her own, "You prefer purple. Yes?"

She grinned back at him as she lifted the sheets that now covered them, and referencing the tangle of wires hooked to their chests, and limbs below, objected simply "I'm not putting them on now. But I promise to model them if we wake in the morning ..." she trailed off. But before her eyes drooped again she leaned over and kissed him, making an image that might well have resembled two hydras nestling together.

Their long embrace silently slumped into a singular snuggle as together they drifted into the dark abyss.

On a branch outside the window, a giant Owl watched as the weary lovers succumbed to sleep.

Chapter 71

INSIDE THE WALLS OF THE HEART

Lud dub, lud dub, the red cells pulsed in and out of Lucy's fatigued heart. She was already sound asleep, but yet to hit REM.

Four days ago she had been on the receiving end of a sneeze, one laced with 40,000 droplets of infectious H9N2. The flu's hemagglutinin viral protein had been initially cleaved by a defensive host protease in her mouth, and subsequently in her throat and lungs, as excess inoculants slipped inside her body.

It was a highly infectious version of the flu, favoring easy transmission over most other traits. Indeed that was how it had been engineered. Unfortunately it had also been virulent enough to attract defensive attention of various proteases, home-team players that inadvertently took the infection throughout her body, including deep inside tissues that included her heart and lungs.

Such pervasively penetrative strains of flu were not often as infective as the H9N2 that coursed through Lucy's internal super highways, but what they generally lacked in infectivity, they made up for in lethality. This particular strain, however, was luckily more or less benign, so that, unafflicted by another compromising infection, healthy bodies such as Lucy's stood an excellent chance of fighting it off.

True to those reasonable expectations, Lucy's host defenses had been engaged in brutal skirmishes throughout her body. Even so, the virus hijacked host synthetic machinery and used it to amplify its own viral proteins, replicate its genetic material, and assemble that RNA to make new virus.

In the midst of this, Lucy labored under the symptoms of her body's own defenses—the aches and fatigue caused, not merely by her lack of sleep, but, just as significantly, by the interferons released internally to dampen the virus' replication, and the subsequent inflammatory chaos caused by macrophages mopping up discarded dead cells left by the high-jacking intruder. And as she labored she barely noticed the mild heart palpitations and ventricular arrhythmia that could turn seasonal infections into life terminators.

It was while these battles raged that Lucy had kissed Hiroshi, ensuring entrée to the compromising Coxsackie.

$+$

For its own part, Coxsackie, though rarely fatal, wrought plenty of havoc on the human body. Particularly significant over the last fortnight was its propensity to bind to a protein previously named in its honor, the CAR, or Coxsackie Adenovirus Receptor. CAR played the crucial role of conducting electrical signals from the atria to the cardiac ventricle, making it fundamental to the heart's normal rhythm.

Electrical abnormalities that precipitated heart arrhythmias, consistent contributors to sudden death, were not entirely uncommon in humans. The heart, however, traditionally displayed a robust ability to quickly reestablish working order. Unfortunately, at this moment, potassium ions were decreasing around Lucy's heart, shorting the repolarization reverse, or, in layman's terms, the final fail-safe against an electrical storm.

Throughout the world these channelopathies—in combination with the muscle paralysis that accompanied deep sleep—opened the door to the flu's latent, but rarely actuated, ability to kill quickly and quietly.

$+$

Heart attacks increased annually with flu season, but never before had influenza had a co-conspirator like this new Coxsackie. It was as if they had been designed together!

Lucy's eyes flitted back and forth, she was drifting into that now-lethal dream-state.

Inside of those fluttering eyelids, Lucy saw carriages steal in through a winding dark tunnel and disgorge red blood cells into a cavernous station. This was no Shinkansen, and with a constriction of the station walls the heart sent the train out the next tunnel, towards the lungs. It was rush hour, but life was passing in time-lapse. The day was grinding to a halt as the inevitable last train pulled in from the vein-tunnel.

Lucy watched dispassionately, somehow knowing that, not just for the *day*, this was quite possibly the last train *ever*.

And still there was hope.

Deep in her body there another battle was being waged, one between competing invading forces. Where Hiroshi's Coxsackie opened the path to an electrical storm, the storm-troopers of Wei Lin's soupy cocktail were determined to re-up the potassium levels, and re-set the fail-safes.

In her sleep, Lucy squinted. There was movement way down inside the bloody tunnel, not another train, but straining, she could see workmen on the track.

In the bed beside her, with the same malevolent pathogens coursing through his veins, Hiroshi's eyes flitted as he too descended into deep sleep.

Chapter 72

THE SHOWDOWN

"What are we looking at?" President Pollack demanded.

Patches of purple and yellow alternated across the globe, swaths of color here and there forming a tessellated quilt. China's homogeneous purple contrasted markedly with the heterogeneous mix in the US.

A dozen principals and three-dozen assistants all watched their own renditions of the map on video monitors across the country. They were what remained of the top brass. The president himself watched from his hospital bed inside the negatively pressurized isolation chamber, specifically designed to prevent the spread of infectious disease.

Lucy had spoken with Jackson an hour earlier, but the reassurance she'd hoped for from the five-star General was surprisingly lacking. Jackson had, without fanfare, assured her he would handle the logistics behind mobilizing the required forces, but he'd spent more time guiding their discussion on the potential roadblocks and obstacles that the other participants of the teleconference might present. Most significantly, how to manage their competing interests and egos. Jackson provided sage advice, but his uneasiness gave Lucy pause and now guided the careful consideration with which she trod.

On the plus side, it appeared that Director Havamyer, who had been running the White House staff ragged since Lucy's call last night, was now in her court. That said, she recognized that her harsh manner yesterday might turn him if the newly appointed Commander Marshall (who was watching from the PharmaCo boardroom) decided to defend his industry connections to the bitter end.

In short, the mood was tense.

Lucy, still at Wei Lin's facility, was indicating features on her map with a stylus; explicating the dire situation that they, and the rest of the world, faced. "Yellow is H9N2. Purple is Coxsackie."

She was using the food truck deliveries that had caused disruption up and down the West Coast to illustrate how, in stark contrast to contact within a similarly infected population, which was fine, contact between oppositely infected populations led to waves of death. Through the clutter of video screens it was difficult to tell whether she was getting through so she turned back to the initial outbreak.

Lucy reset the graphic to the blank white map of the world before the outbreak. She restarted the infection clock and, with her stylus, drew everyone's attention to Kazakhstan. A thin strand of purple emanated from Almaty weaving and wending its way across the globe. Meanwhile, a yellow strand, radiated in tendrils from Fresno. Eventually the purple and yellow touched ends in New York City in a dramatic red splotch. Behind the red point of contact, the two strands fattened in a graphic representation of the paths along which the separate infections had spread.

Lucy froze the image, highlighted the clock at the bottom, and noted how widely spread both infections already were. "We live in a world of unprecedented travel. If either of these pathogens had gotten a week's head start, one might well have covered the globe before the other got started, and the epidemiology would have looked very different; much closer to a traditional single-virus outbreak."

She started the clock again, allowing tentacles of yellow and purple to emanate and collide around the world in more splotches of red. For a moment Lucy turned off the yellow and purple, "As you can see, when all we saw were these red patches—the IF-zones—there were no trails of bodies, just random clumps of deaths." After watching the easily trackable spread of yellows and purples, the new visual was striking in it's random nature. Splotches of red exploded around the map without warning. This elicited nods of comprehension around the virtual room that reassured Lucy she *was* getting through.

Flicking the purple Coxsackie back on, she reset the infection clock to zero and, this time, carefully followed the purple strand out of Almaty, "Doctor Wei Lin of the Chinese CDC visited the Kretsky facility the day of the outbreak, and was, in all likelihood, the innocent disburser of Coxsackie. Moreover it's a sound conjecture that Doctor Wong—who passed through JFK, and met Agent Johnson the day before he died—was one of the early points of entry of Coxsackie into the United States," she paused for dramatic effect before clarifying, "he also worked at the Chinese CDC and we now know he and Wei Lin met between Wei Lin's return from Kretsky and Wong's departure to the US."

Inside his isolation chamber, all the walls of which bowed in towards him, in a perfect metaphor of the pressure he was feeling, President Pollack was unimpressed. "Well so much for the Kazak's safe infective vaccines!"

Lucy had expected such a sentiment from someone and was ready to parry, "They're not the only ones in the business of making infective vaccines. Amanet, who worked at Kretsky, just happened to be visiting the US the week before everything happened."

Director Havamyer interrupted a clarification, "Amanet was the man the NCS identified in conversation with Magjan Iglinsky in the Almaty Airport."

"Thank you, Director." Lucy was happy to see Havamyer helping, "We believe it was Amanet who passed the H9N2 virus to Mr. Iglinsky at the Almaty airport. And we believe it originated in PharmaCo. Thus the yellow originating from Fresno."

That was the first bombshell, and it elicited the expected response from Marshall, "That's outrageous!"

Again, Lucy was prepared, "Cars and alcohol are both accepted parts of modern life, but together they make a lethal combination. What we've got are two more or less benign agents acting in concert."

President Pollack looked unswayed, "I walked into a room with a cold and the Chinese leadership is dead!"

"Sir, with all due respect, I didn't advocate a trip to China. And I wasn't consulted on relaxing domestic quarantines."

"No, you just break quarantine when it suits you."

"Do you realize Prime Minister Maqtaly was found dead yesterday?" Marshall added with rhetorical ire, "If–"

But Lucy wasn't ceding the floor to him. Instead, she acknowledged Pollacks' quip about quarantines by playing an obtuse sympathy card, "And in consequence Mr. Sugimura and I are both infected with H9N2 and Coxsackie."

Whatever sympathy that revelation may have elicited from Marshall, it was irrelevant to Pollack who simply advised her to get a pacemaker. Again though, Lucy was prepared.

She made a direct appeal into her video camera; she had to reach the President, "That might jump-start your heart when the Coxsackie takes deep sleep to a flat-line, but the Coxsackie virus will prevail. At best a pacemaker might buy you a couple of days." In reality, her personal welfare was not the issue. Lucy simply needed everyone on the call to understand her grasp of the science behind the pandemic.

With a view that it may well come down to the will of the President against her own, Lucy decided to risk putting the President on the back foot. It was a calculated play she'd conceived before the call opened, and she hoped that it would not only instill in everyone a respect for her knowledge and understanding of the situation, but that it might simultaneously unsettle Pollack, and thus bolster her position in the event of a showdown. "Mr. President, we have a seven billion person problem, and, thanks to your quarantine management, half of America might be dead tomorrow."

But it was Marshall who knocked on the door she was waiting to open, "What do you propose?"

"A third infective vaccine."

For a moment the only sounds on the teleconference were background static and audible gasps, and then President Pollack struck back, "That's precisely the logic that caused this disaster!"

The objection was predictable. Lucy was glad that it had come from the President himself, thus saving her the need to alienate anyone else. She drew a breath and launched into her prepared rationale "Sir, there's a second Coxsackie strain, let's call it Chinese-Coxsackie, the one Wei Lin inoculated the Chinese piggeries with. Without the H9N2 it's less benign, but in combination with the H9N2 it's nothing like the activated Kazak-Coxsackie/H9N2 hit. Most importantly, the Chinese-Coxsackie out-competes Kazak-Coxsackie, meaning a subject struck by both will exhibit Chinese-Coxsackie symptoms. I conjecture that the Chinese-Coxsackie/H9N2 hit is not lethal. It works in pigs. And, based on a two-subject-one-night test, it works on humans too."

The virtual faces around the video conference room were suddenly blank. In her haste to elucidate, Lucy had obfuscated.

It was a classic lecturing blunder, information overload. The faces in the video feeds reminded her of a class of freshmen, bamboozled and totally un-intimidating. President Pollack was now a weirdly impotent human wrecking ball, contained by a plastic tent with an air-evacuation pump. Even turned loose he would infect but a small cohort around him, and he was no threat to Lucy, who no longer bore the Kazak-Coxsackie.

"Hiroshi and I trialled the Chinese-Coxsackie last night, and here we are today. Still alive." Lucy summed it up.

"That's all very well," Marshall broke back in, "but even if it does work, how long will it take to make your vaccine at scale!"

Marshall was sharp. Even if Lucy was right, amplifying the vaccine was still a big problem. The real issue was not the men and women on this call, but the millions of men and women around America—the billions around the world—who were soon to be, or even already were infected with Kazak-Coxsackie and H9N2.

Chapter 73

DECISION TIME

It sometimes took an outsider to jolt the system into action. Lucy was happy to be that agent of change, and through a collaboration with Wei Lin she had hope things would end as well as they could.

Courtesy of the work for the Chinese piggeries, Wei Lin had already had the vaccine at scale. Indeed, the US facility in which Lucy was sitting at that very moment had harvested in excess of 10,000 liters last week, though thanks to an impressive feat of coordinated mobilization, only about one hundred liters—to be used as the new starter—remained on the premises.

Even in the best of times it was an incredibly non-trivial problem to coordinate a massive public vaccination. Not only was it non-trivial to culture inoculants, stabilizing them and ferrying them to delivery points presented a plentiful array of its own problems.

Beyond that, live attenuated vaccines had additional potential snags. There was the very real potential of incidence in which those vaccinated exhibited unwanted and deleterious side effects. Still, such risks had a way of looking rather academic when framed in the context of what had happened over the last couple of weeks.

From the sister plant of the one in which Lucy now sat, Wei Lin had already mobilized a massive Chinese response. Planes were landing throughout that country delivering starter cultures to every conceivable biotech facility that might be able to amplify the samples and create vaccines.

"Havamyer, is this true?" Pollack directed his question to the head of the bureau, who had become his default investigative lead.

Havamyer certified that, yes, CIA satellite images did confirm increased air activity over China, in line with Lucy's assertions.

Lucy knew what she had said made sense, and she knew, moreover, that irrespective of that, her track record over the last hour and a half gave her the benefit of the doubt among many on the call.

Somehow, Marshall still stood in opposition, "Commander Topp your wild speculation–"

But Lucy wasn't in a listening mood, and, ignoring his objection, she cut him off again, continuing her analysis, "I'm exhausted."—why was it people didn't listen, even when you were laying it all out for them— "And if my heart had slowed during deep sleep last night . . ." she let the thought hang in the air; pregnantly for everyone to absorb. "I've already gambled my life, and based on the results I believe our only course of action is to disburse Wei Lin's inoculants as widely as possible."

She wanted to go toe-to-toe with the President alone, albeit from the relative safety of a video-conferencing monitor, but, though everyone else watched her in awe, Marshall was not about to cede his position without a fight, "Mr. President, you have to run trials. You–"

"We don't have time for trials," Lucy retorted. "If we wait, people will die unnecessarily."

"If you're right!" Marshall was seething, "And if you're wrong?!"

"People will still die."

There it was, the bald reality for all to absorb.

Lucy saw Ulman nodding, and for some reason, the younger woman's reference to her erstwhile relationship with Marshall shouted out in her head. She repeated it for the room, "With two you tango." it was an apt encapsulation. "The pandemic isn't over, that you can count on. We still need the National Guard. They still need to enforce the segregation of oppositely infected regions. And under no circumstances should we permit travel between oppositely infected regions." Lucy took a breath, "I'm not advocating action and sitting back, but inaction poses a greater risk."

It was General Jackson's soothing voice that broke in and galvanized support. His timing was impeccable, "Mr. President, with due respect, this is not a political problem, this is a scientific calamity and the only resolution to be had is through science itself. One person cannot be in charge of all decisions, not even the President. Commander Topp is by far the most expert resource we have on this issue. And, not to overstate things, the fate of the human race hangs in the balance."

President Pollack was eerily unemotional, "General Jackson, what you're suggesting might well be considered treason."

It was a true testament to Jackson's cool, that in spite of having already committed the acts that gave teeth to his expressed sentiments, and indeed guessing that the President knew this, he continued his calm tone, "Sir, the Chinese have already come to the same conclusion."

Lucy returned her focus from the sunrise outside her window, "Mr. President, you have experts to advise you on decisions that they are better qualified to make, but just as you couldn't do this without us, we can't do it without you. You need to make a national address imploring the public to visit their designated local mall."

"This is unprecedented," came Pollack's even, if unhelpful, response.

"That's not actually so, Mr. President," Lucy countered. "Between 1962 and 1965, we had over 100 million Americans immunized with a live attenuated vaccine for Sabin polio virus."—and the little difference— "We're just going to try and do three times the job in a handful of days."

There was a long moment of silence.

Lucy breathed comfortably, she was drawing strength from General Jackson, "As we all know, the world is a much more highly connected place these days, and though that might cause problems, it also offers new possibilities."

Hiroshi looked at Lucy and smiled. This wasn't his native tongue, but even he could see she was winning the room.

Chapter 74

HOKKAIDO AGAIN

"Keep coming," Lucy implored him.

There it was again, the characteristic two-note call and response—so synchronized that to the unfamiliar listener it was easily mistaken for a single bird. And they were here, ascending the tree in the hope of happening upon a hatchling.

Hiroshi was without a doubt a skilled climber and it was fun to have a partner in the canopy, but, as Lucy noted to herself with a mischievous grin, it was he who would be learning from her where rope-work was concerned.

The two weeks of chaos during the height of the pandemic had been a wonderful harbinger for how their relationship might grow. A puzzle in two pieces, so much richer as the sum.

A rising shrill shriek from the trunk, two trees to her left, arrested her attention. They were near the nest. And then she appeared, the mother bird, soaring through the branches, a glistening fish flopping in her talons.

Lucy and Hiroshi watched as the baby welcomed the sustenance.

Lives ended, and life went on.

Around the world people had been unsure what to do but cautiously interact with one another and then go to sleep.

Later, with the rising sun, people woke again, happily discovering, day after day, that their lives continued, until at some point the novelty wore off and other concerns reentered their existences.

+

Quite in contrast to sentiments expressed in the heat of battle, Pollack had since honored Lucy with a Presidential medal. The irony of the medal never escaped her, though she had to acknowledge that Pollack was big enough to admit his mistakes. She was not a woman Pollack would ever really understand, but his respect for her intellectual insight and fortitude in the face of apparently insurmountable obstacles kept growing as hindsight added clarity to the calamitous events that had unfolded around them.

Nevertheless, all the accolades, academic and otherwise, were just that: academic. For Lucy, science had been her life, and though it continued to be so, there was now a new and growing dimension, one her mother had campaigned for throughout her years.

During the wedding ceremony, Lucy had cried tears of happiness, but an additional few for the fact that Ellen was not there to share the moment with her. There was at least comfort in the thought that her mother had met, and emphatically approved of her man.

Lucy looked down again. She was working on her habit of getting lost in thought. It was time to return to the moment, to the man who made her whole, to enjoy their honeymoon together.

She turned to Hiroshi, secured her slack and leaned forward kissing him again.

Thank You

Thank you for taking the time to purchase and read this book! And an extra big thanks for those who are inclined to rate it, or, better still, leave a review on Amazon or Goodreads!!

Some of you might be curious about me and my past. For those of you, I was born in Australia and earned a PhD in Number Theory at Harvard University. I subsequently wrote and directed a feature film loosely based on the Chinese philosopher Chang Tzu's famous butterfly dream. My father, Keith Williams, is a biologist who worked at Oxford University and the Max Planck Institute in Munich. He also founded the biotech company Proteome Systems, named after the ground-breaking research he spearheaded in his lab that coined the term proteomics.

I collaborated with my father on the story behind *The I.F. Zones* to bring you a thought-provoking novel grounded in real science. I then took that framework and brought it to life with characters led by Lucy Topp, who, like me, enjoys climbing; though I prefer real rocks over Lucy's favored environment, the wilds of treetops.

When I directed *Butterfly Dreaming* I had a saying I liked a lot: "You can't use feedback you never hear." Directing is nice in that you're constantly bombarded by ideas and input from gaffers to cinematographers, from background extras to main stars. Writing is a little more solitary—not as solitary as mathematics, but more than directing.

Anyway, it's in this context that I'd encourage you to reach out if you have feedback. This is my first book, but I doubt it'll be my last (I'm well into my next one, which is also an adaptation of a screenplay I once wrote), so all thoughts are very welcome! I can be reached at @primedrufus on Twitter, and rufus@primedminds.com on email, and I will try my best to respond to everyone who contacts me.

All the best.

Cheerio
Rufus Williams

POSTSCRIPT – IMPORTANT FACTS

This book was written before the COVID-19 outbreak.

Today, July 1st 2020, there are more than 10 million confirmed cases of COVID-19 and half a million dead. And we're just at the beginning.

To be clear, *isolated fatality zones* is a term I made up. I did so because it helps shine a light on the specific epidemiology of the pandemic I described in this book. The ideas it encapsulates are, like most else in this story, based in reality.

Specifically, the Coxsackie strain B3 is a leading cause of myocarditis and pericarditis, which can result in fatal inflammation of the heart. It can be transmitted by touch.

Flu, including H9N2, is highly transmissible and can exacerbate other conditions such as cardiomyopathy. If Coxsackie virus B3 and H9N2 combined in the real world, their more natural gestation periods would complicate diagnosis and obfuscate understanding of the underlying issues. These considerations motivated my choice to accelerate the rates of transmission in our story to unrealistic levels; I believe it kept the plot cleaner and simpler!

Could this happen?

As I said above, before I wrote this, there was no COVID-19. To quote Hiroshi: "Today is not tomorrow.""

Made in the USA
Monee, IL
17 November 2020

48010265R00167